Saint

Gateway Series Book 2

Brian Dorsey

Chapter 1

"Gotcha, bitch!" declared Cassandra Orion with a smile as the ship in front of her rocked from the impact of *Hydra*'s salvo of plasma rounds. "Let's go get 'em," she added, banking *Hydra* sharply alongside the damaged slave ship. "*That last shot did the trick; their propulsion is down,*" reported Orion over the ship's intercom. "*I'm lining us up to their docking port.*"

***

"Roger," answered Tyler Stone as he racked the first round into his rifle. Standing in the docking tunnel, he looked back toward the rest of the assault team. "Ready?" he asked.

Beside him stood Major Mori Skye, holding a riot gun in her left hand. As she slid a pistol into the holster on her hip, she looked toward Stone and smiled.

With the success of the mission against the Venato base, Mori had been promoted to the rank of major and elevated by the Longhouse Council to a Ka-itsenko, the honored Terillian title given to their ten best warriors. As such, she was authorized to wear the traditional war paint of her people into battle. The red and yellow diagonal stripes covering her face and the black handprint covering her lower jaw only accentuated the power of her brilliant green eyes, which burned with the same determination as the day Stone first saw them. Her raven-colored hair, tied tightly into a set of three-weave braids, fell over the front of her shoulders. A badger tail was woven into the hair and hung about ten centimeters from the end of her braid. Nodding in acknowledgment, Mori brought the riot gun to the ready. Three more Scout Rangers, also Ka-itsenko, stood in close order behind her.

First in line was Thay Flint. Thay's thin, leathered face was completely black with war paint, save a red diamond around each eye. Thay had been authorized by the Iroqua matrons to carry out a mourning war of vengeance against the Xen and their allies until his grief for the death of his brother was satisfied; one tomahawk was etched with thirty-five notches to represent the Humani and slavers' lives he had taken so far. His head was bald except a small tuft of prickly black hair running over the middle of his scalp. Holding a pistol in one hand, he reached down to ensure his two tomahawks were secured on his waist belt for quick access when needed.

Behind Thay was the Akota, Henry River. His lower face and jawline were painted a brilliant white, which stood in stark contrast to the charcoal-colored paint from his nose to his hairline. Henry's dark hair fell just over his ears and was intertwined with small white-tipped feathers. Confident, lean, and well-muscled, he held an assault rifle at his waist, but Stone's attention was drawn to the countless number of knives and other edged weapons attached to his assault gear.

In the rear knelt Sandwick Hill of the Siksika, his lower jaw painted red with two thin red lines running from his jaw over his cheekbones to each eye. His hair fell freely over his shoulders with a small lock running down the center of his forehead to the bridge of his nose. The youngest of the group and first son of the primary chief of his people, Sandwick held the butt of his assault rifle to his cheek for a quick look down the barrel. Although the rifle was his primary weapon, a riot gun was slung over his back and a pistol was held at each side.

Stone was still learning the nuances of Terillian culture, and the battle dress of the Ka-itsenko was no different. He had seen only three of these super-elite soldiers in his career with the Elite Guard. One had killed three Elite Guard troops before evaporating into the forest of Sierra 7, another was killed by Captain Emily Martin after a drawn-out hand-to-hand fight, and the third had planted a knife into Stone's bicep before he was able to put two rounds into the warrior's torso and force him to retreat.

"We're ready as well," snarled Magnus.

Stone turned his head toward Magnus. He could see Magnus's thick, long hair puff out, stiffening like a Humani war dog. Stone sometimes forgot about the changes caused by genetic mixing of wolf and human DNA that resulted in the creation of Magnus and his clan. Behind Magnus crouched Katalya, Mori's genetically altered sister—and Magnus's mate.

Despite the impending assault, Stone paused to reflect. Less than a year ago, the Terillians were his sworn enemy and he had no idea Magnus and his clan existed. In this short time, however, Stone had undergone an unbelievable transformation — from Alpha Humani's most highly decorated soldier and fiancé to the daughter of one of his planet's most powerful men — to his current situation: fighting in a clandestine mission in the company of his former enemy.

But Stone knew he had no choice in the matter. Once he became aware that his planet's elite, the First Families, were in league with their Xen masters who had, in fact, conquered Alpha Humana generations ago and set up the civilization he grew up in as a fallacy to maintain control, he realized the only way he could save his people was to become their enemy. Convinced of the truth by his former enemy and now lover, Mori, and by the revelations of his once fiancée, the Lady Astra Varus, her father, and by the treachery of General Cataline Tacitus, Stone now knew that the current war between the Xennite Empire and the Terillian Confederation had been purposely manufactured by the Humani First Families to placate their Xen master's need for more slaves on their home planets — a move necessitated by the spread of a deadly virus killing off large portions of the Xen's human chattel.

Much had happened since Stone's decision to turn against his native world. Stone and his new companions, including the colorful crew of the *Hydra*, had managed to destroy a clandestine Xen base on Venato that had been created to manipulate the virus for two nefarious purposes: first, alter human DNA to simultaneously survive the virus and create a docile slave population; and second, weaponize the virus for use against Terillian and other worlds.

After their escape from Venato, Stone, Mori, and the crew of *Hydra* took refuge near the border of the Terillian Confederation. On the borderland, the remainder of Magnus's clan, having escaped Venato on *Hydra*, chose a remote planet just inside Terillian territory to make a homestead for themselves. Still seeking vengeance for the atrocities carried out by the Xen, Magnus and Katalya left their clan behind to continue the fight. And Mori, now elevated to a Ka-itsenko, was provided a hand-picked team of warriors and told to continue her personal war against the slavers in the Dark Zone, the no-man's-land of several systems that lay between the two powerful civilizations.

"Hold on!" echoed Orion's voice over the intercom. "We're lining up with their gravitational reference."

Stone quickly regained his focus and thanked his luck that Orion was *Hydra's* pilot. Breaching a hull and jumping from one's own deck onto the overhead of another ship always meant a bad day. He had seen three Guardsmen break their legs when the floor they thought they were jumping onto was in fact the overhead of a six-meter high cargo hold. Stone slightly shifted his balance as Orion oriented *Hydra* to the slave ship's reference horizon.

Hydra shuddered, and a low metallic thud signaled that the docking bay had made contact with the slavers' ship.

"Go get 'em!" came Orion's voice over the intercom again as the inner docking door locked shut and the outer opened to expose the outer hull of the slavers' ship.

Stone looked to Mori and nodded.

"Since their ship isn't designed for docking transfers," said Mori to Magnus, "we're gonna need to blow the hatch."

As Mori spoke, Stone watched Thay and Sandwick attach a large rectangular pad to the hull of the slavers' ship and then fall back into their stacked positions.

"Cover!" shouted Mori. "Three, two, one ..."

As Mori finished the countdown, Sandwick activated the blast mechanism. The explosion from the shaped blast was muffled by the protective pad, but pain shot through Stone's ears as they popped, the rapid mixing of atmospheres between the two spaces equalizing the pressure across his eardrums.

"Go, go, go!" shouted Mori. She led the way as she leapt through the hole in the slave ship's hull, her riot gun held close to her shoulder.

Stone entered the breach as Mori was still midair. Pivoting to his left, he saw the flash and heard the blast of Mori's riot gun. He saw a slaver on his knees directly in front of him. Still recovering from the blast of the breaching charge, the slaver sluggishly swung his pistol toward Stone. Stone squeezed the trigger and a salvo of three rounds exploded from his rifle, tearing into the slaver's chest.

As the echo from the shots cleared, Stone heard Mori call out.

"Clear."

"Clear," repeated Thay, now positioned to the right of the breach.

"Clear," responded Stone as he turned to examine the rest of compartment.

Behind Mori lay the body of the slaver that drew her fire as she entered. Between Stone and Mori knelt

Magnus and Katalya. To Mori's right were Henry and Sandwick with Thay to the far right.

Stone saw Mori turn toward him, her braids swinging around to catch up to her glance.

This is the first time Stone had seen Mori in command of an operation; she was born to it.

"Magnus, Katalya," she ordered. "Clear the bridge."

Magnus nodded in acknowledgment then he and Katalya quickly moved toward the entrance of the compartment. As Katalya passed Mori, she stopped and lowered her forehead to Mori's.

"Stay safe, *tanka*," spoke Katalya softly to her younger sister using her native language.

"You too, *c'uwé*," answered Mori.

Katalya turned back toward Magnus and they quickly exited the compartment.

"Henry and Sandwick," continued Mori, "clear the crew berthing."

"*Hau*," replied Henry in acknowledgment as he looked toward Sandwick, himself shifting from his assault rifle to the riot gun slung over his shoulder.

"Ready?" asked Henry.

Sandwick acknowledged with a slap to Henry's back and a nod.

As Sandwick and Henry exited the compartment, Mori turned back toward Stone and Thay.

"Let's clear the path and get down to the cargo hold. That's where they'll keep their captives," Mori ordered as she reloaded her riot gun, replacing the round she had expended on the slaver. "Thay, you take point."

Without a word, Thay holstered one of his pistols and drew a tomahawk from his waist belt. As Thay looked at Mori, Stone saw an opportunistic smile come to warrior's face. A pistol in his left hand held extended forward and his tomahawk close to his waist, Thay loped toward the passageway outside the compartment.

Moving quickly and quietly, the three made their way to the midlevel of the slave ship. The group entered what appeared to be another storage room divided into three lanes by two large storage racks running the length of the space. Entering the room, Stone saw a slaver jump from behind the far end of the right storage rack. "Contact!" he shouted and all three dove for cover as the air filled with pellets from two rapid blasts from the slaver's weapon.

Stone curled himself into a ball and grunted as the pellets ricocheted off the bulkhead and pelted his body. Their velocity reduced by the force of the impact with the bulkhead, the small steel balls peppered his back and sent a flash of pain through his body.

He looked to see Mori curl her body toward one side and wince in pain from her own pelting.

"Damn it!" she grunted.

The welts were already forming on his back when another blast sent a second hail of pellets ricocheting in his direction.

Mori answered with two shots from her riot gun. "Let's see how he likes it," she grumbled as she fired a third round.

Thay burst from his position and sprinted past Stone, who could only watch as Thay ran straight down the alley that only seconds ago was filled with deadly pellets.

The slaver shifted his body and leaned into view to send another round toward the three, but Thay had covered too much ground. As the slaver's gun extended from the cover of the storage rack, Thay directed the barrel away from his body and, in a sweeping movement, slammed his tomahawk into the slaver's skull. The blade sank deep into the man's head as he fell to the ground.

Another slaver leapt from cover behind a nearby storage crate and sprinted down the passageway to make his escape. Stone raised his rifle to fire but Thay's second tomahawk was already in flight. The slaver's scream echoed through the passageway as the tomahawk tore into his spine. The wounded man fell to his knees screaming as he reached frantically for the weapon embedded in his back.

Thay was on him instantly, leaping into the air just before he reached the slaver. Still airborne, Thay grabbed the man's hair as he passed and drove his face toward the floor. Stone heard the thud and crack of facial bones breaking as the slaver's head impacted the metal deckplate.

Thay pulled himself to his knees using the slaver's hair as leverage and pivoted to a position straddling the slaver's lower back. From his knees, he jerked the tomahawk from the man's back, resulting in another ear-piercing scream. Thay quickly spun the handle of his tomahawk and planted the thin-tipped point of the tomahawk in the back of the man's head with a grunt.

'This guy is good,' thought Stone as he and Mori reached Thay after clearing the remainder of the room.

Thay drew a large knife from his tactical vest. Grabbing the dead slaver's hair, he placed the blade to the man's scalp.

"Thay!" shouted Mori. "No! Don't!"

Thay's grip on the slaver's hair tightened.

"Iah tetkaie!" ordered Mori in Thay's native language.

Thay paused and looked up toward Mori, still holding the hair of the dead slaver.

His dark eyes glared back at Mori.

"Don't fret." He smiled and added, "It's only symbolic." He moved his blade over the man's head as if he was taking the man's scalp and let the victim's head fall back to the deck. Still straddling his victim, he again withdrew his tomahawk and began to etch new marks into the handle.

"Why do you care what I do with this pig anyway?" asked Thay as he finished etching his tomahawk.

"I just want them dead," replied Mori. "After that, I think of them no more."

"I like to think about them," Thay said, smiling. "Their deaths warm the lodge fires of my family and clan."

Growing uncomfortable with the conversation and realizing they had not completed their mission, Stone interrupted.

"Mori, Thay, we need to get to the cargo bay."

"Yes," replied Mori, clearly embarrassed by allowing herself to lose focus and by the unseemly conversation between her and Thay. "I'll take point," she added with a quick glance toward Thay.

In a few minutes the three had made their way to the lower level of the ship. At the bottom of the ladder, Mori pulled out a small digital device and flipped through several screens.

"Looks like there should be one more compartment before the main cargo bay," she said, placing the device back into her pocket.

"If this flying trash can is still per original design," added Thay.

"Either way," said Stone, pointing toward the closed armored doors in front of them, "we're going that way."

"Then let's get to it," replied Mori.

Stone took position on the starboard side of the hatch. Crouching down with his right shoulder toward the bulkhead, Stone held his rifle at the low-ready position. He looked across to Thay, who had taken a position opposite him. Once both were ready, Stone turned back toward Mori.

"Ready," he reported.

Mori placed an electronic entry box on the control panel, holding the pistol grip of her riot gun in her right hand. "Stand by," she warned.

Stone gripped his rifle tightly and took a deep breath.

"Firing!" shouted Mori as she flipped the switch causing the armored door's circuitry to be overridden.

The door slid open.

Someone burst through the hatch toward Mori. A shot from Mori's gun rang out and the assailant tumbled backward. Stone's heart jumped as he recognized the uniform; it was a Guardsman.

Dumbfounded, he almost failed to notice a second man step into the opening and swing his sword toward Stone's head. Falling backward, Stone heard the metallic singing of the sword and the brush of air as the blade missed his head by millimeters.

The Guardsman stepped toward Stone. Over his attacker's shoulder, Stone saw Thay stand to fire his pistol only to be attacked by another Guardsman. Refocusing on his own defense, Stone swung his rifle above his chest to block the Guardsman's next attack. The attacker instantly recovered and positioned his sword for a downward stab.

"It's the Traitor!" shouted the Guardsman as he recognized Stone.

Then the face registered with Stone. It was Lieutenant Ghant from Second Battalion. The two warriors locked their gazes on each other; Stone could see nothing but hatred in his opponent's eyes.

Ghant shifted his weight as Mori lunged toward him, her sword drawn. From his back and with his reflexes stunted from the shock of seeing Elite Guard troops, Stone could only watch as Ghant parried Mori's thrust and countered with a strike to her right jaw. Mori grunted from the impact and stumbled but quickly regained her balance and lowered her shoulder into the man's rib cage. Slamming the man against the bulkhead, Mori landed two blows to her opponent's rib cage in rapid succession. The Guardsman curled his body inward in pain but responded with a series of elbows to Mori's shoulder blades, knocking her to the ground. Hitting her knees, Mori reacted to block the Guardsman's knee and punched the inside of his right leg.

"Tyler!" shouted Mori as she struggled with the skilled combatant.

Mori's cry was like a bolt of electricity to Stone. As Mori and the Guardsman continued their fight above him, Stone grabbed Mori's knife from her waist belt and plunged it into the man's thigh.

Ghant let out a moan and fell on top of Stone.

"I'm going to kill you," grunted the injured Guardsman. Pain erupted in Stone's ribs and radiated toward his spine as Ghant crashed an elbow into his side.

Grunting, Stone felt the weight of the Guardsman's body then wrapped his right arm underneath Ghant's chin and locked his left behind his head. He struggled to maintain his grip as Ghant worked to pry Stone's left arm loose.

The weight on top of Stone increased as Mori landed on top of Ghant, crashing her right knee into the Guardsman's sternum. Stone heard Ghant's ribs crack, quickly followed by a painful grunt from the Humani warrior. Ghant loosened his grip and Stone capitalized by locking in his choke hold, squeezing tightly as he planned to choke the man unconscious.

Mori's weight shifted, and Stone looked over Ghant's shoulder to see Mori jerk the knife from the Guardsman's thigh and raise it above her head.

"No!" shouted Stone.

Mori drove the long knife into the man's chest with a primordial grunt.

Ghant's body began to spasm and Stone felt a reduction in pressure on his body as Mori leapt to her feet. Stone rolled Ghant's body onto the floor and pulled himself up against the bulkhead. As he stood, he looked toward Thay, who had joined them. The right side of Thay's face was swollen, blood trickled from a gash on his right cheek, and the left sleeve of his uniform was slashed and soaked in blood from a flesh wound.

"You okay?" Mori asked Thay.

"Better than him," replied Thay, tilting his head toward the bloody body of the Guardsman lying on the floor.

"And what the hell was that?" snapped Thay as his attention turned from Mori to Stone. "That second man shouldn't have made it through the hatch."

"You have to remember, Thay," interrupted Mori. "These men were his companions."

Stone was thankful that Mori had his back but could clearly tell she was concerned about the situation he had created.

"That doesn't matter," shot back Thay. He stepped toward Stone, his dark eyes locked in a cold stare. "You're either one of us or one of *them*," he said, holding his bloody tomahawk up to Stone's face. "You need to figure it out. Soon."

"Tha'tetsato-tat!" shouted Mori again in Thay's language.

Thay turned back toward Mori and the two exchanged what Stone knew was a heated argument about him in one of the Terillian languages. After a moment, Thay looked over toward Stone. He could see the frustration and anger in Thay's eyes.

"Us!" shouted Thay as he pounded his tomahawk to his chest, "or them!" He pointed toward the dead Elite Guard soldiers. Thay focused his gaze on Stone, staring straight into his eyes for several seconds before letting out a grunt and walking away.

Stone looked toward Mori. Her green eyes showed both a deep concern for his feelings and frustration at his hesitation in combat.

"Tyler," she whispered, "I know it can't be easy, especially when it comes to your former clan ... I mean ... companions, but you *are* with us ... with me, now. It's for the greater good that we fight."

Stone opened his mouth to speak but Mori raised her hand to stop him. She continued. "You have to come to grips with the reality that many brave warriors and innocent civilians may die in our struggle, but in the end, we'll be victorious and then we all can be at peace."

"I'm sorry," apologized an embarrassed Stone, knowing he had let Mori down and actually endangered her life with his hesitation.

Mori's hand caressed his face as she looked up toward him.

"I know you would die for me, Tyler." She paused. Stone felt Mori's other hand cradle his opposite cheek as she pulled him to her for a slow, soft kiss. After the kiss, she turned his head so that he was again looking directly into her striking green eyes.

"But I have to know you'll kill for me too."

Chapter 2

Astra sat erect in her elaborate chair in the ProConsul chamber. After a small but noticeable sigh, she looked toward the main.

"They are late, ProConsul," stated the lone attendant in the room, save two guards.

"*They*," retorted Astra, "are never late."

"Of course, ProConsul," acknowledged the attendant, lowering his head in subservience.

"Our Advisors are here to provide much-needed guidance and keep us on the path to becoming the glorious civilization that both we and our Xen friends have envisioned for our people."

"Of course, Pro—" the attendant paused and raised a hand to his ear as a communication was passed to him through his earpiece. "ProConsul, they are here."

Astra's attention snapped back toward the entrance. She rose to her feet, took another deep breath, and slowly stepped down from the elevated position maintained by her chair. She reached the ground level just as the massive doors of the main entrance slowly creaked opened.

Astra closed her eyes momentarily as the light from the outer halls pierced the room and was directed toward her chair. As she opened her eyes, she could make out two spectral shapes shuffling through the opening. Squinting, Astra made out the hooded and cloaked silhouettes of the Xen Advisors as they approached.

The Advisors' scaled, greenish-brown snouts jutted from their hoods as they scurried down the lavender carpet laid out in honor of their visit. They stopped in front of Astra.

"ProConsul," the attendant's voice echoed through the vast chamber. "Representatives of the Xennite Emperor and his many allies, Advisor Dlackar the Wise and Advisor Vartor the Clever request an audience."

"Your presence is always welcome, our most gracious and wise allies," responded Astra as she bowed slowly to each Advisor.

"Of course, ProConsul," hissed Dlackar, the Xen elongation of the 's' evident. "As we are pressed for time, we must ask to make this a brief visit."

"Certainly," replied Astra, nodding her head in acknowledgment. Advisors' time was not to be wasted. "Everyone out!"

The attendant and two guards exited the room as if pushed by an unseen force. The doors to the chamber closed and both Advisors dropped their hoods, exposing their elongated reptilian heads.

"Vartor and Dlackar are waiting for your report," directed Dlackar.

Astra nodded her head and began. "We have consolidated our hold in the Sierra system and the planned advance into the Golf system is scheduled with reserves made available following the end of resistance in Bravo. Heavy fighting continues in the Foxtrot and November systems. Our Doran allies, as you have reported, are conducting operations in both India, Mike, and Navato systems."

"Yes," hissed Vartor. "Our allies are performing well. What are your concerns?"

"Yes," added Dlackar. "The Emperor must be aware of any problems."

"Yes, of course," replied Astra. "We have reports of continuing raids on slave vessels in the neutral and contested systems, especially the Foxtrot system. Our intelligence sources believe special operations teams are specifically targeting our transports. I believe this is where the Traitor is—"

"Enough of this Traitor," interrupted Dlackar. "Don't let your need for vengeance cloud your judgment."

"Or allow you to forget the First Families' duty to the Emperor," added Vartor. "Do not make us regret our decision to work with you — instead of incorporate you — into our plans."

Astra's body grew hot. She prayed for the day she could break free of the yokes of her overlords, but for now she had to play the game.

"Yes, of course. Both myself and the First Families understand and will carry out the wishes of the Emperor—with the glory of the Xennite Empire always in our foremost thoughts."

"Good, good," replied Dlackar. "What of your losses?"

"I do not concern myself with our losses, as I and the First Families would gladly sacrifice all for the

Empire, but I can say that our forces have inflicted over two million casualties on the enemy."

The two Xen turned toward one another in silent acknowledgment of Astra's pledge of loyalty and then returned to the questioning.

"And the number of slaves gathered?" asked Vartor.

"Approximately one hundred thousand," responded Astra. "The incursion by Terillian special forces has cost us close to fifty thousand."

"These numbers are not acceptable," hissed Dlackar, stepping toward Astra. "We were promised one hundred twenty thousand per year."

Recognizing Dlackar's anger, Astra went down on one knee and lowered her head to show her subservience. Her teeth ground together as she feigned humility. "I agree, Advisor Dlackar," she conceded. "Perhaps if the Emperor would authorize our Doran allies to support us or provide Xen forces …"

"Silence!" shouted Vartor. "The Emperor will allocate our forces and those of our allies — including the Humani — as he sees fit."

"Of course," replied Astra, placing her second knee on the ground. "I simply mentioned this as a request for consideration of our Emperor."

"Do not forget, ProConsul, that while you rule this planet, you are but one of many that serve the Emperor," responded Dlackar.

Astra took in a deep breath. "Yes. And I humbly offer a plan to replenish the chattel lost to the Terillians."

Dlackar turned his head slightly toward Vartor, who in turn nodded.

"Continue, ProConsul," directed Vartor.

"My agents have been in contact with the ruler of a significant population in the Echo system. We are on the verge of solidifying a deal that will provide more than enough servants for your home world with the promise of a continued supply."

Dlackar's tongue flitted quickly in and out of his gaped mouth. After an elongated hiss of contemplation, he spoke.

"And how will this be possible?"

Astra rose to her feet and slowly smoothed her dress, a smile of satisfaction forming on her face.

"By using one of the most powerful weapons available against humans."

"What's this weapon you speak of?" asked Dlackar.

"Religion," replied Astra with a cold smile.

"Continue," added Vartor.

"It has come to our attention that a leader has arisen in the Echo system and begun to unite the planets through a religious doctrine that gives him significant control of his subjects. He has run into some opposition on Echo 2 and went to the Port Royal Association for financial and military backing; they naturally contacted my agents. We have currently traded some old weaponry with him and in return, he will provide a sample of his followers for genetic alteration. I plan on sending an emissary there to persuade him to assist the Xennite Emperor's interests in a larger role." Astra paused. She despised these reptilian overseers that both ensured and limited her power over Alpha Humana. But for now, they had to be appeased. "This assistance will be a tithe in chattel which can be shipped directly to your home worlds while at the same time allowing us to gain a foothold into the Echo system without firing a shot."

"Interesting," replied Dlackar. "And how will you provide this support?"

Astra took a step toward the Advisors.

"With a humble request for the Emperor to authorize our Doran allies to assist in the Foxtrot system, which would allow us to —"

"You have proposed an interesting plan," interrupted Dlackar. "The Doran allies are not available to assist —"

"But —"

Dlackar raised his clawed hand to silence Astra.

"We will contact the Imperial Court and determine if the Emperor will be willing to support this plan. Until then, you can send your agent to speak to this leader and promise assistance."

"And if the Emperor does not authorize additional forces?" asked Astra, her head tilted inquisitively.

"Then," added Vartor, "you will need to find a way to persuade this —"

"He calls himself the Saint," clarified Astra.

"— this Saint," continued Vartor, "to provide you the slaves we require regardless of support from the Dorans."

"As is your duty to the Empire," added Dlackar.

***

Stone stood outside the final door to the cargo bay of the slave ship, his rifle at the ready. His heart pounded in his chest and sweat ran down his forehead. *'Damn it, Stone, pull your head out of your ass.'* He had no idea what was behind the door, but if it were another Guardsman, he would have to kill him.

His mind raced with a thousand scenarios of what would happen when that door opened. As Stone readied himself for the possibility of killing another former comrade, his body pulsed with each heartbeat and his knees started to buckle as he stared at the door. *'Greater good. Mori's right,'* he reassured himself. *'If Ghant was here, maybe Captain Desro's on the other side of the door. Or Sergeant Lowstreet.'* Or ... Stone shook his head to regain his composure. *'Focus,'* Stone ordered himself. *'Focus on the door, not what's behind it. The door ... and Mori's words.'*

"Breaching!"

Mori's voice jolted Stone back to his task as the doors to the cargo bay opened.

Stone brought his rifle to his shoulder and peered down the sights as he rushed into the compartment. Breaking the plane of the door, Stone felt Thay and Mori move into the compartment covering his right and left. Stone scanned for targets.

Twenty meters in front of Stone were dozens of people sitting in a tight circle at the far end of the cargo bay. Stone examined the crowd, his weapon at the ready.

"Careful," added Mori as she and Thay flanked the crowd.

"Something's very wrong with this," Stone thought out loud.

"Everyone down on your face!" shouted Thay.

The group remained still. Thay repeated the order.

No one moved.

The tension grew heavy. Freed slaves or captives didn't act like this. This was all wrong.

"Magnus, Katalya, get down to the cargo bay," ordered Mori into her comms.

The focused look and tense stance taken by Mori told Stone she was concerned and the request for backup only heightened his own apprehensions. Stone examined the group more closely. They appeared to be unarmed but he couldn't be certain due to their positioning.

Each wore gray woolen trousers with brown suspenders and white cotton shirts. Around each neck was a bright red scarf and their hair, regardless of the color, was grown thick and to the neckline in the back with two long tufts running the length of their face just forward of their ears.

"Are they slaves?" asked Mori, her riot gun pointed toward the crowd.

"There are no slaves here," came a low but booming voice from the center of the group.

Stone, Mori, and Thay instantly shouldered their weapons toward the center of the assembly. Stone tightened his grip on his rifle and slid his finger inside the trigger guard as a man slowly rose from the center of the crowd.

The man was clearly different than the rest. He wore a dark hooded cloak that made it impossible to see if he was armed.

"Put your hands in the air!" ordered Stone.

The mysterious man slowly complied and raised his arms above his head. The sleeves of his cloak fell to his elbows, exposing forearms covered in tattoos.

"Get down here now," Mori whispered into her comms to hasten the arrival of Magnus and Katalya.

"Don't be concerned," said the hooded man in a guttural voice. As he spoke, he slowly lowered his hands to remove his hood.

"Hands in the air or I'll drop you where you stand!" ordered Mori.

As the man raised his hands again, Stone noticed more tattoos covering the man's neck and a large six-point star imprinted on his forehead. His face was clean shaven as was his head except for a tightly woven braid that fell from the top of his head to the back of his neck. His gaze still locked on the cloaked man, Stone noticed Thay slowly shifting his position to move behind the peripheral view of the stranger.

"Your friend can move behind me if he likes," spoke the man, "for I have hundreds of eyes. My flock is ever vigilant."

Stone looked to Mori, who motioned for Thay to return to his previous position.

"With one hand, slowly remove the cloak," directed Mori.

The man obliged and loosened the clasp of the cloak.

"Weapon!" shouted Stone as the cloak fell, revealing a sidearm and several edged weapons.

The removal of the cloak also revealed a bare, well-muscled torso covered with tattoos of what Stone surmised to be script.

"Drop the weapons!" shouted Mori.

The man turned directly toward Mori. As he did, Stone read some of the script covering the man's back:

The Believers do not fear death
Death brings the ultimate truth
Death brings the ultimate order

'*This is going to go bad*,' Stone thought to himself.

"You must be the leader," spoke the stranger to Mori.

"Why are you here?" she asked.

"For their salvation. For my salvation," the man smiled and took a step toward Mori. "For your salvation."

"One more step and I'll put you down!" warned Mori.

"You can shoot me where I stand if you like," replied the stranger. "Or you or one of your men can face me in individual combat so that the Word can be heard."

"Yes," blurted Thay.

Without turning, the man continued. "It seems as though one of your followers has accepted."

Stone could see the concern on Mori's face. They had been ready for a shootout with slavers or even prepared to tangle with the Elite Guard, but this was different.

"She doesn't choose who I fight," said Thay. "I accept your challenge."

Stone watched as Mori nodded in frustrating acknowledgment. Terillian military discipline was so different from the Humani.

"Very well." The man smiled.

With Stone and Mori covering him, the man slowly withdrew his pistol. Once in his hand, he ejected the clip and removed the round in the chamber. With the same deliberate motion, he returned the weapon to its holster.

Thay made his way to Stone's side, his eyes glistening. For a split second, Stone thought of the look in Emily Martin's eyes prior to combat. But this was different. Where Martin craved the excitement and rush of combat as the ultimate proof of her abilities, Thay's motivation was much baser. It was pure, old-fashioned, grief-driven vengeance.

"I'll show you how to kill without hesitation." Thay grinned as he withdrew one of his tomahawks and slid a long single-edged blade from its sheath on his tactical vest.

"I am ready," the man stated. "Followers rise!"

With his command, the entire group rose to their feet and turned toward the entrance of the cargo bay.

Stone's pulse quickened.

"Stand easy," said the man. "They are simply waiting to see what will come next."

"What do you mean 'next'?" asked Stone.

"These people are under my charge, and as their priest it's my duty to ensure safe passage to the Divine City so that they may serve as followers of the Saint."

"Who's the Saint?" asked Mori.

In unison, the entire crowd shouted, "The Saint embodies the Word. The Saint is the vessel of the Word. The Saint is the only true interpreter of the Word. The Saint is the well of faith from which the Word flows."

Stone quickly glanced to Mori. Her eyebrows were raised and her lower jaw tightened in a look of puzzlement.

"Who the hell are you people?" she asked. "We are here to help you. Don't you know this is a slave ship headed for the Xen Empire?"

"We serve the Saint," replied the priest. "And we are on a pilgrimage to the Divine City. It's the will of the Saint." The priest turned slightly to acknowledge Magnus and Katalya as they entered the room, their weapons ready. "And I will defend my flock until I fall." He turned toward the group of followers behind him. "Then they will defend the Word. Because what is the Word?"

Again, the group responded in unison, "The Word is peace. The Word is stability. The Word is order. The Word is undeniable. The Word is inevitable. The Word is truth."

"*C'uwe*?" asked Katalya to her sister in Akota.

"We've got trouble," replied Mori.

Thay spoke next. "What type of devil has these people under its spell? They ar —"

"And what of the Believers?" interrupted the priest.

"The Believers hear the Word and understand. The Believers turn themselves over to the Word. The Believers serve the Saint through the Priest-Bishop. The Believers do not fear death."

"You do know," said Thay as his head turned back toward Mori, "we're gonna have to put all of these crazies down ... after I'm done with this one."

Thay stepped toward the priest. "If this Saint of yours is so powerful," he mocked, "maybe he can transport himself out here into the nothingness of space to save you."

"That won't be necessary," said the priest, smiling. "For while powerful men plan to change worlds, common men bleed to change them." He drew his double-edged short sword.

"Cute," replied Thay. "Then I guess it's time for you to bleed."

"The Saint's will be done," he replied and turned toward the group behind him. "If I fall, remember the Word transcends death."

Estimating over fifty followers, Stone back-stepped to create a larger field of fire between himself and the crowd. In his periphery, he saw Mori, Magnus, and Katalya doing the same.

As the audience looked on, Thay and the priest collided.

Thay leapt toward the priest, his tomahawk extended above and behind his head. As he landed, he brought the weapon down in a powerful, sweeping motion. His first move was blocked by the priest's sword, but Thay thrust the blade of his knife toward his opponent's abdomen. The priest's reflexes were quick, however, and he spun away from Thay's attack and thrust his sword downward at the back of Thay's head. Thay blocked the move with his tomahawk and drove his opponent's sword toward the ground. Twisting his body, he let out a grunt as he drove his knife into the priest's shoulder just as the priest crashed his fist into Thay's nose.

Thay stumbled backward from the blow as a roar of gasps rose from the crowd of followers. Still holding the rifle in the direction of the followers, Stone positioned himself so that he could simultaneously watch the fight and keep an eye on the crowd.

The priest looked down toward the blade still embedded in his left shoulder and smiled. "Pain is an excuse for the weak-willed and the non-Believers," he said as he grasped the knife firmly and slowly pulled it from his body.

Thay countered his opponent's smile with a hungry grin of his own. "Then let's just see how much you really believe," he retorted, the blood from his nose running down his face, painting bright red streaks against his teeth.

Retrieving a second knife from his vest, Thay again lunged toward the priest. When they collided, Thay blocked a downward thrust from his opponent's knife to his right. The priest repositioned his grip on his sword and slashed Thay across the chest. As the blade cut across Thay's body, he drove his knife into the priest's side.

Thay took a step backward as his combat vest fell to the floor, the straps sliced by the priest's blade. The stranger's sword had also found flesh; Thay's uniform was sliced at his chest and quickly staining red as the blood began to flow.

But Thay seemed unaffected. He quickly retrieved his second tomahawk, and with his peoples' traditional weapon in each hand he spoke. "You're skilled, brother warrior, but I don't think you can allow me to leave many more blades inside you."

The priest, his body slightly bent with Thay's blade still protruding from his right side, slowly stood erect. "I can feel your hatred," he replied. "You wear it like a coat to keep you warm from the cold, but that same warmth will ignite into a fire that will consume and overwhelm you."

"It already consumes me," replied Thay. "And I welcome it."

"I've looked with yearning toward the day I give my life for the Word, non-Believer," continued the priest. "Unleash your hatred and let the Word flow." A smile came to his face. "Plant your blade one last time and let the Saint's will be done."

Thay turned his head toward Mori, who shook her head, warning him to stand down. Then he turned toward Stone. The blood from his nose still flowed down his painted face and his shirt was soaked crimson from his chest wound. A wicked smile crept across his face, exposing his blood-stained teeth. "Time to see if you are a wolf or a dove," he said to Stone.

"Damn it," mouthed Stone. He knew Thay wouldn't back down.

"Thay," said Mori slowly, "you need to —"

Before she could finish, Thay gave Stone a wink before turning and flinging his tomahawk toward the priest.

The priest stumbled as the blade struck his forehead. After a slight pause that seemed like minutes, the priest's body fell backward onto the deck.

Tension gripped the room and the silence consumed Stone's consciousness. He looked into the eyes of the followers.

Vacant.

"No one is here to hurt you! We are here to free you!" yelled Mori to the crowd.

Silence again.

Still focusing on the crowd, Stone felt with his right foot for Thay's rifle, which was lying on the deck to his right. Making contact with the weapon, Stone flicked his foot to send the rifle sliding toward Thay's position. As the weapon skidded across the floor to Thay, the light metallic scratching sound tore through the stillness enveloping the compartment.

Stone focused on a single young man in the crowd; he could see an odd combination of detachment from what was happening and personal determination on his face. It was about to start.

"Only the Word brings freedom!" shouted a voice from the stirring crowd.

"And the Word transcends death!" responded the crowd in unison and they rushed forward.

"Fire!" shouted Mori and the compartment exploded with gunfire.

Looking down the barrel for his first target, Stone saw a wall of white, gray, and red swarming toward him. He pulled the trigger and his rifle recoiled as he sent round after round into the wave of human flesh. At least eight fell in front of Stone as they closed on him. He stepped back and continued to fire. Three more dropped.

As the wave grew closer, Stone dropped his rifle and reached over his shoulder to grasp his sword. Gripping the handle, he snatched the sword from the sheath and in a single motion slashed downward into the onrushing attackers. The blade cut through one attacker at the neck, slicing flesh and bone then continuing into the left arm of a second attacker. The sword had enough energy to amputate the man's arm but only partially penetrated the attacker's torso.

As Stone withdrew the sword, another attacker impacted his left side. Jolted, he pivoted and brought his knee into the new attacker's head, causing him to recoil. Stone slashed with his sword again, eviscerating the assailant.

Before he could react to the next threat, Stone's feet left the floor as two more attackers hit his right side and both thighs. Falling forward, Stone pulled his sidearm from its holster and twisted his body to face his opponents. He fired two rapid shots point-blank into the attackers as he hit the ground. The first fell dead instantly, Stone's bullet entering just above her right eye and exiting in a cloud of red mist, bone, and gray matter. The second attacker rolled onto his side with a wound to his shoulder. The wounded man put his hand onto the deck to pull himself up again. As he did, Stone fired two more rounds into the man's torso and he collapsed.

Stone pivoted and swung his pistol toward the direction of the attackers. In front of him stood a single young woman, her right arm shredded by a bullet and blood pumping from another wound in her abdomen. She stood motionless three meters from him.

Holding his weapon on the woman, Stone quickly scanned the room. The deck of the cargo bay was littered with dead and dying attackers. Mori stood on the far end of the compartment, her pistol in one hand and sword in the other. Scattered around her were close to a dozen attackers. Katalya was replacing a clip in her rifle and Magnus held his weapon in the direction of the woman in front of Stone. Finally, Stone looked toward Thay, who was removing one of his tomahawks from the chest of a dead attacker.

With the room clear, Stone turned back toward the woman. She couldn't have been more than nineteen years old, her young complexion and attractive face highlighted by tufts of golden hair that boxed in both of her cheeks, almost like a picture frame.

But her eyes still held a vacant, determined gaze as she stepped toward Stone.

"Stop!" shouted Stone. "I don't want to have to kill you!"

The woman looked directly at Stone and spoke.

"Believers do not fear death. Death brings the ultimate truth," she said as a smile of contentment spread across her face.

"You don't have to do this," added Mori.

"Believers do not fear death. Death brings the ultimate truth," the woman repeated, glancing toward the ground. At her feet lay the sidearm Thay had left with Stone when he accepted the priest's challenge.

"No!" warned Stone.

Without speaking, the woman reached down toward the weapon.

A single shot echoed through the compartment as Stone sent a round into the woman's right thigh.

She let out a moan and collapsed onto one knee.

"Damn it, stop!" Stone pleaded.

The woman's face transitioned from a grimace of pain to her previous blissful smile.

"Believers do not fear death. Death brings the ultimate tru —" She lunged for the pistol.

Stone felt the recoil and heard the roar of his pistol resonate throughout the cargo bay as the woman's head snapped backward and she fell to the deck.

"Finally!" bemoaned Thay. "If she said 'believer' one more time, I would have shot her myself."

"Screw you," Stone shot back, glaring at Thay. Stone knew he had to kill the young woman, but he didn't have to feel good about it.

"I don't know if you're a wolf," replied Thay coolly as he walked toward the priest to retrieve his other tomahawk. "But you're not a dove either."

"What the hell was that?" asked Katalya as she and Magnus joined Mori at Thay's side.

"I have no idea," replied Mori. "They had no weapons and still came at us."

"And I haven't seen any slaves look or act like that before," said Stone.

"And this one's highly trained," added Thay as he leaned over to withdraw his tomahawk from the priest's body.

"Regardless of what they thought," reckoned Stone, "they were on the way to Xen territory."

He looked toward Mori, who had just finished taking a DNA sample from one of the victims. She looked back toward Stone and gave him a slight nod of confirmation.

"I take it they're a match for genetic alteration," grunted Magnus.

"It looks that way," replied Mori, rising to her feet and activating her comms link to *Hydra*.

"*Hydra* this is Alpha 1, you can call off the transport, no survivors. It's a mess down here."

"What next?" asked Katalya.

"I don't know, but this is too weird to ignore," replied Stone.

***

Mori looked over the carnage around her as she made her way to the priest's body. Each step she took was over the torn and bloody body of an unarmed attacker. Reaching the body, she inspected Thay's handiwork.

"He knew what he was doing," interjected Thay as he stood next to Mori. "He's as well trained as most Rangers."

"None of this makes sense. Elite Guard troops on a slave ship and slaves that don't want to be rescued," added Stone.

Mori knelt next to the priest's body and read a portion of the text covering his bloody torso:

The Saint embodies the Word

The Saint is the vessel of the Word

The Saint is the only true interpreter of the Word

The Saint is the well of faith from which the Word flows

"We've got to find out who this 'Saint' is and why all of these people were willing to die for him," concluded Mori.

"Magnus, Katalya, did you see the point of origin from NAVSYS while you were on the bridge?" asked Stone.

"Yes," replied Magnus. "Echo 2."

"We don't have any significant forces in Echo," replied Mori.

"As far as I know, neither do the Xen," added Thay.

Mori paused for a moment of contemplation. "Something's going on there. Something new. Something that needed Elite Guard troops to protect it."

"So, Echo?" asked Stone.

"Echo it is," said Mori. "But we need to get more intel."

"Back to the fleet?" questioned Thay.

"Back to the fleet. Then Echo," answered Mori.

Chapter 3

Rebecca Sterling's feet tapped against the marble floor as she and her Association partner stood outside the ProConsul's chamber.

"Stop fidgeting," warned Alden Faulkner.

Rebecca's fellow envoy wore a heavy double-breasted overcoat and jet-black leather boots triple latched with brass buckles. The leather over-vest underneath his coat was concealed by a deep royal purple scarf bunched around his neck. His eyes were hidden behind brass-rimmed goggles and he wore a purposely wrinkled and bunched felt tall-hat.

Rebecca Sterling was similarly dressed in the normal attire for Association members and their high-level employees. A brown felt top hat covered her scarlet hair, except for a long braid which ran over her shoulder and down the front of her body to her waistline. Her black silk, long-sleeved shirt was covered at her torso by a brown leather corset purposely meant to accentuate her breasts. Her brown skirt flowed to the floor and was split on the left side to show long, toned legs and the stocking that protruded from her calf-high laced boots to halfway up her thigh.

"Remember," Alden cautioned, "use formal Humani vernacular and tone at all times."

"Yes, of course. And which one of us will be the eye candy?" asked Rebecca, the junior of the two.

The Association always sent two envoys. One male, one female. And both were required to be as attractive as they were intelligent and personable. Rebecca had been on several political missions within the Dark Zone and even one to Terillian territory, but this was her first time on Alpha Humana and her first encounter with the ProConsul.

"It could be either one of us according to our sources. We'll just have to play it by ear."

"All right," said Rebecca, smiling as she positioned the slit in her dress to show more leg. She could feel the nervous energy welling up inside her. If she pulled this off, she would make enough money for a reserved seat at the Steamworks Bar on Port Royal, a clear sign that an envoy was moving up in the Administration hierarchy. Giving a quick tug on her stocking, she continued. "Even with the scar, I hear she is breathtaking."

"And deadly," warned Alden. "ProConsul Astra Varus isn't your normal political leader. She's smart, intuitive, calculating … and ruthless. And she knows how we conduct discussions so just be straightforward and proper, and let her control the conversation."

"But that goes against our training —"

"Listen," huffed Alden, "if she thinks for a second we are trying to play her, we'll have our asses beaten and thrown back onto a transport to Port Royal ... if we're lucky."

"Understood." Rebecca pouted. "Talk proper, look pretty, and let her run the show."

Rebecca jumped and a bolt of excitement rushed over her as the door opened and a tall, muscled Praetorian stepped through the entrance. *'They might be arrogant assholes, but they do keep themselves in shape,'* she thought to herself as she looked over the guard.

"Envoys Faulkner and Sterling," boomed the Praetorian. "ProConsul Astra Varus will now see you."

"Very well, Praetorian," replied Rebecca with an inviting smile.

Rebecca could see the guard take a second to contemplate what the smile meant but he quickly regained his stoic demeanor.

"Follow me," he ordered.

Entering the room, Rebecca was immediately drawn to Astra. The ProConsul commanded the room from her seated position in the chamber hall. She wore a forest green dress that did an even better job of tastefully showing Astra's features than Rebecca's outfit did for her. Her golden blonde hair fell over both of her shoulders and flowed down the front of her dress. She was stunning.

"Envoys Faulkner and Sterling from the Port Royal Association," announced a page standing near Astra's chair.

"Yes, of course," said Astra. "Please, come forward."

Rebecca bowed her head. As she did, she glanced toward Alden, who was doing the same. Being Alden's junior, Rebecca waited for him to raise his head, then she followed suit. She took in the entire room. Everything. The guards — how many, what weapons did they carry, how attentive were they? The attendants and other guests — what were their expressions? Did they seem on edge or comfortable? How many exits? What food and drinks were being served, if any? What communications, scientific, and other technical equipment was in use?

Rebecca looked at everything, but nothing registered; she was mesmerized by Astra. The only thing not pure perfection about her was a scar on her temple running toward her ear. To Rebecca, the one imperfection made Astra only more attractive. Beyond Astra's physical attributes was the way she carried herself. There was no doubt to anyone in the room the absolute nature of Astra's authority.

"And who is this scarlet enchantress?" asked Astra.

Rebecca regained her focus as a bolt of embarrassment and fear shot through her body. She had been so enamored by Astra that she had forgotten to introduce herself with Alden. Rebecca glanced toward Alden, who was burning a hole through her heart with his eyes.

"Forgive me, ProConsul," replied Rebecca, the high pitch of her response giving away her nervousness, "the grandeur of your chamber and the magnitude of your beauty can easily distract a simple envoy such as myself from her duties. I am Envoy Rebecca Sterling, a humble emissary for the Port Royal Association, and I am honored by your reception of our unworthy party."

"Flattery and self-deprecation," interrupted Astra as she smiled at Rebecca.

Rebecca took in a deep breath to settle herself. As she did, she noticed Astra's gaze drift toward her chest.

"Pretty," commented Astra as she turned toward Alden. "Very pretty." As she spoke, her smile grew flat and her facial muscles relaxed. "But she has a lot to learn about etiquette, would you not agree Envoy Faulkner?"

"Of course, ProConsul Varus," he replied.

Rebecca glanced at Alden. He was not pleased.

"Well, that's enough pleasantries," smiled Astra. "Let us discuss business."

Rebecca saw Astra look toward the Praetorian on her right and slightly wave her hand toward the group of servants and guests in the chamber. The guard instantly responded.

"Everyone exit the hall!" his voice boomed. "The ProConsul wishes to speak in private!"

Rebecca puzzled over the removal of the guests and servants. *'If she didn't want them in the meeting, why did she have them here in the first place?'* Then her training kicked in. Astra wanted her and Alden to see her empty the room in a subtle but definitive display of authority.

As the last of the group exited, Astra turned toward the guard again. "You and your men will exit as well, Praetorian."

Rebecca could see an instant of surprise and hesitation on the face of the guard.

"Yes, ProConsul," he snapped. "We will station ourselves at the entrance if we are needed."

"Very well," she replied.

Rebecca watched as the Praetorians marched to the entrance in single file. Even Rebecca knew it was rare that a ProConsul send all of her Praetorians away. As the last guard exited and pulled the door closed, she turned back toward Astra.

"May we proceed, ProConsul?" asked Alden.

"You may not," replied Astra with a smile.

Rebecca could feel her heart race. Had they— had she—failed the negotiation before it even started? She looked toward Alden. His face was tight in a combination of surprise and frustration.

"Do not worry, Envoy Faulkner," continued Astra. "You have not failed in your mission ... yet. I simply want to negotiate with Envoy Sterling; you will not be necessary. You can enjoy the Capital while we discuss the matter at hand."

"Uh — yes, ProConsul?" replied Alden in quizzical acknowledgment.

Rebecca was surprised the veteran negotiator had slightly lost his composure.

"Is this a problem?" queried Astra in a slightly elevated and pitched voice.

"Of course not, ProConsul," shot back Alden. "But may I have a moment to speak with my companion before I exit?"

Rebecca saw Astra take in a deep breath and close her eyes as if to control an unseemly response.

"Very well, Envoy Faulkner," she huffed.

Rebecca felt Alden's hand on her shoulder as he pulled her in close and turned away from Astra.

"I'm sorr —"

"Never mind that," interrupted Alden softly. "We don't have time. Just listen."

Rebecca focused on Alden's mouth as he talked at a whisper.

"If she doesn't want the Praetorian to hear us then she's told very few people, if any, about her plans. Just listen to her and don't promise anything ... she will try to get you to —"

"That is enough, Envoy Faulkner," interrupted Astra. "Please take your leave."

"Focus on the task and don't become distracted," added Faulkner quickly and quietly. "And I guess we know who she prefers. Use that to your advantage but don't push it," he warned.

"Faulkner!" spoke Astra loudly.

"Yes, ProConsul," he replied as he turned to face Astra. "Of course. May your negotiations be pleasant."

With that, Alden quickly turned and headed for the exit.

Rebecca looked toward Astra as the ProConsul slowly scanned her body. Feeling Astra's eyes take her in, she felt both uncomfortable and excited at the same time.

"I am sure they will be," replied Astra with a smile as she shifted her gaze to Rebecca's eyes. Under Astra's glare, Rebecca felt as if she was standing naked in front of the ProConsul. In a matter of seconds, Astra's fierce, hungry gaze and aura of power had disarmed the highly trained negotiator.

Get it together, Rebecca, she told herself. Focus on the task.

Rebecca gathered her thoughts. "Shall we begin, ProConsul?"

"Of course," smiled Astra in a soothing voice. "Let's get down to business."

Rebecca smiled. "Yes, ProConsul, let us begin."

***

Martin stood at the edge of the door. The smell of industrial sanitizer burned her nostrils and the random squeaking of the orderlies' rubber shoes on the tile floor caused her right eye to twitch.

She hated this place.

Before entering the room, she took in a deep breath; the ammonia from the cleaner that hung in the air immediately turned the twitch above her eye into a sharp headache. Wincing slightly and closing her eyes, Martin adjusted to the smell and exhaled forcefully to ready herself.

Willing herself to move forward, she turned the corner of the door and entered a small, dimly lit room in the Humani military retirement home. In the corner sat a man in an old leather chair. The beams of light coming through the window by the chair highlighted a cloud of lint and dust hanging in the air, contradicting the façade of cleanliness created by the industrial sanitizer saturating Martin's sense of smell.

"Who's there?" inquired a deep but weak voice.

"It's me, Father," answered Martin.

Martin could see a leathered hand rise to a shadowed face to block the light from the window.

"Emily?"

"Yes, Father," she replied with a smile as she stepped toward the light.

Bracing himself on the arm of the old chair, Martin's father slowly rose to meet her.

Watching him struggle to stand, Martin thought back to the man she knew as a child. Strong, muscular, and confident, he was the ideal soldier. Handpicked to serve on the Praetorian Guard, he eventually became Sergeant-at-Arms for the ProConsul's private guard — a position he held with honor and distinction for over ten years and through two ProConsuls. Then it all fell apart.

As she moved closer, Martin could see the genetic regeneration pills that kept his liver from failing. And beside the pills a half-empty bottle of whiskey.

She stood nervously still while the old soldier steadied himself and reached out for her.

"Let a proud father see his warrior." He coughed.

Martin stepped into her father's arms, squeezing him tightly. She heard him let out a small grunt against the strength of her embrace. Loosening her hold, she felt him wrap his arms around her. His arms, which had once enveloped and protected her, were now weakened and frail. With her head on his shoulder, she allowed a single tear to drop from her eye. After a few seconds reminiscing on the man he used to be, Martin forced a smile on her face and stepped back to look at her father.

"It's good to see you, Father," she replied.

The skin on his face, aged beyond his years by alcohol, regret, and betrayal, looked as if it would crack as a proud smile slowly formed.

"I've bragged about you so much," he said, "I think the staff are sick of talking to me."

"I haven't done anyth —"

"Don't be shy," her father interrupted. "The hero of Juliet 3, promotion to major, and now —" He paused for a deep, congested cough. "And now, elevated to the ancient title of Paladin."

Martin bowed her head slightly in a gesture of humility, but her heart felt renewed. Even in his sad state, the praise of her father meant everything. Almost everything.

"Thank you, Father," she replied. "And that's why I've come to see you."

"You can always talk to me," he replied as he slowly, gingerly returned to his seat. "What's on your mind, Paladin Martin?" he asked proudly.

Martin backed up slightly and sat on the edge of a long table by her father's chair. After settling herself, she placed her hands between her knees and rubbed her palms together tightly.

"Something's bothering you."

"My next mission," she began.

"Mission," replied her father energetically as he leaned forward.

Looking into his eyes, she could still see the old fire that had made him a legend in the Praetorians — and to his daughter.

"Yes, Father," she continued. "I'm to track down the Traitor and his concubine."

"And you're torn?"

He still knew her better than she knew herself.

"No," she snapped back quickly. "He betrayed our people, the Guard, me —"

"But you're still unsure you'll act when the time comes," replied her father as he leaned in toward her, taking her hands in his.

His grip was strong again, like when she was a child.

She looked into his eyes, those fiery blue eyes. She could feel her own eyes start to fill with tears.

"He was my mentor, he ... I trusted him. It doesn't make sense that he would turn on us. I thought he was the best of us. I just … other than you, I trusted him more than —"

"Trust doesn't mean anything," he grumbled, squeezing her hands even tighter. "Trust is gained and lost. I trusted your mother and …"

Martin knew that her mother's abandonment of both her and her father to marry into a First Family broke her father and was the catalyst for the alcoholism that robbed him of his career and her of the father she once knew.

"Duty," he continued as he released his grip and gently placed a calloused hand on her cheek. "Duty matters. It makes us who we are."

"Yes, Father," she replied as she wiped the tears from her face.

"You're a Paladin and a hero to our people. You didn't become this because of him, but because of who you are and the way you carried out your duty as a soldier of the Republic. Your feelings for him don't matter, unless they help you carry out your mission."

"But I hate him," she exhaled heavily. "And I love him."

"Then ignore the love and embrace the hate," he replied coldly. "Love will make you weak. It will make you vulnerable. It makes you lose focus. Hatred focuses you and keeps you locked onto your target and your mission — your duty."

Martin thought about what she had lost. Her father's love for her mother destroyed him when she left. She hated and loved Jackson and, in the end, his love for her cost him his life; she would not let Stone do it to her again. She wiped the tears from her eyes — the last she would ever cry for Stone. She took another deep breath and leaned in to give her father a kiss on the forehead.

"I won't let you down," she said, rising to her feet and walking toward the exit. As she opened the door, she looked back to see him pour a glass of whiskey. With a sigh, she stepped out of the room to Arilius Tacitus, the other Paladin, who was awaiting her.

"Are you done visiting Daddy?"

"Yes," she replied, walking past him and toward the exit without giving him the satisfaction of an emotional response. "We've got a traitor and a Ter whore to kill."

Chapter 4

Rebecca slowly opened her eyes against the brightness of the room. The smooth, cool sensation of silk sheets caressed her body. Taking in a deep breath, Rebecca stretched her arms outward and rolled her shoulders as she turned onto her back. Another breath and she smelled the aroma of jasmine and cherry blossoms. The smell took her back to the night before — the best "negotiation" she had ever experienced. As she reminisced, she could still feel hints of the powerful sensation of Astra's body against hers and the bolts of passion that had enveloped her.

"You're awake."

Astra's voice startled Rebecca.

"How did you sleep?" asked the ProConsul.

Rebecca couldn't help but smile as she gazed at Astra. The ProConsul was covered by a large towel with her hair tied in a long braid that fell over her left shoulder and extended to her waist. Small droplets of water glistened on her exposed skin, reflecting the morning light.

"Very well, ProConsul," replied Rebecca. "But how could I not sleep comfortably after a night like last night?"

"Yes. It was enjoyable," stated Astra, dropping her towel and reaching for a dark red dress hanging to her left.

Rebecca's stomach dropped slightly. She was supposed to have enchanted Astra to aid in the real negotiations, but Astra had commented on their night together like it was an everyday, mundane event. Just *enjoyable*? Even worse, Rebecca realized the minor slight had actually hurt her feelings and she began to fear she was the one that had become enchanted.

Rebecca looked on as Astra slid the dress over her body. The dress fit loosely but still displayed her amazing form. She continued to watch as Astra tilted her head slightly to reposition her braid, exposing the side of her neck. Rebecca could remember running her lips over that neck hours ago and having the same done to her.

'Damn it,' she thought to herself. *'Stop thinking about it. Focus on the task.'*

But it was useless. Astra had her tangled in her web.

"I would have asked you to join me for my bath but you were sleeping so comfortably," continued Astra.

Rebecca struggled to not think about her and Astra bathing one another.

"Tha —"

"But now we must discuss Humani and Association business."

Before Rebecca could respond, Astra reached for a comms link near her bed and activated it. "Send them in," she ordered.

A shocked and surprised Rebecca pulled the silk sheet tight around her body as the door to the chamber opened. First through the door were two Praetorian Guards, who took positions on both sides of the entrance. One spoke.

"ProConsul," said the Praetorian. "Senators Marcus Sarius and Julius Lucretia."

Rebecca attempted to pull the covers even tighter, but it wasn't possible. She could feel the blood running to her face and her cheeks flush with embarrassment. As she looked toward the two men, she could tell they were just as surprised.

"Very well, Praetorian," smiled Astra. "Position yourselves outside of the chamber," she added, turning toward the senators. "Marcus, Julius, what news do you have for me?" asked Astra.

"Yes, ProConsul," answered Julius after a quick glance toward Rebecca. "The Patrician Council ..." He paused and Rebecca wanted to melt as he looked again in her direction. "The Council has advised key senators regarding the need to approve the additional funds."

"And what do they think the funds will be used for?" inquired Astra.

"We convinced them the war has greatly increased the need for POWs and political prisoners beyond the capacity on Capro," said Marcus. "And since the war effort requires even our oldest capital ships to remain active, there was no alternative but to create a new prison complex."

"Did they authorize the full amount?" asked Astra.

"The full trillion credits," Marcus said with a smile.

Rebecca struggled to mentally and emotionally collect herself and determine how to respond to the position in which Astra had put her; she was both figuratively and literally naked at the negotiating table.

"But it was not easy, ProConsul," interjected Julius. "Luecentius Malius has many questions and spoke out against spending such a large amount without more details, but eventually our supporters were able to shout him down."

"That old bastard is a thorn in my side," grumbled Astra. "Republican virtues and the importance of senatorial oversight." Her tone was mocking. "That is all that senile, wrinkled fossil talks about."

"There are others," said Marcus as he took a step toward Astra, "that have been heard whispering about the power of your influence in the Senate."

"Let them whisper," shot back Astra. "And we will roar. The days of governmental impotence at the hands of grumbling and elderly men are coming to an end, my friends." Astra stepped toward the two young senators. "We live in a time that requires action. And any impediments to that action must be rooted up, cut out, and thrown aside." She paused to first look Julius in the eyes, then Marcus. "Do you not agree?"

Rebecca, despite her hurt feelings, was enthralled by the ferocity in Astra's words.

"Of course, ProConsul," replied Marcus.

"That is the only way," added Julius. "With the Patrician Council guiding the topics of debate and setting the agenda of the Senate, these relics won't be able to hold us down."

"Will not," interjected Astra.

Rebecca could see the confused look on Julius's face. But even though she was struggling internally with her school-girl crush on Astra, her training told her the senator's mistake.

"ProConsul?" asked Julius.

"Will not be able to hold us down," said Astra as she gave a cold smile to Julius. "Being on the Patrician Council does not allow you to use less than formal language when speaking to the ProConsul, does it?"

"Of course not, ProConsul," he said humbly.

Rebecca could see his face redden with embarrassment. The ProConsul had control of every situation in which she was involved. Rebecca realized she never had a chance. So much for that reserved seat at the Steamworks.

"It will not happen again," he added.

"Good." Astra smiled at having imparted the necessary amount of humiliation to keep the young, brash senator in his place. "Let's discuss the plans. Envoy Sterling?"

Rebecca heard her name and quickly stood to face Astra, her arms firmly holding the sheet around her naked body.

"Yes, ProConsul?" she asked sheepishly.

"Has the Association begun accumulating the necessary resources to start construction of the ships once the payment is made?"

Rebecca thought about Alden's warning to not make agreements or give too much information.

"ProConsul," replied Rebecca, "I would have to verify with —"

"Come now, Rebecca," interrupted Astra. Rebecca's heart pounded as Astra walked over to her. "We do not need to play these silly games, do we?" As she finished her sentence, Astra ran her hand over Rebecca's hair and her arm holding the sheet that stood between her and the world. Astra's touch sent tingles through her body. She could feel her face grow flush again and instinctively looked down toward the floor. Again, she felt Astra's hand as the ProConsul gently cupped her cheek and slowly directed her face upward so that they could look into each other's eyes. Astra then leaned in close to Rebecca.

Rebecca's balance waivered and her knees weakened as the warmth of Astra's breath against her neck overwhelmed her senses. She closed her eyes. All she could think of was the night before.

"Do we?" she whispered.

"Of course not," replied Rebecca as she tilted her head to her side and took a small step back. She was ruined, but at that moment she didn't give a damn. "We have made the necessary preparations to complete all construction and initial testing within ten years," conceded Rebecca.

"Excellent," added Astra, gently caressing Rebecca's arm. Looking into Astra's eyes again, she saw the ProConsul give her a telling smile of satisfaction. Not only did Rebecca know that Astra had her, Astra knew it as well.

"That will be enough for the full complement of a hundred ships, seven thousand fighters and attack craft, and three thousand transports. All off the reports to the Advisors." added Julius.

"The ten-year completion will also allow two years for our strike forces to train with the equipment," continued Marcus.

"And how are our strike battalions coming along?" asked Astra.

"Somewhat slow, but progressing, ProConsul," answered Marcus. "We have about fifty thousand slaves and converts from the Saint currently training, receiving inoculations against the Dominotra virus, and undergoing modification for the Xen virus in the training facilities under construction in the water layer underneath the gas planet Dolus near Capro. The facility will expand at a rate to support an additional eighty thousand per year throughout the project. This will mean we will need to take four million captives, villagers, and POWs each year to be able to meet our goal of compatible subjects and provide the Xen annually with the one hundred twenty thousand alterable slaves as well."

"That should allow for attrition and still provide over seven hundred thousand to man the strike fleet by the time the Xen realize what has happened," said Julius.

"And the Dominotra virus?"

Rebecca felt Astra's gaze once again as she answered. "The Association scientists are confident both the virus and the inoculations are effective. The slaves you provide to the Xen will contain enough carriers so that when they mate with another carrier, twenty-five percent of their children will become contagious when the chemical changes with puberty take place."

Marcus laughed. "The Xen will never expect it."

"It should be quite effective," continued Rebecca. "The virus will be airborne with a seventy-five percent infection rate for the Xen and fifty to sixty percent for Doran and humans. The mortality rate of the infected will be approximately sixty percent for the Xen and fifty percent for the Doran and Humans."

"The Xen social and political structure will collapse," added Julius. "And then we will strike."

"Oh, Envoy Sterling," interjected Astra.

"Yes, ProConsul."

"I must apologize," Astra smiled. "Here we have entered into formal diplomatic negotiations and I have not given you time to prepare yourself. Please excuse my slight." Rebecca again felt the wonderfully distracting sensation of Astra's breath on her cheek as the ProConsul leaned in closely. "You seem to have made me absent-minded with your beauty … and the memory of last night," she whispered.

Even though she knew it was a calculated move on the part of Astra, Rebecca soaked in the compliment.

"Me as well," she replied quietly. "An apology from yourself, while completely unnecessary, is gladly accepted, ProConsul."

"Very well," stated Astra. "Let us give you some time to prepare yourself and discuss these issues in more detail."

"Of course, ProConsul," she replied with a slight bow.

"I shall have my servants assist you with any preparations you desire," Astra said as she stepped over to the communications console. "Praetorians," she ordered, "the senators and I will be leaving shortly. One of you will remain outside this chamber for Envoy Sterling to make herself ready and then escort her to her room."

This time it was Rebecca who moved in close to Astra.

"Last night was amazing," she said quietly as she stared into Astra's eyes. "And I will not be long in your chambers."

Rebecca felt Astra's hand caress her hair and saw the ProConsul's mouth turn upward in a slightly amused smile.

"Yes, dear, it was very nice. I have plans for you, Rebecca Sterling. And perhaps we will do this again," she said with an inviting smile.

"I would very much like that," replied Rebecca with a smile of subservience.

Rebecca's skin tingled with excitement as Astra's hand ran over her hair and then paused slightly as Astra moved her hand to Rebecca's neck and slightly brushed her hair over her shoulder.

"Perhaps," said Astra as she turned to join the senators who were already exiting the room.

Rebecca stood like a statue and watched Astra walk away. After a few steps, the ProConsul turned back toward her.

"And this is not my chambers; this is where I … entertain."

As the doors to the ProConsul's playroom closed, Rebecca dropped the sheets to the floor and sat on the edge of the bed with her head in her hands.

"Stupid," she exclaimed, chastising herself out loud. "You're being used."

She flopped back onto the bed and stared up at the ceiling. She wondered how many others had lain on this bed feeling the same way — frustrated, ashamed, and above all, excited in a way she had never felt before. As she lay there contemplating her utter failure as a negotiator, she noticed the slight hint of jasmine and cherry blossoms in the air and a reminiscent smile came to her face.

***

Once outside her entertainment room, Astra spoke with her senators.

"This is excellent news." She was smiling. "When that scaly *thing* bit into my father's neck, it had no idea the blood that would be pulled from its carcass would be the downfall of his entire race. We have knelt before those reptiles for too long, my brothers. If we are careful, play the willing followers, and stay very, very patient, we will take our rightful place as rulers of the known galaxy."

Astra saw smiles of ambitious pride spread across the faces of Julius and Marcus.

"But patience will be the key," she repeated. "And one day you'll be rulers of your own worlds within the eternal Humani Empire."

Chapter 5

Stone sat impatiently in one of the main briefing rooms adjacent to the command suite onboard the Terillian battleship *Winter Moon* along with Mori and most of the team. He could tell he was not the only one growing restless. Henry River, Mori, and Cassandra Orion each displayed their own subconscious idiosyncrasies. Henry, his war paint removed and his hair in two braids, sat on the edge of his chair with his head down and his feet fidgeting back and forth, up and down. Orion kept trying to smooth out the wrinkles in her uniform. Since rejoining the Terillian cause in earnest, she had been returned to her former rank of flight captain and was still getting used to her new wardrobe. Mori, also without her paint but with her hair free-flowing over her shoulders, sat across from Stone and was repetitiously running her right hand through her raven-black hair.

Sandwick and Thay seemed much less concerned. Sandwick sat leisurely in a chair reading a digital letter from his father. Thay was asleep.

"Where's Rickover and TC?" Stone asked Orion, more out of boredom than actual concern.

"What?" replied Orion. Stone could tell she hadn't been focusing on his voice.

"Rickover and TC?"

"Oh, yeah," recovered Orion. "Well TC's too damn big for these chairs, and this room, and Rickover — well, he's Rickover."

Stone knew the answer but at least it broke the monotony of the wait. He looked toward Mori.

"And Katalya and —"

"They didn't want to wait," interjected Mori before he could finish. She was clearly tired of waiting, too.

Stone had leaned back into his chair to continue the wait when suddenly a door opened and a Terillian general stepped forward. Instinctually, Stone came to attention. With perfect military bearing, he stood motionless. And then he let his eyes glance around the room. Everyone else was still sitting. Slowly relaxing himself, he looked toward Mori.

"Uh, Tyler." Mori smiled, her cheeks flushed. "We don't do that."

Stone put his hands on the table and slowly took his seat. He looked to Thay, who had awakened just in time to see Stone's faux pas. Thay returned Stone's glance with an audible laugh. Stone clearly still had a lot to learn about the Terillian military.

"Ino'ka, Ohcumgache, and Pácanšihuta, we are ready to hear your request," replied the general calling Mori, Henry, and Orion by their Akota names.

"Yes, Uncle," replied Mori as she and the others rose. At least Stone knew the Terillians used "uncle" as a sign of respect.

Stone rose to join them.

"Tyler," said Mori as she put her arm out to stop him. "It's just the Akota. I should have explained to you before."

Stone's blood rushed to his head and his hands started to perspire.

"It's okay," replied Stone. But it wasn't. He hadn't been left out of a military briefing since he was a lieutenant. *'How could the Terillian military be so different?'* he thought. Leaning in to Mori, he whispered gently in her ear. "You owe me a crash course on Terillian military etiquette."

"Of course, Tyler," replied Mori with a smile.

Stone gave her a cold stare; it was starting to not be funny anymore. Looking squarely at Mori, Stone could see she understood.

"And I'm sorry," she added.

Stone watched as the three Akota walked into the command suite. As the doors shut, Stone turned to face Thay and Sandwick, both of whom were staring directly at him. Judging. Again, an embarrassed and defeated Stone skulked his way back to his chair and sat.

"You really don't know much about us, do you?" asked Sandwick.

"It's odd that in only a few hundred years, you Hanmani have completely forgotten yourselves. Perhaps the shame of defeat made it easier," added Thay.

Anger enveloped him. He knew Thay disliked him, and Stone was quickly growing to hate him as well. How could Mori and this psychopath be of the same people?

"I think it's time someone knocked that smartass smirk off your face," Stone shot back as he overtly gripped his sword.

Thay sprung from his chair, presenting his tomahawk. "Let's see you try, Humani."

Stone could hear the sound of Thay squeezing the leather grip of his tomahawk.

"Stop it!" shouted Sandwick as he put his hand over Thay's and gently directed the warrior to lower his tomahawk. "Thayendanegea, your hatred for our enemy has clouded your perspective. This Humani," Sandwick shot a glance toward Stone, "has given up his entire world when he realized the truth. You, of anyone given the power of kinship among the Haudenosaun, must understand — what if you had to face friends and family as enemies?" Sandwick turned toward Stone briefly. "Haudenosaun is what the Iroqua call themselves."

Stone had not heard Sandwick say more than two sentences in the two months he had known him. Now the floodgates had opened to support Stone.

"Thank you, Sandwick," replied Stone.

"And you, Stone," countered Sandwick sternly. "You're a skilled warrior, but I can see the doubt in you at every turn. Doubt will not only get you killed but us as well and I'm not ready to die yet. You're fooling yourself if you think you can live with one foot in the Humani world and one in ours. You know the truth. You know you are of our people and that the Xen took that away from you. Simply embrace your heritage and pick a damn side."

Sandwick's words hit Stone like a brick. He knew he had to fight against the Xen to save his people, but he had been consumed emotionally with indecision and doubt. Stone so badly wanted his universe to be black and white, but he was awash in a sea of gray. And he needed to get his shit together.

"You're right, Sandwick," replied Stone. "I've endangered you and caused you to lose faith in me. I will regain your trust. I just don't know how in your … our … this culture."

Sandwick chuckled in a combination of frustration and pity.

"It's not *a* culture, Stone. The Terillian are Iroqua, Akota, Siksika, Powhats, Numinu, and Quapaw — each with our own culture and history. We are simply allies in the Confederation."

"Allies and cousins," added Thay. "You, and all the Humani, are part of this history, part of the Confederation of the People."

Stone was realizing just how little he knew about the Terillians and himself. "Mori had told me that our ancestors were from the Iroqua and Akota."

"He must undergo the Dance or the Requickening," concluded Thay.

Stone looked toward Thay. His normal anguished face was replaced by a clenched jaw and a reflective, far-off gaze of contemplation.

"What are those?" asked Stone.

"The right ceremony may cleanse you of the Xen pollution and remove the doubt that clouds your spirit," answered Sandwick.

"If you accept it," added Thay.

"Ceremony. What is it? How do I know which one?"

"We can't tell you about the ceremonies, not until we know which one you will go through," said

Thay. "If you're Akota, it will be the Dance. If Iroqua, the Requickening."

"And then it's the duty of the *wichasa wakhan* or the False Faces, depending on the ceremony," added Sandwick.

"So, a DNA test will tell me which one?" asked Stone.

"No," replied Sandwick, exhaling deeply. "It's not your DNA, Stone. It's about your vision."

"My vision?"

"You must go before the holy men and they will help you to have your vision. From there, you'll know what to do," said Sandwick.

Stone was at the same time hopeful and skeptical. He had to do something to put his mind right with his choices. But how much could he rely on the Terillian — or Akot — or Iroqu — whatever ... How much could he rely on some spiritual mumbo-jumbo to solve his problem? The picture of the Terillian Confederation he had grown up with was a combination of lies, stereotypes, and half-truths. He realized that, until this point, he had simply hoped to use the Terillians to save his own civilization. But now, the truth — so clear the whole time — finally sank in. In fact, it was like a bolt of lightning. The Humani civilization wasn't his; it was a fallacy. A trick. A cruel deception by conquerors that had in fact taken his and his entire planet's culture away from them. He was Terillian.

"When can I do this?" asked Stone eagerly.

"Easy, Stone," interjected Thay. "I can tell you are serious about this and it is good. But things must be done first, people must be consulted.

"Mori?" replied Stone.

"Among others," answered Sandwick. "You are her mate and as an Akota she must seek permissions and …"

"Why hasn't she done so already?" asked Stone. He was now concerned that he was having this conversation with Sandwick and Thay instead of Mori.

"That is for you and her to discuss," replied Thay. "The Akota are, well, different when it comes to kinship. And neither Sandwick nor I would presume to understand the intricacies, especially since her father is dead and she has no uncles or brothers."

"Don't forget," added Sandwick. "There are things about each culture that you will not know unless you are part of it. It's not for us to know why, when, or if Mori will discuss this with you or what she must do beforehand." He shrugged, then continued, "But she's also a female warrior. And a Ka-itsenko — very rare. And complicated."

"I think the Akota call it strong medicine," said Thay. "Lots of people, important people, will be watching what happens because she is involved."

Suddenly Stone realized his relationship with Mori might be more complicated than the politics involving his engagement to Astra. *'Leave it to me to fall for the most complicated woman in the Terillian Confederation.'*

Realizing he wasn't going to get much more out of the two but desperately wanting to capitalize on their willingness to talk, Stone changed the subject.

"Why couldn't we go into the briefing?" he asked.

"This is an Akota ship," answered Sandwick. "Each ship, except command ships for large fleets, is made up of troops from the same people."

"Are they different, the ships? I've only seen the same classes of ships."

"You really don't know the big picture, do you?" asked Thay as he leaned forward in his chair toward Stone.

A wave of uncertainty passed over him with Thay's question.

"I guess not."

"With the exception of the Scout Rangers, which is open to all that qualify, every *Terillian* you or the Humani have faced have been Akota."

"But the First Terillian War?" asked a stunned Stone.

"From your perspective, all Akota," answered Sandwick. "The entire Dark Zone is dotted with former Akota colonies and Alpha Humana was the most remote."

"With a small band of Iroqua included as part of a Confederation agreement," added Thay.

"From my perspective?"

"There was no 'first' war," said Sandwick. "We have been in continuous conflict with the Xen and their allies for over three hundred years. The Siksika and the Numinu have been fighting the Dorans from the beginning. The Powhats have provided equipment, logistical support, and at times allowed entry into the Rangers. The Quapaw allow individual clans to fight with the Siksika. And the Iroqua nation —"

"The Iroqua have so far chosen only to allow individual warriors to fight," grumbled Thay.

"Just the Akota?" Stone was dumfounded.

"Since this sector affected only the Akota and their colonies, it was they who agreed to the Accords and the creation of the Dark Zone, as well," said Sandwick.

"Because my people didn't come to their aid when it was needed," muttered Thay.

"Maybe this time it will be different," replied Sandwick in a conciliatory voice.

"Perhaps. But until they do, we'll be stuck in this eternal stalemate."

Stone suddenly felt very small. The war that he thought to be the biggest war in the history of the galaxy didn't even include all of the Terillians.

"Are they that important?"

"The Iroqua joining the war would almost double the size of our fleet and increase our forces under arms by seventy-five percent."

"Then why haven't they joined?"

"The Akota are holding the line in this sector, my people and the Numinu are keeping the Dorans bottled up, and the Jukaro effectively remove any threat from their sector."

"The Jukaro?" inquired Stone. "Another Terillian civilization?"

"No," replied Thay. "They lay on one of the far edges of the Dark Zone. The Xen attacked them about one hundred years ago and were stopped dead in their tracks."

"The Akota and Powhats tried to ally with them but they refused. The Powhats have occasional contact with them through an embassy, but basically they want no part of this war but are strong enough to repel anything the Xen can throw at them," added Sandwick.

And Stone's world continued to shrink.

"I think that's about all the reality I can handle right now," said Stone. In the last ten minutes, the world he no longer understood had become even more complicated. He sat back into his chair and tried to come to grips with his new place in the universe. After the revelations of Thay and Sandwick exponentially complicated his relationship with Mori and changed his entire perspective on the conflict between the Xennite Empire and the Terillian Confederation, Stone was glad the room had again become silent.

But the silence only allowed him time to think about everything he had just learned. Luckily, after a few short minutes, Mori, Henry, and Orion entered the room.

"Everyone listen up," barked Mori, stepping to the head of the table and turning on the data screens that were immediately behind her and at each person's chair. Stone pulled up and expanded the map on his screen as Henry and Orion took their seats. It was the Echo System.

"Based on the information we gathered and intel from operatives in the Echo System and on Port Royal, this is what we have." Mori took a step back from the table and with a digital pad manipulated the images on the larger screen while she spoke.

"It looks like this Saint we heard about has popped up out of the blue and is making a grab for control of the entire system. The intel shows he suddenly appeared on Echo 4's moon and took control of the abandoned Xen airbase there from the warlord, Syra. His believers think he's an orphaned child of farmers found by a mystic who raised him in the forest, where he became one with the Word …

whatever that is. From there, he started converting people to his doctrine about shared community wealth and a quest for communal consciousness that will remove the mortal bounds that cause pain, fear, and so on."

"So, he's crazy?" asked Sandwick.

"Like a fox," Mori replied. "It looks like there was some tech left on the base, which he has renamed the Divine City, and he took full advantage of it."

"Do we have details on the tech?" asked Thay.

"Some, but it's spotty," replied Mori, pulling up another screen with weapons and spacecraft schematics. "For the most part it's all first-generation stuff with a few jump-capable ships — nothing bigger than corvette size."

"Because of this," interjected Orion as she took control of the big screen from her chair. "This Saint has control of all non-jump-capable ships in Echo. And he is apparently the only one with jump capability."

Mori continued. "From his Divine City, he spread to Echo 3, where he gained control after a bloody campaign against the combined forces of the two ruling governments."

"Echo 3 is fairly advanced for a Dark Zone city," mused Stone. "Combustion engines, supersonic flight, even basic nuclear weaponry."

"And they used all of it — even on their own cities," replied Mori. "But the Saint and his army, called the Crucesignatis, picked up three recruits for every one killed. His 'share the wealth and classless society' line, combined with a promise of your own fiefdom for eternity if you die in his service, is pretty compelling to worlds ruled by tyrants, warlords, and oligarchies."

"Even with that," Stone said, shaking his head, "they should have been able to hold out longer."

"You would think so, but the intel also indicates he has been in contact with both the Xen through Alpha Humana and with the Association at Port Royal."

"Don't forget the Elite Guard on that slave ship," added Henry.

"What has the Association said?" asked Stone, knowing they played the neutral card but actively worked both sides for their own profit.

"They've said they don't know anything about the Echo System, which means they're ass-deep in it."

Mori paused to pull up a map of Echo 2. "Echo 2, now called the Promised City by the Saint. Currently, the Crucesignatis occupy one of the three primary landmasses and is currently fighting for control of the second, called Talia. A warlord controls the majority of Talia — his name is Ya-ling. He's allied with a warlord called Barca and an oligarchy of merchants and mercenaries on the third landmass to create what they call the Triad. They are only slightly less technically advanced than Echo 3 but have a large population. It seems the Saint, even though he has the capability, isn't using nukes or bios, so it's an old-fashioned slug-fest. Now he is bogged down on Echo 2 and the chatter between the Divine City, the Humani, and the Association has increased."

"Any other great news?" asked Thay.

"It's all speculation after that," replied Mori. "This Saint could be a Xen agent, working with them out of necessity, or just maybe he's just a lunatic."

"Or a combination of all three," interjected Stone.

"Either way there's only one way to know for sure."

"Looks like we have our next mission," concluded Thay.

"You guessed it," replied Mori. "We'll jump into the Echo System and do a silent insertion into the Talia landmass." She turned to *Hydra*'s pilot. "Orion, after *Hydra* drops us off, pick a nice quiet spot somewhere in the system and wait for our recall. Count on it being a few weeks."

"I'll have TC stock up on TP, booze, and porn." She laughed.

Stone could only imagine — although he wished he couldn't — what would classify as pornography for a Scapi.

Mori ignored Orion's remark and continued. "From there, we'll observe and, if it seems worthwhile, link up with the resistance forces to get more info. Once we've gathered enough intel we'll contact *Hydra*, get picked up, and decide our next move."

"When do we go?" asked Orion.

"We leave in a week," answered Mori. "Let's start making preps."

Stone and the others rose from their chairs as Mori turned off the data screens.

***

Later that night, Stone lay awake with Mori at his side. So many things weighed heavily on him. He knew he was Terillian, or more specifically either Akota or Iroqua. But knowing wasn't feeling. Maybe that's what the ceremonies mentioned by Thay and

Sandwick would do, just like the Elite Guard induction. That had all been a lie, but a lie that still felt very real on so many levels. And what would Mori have to do in order for him to go through the ceremony, and just how important was Mori and her 'strong medicine' to the Akota? To top it off, his whole sense of place, even as disjointed as it was after his defection to the Terillians, had been destroyed by the realization of just how small his little war and even Alpha Humana itself had been in the big picture of galactic events.

Staring into the overhead of their stateroom, his mind wandered. Every answer to a problem brought more questions. Growing more frustrated, he exhaled heavily. As he did, Stone felt Mori move beside him and her arm come to rest on his chest. Rolling over, he looked directly into her mesmerizing green eyes.

"What is it, Ty?"

Stone slowly ran his hand through her hair. Even after all these months, her beauty still captivated him. "Thay and Sandwick talked to me today about accepting my Terillian heritage and going through some ceremony."

Mori's forehead tightened. Stone felt her move his hand from her cheek as she sat up in the bed. "I wanted to wait longer," she protested. "They shouldn't have —"

"Why wait?" he interrupted. "Aren't you sure about us?"

Mori's tightened jaw transitioned to a smile. "Of course I am, Tyler," she replied, placing her hands on his cheeks. "You're meant to be with me. I've seen it. There's no doubt."

"Then what's wrong?"

"I wanted you to learn more about us naturally, over time. I didn't want to force this on you."

"I understand, but it sounds like the ceremonies will help me with my transition."

"These aren't simple ceremonies, Tyler. We don't undertake them lightly and they have real implications. You must be ready first."

"If this can help me adjust and make the rest of the team more comfortable with me," replied Stone, taking Mori's hands in his, "then I don't have time. I have to be ready now."

"You can be tested only once and if it's too soon, you could face ostracism."

"More than now?" he shot back, eyebrows raised.

"Yes," replied Mori. Stone could feel her squeeze his hands hard. "If you're rejected I can't be with you — the Shirt-Wearers would not allow it."

"The Shirt-Wearers?" Stone's fingers were going numb under the pressure of her grip.

"They are chosen to maintain order among my people. I am a Ka-itsenko and a woman. If it was determined you were not suitable, we wouldn't be allowed to stay together, so I would have to give up my title."

"You would —"

"Don't be stupid, Tyler," she interrupted. "You did the same for me. You know I'd give up my title for you. I'd hate it and I'd be betraying my own vision, but I would do it."

Stone looked into those green eyes once again. He could actually feel them pulling him toward her. "I'd never ask that, Mori. But I'm a danger to you and the others as long as I live between these two worlds. And if this ceremony will help ..."

She looked down toward the bed. Neither one of them wanted to endanger their relationship, but neither wanted to endanger the other even more. After a few seconds of silence, Mori again raised her head and Stone's gaze immediately went to her eyes.

"Of course, you're right," she said.

Stone felt the pressure on his hands lessen as she released her grip.

"Are you sure?" he asked. He wasn't.

"I know who you are, but you don't. In your head you know you're Terillian, and Akota, but in your heart, you're still lost, like all Hanmani. The only way to find yourself is through the Dance. And I must trust that the Great Spirit has the same vision for both of us."

Stone felt a clarity he had not experienced in years. Would this be the answer to what he was looking for, even before the incident at the Gateway Station rekindled the war?

"It's settled then," she continued. "I'll do what must be done tomorrow."

Despite the ominous sound of Mori's statement, Stone felt more at ease than he had in months.

With Mori curled up against him, he soon fell into a deep sleep.

***

Stone hurriedly made his way through the passageways of *Winter Moon*. The news of yesterday still had him frustrated and anxious, and to make things worse, *Winter Moon* was still a maze of compartments and passageways to him. He had been able to reserve range time but now he had to find the damn range. He looked back and forth between his digital reservation and the bulkhead locators as he fast-walked through the ship. Terillian compartment identification was a confusing mixture of symbols and numbers unlike the alpha-numeric system of the Humani, and he was having a hell of a time.

"Seven, One-Four-Eight ... is that a bird? And Charlie," he said out loud as he searched for the range.

Stone turned a corner, his head still buried in the digital reader. Before he could react, he collided with another crewmember.

"I'm sorry," offered Stone, "I —"

Stone went silent when he saw the man looking back at him. It was Navarus Nero, the man who had led the assault that destroyed his regiment and ended in the deaths of both Emily Martin and Hugh Jackson. He could feel his body grow hot with anger. Without realizing his actions, Stone drew his sword and pinned it against the bulkhead.

"Stone, wait!" gulped Nero, Stone's blade pressed against his throat.

"Wait?" replied Stone with a grunt. "You traitorous son of a bitch. You killed them!"

"I'm not a traitor, Stone," Nero pleaded, struggling to talk against the pressure of Stone's sword against his neck. "I'm no different from you. I only want to free our people from Xennite rule."

Stone pressed his forearm further into Nero's chest and his jaw clenched tightly. All he could see was Jackson and Martin and then the explosion that enveloped them.

"Stone, we're on the same side," begged Nero.

Stone finally had a flash of reason through his rage. He slowly released the pressure of the sword from Nero's throat but kept him pinned to the wall with his forearm.

"Talk," he ordered.

Nero took in a deep breath and began to speak.

"I assume that you know most First Family leaders know the truth?"

"Yes."

"Not all of us want to be ruled by them. My treason against ProConsul Maximillus was an attempt to overthrow the government so that we could share the truth with our people and rise up against the Xen. But once the first stage failed, the rest of the leaders remained quiet to protect themselves and wait for another opportunity."

"Others?" asked Stone, lowering his sword.

"Yes, other powerful First Family leaders feel the same as I — as we — do. The Malius, Vanari, Plaxis, Centius, Juli, Vae, and Scarus families, or at least some members, were ready to support the coup had the assassination been successful.

"General Darous Vanari and Admiral Carsis Plaxis?" asked Stone.

"Yes," replied Nero. "And other officials and officers."

"I had just assumed —"

"Don't think so little of your own people, Stone. Our society may have been corrupted by the Xen, but don't lose faith in the Humani people. They can't be held responsible for the shortcomings of our forefathers and their current leaders."

"I had no idea," replied a calm, humbled Stone. There was hope for his people yet, from within as well as from an outside power.

"One day we'll return home and fight for the freedom of our people," declared Nero as he placed a hand on Stone's shoulder. "But until then, we must fight against both the Xen and the First Families. Even if it means we fight our own, misguided people. Just like Juliet 3. I am sorry for the loss of your men."

Stone understood but did not have the words. Instead he nodded his head.

Nero returned the nod and gave Stone a quick pat on his shoulder.

"I hope to see you again soon, Tyler Lucius Stone, but I am only onboard *Winter Moon* for a briefing and must return to my men soon."

The two Humani warriors, once adversaries and now both traitors in the eyes of their people, gave one another a long look of understanding that only they could share. And then they went their separate ways.

***

Preparations for the long mission to Echo 2 and the unbearable anxiety from waiting on permission to move forward with the ceremony that might bring him closure had consumed his thoughts.

With two days left before the mission was to start, Stone sat in his stateroom waiting on Mori to return. As a Ka-itsenko and a female without a senior male warrior in her family, she was forced to make the request of the Shirt-Wearers herself. Mori had told Stone that her status as a Ka-itsenko assured the Shirt-Wearers would hear her request, but it didn't mean they would approve it.

As Stone sat waiting for Mori's return, he flipped through data screens on the terrain and population centers for the Talia landmass on Echo 2. Mindlessly shifting from one screen to the next, he soon realized he wasn't retaining any of the data; all he could think about was the pending decision of the Shirt-Wearers. Restarting from the beginning data screen, he started over, this time reading the data aloud.

"Climate: Seasonal ranging from four to twenty-seven degrees Celsius —"

The sound of the door to his stateroom opening instantly brought his review to an end. He quickly stood and turned toward the entrance. Before Mori could make her way into the room, he spoke.

"Any word?" He tried to read her face but it was surprisingly vacant. "Mori?" he asked again.

"They said yes," she replied flatly, her face blank. Stone smiled at Mori, but she turned her head away and looked toward the floor. He knew she was worried about the outcome of the ceremony but had hoped she would have at least been happy it was approved.

"I know you're worried," he replied, walking toward her. "But once we get back from Echo 2 and —"

"You'll have your vision tonight and undergo the ceremony tomorrow," replied Mori as she looked up toward Stone. Her face was pale, and she still refused to look him in the eyes.

"That's too soon," blurted Stone.

"If you refuse, you'll be forced off the ship. If you fail, you'll be forced off the ship." Finally, Mori looked up toward Stone. He could see tears welling up in her eyes. "This is what you asked for, Tyler. The Shirt-Wearers have decided … it's all or nothing."

Stone took a deep breath. It would be tough, but if anyone could get him ready it would be Mori.

"Well I guess you're gonna have to give me a crash course." He smiled, hiding his concern.

"I can't," she replied. "I can't see you until after the ceremony."

"But how will —"

"You have to trust the vision will lead you to your — to our — destiny," she replied as the tears started to flow. Mori moved in close to him. She put her arms around him and gave him a deep kiss.

He couldn't help but wonder if it was their last.

Chapter 6

"The Saint will see you shortly." The teenage girl smiled, her smooth blonde hair falling to her neckline with two sharp tufts running the length of her jawline.

"Very well," replied Rebecca, returning the smile.

As the girl turned and walked back into room, Rebecca inhaled deeply to calm herself. This was her first mission working for both the Association and ProConsul Astra Varus. She knew that if the Association found out about her she would simply disappear somewhere in the chaos of Port Royal. If she double-crossed Astra Varus, however, she knew the outcome would be very public, very painful, and very final. *'This will be worth it,'* she thought to herself. The Association offered her enough money and prestige to enter the upper crust of their culture. But Astra offered so much more. She thought back to her discussion with Astra the day after their "private" negotiations.

"So, all you need from me is to report to you the same information I report to the Association Council members?" asked Rebecca.

"Yes. And in return whatever monetary and civil titles on Port Royal you are being offered will be … meaningless.

"Meaningless?"

"Would you rather have a few hundred thousand credits and a reserved table in a bar in the middle of the Dark Zone or a continent to govern in my name on a Terillian or Doran world?"

Rebecca could still remember the feeling of Astra's hand on her cheek when she offered the proposition.

"And the Saint?"

"Just get his agreement to provide the necessary converts and slaves in return for the Association technical support and the possibility of Humani military advisors."

"You are offering a lot for a little, ProConsul."

She also remembered the angered look on Astra's face as she pulled her hand away.

"You do not need to be concerned with why I do anything, Envoy Sterling. But if you must know, I simply want to make sure I know everything the Association knows."

"Yes. Of course, ProConsul. I am sorr —"

"No need to apologize, my little peach. Just get the agreement and tell me everything you find out from the Saint and the Association Council."

"Yes. Of course."

"Good. I will send one of my Praetorians disguised as an attendant to ensure your safety … and your loyalty."

"The Saint is ready for you."

"Very well," replied Rebecca with a smile as the girl's words brought her back to the present.

"Follow me."

Rebecca turned toward Praetorian Marcus Hamrahi. The tall, powerful-looking babysitter assigned to her by Astra was dressed in the tan, black, and white mixture of silks and leather that was common among Association employees. She motioned for him to follow the girl as if she was his superior and then followed the two into the chamber.

As usual, Rebecca took in the room. She was instantly struck by the stark contrast of the room compared to that of the ProConsul's chamber on Alpha Humana. The room was dimly lit by large candles lining the walls of the space. The overhead lighting consisted of muted gas-filled lights. Their illumination was so poor that the flickering iridescence of candles on the walls several meters away only created flashes of light as she walked toward a man positioned in a chair on a small stone platform at the far end of the room. In contrast to the rest of the room, the area around the chair was well lit, shining like a beacon in the darkness of a storm.

She also noticed several others milling about the room wearing the same attire and hairstyle as the girl in front of her. Breaking the pattern of white and gray clothing were a few men wearing hooded cloaks. As she neared the opposite end of the chamber, Rebecca saw the girl stop just short of the figure in chair and kneel. Rebecca's eyes slowly adjusted to the difference in light between her and the mysterious figure, who slowly came into view through the flickering light.

The man slowly rose. As he did, everyone in the room dropped to their knees. Rebecca quickly did the same to ensure she wasn't violating any protocols. From her knees, she looked toward Marcus. The proud and stubborn Praetorian stood erect, even in disguise. Rebecca quickly reached for his trousers and gave them a tug. With an audible huff, Marcus lowered himself to his knees.

"Do not tell the ProConsul of the affront to her," he grunted under his breath.

"Shut. Up," grumbled Rebecca through her teeth, frustrated with the Humani hubris.

"Welcome visitors, please rise," directed the man.

Rebecca raised her head as she pulled herself to her feet. The man before her wore a brown cloak with what appeared to be gray trousers underneath. Despite his humble attire, Rebecca could tell he was far from normal. His sandy colored hair flowed perfectly to his chiseled jawline, which was covered by a light beard. Even more prominent were his brilliant blue eyes; they almost sparkled in the dim flashes of light. Rebecca could only image how striking they were in the light of day.

"Thank you, Saint," she replied.

The man stood silent for what seemed an eternity. His piercing blue eyes were hypnotic.

Rebecca, beginning to feel uncomfortable, spoke once again.

"I am pleased to have the opportunity to speak to you for the Association Council as well as the ProConsul of Alpha Humana and Matriarch of the Varus family, Astra Var —"

"Of course." He smiled. "The brokers of sin and the oppressors come to ask for my assistance."

Rebecca clenched her teeth underneath her smile. She had been trained to deal with the boasts and slanders of self-important leaders and politicians;

no doubt he was taking such a stance to show strength since it was he who had initially contacted the Association for support in his holy war.

"Your strength and wisdom would obviously be in high demand during such trying times," said Rebecca, trying not to choke on her words. "Perhaps I could discuss these matters with you in private?"

"There will be no discussion," declared the Saint.

Rebecca's jaw tightened and her eyes squinted slightly, surprised by his response. She knew he had propped himself up as a messiah for his followers and had read in the reports that he was eccentric to say the least, but refusing to talk made to no sense to her.

"But Sa —"

"Enough of this charade," interrupted the Saint with a smile still painted on his face. "It is true that I had contacted you for assistance, but that was before I had reached full synthesis with the Word."

Rebecca began to wonder if he actually believed what he was saying. She could feel her pulse quicken at the thought of what that might mean. Looking to her left, she saw the Praetorian tense his body and begin to scan the room intently.

The Saint continued, "Since my singularity with the Word, I have realized associations such as the one you're about to propose will corrupt and distort the purity of the Word, so I must decline your proposed alliance."

"This won't be taken well by the Association or ProConsul Varus," shot back Rebecca. "To challenge either would be a mistake."

"The Saint doesn't make mistakes," shouted one of the cloaked warrior-priests as he stepped from behind the Saint. "The Word is truth."

"The Saint embodies the Word!" replied the followers in the chamber in unison.

Rebecca could sense the room grow smaller as those in the followers began to move toward her and Marcus.

"This is madness," pled Rebecca.

"Madness." The Saint laughed, shaking his head. "This is clarity. This is purity. This is ... the beginning."

Rebecca felt a hand grip her arm.

Before she could react, she heard the whistle of a blade unsheathing and saw the blur of Marcus's body as he drove a hidden knife into her attacker's chest. Instinctively she fell to the floor and covered her face. Curled in a ball on the floor, she could hear the rush of priests moving toward Marcus followed by the slashing of swords and the screams and groans as the weapons found their mark. In a few seconds, she heard a loud moan, the thud of a body hitting the floor, and then silence.

She slowly opened her eyes to look directly into the dead, vacant eyes of Marcus as he lay on the floor with the bodies of two priests. She felt warmness on her hand and looked to see a pool of blood flowing toward her. Rebecca let out a shriek of horror and quickly scrambled away from the gruesome scene. Almost instantly, however, she felt the grip of several hands on her body. Looking up from her position she saw several followers above her. Her body jerked upward as they pulled her to her feet and held her tightly in their grasp. Fear raced through her body.

"Butchers!" she cried as she looked toward the Saint.

"Butchers?" the Saint asked with a chuckle. "Does the farmer butcher his field before planting his crops? Or is he simply removing the chaff and the weeds so the crop may flourish?"

"We're here on a diplomatic mission," she sobbed.

"No!" he shouted as he walked toward her. "You were bringing the diseases of corruption, privilege, and excess. So I'm forced to purify you."

Rebecca's body shook with anxiety.

"You'll face the power of both the Association and Humani for what you've done," she warned, hoping to bring the Saint to whatever senses he had left.

"Power?" retorted the Saint. "You don't have power. The Humani have technology and the Association has wealth. Those things aren't power." He smiled. "Let me show you what true power is, girl."

The Saint turned toward the girl who had directed them into the chamber. "Come, my child," he directed, and the girl quickly positioned herself in front of the Saint and knelt before him.

The Saint stepped around the girl, reached down toward Marcus's body, and pulled a blade from the Praetorian's back. Stepping back, he looked down toward the girl and spoke. "Rise, child."

The girl rose to her feet, her head still bowed.

The Saint placed his hands on the girl's shoulder and slowly turned her so that she was facing Rebecca. "Look at the nonbeliever," he said gently.

The girl slowly looked upward into Rebecca's eyes. She had a calm, pleasant look on her face. With his hands still on her shoulders, the Saint leaned in toward her cheek.

"Tell her about the believers?" he asked.

Rebecca saw a smile of contentment on the girl's face.

"The believers hear the Word and understand. The believers turn themselves over to the Word. The Believers serve the Saint through the Priest-Bishop. The believers do not fear death."

"Correct, child," he smiled as he ran his hand over the tuft of hair over her right cheek. After stroking the girl's hair, he gently placed the blade into her hand.

Rebecca swallowed hard and the blood rushed from her head as she tried to come to grips with her last seconds of life.

"Now child," he continued as he placed his hand back on her shoulder. "Show this nonbeliever the power of the Word."

Rebecca's knees gave out, but the other followers held her erect.

"Yes, Saint," the girl replied as she raised the blade.

"No!" screamed Rebecca as the girl put the blade to her own throat and in one motion sliced her neck from ear to ear. Looking on in shock, Rebecca was drawn to the smile locked on the girl's face as blood sprayed from her neck, covering her clothing.

As the life-blood flowed from the girl's body onto the floor, the Saint released his grip on the girl and she crumpled to the floor beside Marcus and the others.

"That … is power," exclaimed the Saint as he stepped over the girl's body and leaned close to

Rebecca's face. His fierce blue eyes gazed into hers, but all Rebecca could focus on was the young girl's blood splattered on his face.

"You're insane," she cried.

"No, Envoy Sterling. I'm the vessel of the Word. And in time you'll come to see that," he said to her.

"What are you going to do with me?" she asked, half grateful he wasn't going to kill her immediately but terrified of what was next.

He ran his hand over her smooth red hair. "I'm going to cure you of the diseases of your past life and welcome you into the peace and comfort of the Word."

The Saint stepped back and slowly wiped the blood from his face. Looking again toward Rebecca, he spoke. "Take her away."

Chapter 7

Stone stood naked in front of the medical team. He felt the cold sticky sensations on his body as a nurse attached an electrode to his temple, then another to his chest. Suddenly feeling pressure near his groin, he quickly looked down to see a second nurse attaching yet another to his thigh.

"Ya know," said Stone, "maybe we could turn up the heat in here a little bit. It's very cold."

The second nurse, having attached the electrode, rose to face Stone. She had sandy-colored hair tied into a tight bun, beautiful brown eyes, and a smooth dark complexion.

"I think the temperature —— and everything else —— is just fine." She smiled at him.

Stone, now even more embarrassed, returned the smile.

"Yala," interjected the other nurse, a slender, tight-lipped woman to his right.

"I was just playing," Yala replied. "If the rest of the Hanmani look like this ——"

The other nurse stepped toward Yala and placed her mouth next to her ear. She spoke in Akota and attempted to whisper but Stone could make out Mori's Akota name. As soon as Yala heard the name Ino'ka, she involuntarily took a step backward.

"I'm sorry. I meant no disrespect to you or Ino — I mean Major Skye," she stammered, her hands shaking as she placed another electrode on Stone's body.

"It's okay," he replied.

Stone took in a slow breath and focused on the wall and not the nurses' hands on his body. He also began to wonder just how big of a deal Mori was in her society. She had a direct line to the highest levels of her government, she was able to handpick a team of some of the best warriors he had ever seen, and apparently just her name scared the shit out of the nurse.

"You can put this on now," said Yala nervously, forcing her eyes toward the overhead of the medical room. Stone looked down to see two pieces of cloth held together by a band with a buckle.

"What do I do with this?" he asked.

Still refusing to look directly at Stone, the nurse replied, "You put it around your waist."

"What's it —"

"You're ready for the doctor now," she stated quickly as she pointed toward another door and then turned and walked away.

Stone attached the cloth around his waist and walked toward the door. A digital nameplate read PREPARATION. He was lost in contemplation of what exactly he was being prepared for when the door slid open. Inside the room was another woman sitting behind a large desk.

"I am Doctor Kami Crow. Please, come sit down," she said as she rose and pointed to a medical chair to her left. Dr. Crow was slightly older than Stone, in her early fifties, but still looked as fit as a twenty-year-old; it seemed to be the norm among the Terillians.

"I guess you'll be 'preparing' me," asked Stone with a nervous pitch in his voice.

"Yes," replied the doctor matter-of-factly. "Come. Sit."

Stone slowly moved to the chair and gingerly lowered himself into the medical seat.

"Don't worry," she said without a hint of emotion. "*This* will be painless."

The doctor's emphasis on the word "this" did not help to lessen his anxiety.

"You're going to take this injection," she continued as she held up a small hypodermic. "In the old days, you would have had to go days without food, sweat in a room at thirty-six degrees Celsius and one hundred percent humidity for a few hours, then eat some nasty tasting herbs and inhale some vapors from some other nasty smelling plants. Luckily, we have advanced a bit; now it's all here in this little injection."

"So, you're drugging me," asked Stone as he involuntarily pulled his arm to his body.

"Not drugging, Hanmani. Opening up your spirit to receive your vision."

"Then what?"

"Well, that's up to you. And the *wichasa wakhan* and the False Faces. Using these electrodes, they will read your responses and interpret your vision to determine what your fate will be."

"When —"

Stone's question was cut short as the doctor injected the serum into his leg.

"Thanks for the warning," sulked Stone as he rubbed his leg. "How long until th —"

Suddenly, Stone's mouth grew unbearably dry and his stomach contracted as if he hadn't eaten in days. He attempted to push himself up in the chair but his muscles didn't respond. His vision grew blurred and he felt as if he was sitting in the center of the Great Desert on Alpha Humana. He tried to focus on the doctor's face but everything went black.

Stone opened his eyes but he immediately closed them again against the bright rays of a yellow star. Lying on his back he felt the soft, warm support of heavy grass. His eyes finally adjusted to the light and he looked to his left and right. The grass was almost a meter tall, gently wafting back and forth against a comforting breeze. As he looked toward the sky again he saw something floating gently on the wind. The object slowly made its way above him and settled on his chest.

It was a feather. An eagle feather. Stone picked up the feather and held it above his head. He gazed upward toward the sun and watched the vanes of the feather shimmer against the backdrop of the sunlight and ripple against the wind. Stone took in a deep breath and the earthy smell of the prairie filled his nose.

The sun and the breeze soothed him and the grass underneath him felt as if it was slowly caressing his body. After a few seconds, the caressing sensation turned to a vibration and then a rumble.

'An earthquake,' he thought.

But it was different. As the rumbling continued and intensified, Stone's heart pumped harder and his adrenaline spiked, not in fear or anxiety but excitement. Stone pulled himself to his feet and looked across the flat land. Off in the distance a cloud of dust rose above the horizon. As he watched, the rumbling increased and the wind became more intense. Suddenly the wind ripped the feather from his hand. He watched as the feather floated quickly toward the sky and disappeared.

Next, the rumbling became a roar and Stone turned back toward the cloud. At the base of the cloud, he could make out small black dots. As the cloud of dust and the dots grew closer, the pounding in his chest intensified and his feet involuntarily moved side to side and back and forth. He could now feel the wind pressing hard against his body. Looking down, he saw his skin ripple against the force.

A loud snort immediately brought Stone's attention back to the approaching cloud. Peering into the brown haze, he saw a massive animal burst from the cloud. It was covered in heavy blackish-brown fur with large horns on each side of its huge, dark head. The animal charged toward Stone, but he was not afraid. It felt ... familiar.

In a flash the animal roared past him. He could smell the musty air and see the beast's flared nostrils. His heart felt as if it would explode with a vitality he had never before experienced. He felt another enormous animal rush by him. Looking back, dozens were coming his way. His body was shivering with anticipation. '*Run!*' The thought shot through his head like a lightning bolt. Stone turned and took his first, powerful stride. Then another. And another.

The ground recoiled and pushed back against his bare feet with each stride. Stone picked up his pace and was soon in the middle of the pack of the majestic beasts racing across the prairie. His lungs filled and then contracted quickly and his arms pumped with each stride. He felt wild. He felt powerful. He felt … free.

He had run with the herd for what felt like a blissful eternity when he saw a group of trees appear on the horizon. Pushing on, he raced forward. As he drew closer, he realized the trees were just the beginning of a vast forest.

Suddenly the herd split in two to bypass the forest — all except the first, massive animal that was in the lead. Stone pushed his body hard to catch up to the beast as it rumbled directly toward the forest. In a flash, the two passed into the forest and the prairie disappeared. Stone leapt and bounded through the forest, trying to keep up with the beast as it tore through the dense undergrowth. He pushed himself with all of his heart, but the animal slowly pulled away and vanished into the maze of trees and underbrush. Stone gradually slowed his pace until he came to a stop next to a gently flowing river.

Stone walked to the edge of the river. The soft mud of the riverbank on his feet and the cold air against his skin cooled his overheated body. Taking another step, the icy sting of the water shocked him at first, but he was soon refreshed by the rush of cooling air flowing around his body. He knelt down and let the water run through his hands, moving his fingers playfully. After a moment, he cupped his hands and pulled a handful of water to his mouth for an exhilarating drink. Letting out a breath of contentment, Stone looked across the water. As he did, he saw something break the surface and then disappear again.

Moving along the edge of the water, he investigated the source. Then he saw it; a beaver raised its head above the water and swam to his side of the river. He watched intently as the animal exited the water and scampered up the bank.

Stone followed as the beaver made its way under felled trees, over moss-covered rocks, and through the undergrowth. Eventually, it hopped onto a large fallen oak tree, looked back toward Stone, and then disappeared over the opposite side of the massive tree. But when Stone reached the tree, there was no sign of the beaver. He also realized that he had been so enthralled with the mannerisms of the little animal that he had lost track of how long he had been following the determined creature. The last rays of sunlight were flickering through the trees onto the forest floor. Looking beyond the tree, Stone saw a single, long bark-covered shelter in a small clearing. In the opening of the shelter there was a glimpse of a flickering fire. Then it went dark.

Stone made his way to the shelter. It consisted of long saplings bent over to form a frame covered with formed tree bark. Looking inside, he saw a long single room with a central fire pit. Stone stepped into the lodge and walked toward the pit. The pit was over a meter in diameter and surrounded by large round stones. The fire itself was almost out, with only a few dim embers struggling to remain lit.

Stone suddenly felt the cold chill of an evening breeze and saw the cold mist from his breath. The fire needed to be rekindled. He looked around the lodge but couldn't find any wood. He would have to find some from the nearby forest.

Stone rose to his feet and walked toward the exit of the lodge. Through the entrance into the night, he saw a landscape illuminated by a bright, full moon. Stepping outside, he heard the crunch of a twig underneath his feet and looked down to see a bundle of dry branches.

Stone didn't remember seeing the branches when he entered the lodge and quickly scanned the area. To the left of the lodge, he saw a small pile of logs, several centimeters in diameter. Each looked as if they had been chewed into lengths perfect for the fire. He was trying to formulate an explanation for the appearance of the wood when he heard a disturbance behind him. Quickly turning around, he saw the flash of a flat beaver tail as the animal disappeared into the darkness of the forest.

'*Son of a bitch,*' he said to himself as he gathered the fuel.

He had the fire rekindled and burning strong in minutes. The warmth of the fire comforted him and he fell into a deep sleep.

Stone was suddenly torn from his sleep by an intense piercing pain to his chest.

Grunting against the intensity of the pain, he looked down to his chest. Each of his pectoral muscles had been penetrated by a small bone-like spike. Attached to each end was a leather lanyard leading up to a bright light above where he lay. Breathing heavy against the pain, he heard the screech of an eagle and then a bolt of pain passed over his body as he felt himself lifted off the ground by the lanyards. The pain was unbearable. His head grew heavy and he lost consciousness.

Again he awoke.

Still dazed, Stone's chest ached and he felt weak, hungry, and dehydrated. He attempted to reach for his chest but realized his hands were tied behind his back. He struggled to free himself but the bonds were too tight. Looking around, he realized he was back in the lodge once again. The warmth of a fire on his bare skin soothed him and he looked toward the source. At his feet was the fire he had rekindled.

"Here, brother. This will comfort you," came a familiar voice to his left.

It was Thay. He knelt next to Stone and placed a piece of meat to his mouth. Stone quickly snatched the food from Thay's hand with his mouth. The warm savory taste of the meat, which he could tell was slightly raw by the fluid warmth, immediately improved the hunger pains.

"Now drink," Thay added.

"What's happening?" asked Stone. "Untie me."

Thay put a wooden cup to Stone's lips and tilted it upward. The cool water quenched his thirst and ran down the corners of his mouth and onto the wounds on his chest. Stinging at first, the burning pain from his torn chest soon felt much improved.

"Thay," pleaded Stone. "Get me out of here."

"Not yet, brother," replied Thay. As he answered, he reached down toward the fire and pulled a burning piece of wood, one end white-hot, from the fire.

"I need to welcome you," Thay smiled and he placed the glowing ember to Stone's bare leg.

Stone cried out from the pain.

"I must keep you warm, brother," added Thay as he next placed the hot wood against Stone's arm.

Stone again lost consciousness.

When he came to, Stone's entire body ached and his head throbbed. He slowly opened his eyes and felt the pressure of another hand against his. He looked up into a pair of enchanting green eyes.

"You made it," said Mori.

His focus returning, he could see a huge smile on her face. "Wh —" Stone tried to speak but his mouth was so dry it was no more than a whisper.

"It's okay," replied Mori. Stone felt her other hand on his head. "It will take a few minutes to come out of it completely."

Stone ran his tongue over the roof of his mouth, the dryness starting to fade.

"What?" his voice cracked. "What happened to me?"

"You're finished," she smiled.

"The vision?" he asked.

"All of it," Mori replied. "The Shirt-Wearers felt you had to be tested immediately for my sake so some of the normal traditional practices were waived. The *wichasa wakhan* were consulted and agreed to the accelerated test but required the Iroqua False Faces to be consulted as well on the off-chance you were Iroqua."

"Was it real?" he asked.

Stone felt Mori's hand move to his chest. She ran her fingers over his right pectoral causing Stone to let out a grunt of pain. Looking down, he saw bandages covering his chest. Quickly looking toward his left arm, he saw another bandage.

"Thay," blurted Stone. "He did this."

"To welcome you, brother," came a voice from the corner of the room.

Stone turned toward the voice. It was Thay.

"You bastard," he shot back. "You burned me."

Stone started to pull himself from the bed but was slowed by the myriad of tubes and wires connected to him as well as his weakened state.

"Wait," interrupted Mori as she placed her hands on his. "Let him talk."

Stone turned back toward Thay, confused and angry.

"Your vision convinced the holy men that you are half Akota and half Iroqua. Because of this, and direction from the Shirt-Wearers and the Iroqua Matrons, it was directed that you undergo both the Akota Stellar Dance and the Iroqua Requickening ceremony."

"No one has undergone both ceremonies in generations," added Mori. "It's usually not allowed."

"And I'm sorry for the pain inflicted," replied Thay. "The ceremony is a mixture of your visions in the spirit world and action here in the physical."

"The huge beast —" asked Stone, turning back toward Mori.

"A buffalo," she answered. "Very powerful medicine."

"And the beaver and the lodge?"

"Iroqua symbols," added Thay. "Strong and important ones."

"What does it mean?" he asked, still trying to comprehend what he had just experienced.

"Your vision and what you get from the Dance is for you to decide in due time," answered Mori.

"But the *wichasa wakhan* and the Shirt-Wearers are pleased."

"And the Requickening," added Thay as he stepped forward and put his hand on Stone's shoulder, "washes you of your old existence and welcomes you as kin."

Thay smiled and for once it wasn't an evil or guilty smile but a welcoming one. "I am glad to call you brother."

"Brother?" asked Stone. Only a few days before he and Thay had almost come to blows.

"Yes. Brothers. The night of your vision, a spirit came to me in my sleep and told me I would soon be able to end mourning for my brother. The next morning, I learned you would undergo the Requickening. My heart was made even stronger when I found out your dream rekindled the lodge-fire of my people."

"What does it mean?" asked Stone.

"It's yet to be seen, but I believe your arrival will bring about Iroqua entrance into the war."

"How?" asked Stone, his head was spinning.

"Time," interrupted Mori. "All of this will come with time." She leaned in and kissed Stone gently. "What's important is that you have taken the first step toward fulfilling the Great Spirit's plan for you."

"For now," said Thay, "know that I am proud to call you brother and give you the name Tadodaho, Keeper of the Fire."

"I knew from the first day I saw you," said Mori as she turned his head toward her, "that you were going to change everything."

Stone, although confused and full of questions, felt an odd sense of contentment and place as he looked into her eyes.

"And besides," she added, "we're leaving for Echo 2 tomorrow. Better rest up, Magakisca."

"What does that mean?" asked Stone.

"It's your Akota name. All Akota will now call you Duck."

"Duck?" replied a perplexed Stone. "My warrior name is Duck?" He had wondered what the naming would be and had hoped for a powerful name such as bear, or wolf, or lion. But Duck?

"Don't worry, brother," replied Thay. "Duck is a good name. And very fitting. The duck returns home in the dangerous winter season, just as you have done."

"And," added Mori with a smile, "they're calm and relaxed above the water and frantic underneath, just like you."

She knew him too well. "Thanks," replied Stone sarcastically. He felt Mori grip his hand again.

"It is a good name. A proud name. And you have returned home."

Chapter 8

Stone stood in *Hydra*'s cargo bay with the rest of Mori's team. On the table in front of him, combat packs, food stores, electronic equipment, and weapons — a lot of weapons — were spread out for preparation. Running through a mental inventory of his equipment, Stone busied his hands by affixing a combat knife to his tactical vest resting on the table. With the exception of some stiffness in his chest, Stone had fully recovered from the effects of his visions and ceremonies a week earlier. The rest had Stone feeling physically and psychologically rejuvenated and he was looking forward to the mission as an opportunity to prove himself to the others.

"Looks like we're here," said Katalya as she packed her gear for the mission.

"Orion should be putting us into orbit in a few minutes," replied Mori as she handed pemmican strips to Katalya to include in her pack. Stone had immediately liked the meat, oat, berry, and animal fat mixture the first time he tried it. It was just as space-friendly as Humani military food packs but tasted much better. He looked up from his task toward Katalya and Mori as the two sisters exchanged smiles. Even with Katalya's genetic mutations, there was no doubt they were siblings.

Katalya reached for a large metal pack stored against the bulkhead.

"We won't need exoskeletons," Mori said to Katalya. "Echo 2 is only slightly above the gravity of our home worlds, so we just need to pack the heavy gravity injections."

'Gravity sucks,' thought Stone. Luckily, most planets of military importance had gravities that were within the tolerable range, at least when one used the injections to boost muscle response, bone density, and oxygen exchange. The low gravity planets could make people feel invincible but readjusting to normal gravity made it feel like a person was carrying an extra twenty-five kilograms and breathing through a straw. And the heavy gravity, those greater than one and a half times normal, required the injections, forced oxygen, and hydraulic metal exoskeletons to make up for the energy required to overcome the gravitational force. Unfortunately, exoskeletons slowed its wearer down and were uncomfortable.

"*Major Skye to the Bridge*," announced Orion across *Hydra*'s intercom. "We've got company."

"Damn it," responded Mori as she dropped her gear on the table and headed toward the bridge.

Just before exiting the cargo bay she turned back toward Stone. "Care to join me?"

Stone sheathed his knife and joined Mori.

"Last thing we need is for this mission to start off bad," huffed Mori, making her way down the passageway to the bridge. "If there's Humani in the area, you might be able to give some insight on our next move."

Stopping outside the entrance to the bridge, Stone and Mori shared an apprehensive look with each other. "Let's see what the bad news is," he said.

"If it wasn't bad news, there wouldn't be any news," she replied with a smile as she opened the hatch.

"Damn it, TC," Stone heard Orion shout. "I can see it too, just get me a reading."

Stone looked toward the huge Scapi. The rapid motion of his massive blue arms and a steady flow of high-pitched squeaks from the navigator made it obvious to Stone he was irritated even before the universal translator on the creature's vest spoke.

"If you would stop bugging me for ... see, here it is —" More squeaks. "Looks like two ships. Single or double piloted, no jump drive but with fire control systems."

"Probably old first generation fighters," replied Orion. "Can we jam them?"

TC manipulated several switches on his ECM panel and turned back toward Orion.

"Yes, shouldn't be a problem."

Stone turned to Mori, who let out a sigh of relief.

"So, no muss?" she asked Orion.

"Lookin' go —"

Orion was interrupted by more squeaks.

"Additional contacts ... four more probable Gen 1 fighters and something else." TC's huge hands punched on the keys of his electronics suite. "Damn it," he added after more squeaks. "Humani corvette. It's running a full scan on electronics and comms. And it looks like it's linked up with the fighters."

"Shit," interjected Orion, who turned back toward Mori. "I don't know what the deal with the Gen 1s is, but that corvette is up and running with full sensors, so even if we jam the fighters, the corvette will pick up the neutrino spike from our jump soon and pass our location to those fighters."

"They're Gen 1s. Can you take six of them?" asked Stone.

Orion looked back toward Stone, her forehead contracted and one side of her jaw tightened. "I'm good, but nobody's that good, at least in this old bucket." Orion turned slowly and placed her hand on *Hydra*'s control panel. "Sorry, girl. You're still the only one for me." After apologizing to *Hydra* for the slight, she turned back to Stone and Mori. "Anyway, we've got about five minutes before that corvette picks up our signature, about five more for them to figure out we're not supposed to be here and contact those fighters, and then about ten more until they're on us."

"Damn it." Mori slapped her hand against the bulkhead.

"Damn it is right," agreed Orion.

"I didn't come all this way to turn back," grunted Mori.

Stone wanted this mission to be a go. He needed it to be a go. "So, we have twenty minutes?" he asked.

"Nineteen," answered Orion. "And that's not enough time to put down on Talia and get our shit unloaded quietly. They'll know right where we're at."

"Plot a jump to get us the hell out of here," conceded Mori, shaking her head in frustration.

"Wait," interjected Stone.

"What is it?" asked Mori. "This mission is over before it even started."

"Eighteen minutes," added Orion.

"Hold on," directed Stone as he raised his hand to the two. He looked quickly toward Mori; she wanted this mission too. "Are you trained on HALO inserts?"

"HALO — what the hell is that?" asked an increasingly frustrated Mori.

"High altitude para-drops."

"Oh," replied Mori, her mouth slightly open in both acknowledgment and contemplation. "We call them iono-jumps."

"So, you're trained?"

"Yes. And so are Sandwick, Henry, and Thay … there's no way Katalya and Magnus have been."

"*Seventeen minutes.*" Orion continued her countdown.

Mori's eyes focused on the floor for a few seconds of contemplation before she spoke.

"Let's do it," she declared. "Orion, get us into the ionosphere and find the biggest population cluster that isn't in a city. That should be an army. We'll jump about thirty kilometers away from them."

"We've got to be fast," added Stone.

"Yes, get back to the cargo and get them moving — the jump suits are in two-tach-four-zero-tach-three storage. Have Katalya and Magnus grab the comms equipment and as much gear as they can and put them into a drop pod. Orion can jettison it when we jump and pin its navigation system to your landing zone."

"What about us?" asked Orion.

"Once we bail out, jump to Echo 8 — it's a gas planet so no one should look for you in orbit there. Hang out and go passive; we'll link up for data bursts so you'll know when to come pick us up again. Katalya and Magnus will stay with you."

"Sounds like a plan. I don't know if it's a good one, but it's a plan," she replied. "Sixteen minutes."

"I'll get the suits," declared Mori, turning toward Stone. "Go!" she shouted, but Stone was already turning toward the passageway.

Stone rushed through *Hydra* and in less than a minute, burst into the storage compartment.

"We've got a Humani corvette out there and they'll be on us soon."

"What's the plan?" asked Henry.

"HAL — I mean iono-jump," he answered.

"That's what I'm talking about," replied Thay. "Where are the suits?"

"Mori's on the way with them." Stone then turned toward Katalya and Magnus. "You won't be able to make the jump because you're not trained on the suits. Mori wants you to stay here for this one."

Stone could see the anger grow on Magnus's face as his canine teeth flashed in a low snarl.

"I'm sorry, Magnus. We'll miss you and Katalya, that's for sure."

"Fifteen minutes" was announced across the intercom.

"Shit," uttered Stone as the urgency hit him. "Magnus and Katalya, load up the drop pod with our additional gear, stores, and comms equipment and get to the jettison bay quickly."

Stone could feel the frustration radiate from Magnus. He didn't have time to placate him.

"Magnus. Now," he repeated.

Magnus returned a stare.

"Magnus," added Katalya as she grasped his arm. "We must do this now."

"Yes, of course," he said angrily. "You will show me this i-no-jump thing after this mission. I won't miss another —"

"Yes," shouted Stone. He knew this was a bitter pill for Magnus, but he didn't have the time.

"Come," repeated Katalya, pulling Magnus toward the gear on the table.

With a growl, Magnus conceded and he and Katalya quickly started gathering the equipment on the table.

"Fourteen minutes."

Mori entered the room, followed by the lumbering TC. In his arms were a bundle of jumps suits and gear.

"This shit's heavy," declared Mori as she dumped an armful of gear on the table. "Katalya and Mag —"

"Loading the pod," Stone answered quickly.

"And he's pissed about it," added Sandwick.

"It sucks," replied Mori as TC dumped the jump suits on the table. "I hate going in without everyone, but we don't have a choice."

"Thirteen minutes," counted Orion over the intercom. "Picking up comms from the corvette to the fighters."

Mori flipped the toggle switch for the comms circuit at the table. "Are they on to us, Orion?"

"Standby." Stone heard more squeaks from TC in the background. "Damn it, they're good," declared Orion. "They got us. We just lost three minutes. They'll be on us in ten."

"Son of a bitch," grunted Mori. "Get us over the drop zone."

"Roger," replied Orion as Stone felt *Hydra* bank and accelerate.

"Grab your shit and get ready," ordered Mori to the team.

Stone quickly unhooked the belt holding his sword and sidearm and had a jumpsuit in his hands before they hit the deck. Stepping into the suit, he slid his feet through the leggings and quickly secured the pressure bands around his feet. Stone then grabbed the lanyard for the suit and pulled it to his neck.

"Nine minutes," reported Orion. "Fighters changing course to pursue."

Now the hard part. He had done dozens of jumps with Humani equipment but the Terillian gear was different. Looking over the table, Stone saw sets of double-cylinder canisters. *'Must be O_2,'* he thought. He grabbed the canister. *'This goes … right here.'* Stone slid the containers into a pouch on his right thigh. A quick look and nod of approval from Henry told him he was right. "Now the —"

"Your vest," said Sandwick as he threw his own vest over his torso.

Stone picked up the tactical vest from table and threw his right arm through the arm hole, then repeated the same for his left arm. He felt for his knife in the vest. *'Still there.'*

"Eight minutes."

Stone hefted the drop pack containing the parachute over his shoulders, connected the latch across his chest, and tightened the apparatus with a strong pull on the straps.

"The chute pack has a sheath for your sword," said Mori as she picked up Stone's sword and slid it into place over his right shoulder.

Stone picked up his belt, checked his pistol was secure, and reattached it to his waist.

"Entering the ionosphere," reported Orion. "We'll be over target in four minutes."

"Let's hustle," shouted Mori as she attached her assault rifle to a clip on her vest and secured it with a lanyard.

"Seven minutes 'til the fighters are on us."

Stone quickly followed Mori's example and then reached for the face mask that would keep his head from becoming frostbitten and provide direct oxygen to him during the jump.

"Where's the rest of it?" he shouted looking for the head piece.

"We don't use those," shouted Thay. "Pull this over your head then put the mask on," he instructed as he tossed Stone a fabric hood.

Stone caught the hood and paused to inspect it.

"It works just as good," promised Sandwick just before he pulled his own mask over his face.

Stone shoved his head into the hood and was picking up his mask when Mori grabbed his arm.

"You got this?" she asked.

"This line goes to these canisters and this one goes into the suit, right?"

"You got it." She smiled. "The pressurization and depressurization are automatic based on altitude after you activate this button," she added as she pointed to green LED button on the portion of the canister protruding from the suit. "And this lever —"

"Is this for manual control if it fails," added Stone.

Mori gave him a quick smile. "Looks like you're good to go," she said as she shoved the control console for the comms equipment into a pouch on her vest.

"Oh, almost forgot," added Mori.

Stone felt a sharp pain in his right arm and a sudden rush of energy. He looked over to see Mori pulling an ejection pen from his arm.

"What the hell?" he asked.

"That'll purge some nitrogen from your body and give you an oxygen boost for the jump ... You're welcome."

"Six minutes 'til contact. Over target in three."

Mori activated the comms toggle switch again. "Katalya, is the pod ready?"

"Ready and loaded into the jettison bay. Good hunting, tanka" came the reply.

"Stay safe, c'uwé," said Mori before she disengaged the toggle.

Stone slid the mask over his face and tightened the bands. Once tight, he checked the seal and connected the hoses.

"Over target in two."

"Let's get to the boarding compartment," ordered Mori to the group.

Stone and the others rushed toward the compartment. Despite the added bulk, they made it in thirty seconds. Inside the compartment, Mori turned to speak.

"Stack up!" she ordered.

Stone took his position behind Mori and Henry, with Sandwick and Thay behind him.

"We're in," Mori reported to Orion over the intercom.

"Roger. Depressurizing," replied Orion. "One minute until green light."

Stone felt the air fill his suit as the compartment depressurized. Holding his left wrist to his face mask, he verified the data screen read the correct data.

Altitude: 84 km
Temp: -90C
Suit Temp: 22C
Press: .04 ATM
Suit Press: 1.00 ATM
Drop Target Pin: Activated
Degrees off target: 5

"Opening outer hatch," warned Mori.

Stone looked out of the hatch into the void and saw the darkness of space mixing with the atmosphere of Echo 2. Looking over the curvature of the planet, a pang of excitement ran over his body — excitement he hadn't felt since he was a young lieutenant. Maybe he had come out of the ceremonies a new man.

"Standby for go," reported Orion as the light in the compartment turned red.

He looked up toward the counter above the hatch: five, four, three, two, one …

Stone took in a deep breath of the canned air flowing through his mask; the light turned green.

Mori stepped forward and disappeared. Then Henry. Stone stepped toward the opening and fell forward. He instantly felt the acceleration of the planet's gravity and the airflow of the suit adjust to his rapidly decreasing altitude. He placed the data screen to his face:

Altitude: 79 km

Temp: -85C
Suit Temp: 21.5C
Press: .03 ATM
Suit Press: 1.02 ATM
Drop Target Pin: Activated
Degrees off target: 2

After a second, Stone turned on his back to look back toward *Hydra*. Blue haze encompassed the ship as *Hydra* initiated a jump, disappearing in a brilliant, bluish-yellow line heading into deep space.

Falling toward the planet, Stone shifted his body to keep himself on target for the pinned drop zone.

Altitude: 25 km
Temp: -34C
Suit Temp: 21C
Press: .4 ATM
Suit Press: 1.00 ATM
Drop Target Pin: Activated
Degrees off target: 1

Stone continued his rapid descent. To the north he could make out fires lighting up the night sky and to his east, what looked like a large city.

Altitude: 10 km
Temp: -5C
Suit Temp: 22C
Press: .68 ATM
Suit Press: .98 ATM
Drop Target Pin: Activated
Degrees off target: 1

Looking toward the ground below him, he saw only darkness. Orion had definitely picked an out of the way drop zone.

Altitude: 2.5km
Temp: 5C

Suit Temp: 21C

Press: .99 ATM

Suit Press: 1.00 ATM

Drop Target Pin: Activated

Degrees off target: 1

Stone felt his suit fully deflate and he took a quick moment of reflection to listen to the roar of the air and feel its exhilarating sting as he sped toward the ground.

Altitude: 2 km

Temp: 10C

Suit Temp: 21C

Press: .92 ATM

Suit Press: 1.00 ATM

Drop Target Pin: Activated

Degrees off target: 0

Activate — activate — activate read across the data screen.

Stone reached toward the lanyard and activated the chute. He heard the compressed air rush through his parachute system as the chute deployed. The chute caught the air and jerked his body out of the free fall, causing him to let out a small groan.

"Report deployment of chutes," ordered Mori over the short-range comms.

"Good," reported Sandwick.

"Hoka-hey!" shouted Henry.

"Good deployment," Thay stated.

Stone was last. "Good to go."

"Roger all," replied Mori. "Once you're on the ground, move toward the drop-pod signal."

Stone looked toward his data screen. The altitude read five hundred meters. Focusing on the ground below, he could start to make out shapes below him.

Three hundred meters. "Trees...shit," he said out loud as he recognized the shapes. *'This is gonna hurt.'*

Fifty meters.

Stone crossed his arms and bent his knees slightly, as he anticipated impact. He heard the snapping of tree limbs followed by a hard impact to his right leg. Whipped sideways by the collision, he then felt sharp blows to his right arm and ribs as he tumbled through the heavy foliage.

Suddenly it stopped with a thud as he hit the ground. Sucking in a breath, Stone took a second to assess the damage. Although his ribs throbbed and he was sure he had a nice collection of bruises, everything seemed to be moving.

Stone pulled the face mask off and slowly reached for the latch on his chest to disconnect the chute. Next, he pulled himself to a kneeling position and shrugged off the heavy jump apparatus. Free of the jump gear, he pulled a pair of light-enhancing goggles from his jump pack and slid them over his face. Instantly the darkness of the night was transformed into daylight as he detached his rifle, brought it to the ready, and scanned the forest for movement.

Stone soon felt the weight of the rifle straining his muscles and his breathing grew labored. *'Damn it ... gravity,'* he remembered. Taking an injection stick from a pocket in his trousers, he flipped open the cap and drove the needle into his thigh. In a few minutes he began to breathe normally and the rifle, once again, felt like an extension of his body.

With the area clear and his body adjusted to the gravity, Stone quickly removed the rest of the jump gear and rearranged his combat equipment. He quietly rolled the chute and jumpsuit into a ball and found some branches and leaves to cover the pack. Luckily, he had brought half the forest down with him as he tore through the heavy foliage so there was plenty of camouflage for the equipment. Once the gear was hidden, he headed into the forest to find the pod and the others.

***

Martin watched the artificial light reflect off the blade of her combat knife as she spun it on the wooden desk. As the tip dug into the surface, she let out a sigh of impatience. Martin and Tacitus had been given the corvette *Cerilus* and a company of Marines to carry out their hunt for Stone and Mori. And they had sat for days in the space between the Foxtrot and Echo Systems waiting for intelligence that might lead them to their prey.

"Do you have to do that?" complained Tacitus, sitting across the empty room from Martin.

Martin looked up toward Tacitus. The longer the two were together, the more Arilius Tacitus's First Family traits drove her insane. Martin knew he was a great soldier and she would trust him with her life in the field, but damn it, he was a pompous pain in the ass the rest of the time. At least she could always infuriate him with her blunt approach to, well, everything.

"Would you rather I do something more sophisticated, Paladin Tacitus?" Martin smiled as she stood and curtsied toward Tacitus. As she rose, she raised her right hand, still holding the blade, and presented her middle finger. "Better, milord?" she quipped.

Martin could see Tacitus's jaw clench and his shoulders tighten. "Why must you constantly push the limits of behavior and purposely antagonize me?"

"Why must you constantly have a stick up your ass?"

Tacitus rose from his seat. "Do not forget, Martin, that I am the senior officer —"

"Not so sure about that," interrupted Martin. "We're both majors and I don't remember her highness, the exalted queen bitch, saying which one of us was senior when she made us Paladins." If Martin knew anything, it was how to piss off First Family members. She had actually transformed it into an art form. "And," she continued, "like the ProConsul said, we're bloodhounds, not the fancy little purebred fur balls that infest the First Family houses. Maybe it's time you got down off your high horse and played in the filth with the rest of the dogs. Or maybe I'll just have to rub your nose in it." Martin paused. '*Should I go there?*' she thought to herself. '*Yes.*' She continued, "Don't forget, all of your First Family fanciness didn't stop your precious ProConsul from taking title of all of Cataline's holdings after the Traitor beheaded him."

"I've had just about enough of your tongue, commoner," retorted Tacitus.

Martin saw Tacitus place his hand on his sword. Other than Stone, Tacitus was the only other Guard member still alive she thought of as her peer in combat. Maybe it was time to find out who was top dog.

"Why, Arilius Tacitus," she said as she smiled and gripped her sword, pulling it from its sheath. "Are you asking me to dance?"

Martin heard the metal of Tacitus's sword sing as he yanked it from his sheath and brought it to the ready. Then he paused. Martin saw his brow furrow as he let out a slight puff of an exhale.

"This is ludicrous," he declared. "We have a mission and we are about to fight one another. There is no need for this, Paladin Martin."

Martin knew goading him into a fight was bad — bad for the mission and maybe even bad for herself. But she never backed down. Never. His pause had left her an escape from her own stubbornness. Half relieved she was able to escape the consequences of her loud mouth and half disappointed she hadn't been able to find out who was the better swordsman, reason prevailed. She slowly returned her sword to its home. At least Tacitus had blinked first. Even if it was more out of logic than fear, she would take it. "You're right, of course," she conceded. "But don't forget you're the one that cried uncle." She couldn't help herself.

"You just don't know how to keep your damn mouth shut do you?"

"Excuse me, Paladins," interrupted Commander Talendo, *Cerilus*'s executive officer. He had entered the room sometime during the argument and finally made himself known to hopefully bring it to an end.

"What is it, XO?" asked Martin.

"Our listening station in the Echo System picked up something. It doesn't seem like much, but you said you wanted word of anything."

"Yes," replied Tacitus. "What is it?"

"We picked up two neutrino concentrations near Echo 2. Both were within less than an hour of each other. We picked up a small craft, most likely a falcon class, but it apparently jumped before identification could be made."

Martin looked toward Tacitus. She could tell he was thinking the same thing as her.

"HALO?" he posited, knowing he was right.

"That's them," she declared. She turned toward the executive office. "XO, get us to Echo 2. Get us a transport and the best pilot you have and tell them to plot and follow the track of that ship to the letter."

"Yes, Paladin Martin," acknowledged the XO with a salute.

"And tell Captain Parsons I want him and twelve of his best marines on that transport with us."

"Yes, Paladin," replied the XO again before he turned and hurriedly exited the compartment.

"I think we've got them," said Tacitus.

"And I guess our dance will just have to wait." Martin smiled as she stepped in close to Tacitus. "But don't forget, I like to lead."

Chapter 9

The transition of the thrusters from a roar to a low hum told Martin the transport had touched down and the engines were powering down. As the door opened, she felt the rush of air over her face and heard the rumble of Captain Parsons and his marines rushing past her through the opening. Although they were loud, obnoxious, and basically a blunt object of war, Martin also knew the marines to be resilient, loyal, and brave. And it never hurt to have a pissed off, bullheaded marine on your side in a firefight.

The injections hadn't yet taken full effect and Martin felt the increased weight of the pack and her weapons as she stepped through the opening and scanned the landscape. The transport had put down at the edge of a large field of golden-brown wheat near a large deciduous forest. In the distance was a small mountain range, its peaks encased in grayish-black clouds.

"That's better," said Tacitus as he stopped beside Martin.

Martin could see the relief on his face as her own load grew lighter by the second. "We need to head that way," declared Martin, pointing toward a dip in the mountain range.

"Agreed," replied Tacitus. "They would want to make it to the front lines without too much attention."

"That's what I would do. And if they came down into this forest up ahead, they could move along that ridge and then through that pass."

As Martin looked toward Tacitus, she saw him flip through a data screen he had pulled from his pocket. "Looks like the heaviest fighting is near the city of Yali, about a day or two beyond the pass."

"Well, we better get moving then," replied Martin. "Parsons!" she yelled as she turned away from Tacitus and toward the captain.

She watched as the captain rose from cover and jogged toward her.

"Paladin Martin," he reported with a salute.

"Have the pilots put the transport right on the edge of that tree line and camouflage it so it can't be seen from the air."

"Yes, Paladin."

"Also," added Tacitus, "you and your men set up a perimeter and wait for our call."

"We won't be joining you?" asked Parsons.

Martin could see the frustration on Parsons's face. Marines didn't like being left behind.

"No," she replied. "We need to move fast and quiet. Besides," she continued, "when it hits the fan, you guys get to ride in and fuck some shit up."

Martin saw a contemplative look on Parsons's face. No doubt he was envisioning his marines saving the day, emerging from an epic, cinematic explosion with guns blazing and war faces shining.

"Understood, ma'am," he acknowledged.

With Parsons appeased, Martin turned toward Tacitus. He placed his data screen back in his pocket, pulled out a pair of UV glasses, and slowly slid them over his eyes. "You ready, Martin?" He smiled.

"Always," she replied, sliding on her own glasses. "Let's go hunting."

***

A slow, steady drizzle of cold rain impacted the foliage and caused a low rumble as Stone peered through the scope of his sniper rifle. A small town was just becoming visible through the fog as the daylight broke. In the days since their high-altitude jump, Stone, Mori, and the others had what each would have called a typical mission experience — constant rain, freezing nights, and a general lack of sleep. Avoiding populations, they had clandestinely moved closer to the front lines of the fight between the Saint's Crucesignatis Army and the Triad Alliance that was trying to stop it. For the last two days the team had seen several motorized convoys and both supersonic and subsonic aircraft fly overhead.

Stone watched the edge of the town from his concealed position. Fossil fuel cars darted back and forth and the townspeople seemed to be about their daily business. In the distance, however, he could hear the concussions of large explosions. The front lines were not far away.

"Anyone down there armed?" asked Thay from his position next to Stone.

"Doesn't look like it," he replied. "Just normal everyday — check that —" Stone paused as a truck speeding into his view drew his attention. The large truck, with military markings, stopped at a park on the outskirts of the town and about ten armed men jumped from the back then took up positions around the park. Two more trucks pulled into the area and more men poured out and lined up in a formation in the center of the park.

"Armor," commented Thay.

Stone scanned the area with his scope. A few hundred meters behind the trucks rumbled two armored vehicles. In the lead was a wheeled vehicle with a twenty-five millimeter cannon mounted on a turret. Behind it rattled another a massive, tracked behemoth with a gun of at least one hundred twenty millimeters and several other smaller guns jutting out from the armor shell.

"*You guys picking this up?*" came Mori's voice over the comms circuit.

"Roger," replied Thay. "We've got about thirty armed men and some armor out to the southeast."

"Copy. We see 'em."

Stone heard a rustle in the brush behind and turned quickly to see Henry River take up a position to his left.

Stone looked down from his position toward Mori's. Although he couldn't physically see her, he knew both her and Sandwick were a few hundred meters from the entrance to the park, concealed near a bridge that stretched across a small stream.

"*Triad troops, I'm guessing,*" came Sandwick's voice.

"Must be," replied Stone. "The action is still a day or so to the north. They must be reinforcements."

"*Let's stay concealed and observe,*" directed Mori. "*We don't know enough about either side yet.*"

As Stone looked through his scope, he saw the streets now empty except for the troops. "Looks like the locals have cleared out," he reported.

"*Yeah. They're all gone,*" replied Mori.

Stone felt uneasy. If these troops were reinforcements to defend against an invading horde, why did the townspeople evaporate when they arrived? "I've got a bad feeling about this," Stone warned the others.

"*Me too,*" replied Mori. "*Thay, Henry, make your way down to us. Tyler, cover us if shit goes bad.*"

"Roger," replied Stone as he felt Thay rise from his position.

As Thay and Henry quickly disappeared into the bushes, Stone activated the data information for his weapon. It displayed wind speed, humidity, and range. As Stone focused his crosshairs on one of the trucks, it read two thousand meters. "Easy day," he whispered to himself as he laid out four magazines for quick access.

"*We've got movement,*" reported Mori over the circuit.

Stone peered through the sights. The formation had broken up, the men spreading out to search the nearby buildings. From two thousand meters, Stone watched and listened to the other's comms circuits.

Suddenly a door on one of the buildings flew open and two men from the town exited, followed by one of the armed men. Panning to the left, he saw more men moving toward the park, followed by more soldiers.

"*Looks like they're rounding up the men,*" reported Mori.

Stone could hear the tension in Mori's voice and he instantly remembered the incident with the slavers in the November System. Stone turned his weapon toward Mori's position. As his sighting system focused, he saw Thay and Henry moving along the bank of the stream to take a flanking position.

"*Tyler*," came Mori's voice over the comms circuit.

"Yes," he replied.

"*If anything looks wrong, open up on them.*"

"Roger," he replied as he trained his weapon on the park.

"*Henry, can you hear anything?*" asked Mori.

Henry, now closer to the park, answered. "*Sounds like a conscription party. The officer near the center of the park keeps talking about duty to the Triad and that it's their duty to die fighting the enemy hordes.*"

Stone was conflicted. Did they have the right to stop forced conscription by the governments in power against an invading army? The Humani conscripted. But was he even Humani anymore? '*Stop thinking so much*,' he chastised himself as he peered through the sights again. He saw another door burst open. This time it was a girl, maybe in her teens. She ran across the street and latched onto a man standing among the new conscripts. One of the guards pulled her away from the man; she jumped back up and ran toward him again.

"*Henry, what the hell's happening over there?*" asked Mori.

Stone perceived anxious energy in Mori's voice.

"*I can't tell*," he replied. "*They just pulled her away again.*"

Stone saw the girl try to stand, only to receive a kick to her ribs and fall again. The man in the ranks stepped forward but was knocked to the ground with the butt of a rifle.

"*This is going sideways,*" declared Mori. "*Get ready.*"

"Shit," said Stone out loud as he shifted the safety to off on his rifle.

The girl rose again. This time an officer walked over to the girl and raised his pistol to her head. Stone centered the crosshairs on the officer's chest. Range: nineteen hundred fifty meters. He saw the recoil of the officer's pistol and the girl crumple to the ground. He didn't need to wait for the order he knew was coming. Before he could hear the crack from the killer's pistol, the thunderous boom of his own rifle rang out and he felt the force against his shoulder as he fired. Looking down the scope he saw the round impact the officer and his chest explode in mist of red.

Stone turned toward the officer perched atop the large tracked tank. As he heard the burp of automatic weapons from Mori and the others, he fired again. The officer jerked backward and then slumped forward and disappeared into the open hatch.

"*Moving up!*" shouted Mori through the circuit.

Stone glanced toward her position and saw Mori and Sandwick rush across fifty meters of open ground and take cover behind a concrete embankment. As they dove behind the cover, the large tank fired and the shell exploded on the other side of the embankment, showering Mori and Sandwick with debris.

"*You good?*" shouted Stone into the circuit.

"Y-Yeah," coughed Mori. "*Thay, try to flank that armor.*"

"*On the way,*" he responded.

Stone turned his attention on the wheeled armored vehicle. It turned and started rolling toward Mori's direction, spewing twenty-five millimeter shells as it advanced, the *thud-thud-thud* of its firing booming over the automatic small arms fire. He focused his sights on the rear of the vehicle, activated the data screen, and flipped through the data with a rolling toggle near the handgrip. It didn't take long to find the data he wanted. Material: *steel, thickness: 2–2.5 cm.*

"Gotcha," he said to himself.

Stone rolled on to his side and grabbed the clip with a yellow marking indicating heavy metal rounds. Slamming the clip into the rifle, Stone looked down the sights. The vehicle was only a few meters from Mori.

Three quick rounds from Stone's rifle sent smoke billowing from the rear of the vehicle as it slowly came to a halt almost on top of Mori and Sandwick.

"The wheeled one is down but watch out for the gun," reported Stone.

"*Roger,*" acknowledged Mori.

As Stone looked on, Mori jumped from behind the embankment and sprinted toward the disabled vehicle. He watched as Mori pulled a shaped charge from her pack and slapped in to the side of the tank. He was watching her arm the charge when he saw the hatch for the tank open and a man climb out with a rifle in hand.

"Mori — turret!" he shouted as he pulled the trigger.

Stone was over nineteen hundred meters away, however, and before his shot could reach the man, Mori's and Sandwick's rounds tore the tanker apart.

Stone saw Mori finish setting the charge and then dive back over the cover as the explosion blew a hole the size of a man in the side of the tank. Flames erupted out of the open turret and barrel of the main gun as the weapons inside cooked off. Mori and Sandwick moved forward past the burning hulk and toward the buildings on the opposite side of the park.

Stone next turned his sights on the massive tracked tank. He pulled up the armor data: *composite-layered and 4–5 cm.*

"Damn it," he said in frustration. His rounds would not penetrate its shell.

"You're gonna have to take that big bastard out up close," he warned Mori and the others.

"*Roger,*" she acknowledged. "*Keep our asses covered!*"

"You got it," he answered as his rifled recoiled again; nineteen hundred thirty meters away, a man fell out of the second story of a building.

"*We're clearing the building east of the park,*" reported Thay. "*Eight down.*"

"*Roger,*" acknowledged Mori.

Stone figured between the others and his sharpshooting, there probably weren't more than seven or eight combatants left. But there was still that armored monster. Stone saw the tank pivot and accelerate toward the building Thay and Henry were clearing. Suddenly it stopped and sent a round into the building. The left corner of the three-story structure exploded in a fiery ball with glass, brick, and wood flying in all directions as what remained of the building shifted violently.

"*Thay, Henry, report,*" ordered Mori.

"*We're good,*" answered Henry.

The tank's turret turned toward another building and fired. This time the entire two-story structure crumbled into a pile of burning debris. As the building fell, a twenty millimeter cannon from the tank opened as well, peppering the embankment where Mori and Sandwick had been moments ago.

"This guy's just shooting at everything," noted Stone, realizing the crew was acting more like a scared animal swatting at bees than a trained, disciplined team. "They're not trying to find a good position or —"

Another round flew from the tank, this time impacting a clump of trees across the park. The tank then pivoted and drove over one of its own trucks.

"*These guys don't know what they're doing,*" commented Sandwick.

"*Thay,*" ordered Mori. "*Pop some smoke around that beast and we'll do the same. They're already scared — now let's blind 'em.*"

"*Roger,*" acknowledged Thay.

As the smoke covered the tank completely, the beast fired its main gun again. The round impacted hundreds of meters away, near the stream. In an attempt to cover itself, all of the smaller weapons on the tank opened fire indiscriminately as Stone saw Thay rush through the wall of fire into the cloud of smoke. A few seconds later, he saw Thay reemerge from the cloud and dive for cover as a giant orange ball of flame engulfed the tank. As the roar of the explosion died down a quiet came over the park. Stone heard Mori's voice over the comms circuit.

"*We're all clear. Thanks for the cover. Meet us down here.*"

"Roger," replied Stone. "On the way."

In a few minutes Stone had descended the slope and was making his way across the charred and burning landscape that used to be the park. Although he had seen the battle from his previous vantage point, his other senses were now overwhelmed as he crossed the ground to Mori and the others. The hissing of the fire still raged from the wrecked tank and the crack and pop of small arms exploding from within mixed with the stinging smell of burning fossil fuel and human flesh. At the center of the park, Stone stopped to look at the body of the officer he had killed in order to ignite the firefight. His aim was true; the massive round had destroyed the right half of his chest. Looking to his left, he saw a man with a heavily bruised face and blood streaming from his mouth cradling the limp body of the girl Stone had failed to save. The man looked up toward Stone, tears flowing down his face.

"Why did this happen? Why? We didn't want any part of this war."

Stone stared back blankly. A year ago, he would have spat some patriotic, rhetoric-filled drivel but now "I'm sorry" was all he could say. His gaze locked on the sad scene in front of him, and Stone felt a sense of helplessness and frustration. More and more he had come to see warfare — once thought to be an exciting, honorable endeavor — for what it really was: a dirty, base task that had to be done by someone to eventually put things right. In the past, anytime he was away from the field, he longed for the chaos of battle; now he wanted to be any place but here. He knew he had to be there, but he no longer wanted to be.

"Tyler!"

Mori's voice drew Stone's attention from the heartbreaking scene in front of him. Turning toward Mori, Stone saw her and Henry standing by three men. He pushed the miserable vision of the dead girl and her father from his conscious thought. They would visit him in his dreams anyway.

"What's going on?" asked Stone as he reached the group.

"These assholes were Triad," answered Henry.

Stone had figured as much. Even though the Saint's troops had invaded Echo 2, it didn't mean the current leaders of the planet were any better.

"What happened here?" asked Mori.

A tall, thin man with a heavy beard stepped forward from the group to speak. "You — we are in the land controlled by Ya-ling. Ya-ling required that we give half of our harvest and manufactured goods to his vassals and provide a levy of men and he would let us be, other than selecting young women from each territory for his court. This was when he was at war with the Merchant Alliance before our planet was attacked. Once the Western Continent was taken and Ya-ling lost the cities of Gra-lee, Var-Sa, and Var-Par, the Merchant Alliance, Ya-ling, and the Warlord of the East, Barca, formed this Triad. But the Triad has continued to lose battles and has started conscripting men to fight in their armies."

"How many times have they conscripted?" asked Mori.

"This was the third time in four moons," replied another of the men.

The bearded man continued. "It was volunteers at first and the units were Ya-ling's men, drawn from our own levies. Most of the men from our levies have been killed in battle, so other groups from the Triad have started passing through our town."

"And they don't ask for volunteers," added the third townsman.

"Don't you want to fight for your land?" asked Henry.

The bearded man turned toward Henry. Stone could see a desperate, frustrated look on his face.

"It's not our land," he replied. "It hasn't been since Ya-ling's grandfather overthrew the rightful leaders and established himself as a tyrant. Since then, we just try to survive."

"And to protect our families when we can," added the second man.

"What about the Saint's army?" asked Stone.

"I don't know about his supernatural powers," answered the bearded man. "But they say he promises equality among his followers and shared common property."

"That's more than we have now," stated the third.

"But they're fanatics," replied Stone. "We have seen them. They willfully give their lives for him, for what?"

"And what did these people give their lives for today?" interrupted a voice behind Stone.

He turned to see the father of the dead girl, his shirt soaked red and his hands painted with her blood.

"Why is my Serena dead? Can you tell me?"

Stone still had no answer.

"Because it wasn't for equality or shared property." The distraught father spat the words toward the group. "When the Saint's Crucesignatis army arrives, I will join them and kill as many of these Triad bastards as I can before I die so that when I join my daughter in the afterlife I can show her the price they paid for her life."

Sandwick stepped between Stone and the father.

"No wonder the Saint is getting so many —"

A warm splash of blood hit Stone's face and neck as Sandwick's head disintegrated in a bloody cloud.

"Contact forward!" shouted Mori as she dove behind a nearby concrete statue of Ya-ling and brought her assault rifle to her shoulder.

Stone took cover behind a wrecked civilian vehicle and quickly scanned the ground in front of and around him. Thay was behind the cover of one of the Triad trucks and Henry had dove into the open door of the nearest building. The townsmen had all disappeared except the girl's father, who stood motionless.

The sharp crack from the shot that killed Sandwick echoed across the park.

Five seconds, thought Stone. Almost two thousand meters.

"Damn it," yelled Mori. "Did anyone see where that came from?"

***

"One down," declared Martin from the same sniper pit Stone had used only moments earlier.

"Why didn't you take out Stone?" asked Tacitus as he prepared his rifle.

"I'm taking him and that bitch up close," she responded. "They'll feel my sword slide into their flesh before they die. The rest of them though —"

***

"It came from the same spot I was in," replied Stone.

"That's almost two thousand meters," shouted Mori.

Another round tore a chunk of concrete from the statue providing cover to Mori, showering her with small fragments.

Only a few people could make that shot. Stone knew he could. Sandwick could have but he was dead. So was Martin. That left only one — Arilius Tacitus.

"It's the Guard!" shouted Stone.

"Could be mercs or bounty hunters," suggested Henry over the circuit.

Stone pulled a data screen from his pocket, placed it in video mode, and slowly raised it above the hood of the vehicle. Focusing on his former position, Stone saw a flash. Suddenly the data screen shattered. "Shit!" he declared as some of the fragmented parts cut through his tactical gloves and into his hand. "I don't think that's a merc," declared Stone.

"What's that guy doing?" said Mori.

Hearing Mori's voice, Stone scanned the area. To his left stood the dead girl's father. He was holding a rifle.

"Put that weapon down!" warned Mori.

"You're gonna make yourself a target to them!" yelled Stone.

The man turned toward Stone and spoke. "That's more Triad out there and I'm not going to sit by and —"

A chunk of flesh and bone flew from the man's back as a round found its mark. He fell to the ground, dead.

"Son of a bitch," Stone said aloud. Detaching a smoke grenade from his vest, Stone activated his comms circuit. "Pop smoke and everyone make a run for that alley while I provide cover. From there we can use the buildings for cover."

"What about you?" asked Thay.

"I'll keep their heads down and be right behind you." Stone knew he wasn't going to be able to take a careful aim, but maybe he could throw enough lead in the shooter's direction to distract them for a few seconds.

"Smoke out!" ordered Mori and a series of smoke grenades exploded sending a mist of white smoke over their position.

***

"They're poppin' smoke," shouted Tacitus. "Switching to therma —" Tacitus was cut short by rounds impacting around their position. "Shit!" he replied, regaining his composure.

Martin did not flinch. As rounds tore into the ground and bushes around her, she flipped the toggle to turn her sights to thermal. Drawing a bead on a red silhouette of a running body, she fired.

Tacitus joined Martin and sent a round toward the outline of a man behind a car.

***

Stone was thrown backward as his sniper rifle shattered and fragmented. He felt a sharp pain in his left shoulder and saw a sliver of metal that used to be part of the housing embedded in his flesh. Taking a deep breath, he brought his assault rifle to his chest and looked across the field of battle. A hundred meters away were Mori, Thay, and Henry. Thay appeared to be injecting something into Mori's leg. Stone saw Mori look toward him.

"*We made it,*" she said over the circuit.

"Are you okay?"

"*Took a grazing shot, but I'll live. What about you?*"

"I'm good," answered Stone as he pulled the sliver from his shoulder. But he wasn't. He had a long way to make it to the others and whoever was shooting at him was good.

"*What's next?*" asked Mori.

"Leave me here," replied Stone. "They will come down off that hill eventually and I will take them on then and meet up with you."

"*No,*" shot back Mori. "*You don't even know how many there are. We're not leaving you.*"

"Don't put me in front of the mission," pleaded Stone. "I got this."

Another round slammed into the car Stone was using for cover.

"*No,*" declared Mori. "*We —*"

"Quiet," interrupted Stone. "There's something coming."

Stone could hear a metallic screeching sound from across the park. It steadily grew stronger. Eventually he could feel the vibration of the ground underneath him. "Do you hear it?" asked Stone.

"*Armor,*" answered Thay. "*And a lot of it.*"

Stone quickly peered over the hood of the vehicle and caught a glimpse of a column of large tanks rolling over the bridge at the far end of the park. "They're at the bridge, a full column plus infantry."

"*This battle is getting a little crowded,*" said Henry.

"Just go," pleaded Stone. "I'll find a way out of this."

"*Shut up*," interrupted Mori. "*Stop trying to go all martyr on us.*"

"But—"

"*Just listen,*" she continued. "*They're on thermal so if we make it hot down here you can make a run for it.*"

Stone quickly looked over the area. "The gas tank for that truck," he said.

"That should do it," replied Mori.

Stone raised his assault rifle and fired a round into the tank. A metallic clang rang out and gas started pouring out of the hole. Stone watched as the stream of fuel flowed outward from the tank. In a few moments the pool had made its way to Stone. "Get ready," warned Stone.

"*Do it,*" replied Mori. "*Just get here before shit starts blowing up.*"

"Here goes," said Stone as he ignited the fuel with a fire-start.

A wall of flame shot across the ground and in seconds engulfed the field. Stone readied himself but for some reason his body did not react. Looking at the flames, his thoughts went back to the devastation on Sierra 7 and Juliet 3; he saw the scorched and wrecked bodies in his mind.

"*Tyler, move your ass!*" came Mori's voice over the circuit.

Mori's voice brought Stone back to reality and he leapt from his position and sprinted across the ground. Wincing against the intense heat, he stayed close to the flames to stay hidden from the thermal sights.

***

"Damn it," cursed Martin.

"He's making a run for it," added Tacitus.

"Fuck it," grunted Martin as she opened up with her rifle sending rounds flying indiscriminately into the flames.

Tacitus joined in.

***

Stone heard the *whizz* of bullets around him as he sprinted toward the alley. A sting of pain shot through his arm as a round grazed his bicep, but he kept running. Bursting from behind the flames, he dove for the cover of the alley.

"Glad you could join us," smiled Thay.

"Yeah," replied Stone. "Let's get the hell out of here."

***

"Shit," cursed Martin and she pushed her sniper rifle to the side and stood erect. "We need to get on their asses."

Suddenly a tree behind Martin exploded, splintering into a thousand pieces. Knocked to the ground, a searing pain blasted through Martin's back as it had been peppered with small jagged pieces of wood. Firing on Stone had drawn the attention of the approaching Triad armored column.

"We've got armor and infantry to our right," grunted Tacitus.

Martin saw a shard of wood protruding from his shoulder. "No shit," she replied as she pulled the chunk from his body. "We don't have time for this shit," she added as she activated her comms circuit. "*Cerilus*, this is Hunter 1, request ANVIL from CAP. Say again, request ANVIL."

"Hunter 1, this is *Cerilus*, copy ANVIL. Designate tangos. Reaper 21 and 23 inbound. Time on top five minutes."

Martin brought her sniper rifle into position facing the new threat. "Hawks inbound," she warned as she picked out an officer and fired.

"Targets designated!" shouted Tacitus as he shook off the debris from another nearby explosion.

Martin set her sights on an officer atop one of the forward tanks. She took in a breath. Another explosion almost lifted her off the ground and rocked her forward. With a grunt, she centered her crosshairs on the officer again and fired. Three seconds later the officer tumbled from his position.

"Since everyone's coming to the dance we might as well get Parsons and his marines in on this," yelled Martin over the whizzing bullets and explosions.

Tacitus activated his circuit. "Sandman 45, this is Hunter 2, request immediate support at my location. Engaging armor and approximately a battalion of infantry. Be aware incoming hawk attack craft, over."

"*Roger, Hunter 2,*" came Parsons's voice over the circuit. "*Sandman 45 in route. ETA six minutes.*"

Martin fired again and another Triad soldier fell. She could feel herself growing more anxious every second. Not that Martin didn't enjoy a good fight, but every second she wasted with these locals meant Stone and the others were getting farther away.

"*Hunter 1, this is Reaper 21 and 23, inbound. Keep your heads down.*"

"Roger," replied Martin. "Light 'em up."

Martin looked up from her sights as the entire column of armored vehicles was consumed in a rolling ball of fire. Seconds later, the percussive sound of the hawk assault crafts' supersonic engines drowned out the roar of the explosion.

"Hunter 1, this is Reaper 21 and 23. Switching to guns for second run."

"Reaper 23, this is Hunter 1. Pull off run. Take out all roads, bridges, or moving vehicles from east to west of this town."

As Martin gave the order, the ground where the fireball had just begun to subside erupted in a rising wave of dirt, metal, and flesh, the rounds from hawks' Gatling guns tearing apart what was left of the armor. Martin looked toward the sky and saw one of the hawks peel off from its run to carry out her order.

"Roger, Hunter 1. Reaper 23 copies."

Martin's attention was then drawn toward the roar of a transport passing overhead at combat speed. The craft banked heavily and stopped at a hover two meters from the ground over the now-destroyed park. The rear hatch opened and twelve marines and their officer jumped from transport and rushed toward the bridge and the surviving Triad infantry. Martin soon heard a burst of automatic fire as Parsons and his men began to engage the ground troops. Martin's attention was then drawn to a loud explosion. Looking to the east, she saw smoke begin to rise from that direction.

"Hunter 1 this is Reaper 23. I just took out a bridge six kilometers north of our position. There was a small motorized vehicle ready to cross. I engaged and drove it off the road. Four armed personnel bailed from the vehicle and disappeared into the forest to your northeast."

"That's them," said Martin out loud. She turned toward Tacitus.

"Let's go," he shouted as he sprinted past Martin.

Martin dropped her sniper rifle and followed him. The two jumped, twisted, and bobbed as they sprinted down the sloping hill toward the park.

"Transport 1, this is Hunter 1. Have two hover bikes ready in four minutes," commanded Martin into the circuit as she caught up with Tacitus. Martin sensed her partner push himself and start to gain on her; she did the same and they raced side-by-side down the hill.

At the bottom of the hill, the two burst full speed from the foliage and rushed toward the transport.

"Good job, Parsons!" Martin breathed heavily as she and Tacitus sprinted past the marine officer. "You and one of your marines with us."

The four quickly reached the transport, which had set down in the center of the park. They raced into the open rear hatch and the small cargo bay. In front of them were two hover bikes with their gravity wells activated.

"Thanks," huffed Martin, sliding her assault rifle into a compartment on the bike. "Hop on, Parsons," she ordered, and the captain slid on behind her. A corporal did the same with Tacitus. Leaning heavily, she turned the bike and hit the accelerator to force the bike out of the transport. As soon as she was clear, she engaged the thrusters and the bike rocketed forward with Tacitus close behind.

At one hundred sixty kilometers per hour, Martin and Tacitus raced through the small town and toward the bridge. In less time than it took to sprint to the transport, they came upon the shot-up vehicle.

Martin abruptly stopped her bike and in one fluid motion leapt from the bike, drew her assault rifle, and brought it to her shoulder. Rushing to the vehicle,

Martin quickly looked inside. It was empty but covered in broken glass and blood.

"At least one of them is wounded," she said to Tacitus, who was now standing beside her.

Tacitus quickly examined the ground around the vehicle. "They went this way," he said, pointing toward a densely wooded area.

"Let's move!" shouted Martin, rushing toward the forest with Tacitus and the two Marines close behind.

Martin moved swiftly through the wooded landscape, alternating between a glance at the ground for the blood trail and to her front and flanks for signs of an ambush. After several minutes, she stopped and signaled for the group behind to slow their pace and approach slowly. Ahead was a large river that ended in a fifty-meter waterfall a short distance downstream. The sound of the swift water and waterfall required Martin to nearly shout when the others reached her.

"They crossed here," stated Tacitus as he pointed to a blood-stained leaf at the edge.

"Or they want us to think they did," interjected Martin. "Parsons, you check upstream for more blood. I will check downstream."

Martin moved quickly along the riverbank and soon reached the massive waterfall. Peering over the edge, she saw four figures a few hundred meters away disappear into the underbrush on the opposite side of the bank at the bottom of the falls. Martin raised her assault rifle, took aim, and let a burst fly. The foliage around the last figure twitched as the rounds were deflected by the thick undergrowth. The four turned and sent a volley toward Martin, who took cover behind a large rock as the bullets impacted all around her.

"They're over here," she shouted.

Within seconds, Tacitus, Parsons, and the corporal were at Martin's side.

"They returned fire and disappeared into the underbrush down there," she informed the group, pointing toward the last spot she had seen the foursome.

"Roger," responded Parsons as he grabbed the corporal's arm. "Let's get across."

Parsons and the corporal immediately stepped into the river, with the two Paladins behind them. The river was swift but not too deep. What it lacked in depth, however, it made up for in bone-chilling temperature. Martin inhaled deeply as the swift, cold water sent flashes of stinging sensations over her body. Pushing the cold out of her mind, she slowly waded across waist-high into the river. About halfway across the river, the captain turned back quickly to Tacitus.

"It looks like it's passable up here," he said as he shifted to his right.

Looking toward Parsons, Martin focused on a small clump of mud and leaves resting on a nearby log that was jutting out of the water. Looking more closely, she saw a line connected to the bundle of mud and leaves.

"Parsons, wait!" she yelled, but it was too late.

The captain triggered a device hidden under the log and a sudden, powerful explosion sent water, rocks, and Parsons into the air. The corporal, seeing his commander blown apart by the explosion, immediately rushed toward him.

"Stop!" shouted Tacitus.

The corporal looked toward Tacitus and replied, "I've gotta get to him."

"Corporal," interjected Martin. "That's an ord —"

Another explosion tore the young corporal apart.

As water from the explosion showered Martin, she looked toward Tacitus, who was slowly retracing his steps toward the river bank.

"We're not going to be able to cross here," he shouted over the roar of the water.

"They're going to get away," she shouted as her anxiousness returned. They were so close — she was so close — to exacting her revenge.

"They've got wires all over this crossing," replied Tacitus.

"Son of a bitch," grunted Martin, pacing back and forth in a small patch of the river. "They're right there over the —" Martin paused midsentence and pulled her sword from her waist belt and slid it into the secondary sheath across her back then locked it in place. She attached the butt of her assault rifle to the shoulder D-ring on her tactical vest and tied a quick knot around the barrel to the lower part.

"What the hell are you doing?" asked Tacitus.

"I'm not letting them get away," replied Martin.

Before her partner could respond, Martin pivoted and rushed toward the edge of the waterfall. At the edge she leapt forward and extended her arms above her head. She felt the rush of the air and the mist of the waterfall around her as she plunged toward the water below. The roar of the waterfall instantly transitioned to the bubbling, tumultuous rumbling of the river as Martin's body penetrated the surface of the water. The force of the impact was powerful, but she quickly regained her composure and pushed her body toward the surface. Breaking the surface of the water, she took a deep breath and looked back toward the top of the waterfall with a smile before turning and swimming toward the opposite shore.

In a few seconds she reached the shore. Dragging herself onto the rocky bank, she detached her rifle, scanned the thick undergrowth, and moved into the heavy foliage.

Moving slowly and quietly, Martin looked for signs of movement and listened for the slightest hint of the enemy. She listened for the normal sounds of the forest — birds, squirrels, insects. It was silent except for the rustling sound of the nearby river. They were close —

She immediately spun to her left at the sound of snapping twigs. As her rifle swung around, the silver flash of a tomahawk caught her eye as the weapon was knocked from her hands. She looked up to see another tomahawk coming toward her head.

Martin blocked the downward thrust and brought her right boot against the chest of her attacker. As he fell backward, she could see he was a tall, lean Terillian with a small tuft of hair running the center of his head. His face was painted black with red diamonds around his eyes. Martin saw his eyes open wide and his mouth gape.

"You're Red Wolf," he spoke in Humani. "You're supposed to be dead. The War God has made this my lucky day." Martin saw his shock replaced with hungry anticipation of a fight.

This was more than any Terillian had spoken to Martin in any language. After the surprise passed, she responded.

"The name's Martin, Ter. And I'm far from dead, you son of a bitch" she shot back. "And I wouldn't say what's about to happen to you is gonna be lucky." She drew her sword.

Martin saw a smile come to the Terillian's face. Then he rushed forward.

Martin thrust her sword at her attacker. The Terillian twisted his body and swung toward Martin's midsection. She brought her knee up to block his forearm. Her knee countered his attack, but Martin felt her feet leave the ground as her opponent lifted her into the air and rushed forward. Most of the air left Martin's lungs as she slammed into a large tree. Sucking in a short breath, she brought her forehead down into his nose. The man stumbled backward, but as he did, he flung one of his tomahawks toward her. She ducked quickly, and the tomahawk embedded itself into the tree just above her head. Martin frantically looked for her sword; it was several feet behind her attacker.

"Well, you don't suck, Ter," said Martin, pulling a combat knife from her vest. "I'll give you that."

This time the Terillian moved first, leaping toward her with his remaining tomahawk slashing toward her neck. Martin moved quickly, taking her body out of the arc of the tomahawk's path. Once inside his swing, she jumped forward and brought her knee into his chest. The man recoiled but kept his grip on her leg. Ensnared by the Terillian, Martin wrapped her other leg around his neck and pulled herself onto his shoulders. From there, she brought her knife down toward his chest. The man released her and blocked the thrust but not before she felt the blade partially penetrate his chest. She heard him let out a groan but then felt his hands on her vest as he grabbed her and in a powerful motion threw her onto the ground.

Her back impacted the forest floor and a sharp jolt echoed through her ribs. Wincing against the pain, she looked up to see the pointed edge of the tomahawk coming down toward her head. She quickly rolled to her side and felt the wind from the blade as it sank into the ground where her head had been. Quickly pushing herself to her feet, she tried to block the upward swing of the tomahawk but grunted heavily when the sharp blade sliced through her left forearm. She reached for her sidearm, but a blow to her hand sent it falling to the ground.

The momentum of the warrior's thrust caused his upper body to angle downward and Martin capitalized, driving her left hand into the jaw of the Terillian with the force of her entire body. The pain from her wound shot up her arm and through her body, but she rapidly brought her right boot against the forehead of the Terillian, snapping his head backwards and knocking him to the ground.

She moved forward and let out a grunt as she swung her right leg toward his head again. Just before her boot contacted his jaw, the Terillian blocked the kick and pushed upward in a powerful motion causing Martin to fall backward. Before she could stand, the Terillian was on her, bringing his knee toward her face. She blocked the move with her forearms but let out a moan of pain as the powerful knee made contact with her injured forearm. Fighting through the pain, she brought her right fist toward his knee. The Terillian was fast and blocked her punch with his right hand and while falling forward, spun his body and landed a powerful elbow against her left jaw knocking her on her side.

Martin rolled onto her back and immediately felt the Terillian on top of her. The attacker brought a fist downward toward her face, which Martin blocked and returned with a quick jab to his throat. The Terillian grunted and grabbed his neck. Martin shoved him backwards and in a swift motion twisted her body to lock her legs around the man's neck. The Terillian struggled against her leg-lock but couldn't free himself. Feeling she might have gained the upper hand, she gritted her teeth and squeezed with all of her strength; her muscles strained to choke her opponent.

Suddenly a sharp pain shot through her right hamstring and her grip instantly loosened, allowing the warrior to kick out of her hold. She looked down to see the Terillian had driven a small blade into her leg. She scrambled to her feet, grimacing as pain radiated through her leg. Before she could react, the Terillian crashed into her body and the two tumbled down the bank and over a large boulder into the river.

Martin entered the water with the attacker on top of her and they sank toward the bottom. Martin could feel the force of the current and sting of the cold as their bodies continued to descend. Still sinking, Martin's body tightened as the Terillian wrapped his arms and legs around her. She could tell the Terillian's intent was to drown her, even if it meant his own death.

Deeper still, and Martin could feel her nose and face start to burn from the lack of oxygen. Reaching to her side, Martin pulled the last knife from her belt and drove it into the Terillian's upper back as the two made contact with the bottom of the river. The Terillian released his grip and disappeared into the swift, dark water.

Her head burning from the lack of oxygen, Martin pushed herself off the bottom of the river and began kicking toward to the surface. Her lungs burned and her injured leg ached as she struggled to reach the air. When she broke the surface, Martin let out a heavy gasp, sucking in a deep breath. Still breathing heavily, she scanned for the attacker. He was nowhere to be seen.

"Damn it," she cursed. "That guy was good."

Grunting as she kicked her injured appendages against the current, Martin began to swim back toward the riverbank. Each stroke felt like a lightning bolt of pain, but she pushed herself onward toward land. Pulling herself onto the rocky bank, she lay on her back for a second to regain her breath and gain control of the pain pulsing through her body.

After a moment she rose and headed into the forest. Cursing and grumbling with each step, she hobbled her way back to the scene of the fight. She had just collected the last of her weapons when she heard Tacitus reach her.

"Are you out of your fucking mind?" he demanded. "Wha —" He paused when he saw that Martin was injured. "What the hell happened?"

"Some ..." Martin grunted. "Some fucking Ranger held me up."

"Just one?" asked Tacitus.

"Fuck you, Tacitus. It was one of those painted-face bastards," said Martin as she injected a neuro-med and coagulate into her leg.

"Where is he?"

"I don't fucking know," she replied. "Maybe dead. Maybe floating down the river. Wherever he is, he's not in any better shape than me."

"That's saying something," he replied. "Because you're pretty tore up."

"Thanks, asshole. That Ter son of a bitch was good, but I put as many holes in him as he did in me." Martin paused and looked up from her wounds toward Tacitus.

"What?" he asked in response to her silence.

"He spoke in our language and called me Red Wolf."

"It's not like there are a lot of red-haired female officers in the Guard. Sounds like you've made a name for yourself. And some pissed off enemies."

"They're already my enemies," replied Martin.

"Well, maybe he drowned."

"I hope not," replied Martin as she pulled her attacker's tomahawk from the tree. "We have some unfinished business."

Chapter 10

"He's over here!" shouted Stone as he grabbed the semiconscious Thay, sliding his arms underneath the wounded man's shoulders. Stone grunted as he lifted Thay from water's edge, the Iroqua's waterlogged clothing only adding to the dead weight of the warrior's limp body.

"Is he okay?" asked Henry when he and Mori reached Stone.

"He's got a wound on his leg and looks like a broken nose," replied Stone as he ensured his footing was sound and pulled on Thay's torso.

Thay let out a moan.

"His back," said Mori. "He's got a damn knife in it."

Stone slightly turned Thay's body and laid him face down onto the ground.

"Where are the meds?" asked Stone.

"Here," replied Henry, pulling a pack from his pocket.

Stone snatched the packet from Henry and quickly opened it. It contained half a container of coagulant, a neuro-inhibitor, disinfecting spray, and an adreno-injector.

"Is this it?" asked Stone.

"That's it," replied Mori. "The full kit was with —" Mori paused. Stone saw her face go flat and a half-frown form on the right side of her face. "With Sandwick."

Stone pulled the uniform apart around the blade embedded in Thay's back. Once clear, he gripped the knife and pulled the blade from Thay's flesh. Thay groaned and Stone quickly applied what was left of the coagulant. He slowly rolled Thay onto his back and injected the neuro-meds into his arm.

Stone saw Thay look up toward him. "It was her, the —" he said in a weak voice.

"This should help you out," said Stone, taking the injector full of adrenaline in his hand. Stone took the cap off the injector and in a quick motion drove the device into Thay's chest. Thay's eyes opened wide and he sucked in a deep breath.

"You okay?" asked Mori.

Thay quickly sat up straight, grunting slightly against the pain.

"She's here," repeated Thay, pulling himself erect with the help of a small tree.

"Who are you talking about?" queried Henry.

"Red Wolf," responded Thay.

"It's the meds. Or the injuries. Did he hit his head?" said Henry.

"She died on Juliet 3," replied Mori.

"I saw her," retorted Thay, clearly becoming more coherent and insistent. "We fought. I almost took her to the bottom of the river with me but —"

Thay stopped again, reaching to the location where the knife had been protruding from his back.

"Who are you talking about?" asked Stone. "Who is this Red Wolf?"

"She is a guard officer — the one that killed Thay's brother."

"There's no female guard officers," replied Stone. "The only one died on Juliet 3."

"Red hair, loud mouth, and a fighter," Thay listed off. "I know who it was."

Stone began to put his thoughts in order. Red hair — female — Juliet 3. "No!" he almost shouted. "She's dead. I saw her die. She can't be alive."

"Well, she's alive, brother," replied Thay. "And she lives up to her reputation."

Stone felt light-headed. He had seen the explosion consume Martin and Jackson. *'Could she be alive?'* he wondered. There wasn't another female, or many males, in the Humani military that could have held their own against Thay. And it looked to Stone that whoever it was had more than held their own. Stone's light-headedness started to shift to an uplifting happiness at the thought of Martin's survival.

"Are you sure?" asked Mori.

"It's fucking her!" responded an exasperated Thay.

"Then we need to be on the move," declared Henry. "We have to get to cover and find a good defensive position."

"I need to find her," replied Thay.

"Thay," interjected Mori. "I understand how important it is, but you are in no condition to fight her. If the Great Spirit wills it, you will meet her again."

Stone could see the frustration on Thay's face. "I will have my revenge —"

"Atotat!" shouted Mori, interrupting Thay. "We don't have time for this. If you go after her you'll endanger all of us. We'll need everyone now that Sandwick ... now that we're down a team member."

Stone watched for Thay's response. The proud warrior's face grimaced with a mixture of pain and frustrated angst. His entire body seemed contracted with a spasm of vexation. Looking toward Mori, he saw the determined face of a commander that was placing the mission and the team above the desires of one. The air seemed heavy with tension as Thay and Mori stared at one another.

"You know she's right," stated Henry.

Mori and Thay maintained their tight gaze on one another.

Suddenly, Stone's happiness sank like a rock in the nearby river as a painful truth hit him; these people wanted to kill Martin — in a bad way.

Henry tried again. "Thay, you're injured. There's clearly more than one Guardsman in pursuit of us. And they have support units and air available. If we stay, we die."

Stone felt his stomach fall even further. Not only did they want to kill Martin, she wanted to kill them. And him as well. Tacitus, who might also be in pursuit, thought Stone was a traitor. Why would Martin think any different? Despite his newfound comfort with his Akota and Iroqua heritage, he knew he wasn't ready to face Martin.

"We have to go," Stone heard himself say without realizing it.

Stone saw Thay turn toward him, his face still distorted in anguish.

"Do you fear her, brother?" asked Thay.

"I trained her," replied Stone. "And we should all fear her. She won't stop and she'll use whatever she has at her disposal to complete her mission."

"You trained her?" asked Thay, his expression now contorting to add confusion to frustration. "Well, you trained her well," he spat. "She killed my brother, another Ka-itsenko."

"She was doing her duty," shot back Stone out of instinct. "She —"

"Stop it!" shouted Mori, moving between Thay and Stone. "This is solving nothing. This is complicated, and we don't fucking have time for complicated, so I'll make it simple." She turned to Stone. "I know you will need to process this, but do it later. And don't forget, regardless of what she does or doesn't know, the Red Wolf is *our* enemy and will kill us if she gets a chance." She next turned toward Thay. "Thayendanegea, I understand your right to vengeance. But I'm in command of this mission that you agreed to join, so you'll follow my orders or bring shame to your clan for endangering your fellow warriors."

The tension was even more palpable now. Stone looked toward Mori, whose back was toward him as she stared at Thay. Looking over her shoulder, he looked into Thay's eyes.

"Does everyone understand me?" asked Mori in a slow, determined voice.

Stone saw Thay's rigid face slowly, reluctantly loosen. He nodded ever so slightly to Stone. "Very well."

"And you?" added Mori as she turned toward Stone.

Stone could feel her green eyes burning into his core. Emotions brought up by the realization that Martin was alive tore through him like a tornado. But that was for later.

"Yes. Of course," he replied.

"Good," said Mori. "Now we're going to move to the northwest, take up a defensive position, get our comms up, and have *Hydra* get us off this rock. This shit has gone sideways."

"Good," Henry agreed. "Let's get the hell out of here."

***

Astra looked down toward her son as she held him to her breast. Gently holding her hand against the child's head, she spoke.

"Don't worry, my little Octavius," she whispered to her infant son. "These times will be difficult, but one day you'll be the greatest leader our people have ever known. When they are least expecting it, I'll take my vengeance on our Xen and Doran overlords for the death of your grandfather. By the time it's over, I'll have set the stage for you to become the first emperor of a galactic Humani Empire. An empire that will last for eons." Astra paused. "But first we must find out what is keeping our little Port Royal canary from singing for us."

"Tellia, come take Octavius," ordered Astra to a servant standing on the far edge of the room.

"Yes, ProConsul," replied the servant as she quickly walked to Astra and took the infant from her arms.

Astra activated the communications console. As she looked into the screen, the image of a Humani general appeared.

"Yes, ProConsul," answered the officer. "This is General Macilli Valari. How may I serve you?"

"General Valari, Paladins Martin and Tacitus are operating in the Echo System and I must get a priority message to them. How long will it take?"

"Yes, ProConsul, of course. If we override bandwidth protocols and hierarchy, we can send a message via electron spin burst and they should receive it within the week."

Astra sighed but even she knew she couldn't change physics.

"Very well. Pass this message to them immediately: At the order of the ProConsul, report directly to Echo 4 and make contact with Envoy Rebecca Sterling and Praetorian Hamrahi and report status immediately via fastest communications medium."

***

Stone's mind raced while he slept. In addition to his normal parade of nightmares, the deaths of the young girl and Sandwick made their first appearances. It wasn't long, however, until the vision of Martin in the Battle of Juliet 3 returned. As always, Stone was running toward the wounded Martin as Terillian soldiers rushed toward her. He raised his pistol and fired. This time, for the first time, the Terillian fell before he could strike. In a few long strides, he was with Martin and Jackson.

Jackson held the badly wounded Martin in his arms. Stone knelt down beside her and placed his hand on her shoulder.

"I made it," he said, feeling a wave of relief flow over his body.

Martin slowly looked up toward him from Jackson's embrace. "Good," she replied as she suddenly swung her sidearm toward Stone's face. "Traitor!" she yelled and there was a bright flash as she pulled the trigger.

Stone jumped from his sleep.

"You okay?" asked Mori, kneeling beside him.

Stone could feel the sweat running down his face and his heart racing. "Yeah. I'm fine," he answered.

Mori smiled. "Liar."

Stone felt Mori's hand on his face as she leaned in for a quick kiss.

"Dreams?" she asked.

"Yes," he replied as he looked into her eyes. Those powerful green eyes always seemed to make him feel better. "But my weakness is my problem."

"You don't have to do this alone," she said. "I don't know about the Humani, but we don't bottle up our dreams. And our dreams don't mean we are weak; they mean we are human. Our dreams tell us what we need to know, not what we want to know. When we get back we'll meet with the *wichasa wakhan*."

"But these dreams, they haunt me —"

"Then we'll talk about them," interrupted Mori. "That's how we exorcise our demons. We share them with others and they lose their power."

"I don't think telling other people my nightmares will help," responded Stone with a whisper. Even though he trusted Mori, he felt ashamed at sharing his weakness.

"You're not the only one to have the bad things we do and see follow you into your dreams," replied

Mori. Stone saw her look down toward the ground. "We've all seen and done a lot we regret," continued Mori. "And had a lot done to us that we regret."

Stone instantly felt even more ashamed. He had seen his share of traumatic things, but he had not lived through the hell that Mori had experienced on Capro. "I'm sorry," he said as he put his hand on her shoulder.

"It's okay," said Mori, looking up toward Stone. "When we get back you'll see. It will help. It won't make it go away, but it will help." Mori paused and let out a slow breath. "But for now," she continued. "I've sent a transmission to Orion with coordinates for a pickup tomorrow."

"What's the next move?"

"I think trying to talk with the Triad is a waste, so we're gonna pay a visit to the bastards who seem to have their hands in everything but don't know anything."

"Port Royal. And the Association," posited Stone.

"They're neck deep in this. I can feel it in my bones," replied Mori. "And frankly I'm tired of their duplicitous bullshit."

"Works for me," said Stone, adding, "I'm ready to get off this rock."

"Afraid you'll run into her?" asked Mori knowingly.

Stone inhaled and exhaled heavily. "I'm over the problem I had on the slaver ship. I won't hesitate again. But her ..." He paused. "She is different."

"Why does she matter so much? Have you two ___"

"No!" interrupted Stone. "It's not like that. She's like a, well ..." He paused again trying to find the words. "She's ... special."

"How is she any more special than any other Humani?"

Stone could tell Mori was growing concerned with what Martin actually meant to him. "I trained her. We fought together," he replied.

"Did you not train other officers? And fight with them?"

He felt a headache starting to form as he struggled to get out of the awkward conversation. "Yes, but ... it's complicated."

"You need to understand, Ty," said Mori. "You may hesitate if you face her — and I guess, well I am trying to understand that — but we won't. We can't; she is too good."

"I understand. I just hope if we meet, I will have the chance to talk —"

"To talk?" shot back Mori, almost yelling before she took a moment to calm herself. "You know her better than any of us but ask yourself this: will she give you the chance? Is that in the Red Wolf's nature?"

Stone's head was now throbbing. "I think ... I hope she will." He exhaled. "I don't know."

"Well you had better figure it out, Ty," stated Mori matter-of-factly. "The rest of us already know the answer."

"I don't want you to doubt me," he said as he raised his hand to her cheek.

"I have no doubt you want to do what is right, Magakisca," she said, using his Akota name. "But you may have to do what is necessary."

"I will, Ino'ka. I know it," he replied, lying to himself.

"Good," answered Mori as she gave him a quick, gentle kiss before lying next to him. "Now let's get some sleep."

As Stone placed his head onto the ground, he looked toward Mori.

She looked back into his eyes. "I won't let her hurt you."

Chapter 11

By the time the first sun had risen, Stone, Mori, Thay, and Henry had made their way to the outskirts of a long-abandoned city. Standing on the roof of a six-story building, Stone and Thay scanned the horizon for signs of the enemy, whether the Saint's Crucesignatis Army, the Triad, or Humani. For miles, Stone could see abandoned buildings, elevated walkways, and streets degraded by time and overtaken by nature. Tall grass grew defiantly from any crack in the concrete. Ivy and other vines had also begun to envelop the standing structures as the environment slowly reclaimed what humans had once arrogantly thought of as their own.

"This place is dead," declared Thay. "Not a single unit. I'm surprised nobody is fighting over it."

"Probably the radiation," said Stone as he pulled up the counter on his data screen. "0.1 milliSieverts per hour," he read.

"Not too bad for a few hours," replied Thay.

"But explains why the city is abandoned. Must have taken a ton of fallout or had a power plant accident during the First Terill … I mean, early on in the war. Guessing that's why Mori picked this spot."

"Either way, it's a shame," said Thay.

"*Everything look good up top?*" came Mori's voice through the comms circuit.

"Good so far," replied Stone. "How are you guys doing?"

"*We've rigged the stairs at the entryway and we'll set up on the second floor in case anyone decides to pay us a visit before Orion gets here.*"

"Stone," interjected Thay as he pointed toward the ground below. "We've got movement."

Stone peered over the short wall on the roof. He saw a figure rush across a street a few hundred meters away. It was a Humani marine. The single marine was followed by a squad. Looking toward his left, Stone saw another squad taking up positions along an abandoned subway station.

"Mori," said Stone into the circuit. "We've got Humani marines to the west and south."

"*Roger,*" she replied. "*We'll have a welcome for them down here.*"

"Let's greet 'em," said Thay as he rested his rifle on the wall and took careful aim.

Stone took aim as well, sighting in on the corner of a building he knew provided cover for at least four marines.

Thay pulled the trigger and the quiet, abandoned city erupted in gunfire.

***

Over the muffled crack of gunfire from outside, Mori heard the rumbling of footsteps coming up the stairs. Looking toward the video on her data screen she saw the images from the camera she had set up earlier; turning the corner from the first floor was a Humani marine, then another, and another.

"Hit it," ordered Mori and Henry activated the explosives in the stairwell.

The building rocked and the force of the blast rattled Mori's bones, but she quickly recovered. Pulling up the screen again, she saw a disorganized pile of wood, brick, and the wrecked bodies of four Humani marines. Before the smoke and dust cleared, however, Mori saw three more marines rush over their fallen comrades.

The metallic burst from Henry's rifle let Mori know the enemy had reached their floor. She repositioned herself on the opposite side of the door from Henry and turned to fire down the entryway. As she did, she felt the whiz of a round simultaneously followed with the explosive sound of the marine's rifle as he fired. Mori spun back to cover the wall and looked across to Henry, who was holding his rifle into the doorway and firing.

Mori grabbed a grenade from her vest. She raised the metal canister to her face and pulled the pin.

"Frag out!" she yelled and tossed the grenade into the entryway.

"Cover!" Mori heard one of the marines yell.

The blast was close and both Henry and Mori curled themselves into a ball as the blast tore through the entryway and blew debris into the room. Mori saw Henry turn to cover the entry only to be tackled and knocked to the ground. She raised her rifle to fire at the attacker but glimpsed a flash of metal to her right.

She had just enough time to position her rifle to block the sword from slicing through her. Across from her was a Humani soldier, her bold red hair tied into a ponytail, her eyes opened wide in surprise. It was Martin, or Red Wolf, as the Terillians knew her.

"Finally, got you," Martin smiled as she sent Mori reeling backward with a front kick to her chest.

Rolling backward, Mori quickly rose to her knees and brought her rifle to bear. She felt the rifle recoil, then a jolt as Martin kicked it from her hands. Mori swiftly rolled to her right, pulled her sword from its sheath, and jumped to her feet as she saw Martin standing as well. Her first shot had torn into Martin's thigh, leaving a small chunk of flesh missing. Mori looked into her opponent's eyes. Martin glared back, her jaw tight; everything about her radiated hatred. Looking over Martin's shoulder, Mori saw Henry and Tacitus locked in combat.

***

"They're in the building," shouted Stone as he felt the rumble from the tripwire set off by Mori and Henry.

"Mori and Henry will keep them busy," replied Thay.

Stone fired another burst from his rifle; a marine rushing toward an adjacent building fell.

"If they get into that building across the street, we're screwed," shouted Thay over the sounds of battle.

Rounds impacted against the short wall in front of Stone, causing him to turn his head away from the flying debris. Quickly collecting himself, he reached for another magazine. As he did, a small electrical charge rushed through his body as the magazine contacted the rifle. Looking upward he saw a line of bright blue light streak across the sky above them.

"What the hell is that?" asked Thay.

"I don't —"

Stone was interrupted by an ear-piercing metallic screech. Blue light radiated across the sky, drawing streaks of light and shooting jagged, brilliant lines of light in all directions. Stone's body tingled, an explosion of blue light momentarily blinding him and the roar of thrusters from a ship drowning out the sound of automatic weapons.

***

"Holy shit, that worked!" declared Orion as she brought *Hydra* to a hover near Stone's position.

"I told you it would," replied Rickover.

"So, I guess a jump at atmo is just more than theoretically possible," said Orion as she activated the intercom. "We're here. Magnus and Katalya, go get 'em."

***

Stone couldn't believe his eyes. *Hydra* had appeared out of nowhere. He had never heard of a ship performing a jump into an atmosphere before. He looked toward Thay, who had a puzzled look on his face that Stone knew no doubt mirrored his own.

"Did they just —"

"I think so," answered Stone.

Stone and Thay turned away from the force of *Hydra*'s thrusters as the ship hovered a few meters above them. Stone put his hand in front of his face to shield his eyes from the whirlwind of debris as he looked toward *Hydra*. Through the cloud of debris and dust, he saw an access hatch open and a rope drop. Katalya and Magnus quickly appeared at the hatch and slid down the rope onto the roof.

"Where's Ino'ka?" yelled Katalya, worriedly asking for her sister.

"On the second floor," replied Thay.

Katalya immediately turned and rushed toward the stairway, followed by the other three.

***

Martin lunged toward Mori. In a series of moves and countermoves, Martin advanced and attacked as Mori parried each move but gave up ground until she felt her back hit the opposite wall. Mori saw the enraged focus in Martin's eyes as the Humani thrust her sword at her. She again blocked the thrust and forced Martin's sword away from her body. Pressing downward on Martin's sword, Mori swung her torso upward and crashed her elbow into Martin's left temple. Martin let out a grunt but recovered, and Mori felt the impact of Martin's shoulder into her chest and then the sudden stop as she was slammed against the wall again. Before she could recover, Mori's body slid down the wall to the floor as Martin swept her leg.

Mori hit the ground and instantly kicked Martin just above her right knee, causing her attacker to fall as well. Pushing her body forward as Martin fell to her knees, Mori hurled herself over Martin's shoulder. When she passed over, Mori locked her arms around Martin's neck. Now positioned behind and above Martin, she leaned forward and pressed hard to stop the flow of oxygen. She could feel Martin's body tighten in resistance.

A searing pain suddenly shot through Mori's forearm as Martin sank a knife deep into her flesh. The pain pulsated through her arm and down her spine as Martin, using the knife for leverage, twisted Mori's arm away from her neck. Mori growled against the pain while she struggled to keep her chokehold locked in place. But Martin was too strong and the pain too intense. Letting out a long groan of pain and frustration, Mori felt her grip release and Martin spin free. Her moan transitioned to a shriek when Martin violently pulled the blade from her arm.

There was no time to focus on the pain; she looked up to see Martin thrust the knife toward her throat. Just as the blade was about to find its mark, Mori redirected her attacker's thrust and spun around behind Martin again in an attempt to lock her right arm around her attacker's neck. She strained hard, pushing downward with all of her strength but she could feel her body start to give way as Martin pushed upward. Mori's jaw clenched tight and she could feel her muscles constrict almost to the point of tearing as she tried to control Martin.

But it wasn't enough.

Slowly, helplessly, Mori felt Martin raise her torso and then, in one powerful thrust, rise to her feet with Mori still locked around her neck. Before she could react, Mori felt a second of weightlessness and then the helplessness of falling as Martin fell backwards, driving Mori's back into the floor. The air rushed from Mori's lungs as Martin landed on top of her.

Almost instantly, Mori felt the concussion of Martin's fist against her face but kept her focus. Blocking Martin's next punch, Mori wrapped her legs around her opponent's arm and arched her body to extend it to the breaking point. Both groaned as Martin struggled against the agonizing stretching of her ligaments and Mori pulled on her enemy's arm with all of her strength.

Mori felt a sudden release and heard a loud grunt from her opponent as Martin's elbow snapped.

Martin let out a murmured curse, but the dislocated elbow also allowed her to reposition and swing her leg toward Mori's head. A jolt rocked her head and her vision started to tunnel as Martin's boot slammed into her temple. Releasing her grip on Martin's arm, she rolled to her right and attempted to stand. Before she could, Martin was on her. The air left Mori's lungs again as Martin powerfully lifted her off the ground and slammed her against the wall.

"Terillian bitch!" cursed Martin.

Mori let out a moan as her ribs again slammed against a hard surface of the wall. She struggled to free her arms from Martin's lock as she was repetitively pummeled against the wall. The back of her head throbbed and her back and ribs exploded with sharp bolts of pain with every impact, but she could not break free.

Using the only weapon available to her, Mori leaned her head forward and bit deeply into Martin's neck. As she bit down hard, she sensed the bitter taste of Martin's sweat and blood and her mouth filled with a chunk of her attacker's flesh. Martin growled and Mori felt herself go airborne as she was flung across the floor by the stronger opponent.

Hitting the floor, Mori rolled and quickly regained her footing. As Martin rushed toward her, Mori glanced beyond her attacker and saw Tacitus knock Henry to the floor with a blow to his knee. Her attention returned to Martin as a powerful kick landed against the inside of Mori's leg and brought her to her knees. Hitting the ground, Mori instantly raised her arms to block a knee coming at her face. Pain shot through her already injured and bleeding forearm as she deflected the blow, but Martin recovered and

Mori felt Martin's boot crashing into the side of her head before she could react. Dazed, Mori fell to the ground and hurriedly attempted to pull herself to her knees, when she felt Martin's arms lock around her neck and head from behind.

Mori's head grew heavy and the periphery of her vision grew cloudy as Martin placed all of her weight into the hold. As she struggled against the powerful hold of Martin, Mori glanced up toward Tacitus and Henry, engaged in their own death match near a window at the opposite side of the room. She let out a grunt of frustration as she saw Tacitus open a large gash in Henry's chest with a lightning-quick slash of his sword.

Mori wasn't doing much better. She felt herself weakening as Martin slowly worked to lock in her chokehold. Fading, Mori frantically groped for the combat knife in her vest. Fumbling for her weapon, she watched through tunneled vision as Tacitus pivoted and dove his sword deep into Henry's abdomen.

Finally finding her knife, Mori grasped the handle and pulled the blade from her vest. Struggling to remain conscious, she repositioned the grip for maximum force, and with all of her remaining strength thrust the knife into Martin's upper leg until she felt the blade deflect off the bone. Mori heard Martin moan loudly and sucked in a deep breath of air as Martin released her hold.

Mori turned quickly and brought her knee against Martin's chin as she rose, bending Martin's torso backwards and causing her to stumble. Huffing to bring in much needed air, she quickly looked toward Henry and Tacitus. She watched helplessly as

Tacitus violently twisted and then yanked the sword from Henry's body. Mori quickly glanced toward Martin, who was rising to her feet. Tacitus, his back facing Mori, was preparing a final downward slash to finish off Henry.

There was no way she could fight both of them.

Mori let out a growl of desperation as she grabbed for the last grenade on her vest, pulled the pin, and let the grenade fall to her feet. Before the grenade hit the floor, she turned and rushed toward Henry and Tacitus. She leapt into the air at a full sprint, flying past Tacitus and crashing into Henry. Mori heard the crashing of glass, the momentum of her body carrying both of them through the window. As they fell, a wave of heat and pressure, followed by a shower of glass, wood, and brick, enveloped them.

Everything went black momentarily as Mori hit the ground. Her head filled with a painful, high-pitched ring and her ribs and back radiated pain as she slowly regained consciousness. Struggling to catch her breath, Mori tried to roll onto her side but cried out, pain pulsing through her body from her leg. Looking toward the source, Mori saw a piece of metal rebar protruding from her left thigh.

Inhaling heavily, she tried to pull her leg free. She grunted deeply as she pulled on her leg with all of her remaining strength but could not free herself. Soon her body began to tremble from the pain and she let her head fall back onto the ground.

Breathing heavily, she looked toward Henry. He was sprawled facedown beside her. Blood began to pool under his chest. If he was still alive, he wouldn't be for long. But there was nothing she could do for him in her current state. The anguish over Henry and the pain racing through her body caused her to let out another groan as she pulled a pistol from Henry's holster and scanned the area for more enemy troops. She glanced to her left and saw the body of Tacitus a few meters from her position. His bloody, torn, and broken body had protected her and Henry from the majority of the damage caused by the grenade.

Suddenly Mori sensed movement as a marine rose up from behind cover. Mori spun further to her left and fired two rounds into the attacker, knocking him to the ground. Scanning to her right, she saw a Humani soldier turn the corner of the building. The first thing she noticed was red hair tied in tight ponytail.

"Shit," grunted Mori as she fired rapidly at Martin. "Die already!"

Mori saw Martin dive for cover behind a small pile of rubble. Struggling to hold her pistol level due to her injuries, Mori watched for movement.

Martin rose and fired a burst. Mori returned fire. A searing pain burned through Mori's left shoulder as one of Martin's rounds hit its mark. The impact drove Mori's back toward the ground from her inclined sitting position. Breathing heavily through the pain, Mori balanced her pistol on the knee of her good leg. Her vision was starting to fade but she took another deep breath and concentrated on where Martin was last seen.

Mori sensed movement to her left. Looking upward, she saw a figure jump out of the same window from which she and Henry had leapt. It was followed immediately by a second. The figures hit the ground gracefully and brought assault rifles to their shoulders. A wave of relief came over Mori as she recognized the figure. It was Katalya and Magnus.

Mori raised her head and smiled toward her sister. Katalya returned the smile but it was interrupted as rounds impacted around her. Katalya and Magnus quickly spun, dropped to their knees, and fired. With the threat removed, Katalya turned toward Mori.

"You okay?" asked Katalya.

"Stuck," huffed Mori. Out of the corner of her eye she saw movement from Martin's position.

Mori, Magnus, and Katalya turned in unison and unleashed a hail of fire in Martin's direction, again forcing her to take cover.

"Mori!" shouted Stone as he and Thay rushed toward her.

"Tyler," she returned. "Henry's hurt bad."

Stone and Thay quickly made their way to Mori and Henry as Magnus and Katalya kept Martin pinned down. Thay covered Stone as he tended to Mori and Henry.

"Don't worry about me," ordered Mori as she reached up toward Stone. Her body ached but all she could think off was Henry. "Henry —"

"We've got to get you off this bar first," interrupted Stone.

Looking up toward the sky above Stone, Mori could see *Hydra* drift over their position.

"Take a deep breath," warned Stone. "This is gonna hurt."

Pain exploded through Mori's body and she let out a scream as Stone ripped her leg free of the metal bar. Breathing quickly to hold in another scream, Mori grabbed Stone's arm and squeezed tightly.

"Let's get you out of here," said Stone as Mori felt him lift her into a metal stretcher lowered from *Hydra*.

Her body ached with every movement as Stone strapped her into the cage.

"We're ready," spoke Stone into the comms, straddling the cage.

"I'll ride up with ya," he smiled.

"Henry!" coughed Mori.

"He's coming up next," replied Stone.

As they entered *Hydra*, Mori felt Stone jump off the rig and then the pressure of Stone's arms pulling her out of the stretcher. Each tug was excruciating. Next, she felt the pinch of a neuro-med followed by coagulants. Mori's body ached, but the pain slowly began to recede to a manageable agony. She looked up toward Stone.

"I got ya." He smiled. "You're gonna be okay."

The high-pitched whine of the winch from the stretcher caught Mori's attention and she sat up quickly. The pain in her ribs caused her grimace; at least a few had to be broken. Looking toward the hole in the deck, Mori slowly saw Thay came into view as he sat on top of Henry's stretcher.

"That's everyone," shouted Magnus as he and Katalya rushed into the compartment having climbed the access trunk.

***

Martin sensed the fire in her direction die down as the roar and whirlwind of debris from the transport drown out everything. Glancing over the debris, she saw *Hydra* start to ascend toward the sky.

"Son of a bitch!" shouted Martin to herself as she felt her prey once again start to slip through her hands.

She raised her rifle toward the ship, pulled the trigger, and held it. Round after round rattled from her gun and harmlessly bounced of the *Hydra* as she emptied her clip in frustration. Her rifle empty, Martin threw it to the ground and activated her comms circuit.

"Reaper 22, this is Hunter 1. Attack mission against modified Falcon-class transport at my location —"

Martin's transmission halted as a wave of electromagnetic radiation overrode her order with a dull buzzing sound. Looking upward, Martin saw a field of blue light start to radiate from *Hydra* as the ship's nose rose slightly toward the sky. The blue light grew more intense and Martin could feel the hair on her neck stand from the static electricity. Suddenly a heavy blue light shot skyward from the ship and in a brilliant flash of blue, *Hydra* disappeared.

"Those ballsy motherfuckers," said Martin out loud in a combination of frustration and appreciation.

"*Hunter 1*" came a voice over her comms circuit.

"Never mind," she replied. "They're gone."

***

"Get another coagulant!" shouted Stone as he worked to stop the bleeding from Henry's massive wounds.

Katalya rose and sprinted toward medical storage for more supplies.

"It's gonna be okay, cousin," said Thay, pressing his hands over the wound on Henry's abdomen.

Stone looked down toward Henry. His mouth was filling with blood and his eyes held a far-off gaze. Mori was still lying on the deck, but her gaze was locked on them as they treated Henry. Her mouth was partially opeAZn and her eyes screamed with anxiousness.

"How is he?" she asked.

Stone, his arms covered in Henry's blood, slowly shook his head to let her know it did not look good. Henry had lost a lot of blood and Tacitus's sword had opened up his chest and abdomen in a bloody mess. And the fall, while preventing Tacitus from killing him outright, had probably caused internal damage. If they were near a medical facility, maybe he would have a chance. Maybe.

Stone felt Henry's body spasm and more blood spat from his mouth. He again looked to Mori. She shook her head in acknowledgment and, fighting against the pain, dragged herself to Henry. When she reached him, Mori placed her hand on his forehead and spoke.

"Life's a flicker of the sparrow's wings. It's the crack of lightning in the night sky. It's the sparkle of light from your sword." Mori lowered her head to touch Henry's. "The sparrow has flown and the thunder rumbles across the sky. Now it's time, my warrior brother, to put your sword away and shine no more. The circle is complete and you'll rest with the Great Spirit tonight."

When she finished, Mori put her hand over Thay's and slowly pulled his hands away from Henry's body. Stone took in a deep breath, sighed, and stared at Mori's pained expression as Henry died.

Chapter 12

"Damn it," grunted Martin as she turned her head toward the bulkhead and grasped the railing on the bed in the sickbay of *Cerilus*.

"Sorry ma'am," apologized the medic as he applied more gel to Martin's damaged leg.

"I'm fine," replied Martin. Another bolt of pain shot through her body but she was prepared. Tensing her muscles and closing her eyes, Martin quietly endured the agony of the medic's probing. Looking across the room, she saw the body of Arilius Tacitus covered by a blanket embroidered with the Tacitus family crest. He had been a good officer despite his First Family attitude. Looking at the blanket, Martin felt herself growing hot with anger. How could Stone have turned on his own people? She had trusted him with her life on countless occasions and he had never let her down — until he met that … Terillian witch. And the bitch could fight too, which made Martin hate her even more.

Another spasm of pain pulsated through her body.

"How long until I'm good, doc?" she asked after taking in a deep breath to control her reaction to the pain. She couldn't let the trail on her prey go cold.

"You're pretty torn up, Paladin Martin," replied the medic. "The gunshot to your leg didn't hit the artery but it did some muscle damage and that chunk missing from your neck where …"

"Where that bitch bit me," supplied Martin. She could see the surprise on the medic's face. "It wasn't a fucking pillow fight, sergeant."

"No. Of course, I didn't mean to … anyway, that could become infected. Your right knee is bruised but the problem is your elbow and that knife wound. Your elbow will need … we really need to get you to a proper medical facility to get you to a hundred percent."

"I don't have time for a hundred percent," grumbled Martin. "Just plug the holes and give me some meds." If she couldn't run Stone and his whore down, Martin would crawl after them.

"Paladin Martin" came a voice at the entrance to the medical bay.

Martin looked up to see the ship's executive officer with a digital pad and a message chip in his hand.

"What is it, XO?"

"A message from ProConsul Varus. For your eyes only," replied the XO.

"Great," complained Martin, barely containing her disdain for Astra.

Martin could see an awkward look of discomfort and anxiety as he stood at the entrance.

"Well," exhaled Martin, holding out her hand and waving for the XO to move forward. "Give it to me."

The XO briskly walked over to Martin and reached her the pad and chip.

"Let's see what our illustrious leader has to say," Martin quipped as she snatched the data pad from the XO.

She slid the chip into the pad. After placing her thumbs into the print reader to verify access to the classified information, she punched in her personal code to unlock the message. The message read:

PALADINS MARTIN AND TACITUS SUSPEND TRACKING OF THE TRAITOR AND PROCEED IMMEDIATELY TO ECHO FOUR MOON. VERIFY AND REPORT STATUS OF PRAETORIAN HAMRAHI AND ENVOY STERLING OF PORT ROYAL. DO NOT OBTAIN INFORMATION REGARDING MISSION. PROVIDE SECURITY FOR RETURN TO ALPHA HUMANA. *CERILUS* DIRECTED TO SUPPORT AS NEEDED.

"You've got to be shitting me," declared Martin. She had already lost valuable time and now Stone and his Terillian would be in the wind again. A flood of anger replaced the feeling of pain that pulsated through Martin's body. And this message made no sense to Martin. She could only imagine what scheme the First Families were up to with the Association for her, a Paladin, to not have authorization to the details. And why the hell would she need to provide protection if a Praetorian was with the envoy?

"Paladin?" inquired the XO.

Martin did not answer. Her mission was finding Stone and now Astra Varus was keeping her from her mission — from her vengeance. She thought about ignoring the orders, but even she couldn't bring herself to do such a thing.

"Paladin Martin?" he asked again.

"XO, set a course for Echo 4 moon," she grunted.

"For what purpose?"

"You'll have to ask the ProConsul," she replied as she passed the data pad back to the XO. "I'm just a damn trained dog of Astra Varus."

***

As *Hydra* slowed from jump speed near Port Royal, Stone made his way to his and Mori's room. He had grown concerned for her over the last few days. Since Henry's death, Mori had seemed to distance herself from the others. She had even withdrawn from Stone slightly. He had tried to talk to her, but she seemed too distracted or disinterested in the conversation for anything other than quick, to-the-point answers. He knew she hadn't been sleeping well either and her mood was starting to grow sour. Despite her change, the fierceness in her eyes still remained but it seemed focused on a far-off horizon, one away from Stone and the others. Since the direct route had failed, Stone figured he would give her space to figure it out on her own over the last few days. As he opened the hatch, he saw Mori at the edge of the small bed they shared in the cramped compartment. She looked up to acknowledge Stone entering. To Stone's surprise, Mori was in full combat gear with her traditional face paint applied and her hair in braids.

"I take it we're close," she said as she slid a combat knife into her vest and then methodically loaded a clip into her rifle and racked a round into the chamber. Her face was tight and her determined eyes focused on her weapon.

"Are you okay?" he asked.

"I will be soon," she replied mechanically.

Stone grew concerned. The Ka-itsenko only applied their war paint before battle and he had assumed this would be handled delicately, like everything on Port Royal.

"What's your plan, Mori?" asked Stone.

She did not answer.

"Ino'ka," he said loudly. Finally, Mori looked toward him. "What are you going to do?"

"I'm gonna find an Association Council member and make him talk."

Stone saw that determined look and burning fire in her eyes refocus on the present.

"What about the security force? What about the deals the Terillians have with the Association? If you go in hard —"

"I don't really give a shit," she replied. As she rose to her feet, Stone saw her grimace from the pain in her ribs, still not fully healed from her clash with Martin. After a heavy breath she grasped her knife in one hand and one of her braids in the other.

"What are you doing?"

"What I have to," replied Mori as she sliced through the braid. She let the long braid fall to the ground and reached for the other. "These assholes on Port Royal have played both sides of the fence too long. Too many have already died because the Associate is more concerned with profit and political status than justice." The other braid fell. "And it's time for someone to balance the scales."

"Shouldn't we—"

"You should get ready," interrupted Mori.

Stone paused and looked into her eyes. There was no changing her mind. She activated the ship's intercom. "This is Major Skye. Everyone meet in the cargo bay in combat gear. Orion, I want you there too." She looked back toward Stone. "Hurry up, Tyler," she ordered as she walked past him toward the cargo bay.

He grabbed his rifle and combat pack and started making his way to the cargo bay. On the way, he met up with Orion.

"What's going on?" she asked.

"She wants to go straight at them."

"Well, that's one way to do it," replied Orion.

"Something's wrong. She's withdrawn … I know you've seen it. And now she's in full combat gear, painted, and she just cut her braids."

Stone felt Orion grab his arm.

"She cut her braids?"

"Yes. Why did —"

"Damn it," said Orion through her teeth. "I was afraid this would happen. Henry had been a friend of hers since her commissioning. The hair is a sign of mourning and a pledge for vengeance. She won't let it grow until he is avenged. It means trouble for whomever she's after and a lot of action for us."

"This isn't the smart thing to do," replied Stone. "She knows —"

"It's not always about smart," interrupted Orion. "Sometimes it's about returning the balance. It's our way."

"Even if —"

"She's basically declared her own personal war on the Association."

"What about the others?"

"Thay is already ready for a fight. Katalya, she's Ino'ka's sister, and Magnus, well, you know his feelings toward the Xen, Humani, and anyone helping them."

"And you?"

"What else am I gonna do?" Orion conceded. "We should get to the cargo bay."

When Stone and Orion reached the cargo bay, the others were already there. Stone approached Mori and gently placed his hand on her shoulder. She looked up to him. He could see a mixture of pain, determination, and frustration on her face.

"Are you with me or not, Tyler?" she asked.

"I am," he answered. "I just —"

Stone felt her hand brush his hand off her shoulder. She turned to face him directly.

"Remember when I told you that you would have to be able to kill for me? Well, it's time. This isn't about protocol or politics or any of that crap. It's about justice." Mori pointed toward a large container at the far end of the bay. "Ohcumgache's body is lying in a box right over there and we had to leave Sandwick on that damn planet."

She stepped in closer. Stone felt her grasp his combat vest and pull until he was looking directly into her eyes. "They died trying to find out what is going on and these people have the answers. I'm tired of my people dying on these remote planets while we ignore the fact that the Association is the key. They've been profiting off my people's suffering long enough. It's their turn to pay. Today we're gonna find out the truth."

Mori's words hit Stone like a brick. The pure, simple truth of her words echoed in his thoughts. Damn the implications; today would be pure, uncomplicated ... satisfying.

"I'm with you," he replied, to which he saw Mori give him a determined nod of acknowledgment.

"It's gonna be almost impossible to get through the security to the administration polis," interjected Orion, pulling out a digital pad and activating a map of Port Royal. "We can make it through the market polis without too much trouble as long as we pay the fees for weapons. But once we get to the boundary of the admin polis ..."

"Then what?" asked Katalya.

"We fight our way in," answered Thay.

"We need to find another way in," replied Orion. "It's too well defended, even for Ka-itsenko. We don't have the numbers."

"We're — I'm — getting in there," declared Mori. "Somehow."

"Can we get around the defenses?" asked Magnus.

"The admin polis is a fortress, positioned at the center of the other poli," said Orion. "Before we could get through the defenses they would be all over us."

"If we can punch through and make a rush for the estates —"

"The majority of their security forces are at the boundary to the admin polis and we can't fly into the area. It's all artificial atmosphere and encased. And moving on the ground will take too long to ..." Orion paused, biting her lower lip and lowering her head in thought.

"What is it?" asked Stone. "You've got an idea."

After another few seconds, Orion raised her head and spoke. "We can't go through the polis and we can't go over it. Maybe we can go under it."

"Under it?" asked Magnus.

"The support systems for the admin polis run under the city, so they don't 'ugly up' the scenery," replied Orion. "I'm sure it'll still be guarded, but not nearly as heavily."

"How do we get in?" asked Mori impatiently.

"Access to the main gates would require bribing or threatening a guard or an official, which we don't have time or the money for. The plumbing, however ..." Orion smiled. "Well, we just need to find the right overextended or horny technician. And I'm sure Hanagus will be able to point one out to us."

"Fine," declared Mori. "Contact Hanagus and make the arrangements. Tell him we'll be there an hour after we land and he had better have some names."

Stone looked around the room. The others, except for Thay, were clearly surprised by Mori's statement. "Don't you think that's coming at him a little hard? After all he and Bianca helped —"

Mori responded to his question with a dismissive "hmm" and turned toward Stone.

He stared at her as her brow tightened in annoyance at his comment. "He did it for the money," she added. She then looked directly into his eyes. "And I know what Bianca wanted."

Stone didn't — couldn't — respond.

After a long, dissatisfied look, Mori continued. "I'll be in the armory until we dock," she said as she stepped past Stone and walked away, her shoulder slightly bumping his arm as she passed.

Thay smiled after Mori exited. "She's pissed. I'd better pack up more ammo for this one."

"Is that all you can say?" asked Stone. "She's not herself. She's making rash decisions."

"She is acting like herself," replied Katalya. "You just haven't known her long enough."

Katalya's words both stung and frightened Stone.

"It's her right to go after the Association," added Thay. "And anyone between her and the Association. Maybe she's got a little Iroqua in her."

"This is crazy," Stone declared. Shaking his head, he exhaled loudly and turned to follow Mori.

In a few seconds, he had caught up to her. "Ino'ka," he called out, grasping her arm.

Mori quickly spun around. He could see the anger in her eyes. "What is it? We — I don't have time —"

"Listen to me," he demanded, grabbing her other arm.

"Let go of me," she demanded.

"Ino'ka, just hear me out," Stone spoke in Akota, hoping it would help to clear her senses. "I know Ohcumgache was a friend —"

Stone felt Mori grasp his right hand and force her left arm free. "He was family," she grumbled. "When my parents ... when I was left alone, there were no elder males in my family — they had all died fighting your people —" She spoke slowly as she stared into his eyes. "So his aunt took me in and raised

185

me as her own until I was accepted to the academy. He … he was more than a cousin, more like a brother … but I wouldn't expect you to understand."

Stone's anger grew from someplace deep inside. "How dare you!" he snapped. "Don't you think I have felt loss, seen friends die on the battlefield? I turned against my entire planet and you try to tell me I don't understand."

"Family is just more than a name and a lineage to us," she replied.

"Do you think I don't know that," he retorted. "I thought we were together in this." He eased his grip on her other arm and placed his free hand on her cheek. "You've changed my life and even though I feel like I've been swept up in a tornado, I know I'm doing the right thing. I just need your help to understand why you are being this way." As he looked into her eyes, he saw her facial muscles relax and the normal Mori return.

"We are in this together, Ty," she replied, placing her hand on his chest.

He could see a tear forming in the corner of her left eye and her cheeks grow flush.

"There's just so much," she whispered. "The team. Sandwick. And I still can't forget that, that place the Humani sent me. I haven't been able to talk with the *wichasa wakhan* since we left, and the thoughts are starting to visit me at night again. The guards and the pri —"

Stone pulled Mori in close to him. He could feel her tremble as he held her.

"And then Henry," she huffed as she let her emotions flow. "I need to be strong, a leader, not just

for my team but for our people. It's expected of a ..."
She paused.

Stone could sense her hesitate.

"... of a Ka-itsenko," she continued.

Stone could tell she was holding back, but now wasn't the time to pry further. He gently stepped back so that he could look into her eyes. He understood the weight of command but could only try to understand the hell that was her captivity on Capro.

"You've got nothing to be ashamed of," he said softly. "You're one of the bravest warriors I have ever seen and you did everything you could've to save Henry."

"But it wasn't enough," she said, looking toward the deck.

"All we can do is try." Stone's thoughts went to him rushing toward Martin and Jackson. He pulled her in close and held her tight. "Sometimes we just can't get there in time."

Chapter 13

"Just follow me, honey, and we'll work out the details upstairs," smiled Bianca.

The middle-aged and rotund Technician 2nd Class Yancy was having the best day of his life. His life usually consisted of pawning his furniture to pay a loan shark and working twelve to sixteen hours a day on the administrative polis's environmental conditioning systems to buy it back at a markup. But Yancy couldn't remember such a banner day. He normally left Hanagus's bar filling out IOUs or by signing an authorization for the "establishment" to withdraw from his earnings, but today was different — wonderfully different. In just a few hours, he had won over three thousand credits and even drawn the attention of the house entertainment boss, the beautiful Bianca.

"Sounds ... good ... to ... me," huffed the out-of-shape Yancy as he eagerly but slowly followed Bianca up the two levels of stairs to the relaxation rooms.

Noticing the man was lagging behind, she stopped and turned to smile. "No rush, honey. You'll need to save your energy for what's coming."

Energized by her comment, Yancy picked up his pace, at least for a few steps until his poor conditioning overcame his rush of lustful energy. Finally reaching the relaxation level, Yancy took in a deep breath. His head was spinning from a combination of the excitement of actually winning a game of triples, the thought of seeing Bianca naked, and the lack of oxygen in his lungs.

Bianca paused, allowing Yancy to catch his breath again. "Let's step inside and get down to business," she said with a smile as she unlocked and opened the door to room number eleven.

As he stepped into the door, Yancy's excitement and anticipation were instantly replaced with surprise and confusion. Inside the room stood a group of heavily armed people. He turned to run but was met at the exit by a tall wiry Terillian warrior with a painted face and a small tuft of hair running over the middle of his otherwise bald head.

***

Stone could see the fear on the chubby technician's sweat-coated face as he turned away from the exit, which was blocked by Thay.

"Here ya go," said Bianca, reaching behind Thay and pulling the door closed.

"So, this is our guy?" asked Mori, clearly unimpressed with the sight in front of her.

"He's what you asked for," replied Bianca. She gave a quick glance to the terrified technician. "Exactly what you asked for."

"You can take the money," offered the trembling Yancy. "I knew this was too good to be true," he mumbled under his breath. "Stupid."

Stone stepped toward the man. As he did, Yancy fell backward against the door and onto the floor.

"Please don't hurt me," he pleaded.

"Get up," demanded Thay as he pulled the man back to his feet.

"We're not going to hurt you," said Stone. "Now come over here." He pointed toward a small chair.

"We're probably not going to hurt you," amended Thay with a smile.

Yancy glanced quickly toward Thay and then shuffled to the chair.

"What do you want with me?" he asked. "I don't understand —"

"Just shut up and listen," interrupted Mori as she sat in the chair next to Yancy.

"I always end up in these fucked-up situations," Yancy grumbled.

"Maybe you should think about why that happens," commented Orion with a chuckle. "And maybe get directions to a gym."

"It's okay, honey," interjected Bianca. "Just listen to them. It's not as bad as you think."

Stone noticed Yancy glance toward Katalya and Magnus. As he did, Magnus responded with a growl that showed his unusually sharp canines. Yancy quickly shifted his gaze downward, staring at the desk separating himself and Mori.

"It's usually worse than I think," sulked Yancy.

Stone looked toward Bianca in amazement at the man's sad state.

"Like I said." Bianca smiled. "Ex-act-ly what you asked for."

"Enough delays," declared Mori, leaning in toward Yancy. "I am Major Mori Skye of the Scout Rangers."

"I am —"

"I don't care who you are," Mori interrupted. "Just be quiet while I tell you what you're going to do."

Stone saw the fire in her brilliant green eyes radiate against the multicolored war paint on her face. Her gaze clearly unsettled the already frightened Yancy.

"You clearly have a weakness for gambling and women," she continued. "A weakness, among other obvious excesses, you can't afford."

"But I —"

"I think I told you to shut up," interrupted Mori as she pulled her pistol from its holster and placed it on the desk.

Yancy slouched back into the chair in an act of acceptance and submittal.

"Like I said, you're basically a fat, drunk deviant. But that's okay and today it might actually get you everything you've ever wanted."

Stone saw Yancy's posture straighten at the promise of some reward.

"What do I have to do?" he asked.

"Just give me your access card, passcode, tell us what you know about the security of the maintenance underground, and confirm the schematics I'm going to show you."

"I can't," professed Yancy. "If they find out — and they will — they'll kill me."

"Or maybe you can die right here," offered Thay as he stepped toward Yancy, his tomahawk drawn.

Yancy recoiled and twisted his body away from Thay's direction.

"Wait," ordered Mori. "That won't be necessary … if you cooperate."

"But — "

"Again, shut up," replied Mori, cutting off Yancy's reply. "This is where being a compulsive loser actually pays off for you. We know you can't stay here after you give us the information. So …" Mori looked toward Bianca.

"Keep the credits you have, plus another fifteen thousand," said Bianca. "And Hanagus will make sure you get off Port Royal tonight."

Stone saw Yancy's eyes open wide when he heard the amount Bianca had offered. "Where will I go?" he asked.

"Lima 6," answered Bianca. "There's quite a few little smuggling towns there."

"Just your kind of cheap, low-rent hole-in-the-wall whorehouse and gambling pit infested place," added Orion sardonically.

"And with your new financial status," continued Mori, "you should be able to make a nice little life — well, what you call a life — for yourself."

Stone could see Yancy weigh his options: death at the hands of the Association, death by tomahawk, or the chance to be king-swine in his own little pigpen. It didn't take long for him to decide.

"I'll do it," he said. "But you have to assure me I'll get off Port Royal tonight."

"You'll be on an undeclared flight leaving in four hours," answered Bianca. "Until then, you and I will spend some quality time together in this room."

A contemplative and anxious smile came to Yancy's face.

"Okay then." He smiled. "Let me see the schematics."

Over the next few minutes Yancy verified the accuracy of the maintenance area plans, divulged details about the security protocols, and generally spilled his guts on everything he knew about the administrative polis.

"That's all I know," declared a now-relaxed Yancy.

"I think we've got enough," said Stone. "This might actually work."

"Well, let's hope it does," replied Orion as she rose from her seated position on the bed in the center of the room. "I'll have *Hydra* ready for our inevitable quick getaway."

Mori stood, walked toward the door, and turned to face the group.

"We'll split into two groups and meet at maintenance access 1-863 at 2330. We'll enter the maintenance area and make our way to section 1588, we'll grab Councilmen Ferrous, get the info, and be back at *Hydra* by 0150."

"And we'll get all cozy in here." Bianca smiled as she walked over to Yancy.

"Yes," said Yancy under his breath.

As Stone watched, Bianca straddled Yancy's chair and ran her hand down the length of his arm. He could see the sweat start to bead once again on

Yancy's bulbous face. Suddenly he heard a metallic clink and Yancy's smile turned to a scowl.

"What did you do?" Yancy asked loudly, pulling on his hand, now handcuffed to the chair.

"You silly boy," said Bianca, laughing as she backed away from Yancy. "I'm staying here to keep you quiet, not to keep you happy."

"You bitch!" he yelled. "You sa —"

Before he could finish his word, Mori's knife was pressed against his throat. Yancy froze, afraid to move.

"You're gonna stay right here and keep your damn mouth shut," she whispered in his ear just loud enough for Stone and Bianca to hear. "And if anything you've told us is a lie, I am going to come back here and skin you alive myself."

Mori slid the razor-sharp blade over Yancy's neck, causing it to bleed ever so slightly. She then stepped in front of him and leaned in close. "Betray us and this will be the last face you'll ever see. Do you understand?"

Yancy nodded his head in nervous acknowledgment.

"Good," said Mori as she stepped back from the once again terrified Yancy and looked toward the group. "Let's get going."

***

"This way, Paladin Martin." The teenage girl smiled, her smooth blonde hair falling to her neckline with two sharp tufts running the length of her jawline.

As she entered the room, Martin did a quick tactical assessment. There were a dozen or so dressed exactly like the little lamb that had led her into the room; they wouldn't be a problem. What did draw her attention was the five others positioned strategically in the dimly lit room. They wore hooded cloaks, but she could make out protrusions that clearly indicated weapons of some kind. And centerline toward the opposite wall sat a man in a lone chair. As Martin walked toward him, he rose from his seat to meet her.

"Welcome visitor," he replied in a soothing voice.

Martin looked over the sandy-haired, bearded man with almost luminescent blue eyes. After a moment she spoke. "You must be the one they call the Saint," she said.

The man paused. His lips tightened and his brow furrowed. Martin could tell he wasn't used to being addressed directly. As he looked upon her, she saw several of the people in the room gravitate toward the man. In a few seconds, six or seven of the white-shirted ones stood around the man. He tilted his head slightly in puzzlement.

"I said," repeated Martin more loudly, "you must be the one they call the Saint."

More people in the room moved toward the man.

"Hmm," the man finally responded. "I am indeed the Saint. And as for you ..." The Saint turned toward the girl who had escorted Martin into the room. "My child, what did she call herself?"

The girl turned her head toward the floor. "She is Paladin Martin of Humani, Saint."

"And why have you come to us?" he asked.

"I've come to speak with Envoy Sterling and her companion and escort them back to Alpha Humana by order of the ProConsul Astra Varus."

"Oh yes, I do remember them." He smiled. "You have to give Astra Varus my regards, but it seems after a few days surrounded by the speakers of the Word, they have decided to join us."

"Join you?" quipped Martin. "I think I'd like to see that for myself. And by like," added Martin, "I mean I will need to see it."

"Hmm," he replied as he turned back toward Martin. "So very demanding. And what is this title Paladin? I have never heard of such a thing. I can tell you are Humani by your bluster, but you don't look like a typical diplomat or envoy."

"Because I'm not," replied Martin.

"Well then, what exactly does that make you, Paladin Martin?" The Saint's smile poorly hid his growing frustration. Out of the corner of her eye, she noticed the armed men spreading themselves out in all directions around her. As the men positioned themselves, Martin slowly, methodically raised her hands behind her head and tied her hair into a tight ponytail.

"You will answer me?" repeated the Saint, his voice cracking slightly as his anger showed itself.

Martin smiled. "I'm guessing that even on this rock you've heard of the Humani myth of the raven that heralds the coming of a malevolence?"

Martin saw a smile come to the man's face as he gave out a short, muffled laugh. "So you are Astra Varus's little raven, here to be the harbinger of some wickedness that will befall us?"

"No," she replied coldly. "I'm the thing the raven warns you about."

Martin could see the anger boiling over in the Saint.

"Your arrogance knows no limits, Humani," he growled. "You, a nonbeliever, come into my chambers and in the presence of my followers disrespect the embodiment of the Word."

"I don't know what this Word is, but this is your last warning," said Martin, placing her hand on her sword.

"Blasphemy!" he shouted. "My priests will tear you apart so that this room may be cleansed of your wickedness."

"If that's the case," replied Martin as the metallic reverberation of her sword being unsheathed echoed through the room, "you might want to get some more help for these five."

"Take her!" he shouted, and the five men rushed toward Martin.

Martin braced herself and blocked out the dull pain in her leg and elbow still lingering from her encounter with Mori. She parried the thrust from the first priest and in a lightning-quick counter, slashed his chest open. Shifting her body to her left, Martin spun away from the slashing sword of another attacker. As she tilted away from the weapon, she heard the singing sound of the metal as it passed within millimeters of her face. Countering, Martin drove her sword upward and heard a groan from the second attacker as her sword entered his right side and tore through his abdomen. With her right hand still holding the blade skewering the priest, Martin slid behind the impaled warrior and pulled a sidearm from the man's belt.

She gripped the pistol and looped her arm over the left shoulder of the injured priest. As she did, she saw the flash and felt the impact of a third attacker's bullets on the man she was using as a shield. She squeezed the trigger twice and the third attacker fell with a bullet in his chest and one in his throat. Martin then shifted her aim toward the Saint and pulled the trigger. To her frustration, one of the white-shirted followers dove in front of him and absorbed the impact.

Martin sensed movement to her right and spun to face it with her human shield in tow. As she spun she came face to face with another priest. She saw the determination on his face and felt the warm pulse of his breath as he drove his sword forward. His sword was true and his thrust strong as it sank into her shield's body and out his back. She grimaced in pain as the blade pierced her stomach.

"Motherfu —" shouted Martin but her curse was drowned out by the blast of her pistol as she placed the muzzle against her attacker's forehead and pulled the trigger. Turning again, she fired toward the Saint but another follower willingly sacrificed herself for her leader.

"Stupid bastards," cursed Martin, sending a round from her pistol into her shield's left leg.

As the man fell to his knees, Martin jerked her sword from his body and in a powerful slash decapitated the man. Again, she turned toward the Saint and pulled the trigger but the metallic clicking told her the weapon was empty. Cursing again, she threw the weapon to the floor and lunged toward the crowd surrounding the Saint when the last priest crashed into her right side.

Martin let out a loud groan as the pain from her still-injured elbow shot through her body when it impacted the floor. Turning quickly, she looked up to see the priest swinging his pistol toward her head. Martin grabbed the attacker's left forearm and directed the pistol away from her head as he fired. The blast was deafening but didn't distract her. Kicking her legs into the air, she locked her legs around the priest's head and arched her back to tighten the chokehold. The man's face began to grow bright red and she felt him release his grip on the pistol. Not having time to choke her opponent, she quickly released the man's forearm and pulled her knife from her vest. With a loud roar she drove the blade deep into the forehead of her attacker. She then released her leg-lock on the dead priest, grabbed her sword, and scrambled to her feet.

In front of her was a sea of followers creating a wall between her and the Saint.

"Where are you, you bastard?" she yelled. "I told you five wasn't enough." She walked toward the wall of followers.

"Very impressive, nonbeliever," she heard from behind the barrier of human flesh. "But why would I worry about five, when there are five hundred, five thousand, five million."

Martin stopped a few meters from the crowd and raised a pistol toward the group.

"Get out of the way!" she ordered.

No one moved.

"Move or I will shoot you," she continued as she drew her own pistol.

"Threats will do you no good, Paladin. The believer is unmoved by the nonbeliever. Violence cannot overcome the peaceful lambs of the Word."

"The Word is Peace," shouted the group of followers.

"What the fu …" mumbled Martin. "Fine," she answered more loudly, and she shot one of the followers in the leg.

The girl fell to the floor and after a second was helped back to her feet by surrounding followers. Back on her feet, the young girl looked directly into Martin's eyes. Martin could see the complete lack of personal concern. Instead her face looked calm, determined, even happy. The girl then spoke:

The Believers do not fear death

Death brings the ultimate order

Death makes each Believer a Priest-Bishop

Death allows the Believer to rule over the nonbeliever

The Word transcends Death; The Saint is the Word.

"Fine by me," replied Martin as she raised her weapon to fire again. Then she paused. In her head echoed the Elite Guard Oath she had memorized, proclaimed, and lived by since she was a cadet:

I will stand strong in the face of danger, for my comrades will do the same

I will be unafraid of death for death comes but once and cowardice is forever

I will go close against the enemy, for my will is stronger than his

I will show courage, for it is the one possession that cannot be taken

I will die with pride, for I am fighting for my lineage and my people

I will face death with joy, for I will become immortal — my shining glory never forgotten

Martin lowered her pistol. Crazy or not, she knew every single one of those misguided followers would die for this bastard.

"Shit," cursed Martin as she struggled with how to deal with the zealots. Suddenly, the rush of footsteps at the front of the room caused Martin to spin around.

Martin turned to see another wave of followers flood into the room. As Martin braced herself, the swarm of followers slowly encircled her.

"You can answer peace with violence, nonbeliever," came the booming voice from behind the followers. "Or you can surrender to the Word."

"Fuck your Word!" shouted Martin, throwing her weapons to the ground and preparing to defend herself with her hands.

"Take her but don't kill her!"

In a matter of seconds, Martin disappeared in a sea of white and gray.

***

The sound of Stone's feet landing in the puddle at the bottom of the security ladder echoed through the dimly lit passage. So far, the team hadn't run into any problems. The technician's codes had worked and they had avoided the limited security teams that patrolled the maintenance underground of Port Royal's administration polis.

On the ground, Stone quickly brought his rifle to the ready and moved toward the corner of the vestibule for the ladder way. The underground was warm and humid, and Stone could feel his shirt stick to his body. No stranger to living with discomfort, he pushed the thought of his clingy, damp clothes from his mind. He crouched by the concrete wall and slowly peeked his head around the corner. Scanning the area, he saw a long, narrow passageway poorly illuminated every ten meters or so by overhead lighting. The dim light seemed to flicker as puffs of steam from leaky piping clouded the overhead of the space. Still peering down the passageway, Stone heard the others approach behind him and soon felt Mori's hand on his shoulder.

"Clear?" she asked.

He turned back toward the others. "Looks good," he said.

"Great," whispered Thay. "Hopefully we'll be out of this sauna soon."

Stone took a quick second to savor the fact the environment was getting to the others as well.

"Our fat little friend's info has been good so far," said Katalya. "According to him, about halfway up this passage is the ladder that leads up to the quarters of the council member."

"Or a security office if he's setting us up," replied Mori.

"I think you got your point across that double-cross us was a bad idea," said Stone with a quick smile.

"Let's hope so," she replied as she moved in front of Stone. "Hand signals from here on."

Stone acknowledged and the group started down the passage in intervals. In just a few minutes they reached a ladder leading out of the maintenance underground and hopefully to their target. The group moved up the ladder quickly despite the humidity-drenched rungs. Mori and Magnus had already moved onto the mezzanine of the last level of the maintenance area as Stone neared the top. Looking upward, he saw Mori signal for him to wait. His body tensed when he saw her add the signal for an approaching guard. As Mori disappeared from his view to take cover, Stone wrapped his left arm through the slippery ladder rung and drew his pistol with his right.

Stone pointed his weapon toward the opening at the top of the ladder. He soon heard the echoing ring of boots on the metallic floor above him. A quick look downward and he saw Katalya, her legs pressed against the ladder and her back resting on the opposite side of the access wall. Her rifle was directed toward the opening as well. A little lower than Katalya was Thay. Even in the poor lighting, Stone could see the frustration on Thay's face — frustration in knowing that he would be out of any fight that happened.

The steps grew louder. Stone locked his gaze on the opening. If they had to open fire, they ran the chance of alerting other security forces and their plan falling apart.

Louder still. Stone heard Katalya shift the safety on her rifle to the firing position.

It sounded as though the footsteps were right on top of them. Then a muffled voice.

"Let's head back." Stone could hear someone grumble.

"No" came a reply. "We're supposed to clear all of the ladders on this level too."

"Are you serious?" huffed the first man. "The only thing down here are rats and those creepy maintenance techs."

"I know," replied the other. "But we got stuck on this duty for pissing off Sergeant Reiser. What's he gonna do if he finds out we're half-assing this watch?"

"If you want to climb down that damn ladder, knock yourself out. But who's gonna tell Reiser if we don't? I'm not. You're not. So, I'm pretty sure we're safe unless they figure out how to make rats talk."

"Screw you, Flores. Listening to you got me put on this shitty watch in the first place."

"Fine then," answered the exasperated guard. "We'll go all the way down."

"Shit," whispered Stone through his teeth.

The angry guard continued as Stone heard his footstep growing closer.

"Yes, Sergeant Reiser," teased the guard. "Yes. Yes. I'll walk through the underground. I'll clean the barracks. How 'bout I just get on my knees and —"

"Shut up, asshole," interrupted the other guard.

Stone saw the guard's helmet through the exit hole. He took aim.

"Whatever man," answered the antagonizer.

Stone saw the guard's head turn away from the opening to continue to taunt the other guard.

"You're right, Hayes. We're probably under attack right now," he taunted. "Better get my weapon ready. Cover me!" he mocked loudly.

Stone shifted his finger onto the trigger.

"Watch out, whoever's down there! Security Officers Hayes and Flores are here to fuck you up!"

Stone saw the guard turn and look down the opening. Their eyes locked on each other. Stone could see the shock on the guard's face. Just as he started to pull the trigger he saw a flash leap over the opening and the guard disappeared from his view. Stone started to pull himself up the ladder when he heard a loud groan and looked up just as one of the guards tumbled into the opening. He tightened his grip and tensed his body as the guard tumbled down the ladder way. He felt the impact of the man's torso crash into his shoulder but maintained his grip. Then he heard Katalya grunt loudly. Looking downward, he saw Katalya hanging upside by her legs and Thay shifting to his left to allow the guard to pass. At the bottom of the ladder lay the distorted body of the guard.

"You okay?" asked Stone to Katalya.

"That was close," she replied, pulling her torso upward with a grunt and grabbing the ladder. "Lost my damn rifle though."

"It looks like there's at least one available up top," said Thay.

"*Everyone okay?*" came Mori's voice as she looked into the opening.

"All good," replied Stone. "We're coming up now."

Stone reached the top of the opening to the ladder and took a quick scan of the area. A few meters from the opening lay the body of the other guard. From the looks of his injuries, Magnus had used his teeth to dispatch the guard.

"If that's the best this Association has, we shouldn't have any problems," said Magnus. The blood splattered around his face and trickling down his chin confirmed Stone's assumption.

"Nice work," said Thay as he pulled himself out of the opening. Stone could sense a hint of jealousy in his voice. "The next one's mine."

"Enough patting each other's back," said Mori. "Thay, get that body out of sight."

"No problem," replied Thay, walking toward the guard's body.

Grasping the dead guard by the arm, he dragged the body to the edge of the opening. In an exaggerated movement, as if he was tossing a bag of rubbish into a bin, he hefted the guard's body off the ground enough to direct him over the opening to the ladder. Then he let him go.

"What?" asked Thay as he turned back toward the group. "He's out of sight."

"Fine," answered Mori, her frustration showing. "The entrance to the housing units is through that access on the mezzanine two levels up," she said looking at the hand-drawn map she had been using to navigate the underground.

"And from there?" asked Magnus.

"We cross the street and enter building TI-8. Our target should be in there."

"Let's go get him," said Katalya as she picked up one of the dead guard's rifles.

Chapter 14

Martin slowly opened her eyes. She felt the cold metal of the floor against her cheek. Then the pain in her head began to pulsate with each heartbeat. "Shit," she grumbled.

She took in a deep breath and started to push herself off the floor. She immediately let out a groan and rolled onto her back. The elbow, damaged in her fight with Mori and not yet healed, had obviously been reinjured in her fight with the Saint's followers. Staring up toward the top of what looked to be a holding cell, Martin let a long breath through her teeth and took a moment to assess her injuries. Other than the sharp pain in her elbow and throbbing in her head, there was a dull ache throughout her body, remind ing her of the blows of dozens of followers as she tried to defend herself. After collecting herself and preparing for the pain of sitting upright, Martin pushed out a heavy breath and forced herself into a seated position with a grunt. She then dragged herself to the back wall of her cell and rested her torso against the hard surface to get her bearings.

The cell was small, cold, and damp with a thin stack of hay covered by a cloth blanket in the corner. She could tell her prison was antiquated with metal bars encasing both sides and the front of her cell. Martin could also see other cells across a small hallway.

She was intently studying the condition and layout of her confinement, including a person huddled in the corner of the cell opposite her, when she heard footsteps approaching. She slowly rose to her feet and made her way to the cell door as the footsteps grew closer.

In a few seconds, two men stopped in front of her. They had the same hairstyle as the other followers but wore fatigues and carried stun sticks and pistols.

"This is the one that attacked the Saint," said the guard to Martin's right.

"She killed all of those priests?" pondered the other.

"Despite her skill, the will of the believers was strong and the Word overcame in the end, brother."

"As it always does." Martin saw a smile come to the face of the guard. "You see, nonbeliever, the Word is undeniable."

"It's inevitable," said the other, smiling as well. "And the sooner you accept the Word and the power of the Saint, the sooner you will know peace and freedom."

Martin gripped the bar tightly with the hand from her good arm. "Tell me more of this Word," she said, returning the smile.

"The Word —"

The guard had moved too close to Martin's cell, allowing her to quickly grab his shirt and slam his face into the bars with all of the strength she had left. The sound of flesh and bone crashing into the bars echoed through room. Martin pivoted as the second guard shoved his stun stick into the cell, passing only centimeters from her body. She grasped the man's extended arm and, using her entire body for momentum, yanked it backward against the cell bars until she heard the bone snap and the guard let out a shriek of pain. She slid the man to the floor and was reaching for the keys on his belt when a bolt of electricity sent her tumbling backward.

Her body tingled and her muscles ached with spasms as she looked up toward the cell door. Above her stood a tattooed man in a cloak holding a stun stick. Before she could fully focus on the man, however, she heard the undeniable sound of a pistol being pulled from its holster. Turning to her right, she saw the first guard, his nose broken and bleeding profusely, point his pistol toward her. Martin stared into the man's eyes, daring him to fire.

"Put that away!" shouted the cloaked man.

The guard instantly lowered his weapon. "Yes, Priest-Bishop," he said, "but shouldn't —"

"Is it our duty to question the Word, follower?"

Martin saw the guard turn his head toward the floor.

"It is not, Priest-Bishop," acquiesced the guard. "The believers turn themselves over to the Word."

"Thank you, brother," replied the priest with a smile and a nod. "You and follower Faras should report to the healer and inform the sergeant of the guard that you'll need replacements."

"Yes, Priest-Bishop," answered the other guard as he pulled himself erect with his unbroken arm.

"Good. Now let me have a word with the nonbeliever."

The guards, bruised, broken, and bleeding, gathered themselves and started toward the opposite end of the hallway.

"Now," said the priest as he looked toward Martin. "Let us talk a bit."

She looked over the man. He wore the same style cloak as the other priests she had seen except the fabric was a smooth silk and the color was black with red accents. She could also see the same markings as the others, including the star-shaped tattoo on his forehead. His olive colored complexion accented his amber, almost yellow, eyes and a thick, well-trimmed beard outlined a strong, square jawline.

"Come a little closer, fanatic, and I'll give you one hell of a conversation," she taunted. She could see that the man wanted to take her challenge, but he also had the self-control to resist that urge.

"Maybe someday, nonbeliever. Someday."

"Then what do you want with me?" asked Martin. She felt the effects of the stun stick subsiding and was working through how she could get at the priest. He wouldn't be as easy as the guards — she knew that — but if she could trick him into getting closer ...

"Just to talk. You're interesting to me, nonbeliever."

"And why's that?" she asked as she stood once again, purposely feigning to be even more weakened from the shock than she was.

"Why are you here?" he asked.

"I'm Paladin Martin and represent the ProConsul Astra Varus and the Humani Senate — that's all you need to know."

"Paladin?" mused the man. "That's an antiquated title, isn't it, especially for a member of the Elite Guard?"

"How did you —" Martin paused to inspect her inquisitor more closely. At first glance he looked very similar to the other priests she had faced in the Saint's chamber. But he was different in subtle but significant ways. While the other priests had one single, thick braid of hair on an otherwise bald head and were clean shaven, this man was bearded and was completely bald, with no braid. Martin noticed the man carried a physical confidence that went beyond religious fanaticism.

"I serve at the will of the ProConsul," replied Martin, almost choking on her own words. "Who are you?"

"I'm Priest-Bishop Dan-Lee. And you can quit playing the wounded lamb," he said.

Who is this asshole?' wondered Martin as she stood more erect and walked closer to the cell door. "That doesn't tell me a lot, jerk off," she answered.

"Definitely Elite Guard," replied Dan-Lee as he stepped closer to the opposite side of the bars. "You're arrogant, angry, and probably a handful in a fight or the sack." He smiled.

"What?" replied a Martin, trying to hide her surprise at his lascivious comment. "That's no talk for priest, even a crazy one."

"That's Priest-Bishop, Paladin Martin," he replied without a hint of anger at Martin's derisive statement regarding the Saint. "And you're not going to get a rise out me — at least that kind of a rise."

"Really," replied Martin, thinking she had found her opportunity. "What do you have in mind?" She playfully pressed up against the bars and put her hands through the bars at waist level.

"Oh, you have no idea." The man smiled as he moved closer.

Martin grasped the man's belt with one hand and smiled. He returned the smile.

She suddenly grabbed for his left arm to pull it through to her side in an attempt to gain the advantage. She gripped his sleeve and leveraged her body to pull Dan-Lee into the bars. Feeling the man resist, she attempted to strike at the man's vulnerable privates with her other hand. Before she could make contact, she felt her hand being twisted painfully and she started to lose her balance and fall toward the bars. As she fell, she shifted her body until her back was facing the bars just as she impacted the hard metal. The impact against the back of her head rang through her body and her injured elbow sent out radiant spasms of pain, but she still had control of the man's left arm.

Martin reached across her body with her injured arm in an attempt to gain control of her opponent's hand. She grasped the top of his hand with hers and tried with all of her strength to pull his arm closer to her, but she was too weak from her injuries. And he was very strong. As she struggled with Dan-Lee's hand, her scalp tightened as her opponent grabbed her hair. A bolt of pain rang through her head as she was again slammed into the bars.

"Son of a bitch!" grumbled Martin as she attempted to kick backward through the bars with her right leg toward her opponent's knee.

Her kick found its mark and she heard the man grunt loudly but his grip on her hair did not slack.

"That's enough of that," he said, and Martin felt the man's foot driving into the back of her calf and forcing it, and her, toward the floor. As her knees hit the ground, Martin lost the battle for control of the man's left hand; he pulled her arm through the bars with his other hand still gripping her hair.

Infuriated, Martin let out a primordial groan. Even injured, few warriors would be able to handle her as this man had. She let out a series of frustrated breaths as she remained pinned with her leg held down by her opponent's foot and her hair and injured arm under his control. "You had better kill me now, asshole," she warned. "Because if I get free I will —"

"Relax," interrupted the man.

Martin felt the pressure on leg and arms disappear and her body fall forward against the force of the man's boot on her back.

"We were just ... talking."

"Kiss my ass," she replied as she pulled herself to her feet again.

"Don't worry, Pal-a-din Martin," he continued. "I'm sure the stun-sticks and that injury to your elbow took a little out of you. No shame."

No shame — screw this guy,' thought Martin. No one had ever made an excuse for her and this dick wasn't going to be the first guy.

"Come in here and finish this," she taunted. The pain disappeared; it was replaced with a deep-burning anger that pulsated through her body. "Come on!" she shouted.

"Not today, Paladin," he replied calmly.

Martin simmered, her fists clenched tightly and her gaze locked on the man. "What was all of this about?" she asked.

"Just a chat, Martin," he answered. "And I enjoyed the conversation immensely."

"What?" she asked with a mixture of confusion and fury raging through her.

"We'll talk more, later. For now, let's get that elbow healed."

Martin saw the man toss a medi-pack into her cell.

"Keep that under your bed and don't do anything else to injure your arm further ... if you can manage that."

Martin stared blankly at the man.

"Just keep your mouth shut and regain your strength. We'll talk again soon enough."

Confusion was quickly overtaking anger in Martin's emotional struggle.

"But —"

"Soon, Martin, soon we'll 'chat' again," said the man as he turned and began to stroll toward the exit.

Martin quickly pressed her body against the bars to watch the man leave. "Asshole!" she shouted.

As the far door shut, Martin turned back toward her cell. "What was that shit?" she said out loud to herself as she walked to her bed and knelt next to the bedding.

"Damn," she said as she opened the medi-pack. It contained everything she needed to get back into fighting shape — maybe not one hundred percent, but she didn't need one hundred percent. After injecting a pain inhibitor, neuro-replenisher, and anti-inflammatory cocktail, she rested back on her knees.

The painkiller was just starting to kick in when she heard rustling from the cell next to her. Martin looked over and saw a tall, attractive woman in a tattered dress that looked like the style worn by the dandies and rich bitches on Port Royal. Her hair looked freshly cut into the follower-style, but she could tell this wasn't one of the fanatics.

"You should not fight them," said the woman. "Why did you fight them?"

Martin could tell by the woman's posture and her language she was probably the envoy she was sent to retrieve.

"Because fuck those guys," she replied as she slowly rose to her feet. "Who are you?"

"I am a belie —" The woman paused and shook her head as if to clear a haziness. "I am Envoy Rebecca Sterling, an agent for the Association and the Humani ProConsul, the illustrious Astra —"

"Yeah. Yeah. I know who she is," interrupted Martin. "I was sent to retrieve you and the Praetorian, but I'm assuming he's dead."

The woman lowered her head. Martin saw a wave of chills pass over her body. "It was horrible."

"Dying usually is." quipped Martin. "Unless you do it right," she added with a smile.

"What are we going to do now?" asked Rebecca.

Martin could see the fear and hopelessness in Rebecca's face. She looked like a lost, beaten, and disheveled puppy in a pound. "We're gonna get out of here," replied Martin. "I'm not sure what that asshole that just left has in mind, but I'm pretty sure it doesn't involve me staying in this cell. And if that takes too long … let's just say this Saint jackass has made an enemy of Astra Varus, and that generally doesn't end well for people."

"Does she know?" asked Rebecca.

"She sent me here to get you, so she must think something's wrong. And if I don't report, she's gonna opt for a less subtle option … like a Humani battle group."

"She sent for me?" asked Rebecca intently. "What did she say? Did she have a message?"

"She said to get you," replied Martin matter-of-factly. Martin suddenly paused and tilted her head slightly to contemplate the nature of Rebecca's question. She felt the rage from a few minutes ago return. "No," she huffed as she rolled her eyes and looked up toward the ceiling.

"What?" asked Rebecca.

"You've got to be shitting me," continued Martin as she walked in close to Rebecca. "Tell me the truth … Did her royal bitch-ness send me into this trap to retrieve a piece of ass?"

"No!" replied Rebecca, clearly embarrassed. "I mean —"

"That bitch!" replied Martin as she turned away from Rebecca and made a long walk around her cell to release a flurry of curses focused on First Families in general and Astra Varus specifically.

"But there is the mission as well," said Rebecca in an attempt to calm Martin's tirade.

"Mission? Yes. What is the mission?" asked Martin and she returned the bars next to Rebecca.

"But it is highly classified. I do not —"

Martin reached through the bars and grabbed Rebecca's torn dress, pulling her in close.

"Listen, you little Association skank. If you ever want out of this cell, you're gonna tell me what this is all about."

The wide-eyed look from Rebecca told Martin she had gotten her point across.

"Let's hear it," said Martin.

Rebecca looked back toward the floor and inhaled heavily. She then glanced toward the empty hallway before returning her gaze and speaking. "It's her plan to defeat the Terillian Confederation and free herself from the grips of the Xen Emperor."

"The grip of the Xen Emperor?" asked Martin. "If it wasn't for the Xen, our world would've ..."

"You don't know ..." Rebecca paused. "Of course."

"Know what?"

"It's forbidden," replied Rebecca as shook her head. "I knew I shouldn't have —"

Martin grabbed Rebecca again and pulled her against the bars.

"Listen, you little bitch, I'll leave you here to rot." She pulled a little more so that Rebecca could feel the pressure of the cold metal bars against her cheek. "I'm done screwing around with you. Tell me everything. Now!" she added as she released her grip on Rebecca.

Rebecca quickly stepped back from the bars. "Fine," she gasped. "It was the Xen centuries ago that destroyed your world. They created the culture you know of out of the ashes and controlled you through the First Families."

"Bullshit," replied Martin.

"It's true," answered Rebecca.

Martin felt ill. If there was any food in her stomach, she would have lost it. She took a step backward, shaking her head. "Liar!" she yelled. "It's not true. It can't be." *'Just another Association lie,'* she thought.

"As long as the First Families keep the Xen happy, then they are allowed to rule Alpha Humana. It's not too bad of a deal, really," mused Rebecca. "Instead of devastation at the hands of the Xen, the First Families get to live like kings. And all they have to do is play their part and keep the lower classes in line. It was a very good deal for them."

"There is no way —" Then it hit her like a lightning bolt. The room began to spin and her balance failed her. Without realizing it, she was on her knees. Her entire existence, her entire world … was it a lie? Every fiber of her being told her this woman could not be trusted. She was an Association agent, a master of subterfuge. She was lying. It had to be a lie. She wanted it to be a lie. She needed it to be a lie. But while her heart told her it was a lie, her brain began to ask questions. "And the First Terillian War?" mumbled Martin quietly from her knees, still trying to find the strength to take a breath.

"The Xen offered your First Families an ultimatum. Either offer their own world up for enslavement or attack the Akota of the Terillian Confederation and enslave their colonies."

"First Families," she mumbled. "And who are the Akota?"

"The Akota are one of many cultures that make up the Confederation. The majority of the Neutral Quadrant is made up of former Akota colonies, but the Confederation consists of several other similar civilizations."

Martin's head pounded and her stomach churned as logic and emotion struggled to make sense of what she was being told. *Why would she lie?* she suddenly thought to herself. *What does she have to gain by making this up?* She thought of First Family patriarchs. Could they do such a thing? Then she thought of Astra Varus. Yes. Yes, they could. "Bastards," she moaned.

"I'm afraid there's a lot you don't know about your history, Paladin Martin," she replied.

"Don't call me that!" shouted Martin. "No more damned titles. It's all a lie … it's all a fucking lie." Martin slowly pulled herself to her feet as Rebecca continued.

"The First Terillian War provided enough slaves for the Xen to keep them happy for several generations —"

"The war was about slaves for the Xen?" interrupted Martin. She felt the confusion and pain caused by learning the truth start to turn to anger and rage — first a simmer and then a hot burning flame. "And this war?" she demanded.

"The slaves on the Xen home worlds have been stricken by a virus that is rapidly depleting their numbers. With the Xen culture dependent on slavery, they again offered the same ultimatum, which the First Families jumped at."

Martin gripped the bars tightly until her fingers started to go white.

"So, we have been the aggressors. The Terillians were innocent."

"There's no such thing as innocent, Martin," replied Rebecca. "Just degrees of guilty. Everyone's hands are dirty."

The words sank into her pores. She had killed dozens, maybe hundreds of Terillians for simply defending their homes and families.

"Liars," grumbled Martin. "They told me I was a soldier when I'm just their hired killer."

"If ProConsul Varus's plan is successful, the Xen will pay as well."

Martin struggled to maintain control of her emotions and absorb the flood of truths Rebecca was releasing into her consciousness. Her history, her perception of the world, and even her identity were a swirling mass of disintegrating reality.

"Her plan?"

"The ProConsul has grown tired of being under control of the Xen. She and the Association have worked to perfect a virus to be embedded in a percentage of the slaves sent back to the Xen that will devastate the slave population, the Xen, and even their Doran allies. When they are weakened, the ProConsul will use her genetically modified troops to take control of the Xen worlds. In the end, she will defeat both the Xen and the Terillians and establish a Humani Empire that will last for eons."

Martin could see a spark of mindless admiration in Rebecca's eye as she explained Astra's plan to kill millions and conquer the known galaxy. "You're insane," replied Martin. "Varus is going to go to war with everyone?"

"She is going to bring order to the known worlds."

"She's going to ruin us all," shouted Martin. "Where are these additional troops?"

Martin saw Rebecca's expression flatten.

"You won't be able to stop her," stated Rebecca flatly.

Martin reached through the bars, grabbed Rebecca, and slammed her forehead into the bars. "Don't you worry about that," replied Martin as Rebecca reached for her forehead. "Just answer the questions I'm asking."

"But —"

"Ah-ah," warned Martin, gripping Rebecca's clothing tighter. "Where are they?"

Martin paused and flashed a smile at Rebecca. "Or I can just play bounce-the-bitch-off-the-bars for a while." Martin felt Rebecca start to struggle against her grip. "Easy there," said Martin as she introduced Rebecca's head to the bars again.

"Where?"

"Dolus, near Capro," Rebecca relented as she closed her eyes against the pain. "Now please let me go."

"The gas planet?" laughed Martin, maintaining her grip on Rebecca's dress for another trip to the bars.

"No!" blurted Rebecca. "It's true. The ProConsul gained the funds and the Association contracted the construction of a base and research facility in the ocean layer under the gas atmosphere. While the virus remains dormant until the carriers reach puberty, the growing army will be trained, and the fleet that will claim a new Humani Empire will be built and equipped."

"That's impossible," replied Martin. "That would cost —" Martin paused to ponder what lengths Astra would go through to gain ultimate power. "How many credits did it cost?"

"Almost all of them," replied Rebecca. "But the cost of creating an enduring empire is high. It's even more important to her than capturing the Traitor."

Traitor. The word shot through her consciousness. "Stone," she blurted to herself. *'Did he find out the truth? Was he not the traitor he was made out to be?'* A surge of relief passed over Martin's body as she realized Stone might still be the man she thought he had been —maybe.

"He's a fool," continued Rebecca. "He could have positioned himself at the highest levels of Humani power and instead he's running around the Neutral Quadrant in a dilapidated transport with his Akota concubine."

Martin bounced Rebecca off the bars one more time for good measure and raised her finger to her mouth in a gesture to silence Rebecca. "I think you've talked enough, pumpkin. You should just sit in your cell and keep your mouth shut until it's time for you to go."

"You're still taking me with you?" asked Rebecca. "I thought —"

"But you might not like where we're going," interrupted Martin.

"But —"

"Shhh," interjected Martin again. "You've sung enough tonight."

She watched as Rebecca slowly turned and walked back to her straw bed and lie down with her back to the entrance. Martin then returned to her bedding. Lying down and looking up toward the ceiling, she contemplated her new reality and started planning a way to get back to her former commander and find out his version of the truth.

Chapter 15

"Ready?" asked Mori softly while she and the others stood by the door leading out of the maintenance levels of the admin polis.

Stone nodded his head in acknowledgment. He looked toward Thay, Katalya, and Magnus; they were ready.

"Let's go," said Mori, opening the door and stepping through.

Stone watched Thay and Magnus quickly follow. Now it was his turn. As Stone slowly opened the door, he heard Mori's voice over their short-range voice communicators.

"*Hold positions,*" she warned.

"What is it?" asked Stone as he quickly peeked through the partially open door.

Magnus had taken cover behind a row of shrubbery and Thay and Mori were lying on the grass near a well-maintained copse of trees by a roadway.

"*Security,*" she answered. "*A lot of them.*"

Stone gently let the door shut, leaned against the wall, and clenched his jaw in frustration.

"How many?" he asked.

"*They're everywhere,*" answered Thay. "*Dozens.*"

Stone wondered if they had been double-crossed by Hanagus or Bianca. Maybe the technician had escaped and reported them. Maybe someone reported the dead guards or they missed a report. He looked over to Katalya, who was still in the maintenance area, as well. Her face was tight with anxious energy.

"We can't go through with this," she whispered to Stone.

Stone nodded his head in agreement and activated his comms circuit. "Get back inside," he said to Mori.

"*Roger,*" she replied. "*We just need —*"

"*They've got dogs,*" interrupted Magnus. "*I can smell them.*"

"*As soon as this patrol passes,*" continued Mori, "*we'll —*"

Stone heard the barking of dogs.

"*Contact!*" Mori shouted into the comms circuit, the barking of the dog overwhelmed by the explosion of gunfire.

"We're coming out!" shouted Stone as he reached for the door.

"*No!*" shouted Mori over the comms circuit. "*They don't know you're there. You and Katalya get back to Hydra. Orion will need your help if they're not already captured or dead —*"

Stone heard a burst of automatic fire from Mori's rifle over the circuit.

"*We'll find another way out and meet at rendezvous Bravo in five hours. If we're not there, follow breakdown protocol.*"

"But—"

"*That's an order, Tyler. We don't have time —*"

Another blast of her rifle drowned out her voice.

"Mori?" shouted Stone.

"*Don't worry,*" interrupted Thay over the circuit. "*I've got her back.*"

"*Tyler, go!*"

Stone felt Katalya grab his arm.

"Let's go," said Katalya. "She's my sister and I want to help too, but she's right. And she knows what she's doing."

Stone grunted as the frustration overwhelmed him. "Shit!" He activated his circuit. "Roger, I'll see you in five hours."

He started to move, but his body didn't want to obey. He so badly wanted to help Mori and the others.

"Tyler. We need to get to Orion," said Katalya. Stone could feel her give his arm a good shake to jar him into action. "Let's go!"

Stone looked at Katalya. He could tell in her eyes, so similar to Mori's, that she was concerned too, not only for her sister but for her mate, Magnus. For a second, they both gazed at each other as if to share their fears of what might happen while at the same time steeling their resolve.

"Let's go," acquiesced Stone.

The echoes of gunfire soon faded away as Stone and Katalya quickly make their way back into the maintenance underground. At the opening to the vertical ladder, they paused.

"Mori?" spoke Stone over the comms circuit. "Thay?"

There was no response. Stone hoped the distance and interference from the metal and concrete between their position and his was the reason for their silence.

"We're probably out of range," said Katalya.

Stone saw the concern on her face. He could tell she was asking him as much as telling him.

"Yeah," he replied. "We're on the edge of the range and underground ... definitely out of range." If only he could convince himself.

"They'll make it to the rendezvous," she added.

Stone put his hand on her shoulder. "Of course they will. Mori, Thay, and Magnus ... if any three people can do it, it's them," Stone said reassuringly.

"If?" replied Katalya.

"They'll be there," answered Stone. He was focusing on reassuring Katalya, but was trying to convince himself as well. They had already worked out the contingencies if the mission ran into problems. The Bravo rendezvous was a relaxation house in the recreation polis, far away from Hanagus's establishment in case they were involved. If Mori and the others weren't at that location, there were a series of alternate times and locations cascading all the way to making it to the Terillian controlled planet, Lima 8. It wasn't the first time a mission had fallen apart for Stone, and he was sure it wasn't for Mori or Thay either. *Do your job. Execute the plan,*' he told himself. "You ready?" he asked Katalya.

Katalya nodded as she hooked her rifle into its sling and stepped down onto the first rung.

"Tyler ..."

"Yes?" he replied looking down the opening toward Katalya.

"Thanks for saying what I needed to hear."

Stone gave her a quick smile. "It's true. Now let's get out of here."

Stone followed Katalya as the two descended to the lower level. At the bottom were the bodies of the two guards they had encountered before. The attack by Mori and Magnus, combined with the damage from their falls, had taken their toll. The bodies were twisted and distorted with several gaping wounds. The floor was slick with their blood, forcing Stone to take slow, deliberate steps when he reached the bottom.

"We should get any gear from them that might be useful," he said, but Katalya was already digging through the blood-soaked pockets of one of the guards.

She pulled a hand-held communicator from the dead man's vest. "We can use their comms gear to listen in on what's happening."

As he and Katalya continued to collect additional ammunition and other useful items, the echo of a boot splashing through a puddle of water caught their attention. Stone spun around to see two maintenance technicians, carrying toolboxes and other gear, staring at them from approximately twenty meters away. The techs dropped their equipment and turned to run.

Stone rose to give chase, but Katalya was already two strides ahead of him. He pushed his body hard in an attempt to catch up to her but all he could do was stay close. Turning the corner, he saw the two technicians still running with Katalya only a few meters behind. At a full sprint, she drew her knife and drove it into the first technician's lower back. As he arched his body and fell, she leapt toward the second man and landed on his back with her canine teeth sinking into his neck, the two tumbling forward.

The first technician was attempting to activate his communication device when Stone reached him.

Before the technician could speak, Stone dropped to his knees and slid into the man's body. He grasped the tech's hand and wrenched his arm outward with a powerful twist causing the communicator to fall to the ground. The technician let out a moan that was quickly cut short as Stone extended the man's arm toward him and knocked the man unconscious with a powerful kick.

He jumped to his feet to assist Katalya but there was no need. She was walking toward him, her mouth dripping blood and the dead technician lying in the background. He was still amazed at the skills of Katalya and Magnus. The speed and ferocity of their attacks almost made him feel sorry for their victims.

"Is this one still alive?" asked Katalya as she wiped her victim's blood from her chin with her sleeve.

"Just unconscious," replied Stone as he looked down at the technician.

"Should we leave him?" she asked.

"He's not security. Just some working stiff trying to do his job," replied Stone. But he knew that didn't mean anything. "But the Association might not know how many of us there are. If he talks, they could get more intel."

"I know." Katalya sighed. "Wishful thinking."

Stone was surprised at Katalya's sympathy for the technician given the violent and brutal nature in which she attacked.

"That's what war is," declared Stone. "You start off with a specific goal and end up with collateral damage."

"He probably wouldn't survive his wounds anyway," added Katalya.

"Yeah," answered Stone as he subconsciously felt for the medical pack he was carrying that could stop the technician's bleeding. But then there would be none for him or Katalya if they were injured.

"Wrong place, really wrong time," said Katalya, reaching down and pulling her knife from the man's back. The blood flowed freely from the wound. "Guess it's better to just get it over with," she continued as she brought the knife towards the man's neck.

Stone wanted to turn away but forced himself to watch. This man was innocent, or at least wasn't a combatant, and if he was going to die, Stone at least owed the man the respect of watching his death and feeling disgusted by it.

"Sorry, guy." Katalya sighed again. She paused. Stone saw her take a deep breath. And another. She didn't want to do it.

"Stop," he interjected. "We've been fighting this whole time because we are supposed to be doing right. And this isn't right."

"Are you sure you want to do this?" asked Katalya. Stone could see the wave of relief pass over her face.

His training told him it was a mistake. He paused.

"Yes, damn it. I'm sure." He pulled a coagulant gel pack from his pocket. "This guy isn't dying today because of us."

Katalya rose to her feet, sheathed her knife, and stepped back from the unconscious man.

"You know if Thay were here —"

"I know," interrupted Stone. "But he's not ... it's us, and we're gonna let him live."

Stone knew without a doubt Thay would have killed the man. Magnus too. Maybe even Mori.

"We had better hurry though," cautioned Katalya.

"You're right," said Stone as he applied the gel to the man's wound.

After the gel, Stone injected a heavy dose of neuro-med into the man's leg and rolled him onto his side.

"This should keep him out long enough for us to get out of this maze and back topside." Just as he started to rise, Stone saw a small digital pad protruding from a utility pocket. He withdrew it and activated the screen.

"What is it?" asked Katalya.

Stone flipped the screen and series of photos appeared. Selecting the first one, he saw what appeared to be the technician with his wife and small daughter, no more than eight or nine.

"Just personal crap," he replied as he set the pad in the front of the man's chest. Rising back to his feet, Stone grabbed his rifle and looked toward Katalya. "I think we've done our good deed for the day. Now let's get out of this hole."

***

"Left!" shouted Mori, firing a burst from her rifle.

Magnus and Thay joined her as the two Association guards on an elevated walkway to the left disappeared in a hail of lead.

"Incoming!" warned Thay.

Mori spun farther to her left as an antipersonnel rocket zoomed past her head and impacted against a wall five meters away. The blast enveloped the group, jarring Mori's body and knocking her against a nearby wall and onto the ground. As she hit the ground, she grabbed for her right ear.

It felt like it had been pierced by a hot knife; the concussion had ruptured her eardrum. Her head throbbed, a high-pitched tone reverberating through her good ear. Pushing the pain out of her consciousness, Mori rose to her knees and brought her rifle to her shoulder. Two attackers were on top of her.

Mori pulled the trigger and her rifle erupted at point-blank range. The first attacker's torso twisted backwards awkwardly as his chest was torn apart by Mori's fire. Shifting her aim quickly, she fired again.

The second attacker crumpled to the ground from the combined fire of Mori and Magnus, who had recovered from the blast and fired at the guard as well.

"Thay!" shouted Mori. She looked through the dust still floating to the ground from the explosion. "Thay!"

As the dust and smoke began to clear, Mori saw Thay in a firing position behind a pile of debris created by the explosion. He raised his hand to indicate he was still in the fight.

"Incoming!" Thay shouted, followed immediately by a blast from his rifle.

Mori curled her body tight again as another rocket exploded nearby. When the blast wave began to dissipate, she again took up a firing position.

"Got 'em," reported Thay. "We're clear to move."

"Move!" she shouted, springing to her feet and sprinting toward what appeared to be a nature park.

The ringing in Mori's left ear subsided as she and the others made their way across the hundred or so meters to the entrance of the park. Each step, however, brought a wave of pain that passed over the right side of her face from the damaged ear. At the entrance, Mori took a defensive position by a large concrete statue. Feeling Thay's body as he crouched beside her, she released the empty clip from her rifle, slammed another into place, and depressed the bolt release pin. Looking to her right, she saw Magnus leaning against a large tree covering the group from the rear.

She felt Thay shaking her shoulder and turned to face him.

"Can you hear me now?" he shouted. "Your ear —"

"It's fucked," she interrupted. The acknowledgment sent another wave of pain through her body.

"Here." Thay injected a neuro-med into her thigh. "This should take the edge off."

The medicine acted quickly, and Mori felt the pain subside to a dull ache almost instantly.

"Anyone behind us?" she asked Magnus, turning her good ear toward him.

"Nothing."

She turned back toward Thay and spoke. "I don't think they were waiting for us when we left the maintenance area. They seemed to be casting a wide net."

She saw Thay nod in agreement. "They knew we were here but not where. If we can get back to the underground, we might have a chance."

"Unless they're driving us there," retorted Mori. "But we have no idea where we're going up here."

"Do you still have that map from the tech?"

"Right here," answered Mori, patting her tactical vest. "We'll move along the edge of this park until we find another entrance into the maintenance area."

"They might have locked down the entrance and exits," pondered Thay. "I would."

Mori paused. Her thoughts went to Stone and her sister Katalya. Hopefully they had made it out. She was counting on it as she formulated a plan.

"You're right. If we blow the doors to the next maintenance area entrance we find, they will think we went underground and hopefully shift most of their attention there. If they do, we might be able to make it to an entrance of another polis and start making our way toward the others."

"And what of Stone and Katalya?" asked Magnus.

"They should've made it out by now," said Mori. "If not —"

"If they're not out, they're probably captured or dead," interrupted Thay matter-of-factly.

Mori stared coldly into Thay's eyes.

"It's the truth and you both know it," Thay responded to Mori's gaze. "And this is the best plan we've got."

"I agree," added Magnus. Mori could see he was also stinging from Thay's brutal, but logical, statement.

Mori shook off her anger at Thay's insensitive comment and refocused on the mission as a she slightly tilted her head in contemplative thought.

"What is it?" asked Magnus.

"If they think we went underground and redirect their forces —"

"They'll never expect it," interrupted Thay as a familiar smile came to his face.

"Expect what?" asked a frustrated Magnus.

"We're going back to get that councilman," declared Mori.

***

Stone and Katalya watched from their hidden position as dozens of guards poured into the same maintenance entrance they had exited only moments ago.

"They must have found the technician," said Katalya.

"Maybe. Or they shifted their search for the others." Stone could tell Katalya was hoping their small act of compassion hadn't made things worse for themselves or the others.

He slid further behind the cover and gripped his rifle as two security officers stopped in front of his and Katalya's position. As they spoke, Stone listened intently.

"We've got them now," said one of the men convincingly. "We received a report the intruders entered the underground after they blew one of the security entrances to the maintenance area."

"That's still a lot of space to cover," replied the other. "And I hear they are Scout Rangers."

"I don't know. Even if they are, there's only three of them and we're sending over half our security force down there after them. No three people, even Scout Rangers, can fight their way through four thousand."

A small bit of relief passed over Stone. First, the Association still thought there were only three intruders. Second, he thought using an explosive to access a maintenance door was a little too ostentatious for Mori. It had to be a diversion — one that was obviously working.

"I guess," answered the second officer. "And that ten thousand credit reward in any polis sounds nice too."

"No shit," said the other. "Do you kno —" The officer held his hand to the other to indicate a message was coming through his communication circuit.

"This is Security Officer Stonewright ... Yes but ... Yes, I understand." Stone saw the officer's posture change and his head tilt back and to one side in frustration. "We are on the way."

"What is it?" asked the other officer.

"Damn it!" cursed Stonewright. "So much for the reward."

"What are you talking about?"

"We have been ordered to the private docking bays to secure some smuggler ship named *Hydra* and detain the crew."

"You've got to be kidding me," complained the other officer. Stone could tell from the look on the man's face that despite his verbal complaining, his expression showed relief that he wouldn't have to play cat-and-mouse with Scout Rangers in the underground.

"Maybe we can get a percentage of the sale of the ship if they sell it," said Stonewright. "Either way, that's where we're headed."

"Understood," replied the second officer, turning toward his men at the entrance. "Second squad!" he shouted. "Change of plans."

Stone watched the security teams of Stonewright and the other officer make their way to a transport tube and board a shuttle to the market polis's private docks.

"We've got to get to them," said Katalya.

"They're not looking for us," replied Stone. "If we dump some of our weapons to not look so obvious we might be able to catch up to them."

"What if we don't make it in time?" asked Katalya, dropping her tactical vest.

"We'll get there," replied Stone. "And if we don't, we'll meet up with your sister and the others and then find a way out."

Stone could tell Katalya was still unsettled. He gently placed his hand on her shoulder. "I've been in these situations before, Katalya, and so has Mori … it's what we do." He saw a slight relief in Katalya's pained expression.

"Of course," she replied.

"Good," said Stone with a smile. "Let's go be heroes."

Stone and Katalya quickly doffed the majority of their combat gear and boarded the next tube toward the private docks.

The doors slid shut with a wispy swoosh and the tube quickly accelerated. Stone nonchalantly scanned the other riders. It appeared that even though the Association security was on high alert, they didn't want it to impact their bottom line too much; the car was mostly filled with the typical sort you would expect in the market polis — wealthy Dark Zone barons, gamblers, peddlers, smugglers, recreation girls, and what Stone assumed was either a musician or an escaped mental patient.

And there was the security guard. At the far end of the car stood a heavily armed guard intently scanning the crowd. It didn't take long for him to focus on Stone and Katalya.

"He's walking this way," whispered Katalya.

Stone reached down and grasped Katalya's hand in a move to show they were a couple and to prevent her from withdrawing her pistol. He leaned in as if to give her a kiss. Her eyes burned with anticipation; espionage was not her forte.

"Just follow my lead," he mouthed just before giving her a kiss on the cheek.

Stone looked up from the kiss to the guard staring intently at them. "Why are you two here?" he asked briskly.

"Why is anyone here?" replied Stone as he smiled and looked down devilishly toward Katalya.

The guard stared at Stone coldly and then took a long, lecherous look at Katalya.

"Who are you?"

"I'm Sherman Greene from Bratius Minor," replied Stone using the Port Royal name for Hotel 7. "I run a modest business where I, uh, facilitate things for people."

"Why are you here?"

"Got bored with things there and wanted to … uh …" Stone overtly glanced toward Katalya, "mix things up."

Katalya stood motionless, rigid, and clearly disturbed. But Stone had chosen his story to let that work for him.

"And your companion?"

"Oh," smiled Stone. "From the recreation polis." Stone leaning in toward the guard. "She cost me a fortune," he whispered. "She's been … altered."

The guard had already noticed Katalya was different. Her left ear had protruded from her hair and the pointed tip drew his attention.

"Altered, huh?"

"Yeah," continued Stone. "I don't even know what's going on under those clothes, but I'm dying to find out."

"How much was she?" asked the guard, now staring directly at Katalya.

"Twelve hundred —"

"Shit!" interrupted the guard. "Credits?"

"Humani," answered Stone.

The guard shook his head. "That's almost two thousand credits."

"We'll if you want something new and different," Stone ran his hand down Katalya's back slowly, "You've gotta pay for it."

"What's your name, honey?" he asked.

Katalya remained silent.

Stone saw the guard's playful but lascivious smile turn into a scowl.

"Tell him your name," directed Stone, looking down toward her.

She looked up at him with a tense, tight face. Out of the corner of his eye, he saw her right hand reach toward the knife hidden in the small of her back. Again, Stone ran his hand down her back, but this time rested his hand on hers.

"Your name," he said again.

"Katalya," she answered without emotion, her canines showing as she spoke.

"Damn," said the guard as he leaned in toward Katalya's face.

Stone feared Katalya would rip his throat out with those teeth if he got any closer. "If you don't mind, sir," he interjected to get the guard's attention. "I don't want you to spook her too much … she's obviously new."

The guard looked toward Stone and took step backward into a defensive stance. It was starting to go bad. "Do you have any weapons?" asked the guard tersely.

Stone kept his grip on Katalya's hand. "I thought if I paid for undeclared status, I would be allowed to carry." As Stone spoke, he slowly drew some unmarked Humani exchange cards to show he could afford the cost of play on Port Royal.

"Of course," amended the guard.

Stone felt a sense of relief.

"But just let me check your unmarked pass."

There it was. Now it would get ugly. "Just a moment," replied Stone as he feigned digging through his pockets. "I know it's here."

Stone saw the guard look toward Katalya and then quickly back to him, gripping his rifle tightly.

"Step away from the girl and put your hands up," he ordered.

"Just a minute. I know —"

"Now!" shouted the guard as he leveled his rifle at Stone, the barrel almost touching his chest. In his periphery, Stone saw the other passengers moving away from him and Katalya.

"Okay, okay," replied Stone, "but I just —"

Before the guard could react, Stone directed the rifle away from himself and Katalya then crashed his right foot into the inside of the guard's right knee. The unnerving sound of tearing of ligaments was quickly replaced by the screams of the guard as he fell to his knees. Stone shifted his weight, wrapped his hand around the guard's neck, and with all of his strength drove the back of the man's head onto the floor of the transport tube, knocking him unconscious. As he turned to rise, Stone saw Katalya leap onto the chest of the unconscious guard.

"Asshole," she declared as she drove her knife into his chest.

Stone grabbed the rifle lying on the floor and quickly scanned the transport car. He stood in the center of the car with Katalya still straddling the dead guard next to him, ready to defend himself. Looking over the room, Stone saw the stares of the other occupants. After a tense moment, a large, balding man with a recreation girl hiding behind him spoke.

"We go through a tunnel shortly," offered the man. "I would recommend depositing our friend over the side when the opportunity arises."

Stone had temporarily forgotten he was on Port Royal; no one gave a shit about anyone except themselves. Acknowledging the man with a smile, Stone tossed an exchange card toward him. The bald man caught it and returned the nod before taking his seat and returning his attention to his escort as the rest of the car returned to their previous conversations. Stone looked down toward an astonished Katalya.

"That's it?" she asked as she rolled off of the guard's body.

"Welcome to Port Royal," answered Stone. "Now let's get ready to dump this guy."

As the other passengers went about their business, Stone and Katalya dragged the body to the door. Looking through the window, Stone saw the blur of buildings suddenly transition to darkness punctuated by periodic flashes of light. He grabbed the arms of the dead guard and hefted the lifeless body to his waist. Supporting the weight with his right arm, he searched for a release to the doors with his left.

"Where's the latch?" grunted Katalya as she searched for the release as well.

Stone began to worry they wouldn't get the door open in time as he looked around the edge of the door.

"Mmm," grunted a well-dressed older lady sitting near the door.

Stone looked toward the woman. She appeared to be in her thirties, but Stone could tell the number was probably closer to fifty. *'Probably a manager for the talent at a recreation club,'* Stone thought to himself.

The woman casually tilted her head to her left and upward. "Behind that box," she said quietly.

Stone quickly opened a small box on the wall to reveal a switch. He pulled the switch and the ratcheting rumble and swoosh of the tube exploded into a roar of air highlighted by loud metallic clanking. With a grunt, Stone flung the body of the guard into the darkness. He took a deep breath and activated the switch to close the door just as the darkness flashed bright and disappeared as the tube cleared the tunnel.

"Mmm."

Stone heard the lady clear her throat for attention once again. Looking down, he saw her subtly hold out her hand. Understanding her, and Port Royal in general, he pulled another exchange card from his pocket and placed it in her hand. The woman placed the card in her satchel, gave Stone a quick smile, and turned away to stare out the window. He turned back toward Katalya, still dumfounded by the unemotional response to what they had just witnessed.

"Just a few more stops," said Stone as he led Katalya to a seat, "and we'll be there."

Stone felt Katalya's hand on his arm.

"I know why you did what you did back there," she said. Stone looked into Katalya's eyes, so much like her sister's, he thought to himself. He could see the frustration and anger on her face.

"Talking to the guard," she continued slowly. "Saying I was a ..."

"It was a trick," replied a confused Stone.

"It might have been necessary," she replied. Stone felt her grip tighten. "But never do that again. Never."

"I don't understand —"

"Ino'ka has told you how we became separated, that I was taken by slavers, yes?" He felt her grip even tighter. "Never again."

Stone felt ashamed of his actions and saddened for Katalya, but what else could he have done? He put his opposite hand on hers. "Never. I promise."

Stone sat down beside Katalya and they quietly stared out the window of the tube as the *swoosh* and rattle counted down the few minutes until they reached their destination.

Chapter 16

Councilman Shelton Ferrous nervously looked left, then right, then left again.

The news of an intrusion, possibly by Scout Rangers, had the well-placed citizens of the administration polis on edge. So much so, Council Leader Cooper had called an emergency meeting of all available councilmen. Although he would've rather taken refuge in his quarters surrounded by his security system and personal guards, he needed to look strong in front of the Council if he wanted to challenge Cooper for council leader at the next annual profit and operations conference. Surrounded by four guards and joined by his chief of security, Jameson Rankine, he again scanned the street and nearby structures before he exited his apartment and hurriedly walked toward the opposite side of the street and his personal car.

"I heard three of them took out over twenty security guards, and they still haven't been found?" asked Shelton, trying to make himself as small as possible without looking too sheepish. People talked if the price was right — even his own men.

"Don't you fuss, Councilman," replied Jameson in a deep, confident voice. "Just a bit and we'll have you —"

The sound of a dull thud and sight of the two guards collapsing in front of Ferrous cut Jameson off midsentence.

"Behind me!" Shelton heard Jameson shout as everything began to blur in a torrent of chaos. Before he could focus again, Shelton stood surrounded by the bodies of five guards.

Shelton finally reacted and turned toward his apartment. He had only taken a few steps when he saw a large armed man step in front of his door. Shelton tried to stop too quickly from his sprint and tumbled to the ground. His heart pounded as he scrambled frantically on his hands and knees; eventually he regained his footing and began rushing toward his car. Fear taking control of his body, he turned his head to look back toward the man, who had slowly begun to follow him. His senses too overcome with fear, Shelton tripped over the body of Jameson just as he turned away from his pursuer. Again, he scrambled to his feet and rushed to his car, fearing a bullet in his back with every stride. He saw the car growing closer, but his fear only intensified the closer he came. After seconds that seemed an eternity, Shelton reached his car and dove inside.

"Get me out of here!" he huffed as he rolled onto his back, trying to regain his breath.

Panting heavily, he soon realized the car was not moving. "Go!" he shouted as he sat up in the seat and looked toward his driver. His heart fell into his stomach as his gaze was returned by man with a thin face and a single tuft of hair running down the center of his otherwise shaven head.

"Just be still," ordered the man.

"Who are you?" asked Shelton. "You're ... you're them. What do you want?" he asked, his mind racing. "I have money. A lot of money."

"Just shut up" came a woman's voice from the front of the car.

Shelton's vision started to tunnel and he could feel the sweat pouring down his flushed face.

"You're her," he panted. "The one with the bounty, the Traitor's whor —"

His sentence was cut short by the sight of the barrel of Mori's pistol pointing at his forehead. "Finish that sentence, asshole," she warned.

"I, I ... don't kill me!" he pleaded.

"We're not going to kill you ... yet," she answered.

Shelton jerked to his right and coiled up against the opposite side of the car as Magnus opened the door and sat beside him. It didn't take him long to notice the large canines, the coarse hair, and the pointed ears.

"You're from Venato," he declared.

"You know a hell of a lot about Xen and Humani operations," replied Mori as he turned toward Thay. "I told you he'd know some shit."

"I'll tell you whatever you want," pleaded Shelton. "Just let me go."

"We'll talk about that later," she replied. "Right now, you're gonna escort us out of this polis and tell us everything you know on the way out."

***

Stone crouched low as he turned the corner of the passageway leading to *Hydra*'s berth. He immediately saw the Association security forces taking position around the ship and quickly took cover against a ventilation revetment carved into the wall. He knelt and brought the rifle he had taken from the guard to the ready. Looking down the barrel in the direction of *Hydra*, he felt Katalya take position next to him.

"What's our move?"

"I don't see Orion or the others," he replied. "If you move to the right behind that power supply, we can be in position to put them in an enfilading if they move toward this passage or the utility entrance."

Katalya nodded and rose to her feet, but Stone quickly grabbed her and pulled her back against the revetment.

"What?" whispered Katalya angrily.

"I see them," he replied and turned back toward *Hydra*.

From his vantage he watched as Orion walked from *Hydra*'s main access onto the supporting brow. She was followed by two guards. Next came Rickover. And two more guards.

"Shit," he mouthed as he watched the two walk across the brow to the opposite platform.

"Where's the Scapi?" asked Katalya.

Before he could answer, Stone saw four guards emerge from *Hydra*, two of them facing back into the ship. After them came TC. His massive body filled the access as he lowered his head to step through the opening. Behind him walked three additional guards.

"What now?" asked Katalya.

Stone struggled with his next move. He knew he and Katalya could take out the guards, but he wasn't sure if they could do it without losing Orion, Rickover, TC, or all of them. As he mulled over his next move, he heard a report over the communications radio he had taken from the guard on the tube.

"*Security HQ, this is Blue Team, Second Squad. We have secured the vessel and its crew. Request orders.*"

Then came the response.

"*Copy. You are directed to activate lockdown sequence on the vessel and turnover crew to Humani Elite Guard troops who are in route.*"

Stone cursed under his breath again. If the Elite Guard got hold of them, it would only be a matter of time until they were at the hands of the interrogators or on their way to Capro prison.

"Stone?" asked Katalya again.

"We take them out," he answered, looking down the sights of his rifle. "I'll start in the front, you in the back and we'll work to the middle. On my mark ..."

Stone sensed Katalya level her pistol a few feet from him. Taking a deep breath, he settled the sights on the first guard. He exhaled slowly. He pulled the trigger and saw the first guard fall followed immediately crack of Katalya's pistol. Stone fired again and the other guard next to Orion fell. In a flash it was over.

"Let's go!" he shouted to Katalya as he leapt from cover and ran toward *Hydra*.

Sprinting toward *Hydra*, Stone could see Orion rushing toward Rickover, who was on his knees holding his left arm.

"Is everyone okay?" asked Katalya as her and Stone reached the others.

"We're good ... I think," answered Orion as she helped Rickover apply pressure to a flesh wound on his upper arm.

"Good?" grumbled Rickover. "I'm shot."

"Shut up, big baby," mocked Orion. "It's literally just a scratch."

"We need to get out of here," interrupted Stone. "Elite Guard troops are on the way."

"Damn it," replied Orion. "Let's get back onboard and ..." She paused. "Where are the others?"

Stone looked to Katalya, the concern over her sister and mate was evident.

"We had to split up," he replied, turning back toward Orion.

"This sucks," declared Orion as she kicked a nearby storage box.

"We have to get out of here," added Stone. "They're coming."

Orion looked down toward the ground and inhaled deeply. "You're right," she acknowledged as she looked up toward TC. "TC, let's get back onboard and get *Hydra* ready to get out of here."

Stone felt Katalya grab his arm.

"We're really going to leave them?" she asked.

Stone turned toward her. "We have to stick to the plan —"

"We can't leave them here," she shouted.

He could see tears forming in her eyes. Stone didn't want to leave them either, but countless missions had told him it was the right thing.

"If they lock down this bay we'll be stuck." Orion turned to the Scapi. "TC, go get her ready."

"No!" shouted Katalya as she stepped back and gripped a rifle she had taken from a dead guard. "I'm not leaving my sister. I'm not leaving Magnus."

Stone was at the same time frustrated and empathic as he slowly stepped toward Katalya.

"Katalya, I don't want to leave them either, but —"

"Then don't," she shot back.

"Damn it, Katalya," shouted Orion. "We have to —"

The thud of a round hitting Katalya's shoulder followed by the whizzing of bullets cut Orion short.

"Contact!" shouted Stone as he dove for cover and quickly leveled his rifle in the direction of the passageway.

Stone saw the torso of an Elite Guard rise up behind the very hiding spot he had used minutes ago. He fired quickly and the man ducked for cover again.

"Are you okay?" he shouted toward Katalya.

"Yes," she growled. She was lying on her back behind one of the dead guards, preparing to inject a coagulant into her shoulder. Another round of fire sent a wall of metal flying past Stone and ricocheting off wall opposite the bow.

"TC!" he heard Orion shout. Stone turned toward *Hydra*'s access door. "Get —"

A sound of massive metallic bars locking *Hydra* to the foundation of the docking bay drowned out the gunfire and rattled the floor as the ship was remotely anchored to its position.

"Damn it," shouted Orion.

"Can we override it?" shouted Stone.

"It would take hours."

Rounds again impacted against the storage box Stone had taken cover behind. One round tore through the box and exited centimeters from his face, showering him with metal fragments.

"Shit," he grumbled as the metal shards pelted like a dozen needles jabbing into his cheek.

"We're screwed," declared Rickover, huddling by TC just inside *Hydra*'s access.

Stone quickly raised his rifle and returned fire, but it was just for show. They were in an exposed position and all they could do was try to keep the Guardsmen from having enough time to take careful aim.

"Any ideas?" he shouted to Orion.

"If we could make it to the opposite side of *Hydra* there's a maintenance panel we could access and maybe get clear." Another hail of gunfire interrupted her. "But we'll never make it."

Stone winced as the metal shards embedded in his face reminded him of their presence. Hopefully Mori and the others were having better luck. He looked over toward Orion, who was applying pressure to a wound in her leg.

"You good?" he shouted.

"Yeah," she replied. "But it doesn't matter. They've got us."

He could see Orion pound the back of her head against the container she was using for cover.

"I'm not going to Capro," she shouted. "I'll die here first."

Stone's thoughts flashed back to how Mori looked when he rescued her from Capro. Orion was right; she would be better off dead. He, however, wouldn't go to Capro. His death would be much more public.

The sudden rumbling of the ship's brow drew Stone's attention and he turned see TC emerge from *Hydra*'s access with a heavy machine gun in one hand and a large metal plate in the other.

A flurry of high-pitched squeaks echoed through the docking bay.

"Go! Go! Go!" came the translator as the massive Scapi stopped in the center of the bow and sent a torrent of heavy caliber bullets toward the Guardsmen in the passage.

Stone rose to his feet and fired as he ran toward Rickover. As he passed, he saw Katalya leap into the pit from the brow and head toward the opposite side of *Hydra*.

"Come on," shouted Stone, grabbing Rickover to help him into the pit.

"We can't leave TC!" he shouted.

Stone looked back toward TC. Rounds from the Guardsmen ricocheted off the metal shield he was holding as he rumbled toward Orion's position. Suddenly the Guardsmen shifted their fire and Stone saw several rounds tear into TC's legs. The massive Scapi fell to his knees but quickly rose again and stumbled toward Orion.

"Go," ordered Stone, directing Rickover's hand toward the ladder near *Hydra*'s access.

Rickover conceded and stepped down onto the ladder. "Don't let them get him," he ordered as he looked up toward Stone.

"Just go!" replied Stone, who looked up and took aim at a Guardsman distracted by the Scapi's brave action.

He fired and the Guardsman fell, but a salvo of gunfire drove him to take cover behind the access. Looking on, he watched TC slowly make his way to Orion and covered her as she rushed across the brow and dove into the pit.

The thunderous sound of TC's heavy machine gun suddenly fell silent as a single round passed just over his makeshift shield and tore into the top of his head.

"Damn it," cursed Stone, grabbing a handhold at *Hydra*'s access and diving into the pit.

Hitting the ground, Stone broke into a sprint as he rushed to the opposite side of *Hydra*. When he arrived, Orion was standing at a small access.

"TC?" she asked.

Stone shook his head.

"That fucking big blue bastard," cursed Orion as she punched the access panel repeatedly.

"We've got to go," said Stone as he placed his hand on Orion's shoulder.

Orion exhaled heavily and nodded. Stone stepped into the access, followed by Orion.

"We've got to hurry. They'll be right behind us," said Orion.

Stone reached for a grenade he had taken from one of the guards. "This will slow them down." Orion pulled the pin and placed the lever against the panel.

"Good," replied Orion. "We'll travel down this passage a few meters then it branches off in several directions. We can leave a few more surprises for them there."

"After that?" asked Stone.

"This isn't the first time I've had to make a quick getaway on Port Royal, Stone."

Astra stood at her private landing bay near her personal entrance to the Forum with General Vispa standing at her side.

"They should be here any moment, ProConsul," said Vispa.

Astra let out a sigh. The only time she had to wait was for the Xen or the Dorans.

"What is the status of that religious nut in the Echo system?" she asked.

"Major General Mellius and Vice Admiral Tharus with three battle groups and fifteen thousand troops will be in system in a few days. They will use the orbital destroyers to set up perimeters around the capitals and troop concentration areas and then send in attack craft and ground troops to destroy any resistance."

"Excellent," replied Astra. "That self-righteous prick will see what true power is."

"Of course, ProConsul," agreed Vispa.

"I want every soldier killed and the rest of his followers rounded up into camps." She paused and turned toward Vispa. "And General Vispa, I want his head delivered to me in a box."

"Of course, ProConsul."

"I am serious, General," she added, afraid he hadn't understood her actual desire. "I want it delivered in a box of Perillian wood, engraved in gold with my family crest on the cover."

"Yes, ProConsul," replied Vispa, "it will be done."

"And inform Mellius if he can't deliver this lunatic's head, I will have his." Knowing she had made her point, Astra turned back toward the landing dock as a heavily armored shuttle, with Doran military markings, drifted into position.

"Protocol, gentlemen," said Astra quietly but sternly, looking straight ahead. "Do not embarrass me."

The ship locked into its berth with a metallic thud and the shuttle doors opened. Astra inhaled and forced a smile to her face as Dorans, the first in over a century, set foot on Humani soil. Two guards exited. They wore what appeared to be armored uniforms and exoskeletons to make up for their gaunt builds. Each wore a grayish metal helmet that covered their face and a heavily shaded shield over their eyes, which were illuminated with a slight bluish hue. They mechanically marched into position just outside the access door.

Holding her smile, Astra's eyes opened slightly wider as a massive, humanoid-shaped metallic form rumbled outside of the access. Standing almost two and half meters tall, the thick machine robotically trudged into position a few meters from the access. Coming to an abrupt halt, the mechanized warrior pivoted from left to right and began to hum mechanically as it continuously scanned for threats. Following the machine came two thin, ashen-skinned warriors standing at least two meters tall. While their legs displayed armored exoskeletons similar to the others, their torsos were covered with a plated armored tunic and shoulder pads. Underneath the tunic was a heavy padded shirt, which seemed to replace the more rigid exoskeleton of the others. Over their shoulders they carried a type of rifle unknown to Astra and at each warriors' side was a curved blade half a meter in length. The warrior to Astra's right activated a switch on his helmet, which covered his lower jaw, and spoke.

"Astra Varus of the Family Varus, ProConsul of the Humani Senate and leader of the Republic, I, Captain Navar, officer of the Doran Imperial Guard, have the honor of presenting Lord General Zorlar, head of the Yellow River Clan, cousin to King Vali of the Doran Southern Multi-polis, and combined leader of the Doran Humani Expeditionary Group."

As the warrior spoke, another tall figure emerged from the shuttle. He was dressed similarly to Captain Navar but wore a long sword around his waist in addition to the short sword and was cloaked in a dark blue cape connected around his neck by what looked like wolf's hide.

Astra looked toward General Vispa out of the corner of her eye in a silent warning of the repercussions of failure.

General Vispa stood taller. "Greetings, Captain Navar. I, General Vispa of the Family Vispa and Chief Military Council to the ProConsul welcome the arrival of Lord General Zorlar and introduce the leader of the Senate and Defender of the Republic, ProConsul Astra Varus of the Family Varus."

Astra let out a slight exhale of contentment with Vispa's successful introduction.

"Lord General Zorlar." She smiled. "I am honored with your presence." She waited silently for the response.

"ProConsul Varus," replied Zorlar with what Astra thought was a hint of a scowl. "I hope to serve you well and bring honor to both your family and my clan, and in doing so, honor the Emperor."

Astra bowed her head slightly as the Lord General walked toward her. When he came to a stop, she stood erect, straining her neck slightly to look up toward Zorlar. She maintained her smile. "Please, Lord General, follow me to your chambers and we shall discuss your duties."

"Thank you, ProConsul, but no," replied Zorlar flatly. "I will not require chambers. I will remain with my ship except for official duties requiring my presence on this ... on your planet."

"Very well, Lord General," replied Astra, almost choking on the words. If she had to work any harder to maintain her smile, her skin would crack. She now despised the Dorans almost as much as the Xen. "Perhaps —"

"As my duties have been assigned to me by the Emperor through King Vali, I will assess and support your command staff and, if I feel necessary, proceed to the Foxtrot system and relieve your troops so they may support other Humani efforts."

"Do not speak to the ProConsul in this manner!" demanded General Vispa as he stepped toward Zorlar.

Astra saw the two officers beside Zorlar place their hands on their swords and in the background, she saw the mech quickly twist its torso toward the group as two Gatling guns extended from its arms and began to spin. Out of the corner of her eye, she saw one of her Praetorians take a defensive posture.

"Gentlemen," she said softly, placing her hand on Vispa's chest to gently push him away. "Perhaps Lord General Zorlar and I should speak alone for a while." As she spoke, Astra burned her gaze into Vispa.

"Yes, ProConsul." Vispa relented and stepped back as the Doran guards relaxed their stance and the massive mechanized warrior retracted its weapons.

Astra extended her hand toward the entrance and continued. "Lord General, allow me to show you to the rooms we have reserved for your use … if you so wish."

Zorlar looked down toward her with an expressionless face and nodded in acknowledgment. Astra motioned for the two to step away from the group, leaving the Praetorians and Vispa to stare awkwardly at the Zorlar's troops.

"Your General Vispa seems impulsive, ProConsul, a trait we had heard was common in your species."

Astra wanted so badly to reach up and slap the Doran across the face. But she couldn't reach it and that wouldn't solve her problem. She would have to be patient. "Yes, Lord General," she replied. "Although impulsiveness can be useful in subordinates, true leaders must exhibit sound judgment. Judgment and a sense of one's place in the hierarchy of things." She looked up to see Zorlar's tight expression loosen ever so slightly. "It is important for the leaders of my civilization to feel pride in their status so that the social order can be maintained. Unfortunately, they sometimes forget we are just one ally." She paused "A new ally compared to your Doran civilization, within the greater Xen Empire." She stopped to give Zorlar an ever-so-slight bow of her head. "I have not forgotten."

"Of course," replied Zorlar. "And I fully plan to support you in the Foxtrot system, but I must first stay long enough to ensure my vessels' communications systems are fully integrated with yours, that both the Humani and Doran fire control systems are integrated so as to not identify one another as foes, and to allow a few weeks of joint training so that our battle groups may operate together."

"Understandable, Lord General," she replied. "I just need to —"

"You clearly understand politics," interrupted Zorlar, "and whether you like it or not, you also understand your place in the Empire. I will make the final decision as to the deployment of my ships and men, but in public, I will not challenge your authority directly. Unless I find it necessary."

"Thank you for your understanding, Lord General," she replied with another bow of her head to feign respect and hide her grimaced scowl at his audacity.

Chapter 17

"One hundred," Martin said out loud as she hung from a pipe in her cell and pulled her knees to her chest for another repetition. Over the last few days, the meds provided by Dan-Lee had worked wonders for her, and Martin was well on her way back to fighting shape. She let her legs drop again. Steadying her legs and extending them parallel to the floor, she pulled her body toward the ceiling until her chin touched the pipe. Dull pain still pulsated from her elbow, but she could handle that. "One —"

"Looking good" came a voice from the cell entrance. "You seem to be healing up nicely."

Martin glanced toward the entrance but continued her workout. It was Dan-Lee. "Come in and I'll show you how well I'm healed," she replied. "Two."

"Are you always so quick to invite men into your room?" quipped Dan-Lee.

"Three," she counted out loud, trying to ignore the remark. But she couldn't. As she continued her workout, she spoke. "Men, yes. But I'll make an exception for you. And I promise it'll be a night you'll never forget … because you'll need to eat through a straw after." She pulled her torso toward the ceiling again. "Sev-en."

"So brash and confident," he replied. "You Elite Guard are like spoiled children. Perhaps you need a good spanking."

Martin dropped to the floor and looked into Dan-Lee's eyes. "I'm bored with this. Just come in so I can shut your mouth."

"Not yet," he replied. "But we should talk."

"About?"

"Come closer."

Martin slowly walked over to the entrance and gripped the bars with her hands. She tensed her body — if this jackass gave her a chance she would make him pay.

But he didn't. He stood just out of arms' reach outside her cell.

"What?" asked Martin.

"We are on the same side, Paladin."

Martin laughed. Given her new knowledge about her civilization's greatest lie, the concept of a side meant nothing to her. "And what side's that?"

"I am an agent of the ProConsul."

"Sure," replied Martin as the right side of her mouth curled in skepticism. "You look it."

"If I looked like a Humani spy, I wouldn't be very good at my job, now would I?"

Martin started to put the small pieces of information together. His skill. The amber-yellowish eyes. And his contempt for the Elite Guard. "You're Phelian," she declared.

Martin quickly recalled her history. The Phel inhabited the planet that became Charlie 5 after the

Accords created the Neutral Quadrant. Fierce but primitive warriors, the Phel offered their young to the ProConsul Gaius Craxi generations ago to be trained by the Praetorians and Humani Intelligence as mercenaries and assassins. That all changed about thirty years ago when ProConsul Tradar Epialius learned the Phelian chieftain had been speaking with Terillian agents. Afraid they would switch sides, the ProConsul ordered the destruction of the Phel warrior order. The resultant war of attrition between the Phel and the Elite Guard ended a few years before Martin joined the guard in what was believed to be the eradication of the Phelian warrior class, but as a young lieutenant, she had come face-to-face with a few of these master killers.

"I thought you were all dead," she replied matter-of-factly. "I thought the last of you died on Golf 2 … by my hand."

"So, you were the one," he replied coldly. "Well, a few have survived … no thanks to the Elite Guard."

Martin was puzzled. "If you're Phel, then why the hell are you working for the ProConsul?" She wanted to find out more but didn't want to give away what she had recently learned. If she played the loyal Humani soldier, he might actually help her escape.

"My hatred for the Guard has nothing to do with filling my pockets."

'Not only is this guy a jerk,' thought Martin, *'he has no honor either.'* But he could be useful. "Then why are you here?"

"I was hired when the ProConsul came up with this plan to 'create' this religion to gain more slaves for the Xen and her private army."

"Create? You're telling me all of this shit is Astra Varus's handiwork?" And Martin thought it was impossible for her to hate the ProConsul more than she already did.

"That was the original plan. I was hired to work my way into the higher order if I could and keep an eye on the Saint, otherwise known as Tali Vena."

"Who?"

"Exactly. He was some con-man the Association hired and trained with the ProConsul's blessing. He was given a ton of cash, some preliminary 'followers' like myself, and a doctrine thought to be good to win over the hearts of disenchanted populations in the Dark Zone."

"So, this Word fanaticism — it's all bullshit?"

"Not to the followers. They are drinking in this collective community, reward in the afterlife stuff … but then the Saint started believing too."

"What?"

"The power, the hundreds of thousands — maybe millions — of followers, the constant spouting of doctrine — it went to his head. It's not hard to believe when you hear the same story day after day."

"No shit," replied Martin, almost giving herself away. She released her grip and took a step away from the bars. "Is there any truth left in the galaxy?" she mumbled aloud.

"Truth?" laughed Dan-Lee. "Truth is the near extinction of my people, the subjugation of millions by the Humani and Terillians in the name of their self-righteous causes, it's the desperation of people stuck in the middle in the Dark Zone. Truth is pain, suffering, loneliness, and death. Nobody wants to know the truth; that's why lies are so much easier to accept."

"I just —"

"Maybe you're not the typical Guardsman," Dan-Lee inquired. "For several reasons."

Martin was afraid she was giving herself away. She had always sucked at keeping her emotions in check, but she would have to reign herself in. She stepped back toward the bars. "I am anything but typical," she smiled confidently.

"I bet you are," returned Dan-Lee.

"Maybe someday you'll find out," she replied with a deceptive smile meant to make Dan-Lee wonder just what she meant. "But for now, how are you going to get me out of here?"

"I think you know as well as me that Astra Varus won't take the Saint's betrayal lying down."

"No shit," she replied.

Dan-Lee motioned toward Rebecca's cell, where the envoy was sleeping. "I sent a low frequency coded message when our lost little dove over there was captured. That message should have reached the ProConsul a few weeks ago, along with the distress signal from the ship that brought you likely sent before it was destroyed. My guess is Humani troops will be crawling all over this place within a week at the latest."

Martin knew he was right. That is, unless Astra Varus decided to just nuke the place and find another source for her human chattel.

"What's the plan?" she asked.

"Things will get hectic when the Humani arrive. When that happens, I'm going to release you and we are going to take out the beloved, all-powerful Saint."

Martin considered her options. She could work with Dan-Lee to kill the Saint. Even though it was what Astra Varus wanted, the Saint deserved a bullet as much as anyone else on her list.

"And after that?" she asked.

"I get my money and you get another promotion and praise from your precious Senate and ProConsul."

The thought of praise from the pack of liars leading her planet made her stomach churn, but she played along. If another award put her face to face with Astra Varus again one last time ... "I'm in," she replied.

"Of course you are," said Dan-Lee.

"You just worry about yourself."

"Oh, I never worry about myself ..." She saw and felt him look over her body in that all-too-familiar way. "But I'll definitely be watching your back." He smiled.

She smiled back. "Once we take care of the Saint, we've got some unfinished business."

"Looking forward to it," Dan-Lee replied with a wink.

"You shouldn't."

"See you later, Paladin" He laughed as he turned to walk away.

"You can count on it," replied Martin as she raised her middle finger to his turned back. "Dick."

Martin quickly spun around from the entrance to her cell as if it would make Dan-Lee's lascivious, arrogant attitude disappear. She was frustrated, anxious, and to her own disgust, slightly excited by her encounter with the Phelian mercenary.

"What an asshole," she said aloud as she shook her head and jumped back up to grab the pipe and continue her workout. Pulling her body toward the pipe, she focused on the strain in her muscles and the pain in her elbow; it was easier to take than the emotional pain she felt. "One—"

Chapter 18

Martin spent a restless night trying to come to grips with the possibilities of the shattered foundation that was her reality. She first wondered if she had been too quick to believe Rebecca's tale. But she wasn't one to ponder things to the point of paralysis. It was all about her gut. And despite what she had grown up believing, her feelings about the First Families and the Association made it believable. She just needed verification. And if it was true, what did that make her?

As the night slowly turned into dawn, she lay awake looking for something she could grasp as real. As her mind wondered, the Elite Guard Oath kept coming to her:

I will stand strong in the face of danger, for my comrades will do the same

She thought of her comrades in the Guard. Even though they had all been pawns in the First Families' betrayal of her people, her fellow Guardsmen and their willingness to die for each other was real.

I will be unafraid of death for death comes but once and cowardice is forever

I will go close against the enemy, for my will is stronger than his

I will show courage, for it is the one possession that cannot be taken

'*Courage,*' she thought. '*Courage is real.*'

I will die with pride, for I am fighting for my lineage and my people

I will face death with joy, for I will become immortal - my shining glory never forgotten

A smile came to Martin's face as she realized living her life according to the Oath had not been a waste. She had always fought for her people, not the leaders. All that had changed was the face of her enemy. As a wave of solace washed over her body, she began to drift off to sleep.

Her eyes had just closed as she was jarred awake by the sound of guards rushing down the passageway outside of her cell. Raising herself up, she saw two more guards run by. Martin stood and quickly made her way to the entrance. As she reached the cell door, she was met by Dan-Lee. She could see a controlled sense of urgency on his face.

"It's happening," he replied.

"Humani troops?" asked Martin as her heart began to beat faster with anticipation.

"Yes," he answered, unlocking the cell door. "Two battle groups just blasted through the security fleet and then jumped. No doubt toward here. Should be in orbit any minute."

Martin snatched the assault rifle Dan-Lee offered and grabbed two additional clips of ammunition. A subconscious smile came to her face as she gripped the weapon. "Where is he?" she asked.

"Across the compound in his lower chambers surrounded by his best priests."

"Let's go," she replied as she stepped out of the cell.

"We should wait until the attack —"

A metallic screech drowned out Dan-Lee.

"Down!" shouted Martin as she grabbed Dan-Lee and pulled him to the ground.

The screech grew louder until Martin felt as if it was coming from inside her head.

"What is that?" screamed Dan-Lee over ear-piercing noise.

Martin couldn't hear him but read his lips.

"That," she shouted, "is Astra Varus saying hello!"

The ground rumbled, and Martin felt herself lifted off the floor as the plasma ball from a Humani capital ship slammed into the surface nearby. Holding her hands over her head, she felt small pieces of rubble fall onto her back.

"What the hell?" said a shocked Dan-Lee.

"Never been on the receiving end of planetary bombardment?" asked Martin.

"No. The Guard likes to kill up close."

"We do," Martin replied with a smile. Another salvo landed nearby, shaking the building to its foundation. "Don't worry, it gets worse." She smiled as she pulled herself to her feet. "I think the attack has started."

"Follow me," replied Dan-Lee as he stood.

"Wait! Don't leave without me!" shouted Rebecca from her cell.

"Damn it!" said Martin, throwing her head back in frustration.

The ground rumbled from the far-off impact of another plasma ball.

Martin looked at Dan-Lee. "I guess we need to take her, too."

"Why?"

"She's important to the ProConsul ... probably more money if you return her."

"Fine!" shouted Dan-Lee as the screeching sound of another distant volley filled the air.

"Hurry!" shouted Martin, watching him walk to Rebecca's cell and open the door. Rushing out, she grabbed onto his arm.

"Thank you! Please get me out of here!"

"You've got to be kidding me," said Martin aloud as she walked over to Rebecca and pried her arms off of Dan-Lee. "Just stay behind us, keep your mouth shut, and do what you're told."

Rebecca nodded her head in agreement but shot Martin a scornful gaze.

"Look, bitch," replied Martin to Rebecca's gaze. "I'll just leave you here."

Another blast, this one closer, rocked the building and caused Rebecca to fall to her knees.

"Let's go," ordered Martin to Dan-Lee. "Lead the way."

"Time to make some money," he replied as he headed toward the exit.

"Best keep up, princess," said Martin to Rebecca before she turned to follow Dan-Lee.

Martin, with Rebecca in tow, followed the spy as he rushed down the hallways of the prison toward the exit. In a few seconds, Dan-Lee burst through the exit door and the bright light of morning and the sounds of chaos flooded Martin's senses. Running into the common area outside the prison, Martin saw followers and priests running in all different directions. To her left she saw priests handing out weapons to followers from an armory. To her right, she saw people, some still burning, crawling out of the smoldering rubble of a building destroyed by a plasma ball. In front of her she saw a mounted antiaircraft gun firing into the sky. A few meters away, Dan-Lee had taken cover behind a partially destroyed wall. She looked back to see Rebecca cowering at the exit to the prison. Another salvo of plasma hit a target in the distance, causing the ground to rumble and Rebecca to curl into a ball.

"Damn it," cursed Martin, stopping to retrieve Rebecca.

Just as Martin reached Rebecca, two guards burst from the same exit, almost trampling the terrified woman. Martin took aim on the run and fired a burst from her rifle. The two guards tumbled to the ground directly in front of Rebecca.

"Get up!" yelled Martin as she reached Rebecca.

Rebecca was frozen with fear and stared blankly at the two dead men in front her.

"Now!" shouted Martin as she pulled Rebecca to her feet.

"I can't go out there!" she shouted as another far explosion caused her to jump unexpectedly.

Martin raised her hand and slapped Rebecca across her face. "You either move or I'm leaving you. And I won't come back for you again."

Still shaking, Rebecca nodded her head in acknowledgment.

"Now, pretty please, move your ass," shouted Martin and she took off for Dan-Lee with Rebecca in tow.

Quickly covering the ground, Martin reached Dan-Lee and crouched down behind the wall next to him as Rebecca collapsed behind her. Shaking her head in frustration, she spoke. "Where next?"

"It's about a kilometer that way," shouted Dan-Lee over the chaos.

Suddenly the ground next to them exploded in rolling waves of earth and metal as a Humani attack craft strafed the common area.

Knocking the clumped dirt from her body, Martin looked to her right to see the anti-aircraft gun torn to pieces. She turned her gaze toward the sky to see it was dotted with inbound Humani attack and landing craft.

A Condor fighter soared overhead, its weapons rattling and spewing metal into a follower helo-craft hovering a few hundred meters off the ground. The helo exploded in a ball of flames and fell from the sky. The ground shook and a wave of heat from the secondary explosion passed over Martin as the helo slammed into the rubble of a nearby building.

"We should get moving then," she said. "It's gonna get hot down here real soon."

"Okay, let's go," replied Dan-Lee.

"I can't," shouted Rebecca as Martin turned toward her.

"Damn it! Move!" yelled Martin, grabbing for Rebecca.

Rebecca twisted away from her and scrambled to her feet as the thrusters from the initial wave of

Humani landing craft began to overwhelm the other noises of battle.

"I … I just can't. I don't want to die out here. I'm going back inside and waiting," rambled Rebecca, her voice barely audible over the roar of incoming landing craft.

"Don't," shouted Martin as Rebecca burst from her position and raced toward the prison entrance.

Running across the commons in her ragged dress, Rebecca tripped and fell to the ground. The deafening roar of the transport drew her attention and she looked upward and let out a scream that was cut short by the massive transport slamming into the ground, crushing her.

"Shit," said Martin as she witnessed the sudden end to her annoying companion. "That is not dying the right way," she said aloud, remembering their first conversation. As she contemplated the sudden and unheroic death of Rebecca Sterling, Martin saw a series of small metal portals fall in a circle around the landing craft.

"Move," she shouted as she grabbed for Dan-Lee and jumped to the other side of the wall.

"What?" he shouted.

"Run!" she yelled, turning to sprint away from the landing craft.

As she ran, Martin heard the tell-tale popping of small charges launching long strings of antipersonnel explosives in all directions around the landing craft to clear the perimeter before the troops exited.

"What are we running from?" shouted Dan-Lee, running stride for stride with Martin.

"PLICs!" she yelled. The loud thud of the anchor hitting the ground behind her only pushed her harder.

"Faster!" she shouted. She knew the system well and started counting. "Five … four … three … two … Down!" she yelled as she knocked Dan-Lee to the ground and curled her body into a tight ball.

The pressure wave rocked Martin's body, the wave of heat and debris felt like hot coals were pelting her. Rolling onto her back, she fought to catch her breath and shake the cobwebs from her head, the pain from the searing heat slowly dissipating. After a deep breath, she rolled onto her knees and picked up her rifle.

Martin shook Dan-Lee. "Get up!"

"What was that?" he stammered, grabbing his rifle and slowly standing up.

"Personnel Clearing Line Charge," she replied. "They just started using it for combat landings in close proximity to enemy troops. Pretty much levels everything within a hundred meters of the ship." Martin looked toward the landing ship and surveyed the damage. The wall they had taken cover behind was gone. And so was the front half of the prison. To her right what was left of dozens of followers were strewn in all directions. "They'll be coming now."

Martin watched as the transport doors flew open and troops rushed from the compartment and quickly fanned out. A follower burst from behind the rubble of the prison entrance wielding a large blade. A Humani soldier opened fire and the follower fell. Then another emerged only to be cut down in a hail of bullets from three soldiers. Suddenly, a wave of followers led by a priest scrambled over the rubble toward the transport.

Gunfire echoed against the crumbled structures as the entire platoon opened fire. The wave of followers pushed forward as the Humani fire cut them down like wheat. Only a few reached the Humani positions and they were quickly dispatched, except for the priest. The priest, already wounded, drove his sword into a Humani soldier and dropped another one with his pistol before concentrated fire tore into his body, killing him.

The priest's action had distracted the platoon, however, as Martin saw a single follower, probably no more than sixteen, rush behind the preoccupied soldiers and into the open doors of the transport. A second later, fire erupted from the personnel compartment and a Humani soldier ran from the inferno, his torso engulfed in flames. The soldier fell to his knees, screaming. Martin couldn't let him suffer any longer. She raised her rifle and fired a round into the soldier, ending his agony. "Let's move," she said as she turned toward Dan-Lee. "I'm following you."

Martin held her rifle at the ready as she and Dan-Lee made their way through the chaotic scene of the Humani assault. Hugging the nearby buildings, they had traveled a few minutes when Dan-Lee suddenly halted.

"What is it?" asked Martin as they took cover at the corner of a large brick building.

Before he could answer, Martin felt the rumble and heard the high-pitched whine of a Humani hover tank quickly approaching. She, along with Dan-Lee, quickly moved backward and away from the corner as the massive tank drifted into the intersection. Suddenly, an antitank round flashed down the street from behind Martin and slammed into the armored monster. An ear-piercing metallic *pang* echoed in Martin's head as the round, slowed by magnetically repulsive coils embedded in the tank's armor shell, impacted the triple over-layered armor.

"Get down!" she shouted, pulling Dan-Lee to the ground as the tank's turret rapidly swung toward the street behind her. Martin looked up from the ground as two heavy rotary guns swung outward from the turret. A wall of fire and metal blanketed the street and buildings above and behind Martin as both guns opened fire. She felt the casings of expended rounds from the guns hitting her body, the rattling *thud-thud-thud* of the guns mixed with the piercing whine of the tank's hover engines and the spinning of the gun's carriages. Suddenly everything around her was enveloped in a wave of heat and noise as the tank's one hundred fifty millimeter main gun fired. Her hearing temporarily reduced to a tonal ringing, she looked back toward the tank to see a wave of followers pour over the tank from the opposite direction. As they did, the turret quickly swung three hundred sixty degrees at full turn speed, tearing many of the followers in half. Next, a massive electrical pulse from the coils on the tank activated as an anti-boarding tactic and electrocuted any left alive just before the tank sped away.

Martin slowly rose to her feet. Around her lay the torn and distorted bodies of followers mixed with hundreds of empty casings from the tank's guns.

"It's just a little further," said Dan-Lee, pointing toward a tall building in the distance. "A few hundred yards to that brick building. There's an access on the west end which leads to a secret passage to the Saint's chamber."

Before Martin could answer, a massive nearby explosion almost knocked her to the ground. As she covered her head, glass from shattered window fell around them. "Shit," declared Martin as she shook her head to clear the ringing in her ears.

"The tank?" mused Dan-Lee.

Martin saw a cloud of dust and debris drifting from the location of the tank and sprinted toward the opposite side of the intersection. Stopping and kneeling at the corner, she peered down the barrel of her rifle. "Son of a bitch!" she said aloud when she saw the massive Humani tank burning. All around the tank lay the bodies of more followers. From what Martin could tell, the explosion had come from underneath the tank.

"I knew they would get it eventually," replied Dan-Lee as he reached Martin.

"They must've mined the street," she stated.

"Doubt it. More than likely they distracted the crew by trying to board it again while a few slid underneath it."

"Underneath?" Martin laughed in disbelief. "The heat and pressure from hover engines would have melted the flesh off of them," replied Martin. "They wouldn't have survived three seconds under there."

"Three seconds is enough," replied Dan-Lee. "And the heat alone would ignite most explosives."

Martin thought about the willingness of the followers to sacrifice themselves. "The Humani are going to regret this invasion."

"If they don't stop it here, this madness will spread throughout the Dark Zone. But maybe that's what it needs — a cleansing."

"What are you talking about?"

Martin could see the frustration on Dan-Lee's face as he responded. "You Humani have no idea what it's like to live on one of these planets. For most of us, life in the Dark Zone consists of hunger, fear, and oppression at the hands of warlords and psychopaths."

"Like the Phel?" shot back Martin. She had forgotten they were in the middle of an active battle. Her attention was drawn completely toward Dan-Lee. She could see his face grow flushed and his jaw clench tight with anger.

"You and your damned Elite Guard ... you're all murderers, yet you try to besmirch the Phelian order!" he shouted, stepping toward her.

Martin's blood pumped hard through her body. Her realization of the great lie about her civilization did not ease the sting of being called a murderer. "It's not hard to dirty the name of a forgotten race of mercenaries and assassins," she said, stepping forward as well.

"Humani trash!"

Martin leveled her rifle toward Dan-Lee's head. She could feel her emotions starting to derail her plan, but she didn't care. "Sad little orphan Phel. If your people were better fighters, you wouldn't be the last one."

Dan-Lee's amber eyes burned with anger as he stared, unafraid, into Martin's. "Maybe it is time we finished what we started in the cell."

Martin smiled. She had wanted this almost as much as getting at the Saint. "Sounds good to me," she replied. "But first, why is a Phel working for the Humani? And don't give me that money bullshit."

She saw his eyes show of mixture of rage and determination. She knew the feeling well.

"Revenge."

"What?" replied Martin.

A distant explosion echoed against the walls of the buildings and Dan-Lee started to lunge toward her.

"Whoa, there," she warned as she moved the rifle slightly to remind him she could fire at any second. She could see the frustration growing in her companion. "Why are you here?"

"Bitch," he mumbled under his breath. "I hoped that acting as a spy for the ProConsul would eventually get me onto Alpha Humani and near the ones that ordered the extinction of my people. When I heard a Paladin was captured, I figured I'd hitch myself to you and ensure a trip to Alpha Humani, where I will take the lives of everyone in the lineage of former ProConsul Denara Ragna, the one who ordered my people's death."

"So you're double-crossing them?" Martin felt a hint of respect start to grow for Dan-Lee where anger and frustration had been before. But she knew better than to take a man's word at face value. "And why are you telling me now ... other than the gun I have pointed at your head?"

"Your Elite Guard arrogance and Humani elitism are more than I can stomach. You people think everything is yours for the taking."

He was right. And she had been part of it all. She had to tell him the truth. Martin lowered her rifle slightly. "You don't understand —"

Martin glanced upward as a Humani hawk screamed overhead, firing its guns at a retreating Crucesignatis aircraft. She sensed Dan-Lee moving and looked back toward him, but he was too fast. Martin's rifle was knocked from her hands and a powerful kick to her chest sent her tumbling backwards.

Quickly recovering, Martin stood and twisted her body away from Dan-Lee's sword. "Wait!" she shouted as she grabbed his arm in an attempt to gain control of his sword. She strained against his impressive strength. "You don't have to do this!"

"Shut up!" replied Dan-Lee.

Martin's feet left the ground as Dan-Lee swept her legs. She grunted as she hit the hard, uneven ground but was able to deflect a downward thrust of his sword. Sensing Dan-Lee was off-balance, she brought her knee upwards into his ribcage and wrapped her arm around his neck. Squeezing tightly, she slid on top of Dan-Lee and put all of her weight into keeping his head pointed downward. "You've got to listen to me," she pleaded, knowing he wouldn't be able to talk with her arms around his neck. "I'm not your —" She felt him push upward and she spread her legs wide as she leaned over him, trying to maintain leverage. Grunting heavily and straining her body, Martin pushed hard on her opponent's shoulders and struggled to maintain her arms locked around his neck and head.

"I don't want to fight you!" she groaned as she tilted her head upward and arched her back to hold Dan-Lee in position. Martin's muscles spasmed as the stronger opponent continued to pull on her arm. Her grip slipped ever-so-slightly, and she quickly tried to recover, but her opponent was too quick and strong. Feeling Dan-Lee push forward as she lost her grip on his neck, Martin brought her knee up quickly toward his face but felt him block her attack and lift her into the air.

"I'm ... trying ... to ... talk," she grumbled, giving Dan-Lee four solid punches to the side of his head, causing him to stagger and throw her forward. When she hit the ground, Martin quickly rose to her feet and took up a defensive stance. "Will you stop for a minute?" she pleaded.

"What's wrong?" Dan-Lee smiled. "Too much for you? Your daddy isn't here to help you?" He rushed toward her.

His words tore into her like a knife and sent a spasm of rage through her body. She focused her anger on her target as he swung at her. Ducking below the first hard right hook, she rapidly landed a blow to his kidneys and brought her right foot against her opponent's right knee, forcing him to the ground. As he fell, she grabbed his right arm and, extending it, flung her leg over his body and drove his torso into the ground. Twisting with Dan-Lee's body, Martin landed with her back on the ground and her legs locked over his chest and neck with arm extended over her waist.

"Asshole!" she yelled, pulling hard on his wrist until she felt his elbow start to hyperextend. "You need to learn when to keep your mouth shut." Focusing on torqueing her body to put maximum pressure on Dan-Lee's elbow, she didn't feel him shift his torso toward her until it was too late. Martin felt her knees being pressed against her chest as he rolled on top of her. Unwilling to release her opponent's arm, she wrenched his wrist backward, causing him to let out a groan. Despite his pain, however, she felt his free hand grasp her uniform near her shoulder and again lift her into the air.

"Humani bitch!" he shouted.

Martin felt a rush of air followed by a bolt of pain in her side as he slammed her onto the ground. Before she could catch her breath, he brought his knee into her stomach. The air partially left her body and pain shot through her ribs as she rolled away and rose up to her knees. From her knees she looked up to see Dan-Lee step toward her and swing his right foot toward her head. Pain shot through her forearms as she blocked his kick, but she reacted quickly and grasped Dan-Lee's right leg with one arm and lifted his other off the ground, causing him to fall backward. As he fell, she gripped his shirt with both hands for leverage and jumped into the air, coming down with her right knee on his groin.

She heard him let out a groan as she pulled herself forward onto his body and slammed her fist into his nose, feeling the cartilage snap. "Stubborn prick!" She swung again.

Dan-Lee blocked the punch and pulled her downward, landing a punch of his own against her jaw. She felt her neck twist against the force of his punch but gripped Dan-Lee's torso with her legs like a rider on a bucking horse. She blocked his next punch and drove her head downward toward his nose only to feel a sharp pain in her right cheek as his left elbow crashed into her head and then wrapped around her neck.

"You're pissin' me off," grumbled Martin, spitting out blood and part of a tooth as she struggled to get her arm between her neck and Dan-Lee's chest. "I'm not ..." She grunted loudly as she shoved her arm through her attacker's tight grip, preventing him from locking in his choke hold. "I'm not your enemy. I don't —"

A blow to her ribs sent a bolt of pain through her body. Martin gritted her teeth and let out a growl against Dan-Lee's powerful grip. "Asshole," she grumbled through her blood-filled mouth as she reached for the medical pack in her pocket. She felt for the neuro-injector. When her hand found it, she flipped up the cover and rammed the injector against Dan-Lee's ribs. Martin heard him grunt and felt his body recoil against the injection, but his powerful arms still locked her body in his grasp. Reaching for another injector, she again stabbed the medicine into his ribcage followed by a series of punches. With the last punch, Dan-Lee's grip loosened and she quickly capitalized and pushed her body away from his, landing another blow to his right temple as she did.

Rolling off Dan-Lee, Martin jumped to her feet and into a fighting stance as her attacker did the same. A slight stumble told Martin the overdose of meds was doing the trick and had started to slow Dan-Lee's reflexes. Blocking a powerful but slightly off-balance right hand from Dan-Lee, she pivoted at her waist and crashed her right foot into his ribs followed by left hook to his face. Her target stumbled to his left and Martin attacked again, landing a spinning kick to his chest and knocking him to the ground.

Dan-Lee was back onto his knees when she swung another right foot toward his head. Still fighting, he blocked her kick and swung toward her midsection. Martin pivoted away from his punch and with a loud grunt, spun and crashed her left foot into the back of his head, sending him falling forward toward the ground, unconscious.

"Dick," said Martin, taking in a deep breath. Exhaling, she let her body settle from the waves of anger at Dan-Lee's comment about her father, satisfaction from a good fight, and — she hated to admit it — respect for the lengths he was willing to go through to exact his revenge. "Maybe next time," she said to the unconscious Dan-Lee with a smile as she reached down for her rifle.

Chapter 19

Martin peered around the corner across from the brick building. In the front of the building, the main commons area was covered with Crucesignatis troops and random followers preparing to defend the entrance with their lives. The tops of the building were dotted with troops as well. Then she saw it — an angled, padlocked door at the west end of the building surrounded by a dozen Crucesignatis and several priests. "Shit," she mouthed as she looked for a way to get into the building.

Suddenly, the air around the front of the building flashed bright and the commons area disappeared in a cataclysmic cauldron of fire, smoke, and debris. Martin took a quick breath then turned and curled her body as the blast wave hit her, knocking her off her feet. Gasping for breath, she rolled onto her back as the dust settled around her. Looking upward from her prone position, she saw an eagle bomber banking out of its bombing run.

Slowly regaining her feet, Martin again peered around the corner. The front quarter section of the building was gone, its bricks strewn around the commons area, along with dozens of mangled and charred bodies. She then looked toward the side access; the guards around the entrance remained dug in and ready to defend themselves.

Movement in the commons area again drew her attention. She looked on as one, then two, and suddenly dozens of Crucesignatis troops began to rise out of the destruction. *'Tunnels,'* Martin thought to herself.

"Don't move!" came an order from behind her.

'Shit,' she thought in frustration at allowing someone to sneak up on her.

"Drop the rifle and raise your hands!" commanded the voice.

Martin clenched her teeth tightly and inhaled heavily through her nose before letting her rifle fall to the ground. She slowly stood and turned to see four priests, each with a rifle pointed toward her.

A nearby explosion jarred her and the priests.

"You don't want to waste your time on little ole me —"

A hawk roared overhead, and a low boom resonated through Martin's body as the craft accelerated above the speed of sound.

"Besides, you've got bigger problems." She smiled as she glanced to her right and pointed her upraised hand in the direction of a squad of Elite Guard troops standing with weapons ready. As the priest started to turn, the Elite Guard troops opened fire, riddling the priests with bullets.

As the sound of gunfire died down, Martin picked up her rifle and looked back toward the Guardsmen. "Nice timing," she said.

"Paladin Martin?" she heard a familiar voice call her name.

"Lowstreet!" Martin smiled, recognizing the grizzled sergeant from her time in the Guard. "What the hell are you doing here?"

"The ProConsul's bidding, of course," replied Martin with a sarcastic tone, looking over the other Guardsmen. "Who's in command? Desro?"

"No. He's on special duty on Port Royal looking for Stone and that Terillian Scout Ranger."

"Stone's on Port Royal?"

"Yes, ma'am."

Martin now knew her next destination. She would find him and the truth on Port Royal.

"Sergeant!" shouted an Elite Guard lieutenant just reaching the group with another squad in tow. "What the hell are you doing with this inhabitant?"

"Sir, this is —"

"We've got a mission, Sergeant," interrupted the lieutenant.

Martin looked at his nametag. Braxus. *Figures.* "What's the problem, Lieutenant? Having trouble recognizing your superiors?"

She saw the surprise in the officer's eyes as he recognized her.

"Yes, Major ... I mean Paladin," he stammered. "I was not briefed —"

"Of course you weren't. It's above your pay grade."

"Yes, Paladin Martin," he replied with a salute.

Martin grabbed the lieutenant's hand. "Don't salute me in the field, dumbass," she ordered. "Are you trying to get me shot?" She then turned toward

Lowstreet and curled the right side of her mouth in disappointment.

Lowstreet turned his head away from the lieutenant. "F-N-G," he mouthed.

"I need some of your men," declared Martin. "I'll take Lowstreet's squad."

"Yes, of course, Paladin," replied the officer. "I'll turn command of the platoon over to Sergeant Hall and join you."

"No, Lieutenant, you won't," replied Martin. "Just Lowstreet and his men."

"But —"

"Thanks, LT," she interrupted. "But I will need your sword." She reached down toward the officer's belt and unhinged the sheath. She gave him a smile in response to his stunned, dumbstruck look as she took the proud officer's sword. "Thanks, kid," she added as she gave his shoulder a slap and turned back toward Lowstreet. "Ready, Lowstreet?"

"Yes, ma'am," replied Lowstreet with a smile.

"Good, gather your men —" Martin paused and turned toward the Lieutenant Braxus. "Oh ... you can continue with your mission, Lieutenant; we're good here," she said dismissively.

"Yes, ma'am. As you command." The lieutenant pouted as he turned toward the remainder of his platoon. "Move out!" he shouted, transitioning his anger at Martin's dismissive attitude toward his men.

Martin turned back toward Lowstreet. "We need to get at those bastards over there," she stated as she pointed toward the men guarding the access.

"Easy day," responded Lowstreet.

"That's what I like to hear. We need to occupy them with an enfilading fire on their left flank and provide direct fire from over there." She pointed toward a wrecked vehicle near a partially collapsed building. "We'll shift the base of fire slowly toward their left flank. Once they're engaged, I'll take two of your men and hit them hard from their right."

"Done," replied Lowstreet as he turned toward his men. "Fire team Alpha, you're gonna lay down some smoke and move into position by the building for direct fire. Li, Bradley, you two will follow me around their left flank and engage. Hamari and Dawes, follow Paladin Martin." Lowstreet paused and looked each Guardsmen in the eyes. "Questions?"

Martin instantly missed the Guard. She had dreamed of the day should could get back among her fellow warriors. But she knew too much.

"Good," said Lowstreet, as no one spoke. "Alpha, on my mark ... smoke away!" he ordered and two Guardsmen threw smoke grenades between themselves and the enemy troops at the access.

As the smoke grenades left the Guardsmen's' hands, Martin turned toward the two men assigned to her. "Let's go!" she shouted, rushing forward.

Martin and the two Guardsmen had covered a few meters when she heard gunfire erupt from Alpha fire team. The gunfire grew in volume as she rushed past a burning military truck and bodies of Crucesignatis soldiers and common followers. Her heart raced with the exhilarating rush of combat. As she reached a small fence, she placed her hand on the top and swung her body over in a fluid motion. Landing in a kneeling position with her rifle to her shoulder, she was followed immediately by the two Guardsmen. Two Condor fighters flashed overhead followed by the rumble of a sonic boom as she looked down the barrel of her rifle toward her goal.

Her tactic was working. Several of the defenders were already dead or injured by the heavy fire of the other Guardsmen. Five defenders remained, and they were fully occupied either taking cover or returning fire through the deluge. Martin squeezed tightly with her right hand and held her rifle to her shoulder as she motioned for the two men to move forward with her left. The first Guardsman sprinted toward a civilian vehicle riddled with bullets. He dropped to the ground by the vehicle and brought his rifle to his shoulder as the second man rushed past and knelt behind a tall, thick tree. Martin was on the move as soon as the first man took his position, alternating between the ground in front of her and the enemy troops, she quickly moved past the others and slid into place behind a concrete rubbish housing.

She couldn't help but smile. Martin and the two Guardsmen were in perfect position. *Nothing like working with professionals*, she thought. Without a comms link, Martin raised her hand to signal the other two to select their targets and to fire on her first round. With their acknowledgment, Martin rested her rifle on the edge of the concrete barrier.

She felt and timed her heartbeat.

She took in a slow controlled breath as she moved her finger to the trigger.

She centered her sights on her first target.

And fired.

The enemy soldier fell, and she quickly shifted to her second target as she heard her companion's fire. Taken completely by surprise, the enemy troops all fell before they realized they had been outflanked.

Martin saw a wounded soldier attempt to turn a weapon toward their position, but a burst of gunfire from the Guardsman to her left toppled him backward.

Martin rose to her feet and quickly moved toward the access. Slowing as she reached the position, Martin looked over the scene. The Guardsmen's fire had been devastating. Over a dozen enemy troops and several priests were spread around the access door. As she moved between the bodies checking for signs of life, she heard a low moan to her left. Martin looked down to see a Crustagenios soldier on his side, curled tightly into a ball. Placing her foot on the man's shoulder, she slowly rolled him onto his back.

The dying soldier's eyes met hers. Martin didn't see anguish or despair; instead the man's face was almost glowing in a smile.

"The Word transcends death. And the Saint is the Word," he said softly.

"Crazy son of a —" Martin saw the man's bloody hands open and a grenade roll from his grasp onto the ground. "— bitch!" She turned and dove over the opposite side of the battlement.

The concussion from the blast stunned Martin, and a sharp pain pierced her ears from the rapid pressure change. Still a little foggy from the explosion, she pulled herself to her feet and shook her head as she leaned against the battlement.

"You okay?" asked Lowstreet as he and the others reached her position.

"Uh … yeah," replied Martin with one more shake of her head.

She looked over the barrier. The already devastated area looked like the inside of a meat grinder.

"That one was close," stated Lowstreet.

Martin turned toward the sergeant. "Keep your guard up. These guys aren't afraid to die, especially if they can take out one of us."

"We've been mowing 'em down since we landed," replied Lowstreet. "But they keep coming. It's crazy."

"Faith," she replied as she looked upon the mangled body of a priest. Some of his tattoos were still visible through his hideous wounds. "We need to put them down and make sure they stay down, Lowstreet," she declared. "Keep shooting until you know they're dead."

"Yes, ma'am."

"Good," acknowledged Martin as she refocused. "Let's get this door open and find this Saint asshole."

"Done," replied Lowstreet as he motioned for his men. "Mitchell, Torres, access that door."

Martin watched the two men place a charge on the door as the rest of the squad stacked up along the wall adjacent to the access. Crouching down, she heard the loud *pop* of the breaching charge and rose to leap over the barrier. Swinging herself over the battlement, she fell in line as the squad entered the door and descended a small stairway.

"Contact front!" she heard, followed by a quick burst of gunfire.

"Contact right!" More gunfire.

Moving forward she quickly reached the center of a dimly lit room. Two Guardsmen covered a door at the opposite end of the room as the rest fanned around the space. Near the opposite door lay two Crustagenios troops. To the right lay a dead priest.

"Clear front!"

"Clear right!"

"Clear left!"

A powerful explosion from above shook the room and sent dust and debris raining down from the ceiling.

"Eagles and Hawks have been pounding the entrance. We need to keep moving," Martin declared, stepping behind one of the Guardsmen at the door and peering down a long passageway. Two doors were visible on each side with the opposite end obscured in darkness.

"Alpha clear right. Bravo clear left," she said, turning back to Lowstreet. "We'll cover forward."

Martin and Lowstreet moved into the long passageway with each of Lowstreet's fire teams hugging a wall behind them. Martin dropped to one knee as she passed the first door, keeping her focus on the darkness at the end of the passageway. She heard the doors behind her being kicked open and the rustle of footsteps as each team entered.

"Clear!" came from each room.

Martin was starting to rise when she saw a flash of metal in the distant darkness. Then another. "Contact forward!" she shouted and opened fire as a wall of followers poured from the darkness.

She felt the recoil and picked another target as the Guardsmen behind her opened fire as well. Peering down the barrel, the wave grew closer and she shifted her rifle to full automatic with a flick of her thumb. She matched the rhythm of the recoil with the selection of targets as the wave grew closer by the second. The onrush of flesh reminded her of waves crashing against a rocky shore in a turbulent crescendo a few meters from her position.

Martin dropped her rifle and drew her sword as the wave opened up and five priests pushed to the front of the wave, swords drawn. The first of the priests fell instantly, a round fired by a Guardsman behind Martin impacting with a thud in the center of his chest. The next swung his sword toward Martin's head. She quickly blocked the priest's attack with her sword. She felt the weight of the priest pushing down on his sword and quickly drew a pistol from her waist belt and fired two rounds into his chest, spinning to meet the next attacker. But he slammed into her before she could bring a weapon to bear. The impact of her head and shoulders against the nearby wall jarred her, but she reacted quickly and brought her knee into the attacker's face. Grabbing the man's cloak, she pulled his body erect and raised her pistol toward his head. She was about to pull the trigger when the pointed edge of Lowstreet's sergeant's rapier tore through the front of the man's chest. Martin looked over the man's shoulder to see Lowstreet tackled to the floor by two followers.

As Lowstreet fell, Martin shifted her balance and torqued her hips, slamming her foot into the ribs of one of the followers. The impact was solid as Martin heard the pop of the man's ribcage as several ribs broke. Spinning back to her left, she fired two more rounds into a follower a meter away and quickly looked for the next target. To her front lay a carpet of follower bodies two and three deep. Turning to her rear, Martin saw the bodies of the priests and a few followers scattered among the Guardsmen. She also took a quick inventory of the Guardsmen. One lay dead against the opposite wall with a priest's blade in his chest and the body of the priest lying over his legs. Another was being treated for a nasty wound to his left arm. The rest were unharmed.

"They just don't stop," replied Lowstreet, pushing the body of a follower off his chest and slowly rising to his feet.

"We've got to keep moving," she replied. "Are your men ready?"

Lowstreet turned toward the wounded Guardsman. "You good, Li?"

"Tip-top," grunted the wounded man even though his arm was torn almost to the bone from his elbow to shoulder.

"Good to know." Lowstreet smiled. "Then you can stay here with Bradley and watch our six. If we need to get out quick, we don't need anyone shutting the backdoor on us." Lowstreet looked toward Bradley, who returned a nod of acknowledgment.

Martin could tell the wounded man was frustrated but wouldn't dare challenge Lowstreet.

"Will do, Sarge," he answered.

"Outstanding," replied Lowstreet before turning back to Martin. "Let's get to it."

"Outstanding," repeated Martin as she felt the rumble of a series of explosions from above-ground. "On me."

Martin stepped onto the pile of followers they would have to cross to reach the opposite side of the hallway. She moved slowly with her rifle at the ready, gently placing each footstep on the carpet of human carnage in order to maintain her balance. The soft feel of the bodies as she made her way over the macabre carpet reminded her of the soft red moss on Sierra 7. Eventually the soft, grisly feel of mangled human flesh gave way to the hard stone flooring and she quickly moved a few meters to a large door at the end of the passageway. She looked back toward the Guardsmen; they were in position to face whatever was behind the door. Martin pressed a small green button on the access panel and the doors slid open with a metallic clang.

She shifted her balance to look inside.

Nothing.

"Well shit," exclaimed Lowstreet, stepping beside Martin.

The door had exposed an open lift shaft with no platform. Looking upward, Martin saw two detached cables that appeared to have been mechanically unlatched.

"Looks like they sent those followers up here and then cut the cables for the lift," stated Lowstreet.

Martin turned away from the opening. Her muscles tightened with frustration. She hated losing. After a deep contemplative breath, she turned back toward the opening of the elevator shaft. It appeared to extend several more floors before disappearing into darkness. "Somebody give me a light," she ordered.

"Ma'am," replied a Guardsman as he reached her a light.

She took the light and examined the walls of the shaft. Every 3 to 4 meters was a small ledge.

Suddenly, a massive explosion from above nearly caused Martin to lose her balance. Steadying herself, she turned back toward the opening. Chunks of metal, stone, and other materials knocked loose from the force of the explosion fell down the shaft, eventually disappearing into the darkness. Listening intently, Martin heard the debris impacting the floor of the shaft. "Two seconds," she said out loud. Quickly flashing back to the "mental gymnastics" class she hated as a cadet, Martin let the numbers run through her head, accounting for the planet's gravitational acceleration. "About 50 meters," she declared as she turned toward Lowstreet. "Do we have rappelling gear?"

"Mitchell, get your ass over here," ordered Lowstreet.

The tall, broad-shouldered Guardsman instantly appeared in front of Lowstreet.

"What rappelling gear do we have?"

"Not much, Sarge," he replied. "Most of it's all fucked up from the landing and that explosion that killed Nolan."

"Well, what do you have?"

"Twenty-five meters of line, a harness, and some hardware."

"Looks like we'll have to do this in chunks," replied Martin.

A burst of gunfire echoing down the passageway drew everyone's attention.

"Bradley, status?" ordered Lowstreet over his comms circuit.

"*Contact!*" came the response. "*Multiple —*"

More gunfire.

"Torres, Wilkes, go back 'em up," ordered Lowstreet as he turned toward Martin. "We need to hurry."

"Give me your gear, corporal," ordered Martin to Mitchell.

Martin quickly slung her rifle over her back and locked the rappelling harness into place around her waist.

"*Engaged with multiple targets. We can't hold them much longer*," came over the circuit.

"Shit!" replied Lowstreet. "Mitchell, you go with Paladin Martin. The rest of you with me."

He turned toward Martin. "We'll try to buy you enough time."

"Make 'em pay," replied Martin, knowing Lowstreet was sacrificing himself and his men for her mission.

"No doubt." Lowstreet smiled as he paused to give Martin a perfect salute as if on the parade ground and then turned toward the gunfire. "Move out!" he shouted.

As the rest of Guardsmen rushed toward their deaths, Martin and Mitchell stood at the edge of the shaft.

"We go a floor at a time," she directed, positioning herself for the first drop.

"Roger," replied Mitchell as the intensity of the gunfire behind them grew.

Martin turned her body and, with Mitchell anchoring her, quickly slid down to the next level. Balancing herself on the small platform no more than a third of a meter in length, Martin locked an anchor in place on a support beam. "You're up, Mitchell," she said looking up toward the access.

Suddenly an explosion in the hallway above caused the walls of the shaft to shudder and Martin to tighten her already white-knuckle grip on the support. "You good?" asked Martin to Mitchell. As she asked she realized there was no longer any gunfire.

"I'm —"

Mitchell's response was cut short by a burst from his rifle.

Suddenly the rope went slack and fell toward Martin.

"Go now!" shouted Mitchell.

Martin slid her rifle to the ready and looked up. As she did, she saw the body of a priest flash past her, followed by two Crustagenios soldiers. She shifted her body to see as much of the opening above as she could. She looked up to see Mitchell with his heels at the edge of the shaft. He quickly glanced down toward her.

"Go!" he shouted and turned to fire another burst from his rifle.

Martin checked her harness and pushed off toward the next ledge. As her feet made contact with the wall, she heard another burst from Mitchell's rifle and looked up just as a round tore into his chest spinning him around and knocking him to the ground.

His gaze met Martin's as he lay on his stomach. She could see the cold determination in his eyes. He still had some fight in him.

Martin watched as he pushed himself to his knees and reached for his knife and pistol. She pushed off again and slid another few meters down the shaft. As she drifted downward, she heard the *pop-pop-pop* of Mitchell's pistol and then a loud groan.

Martin looked up to see Mitchell and two followers falling toward her. Before she could react, one of the followers crashed into her shoulder and head and everything went dark.

Chapter 20

Martin's body jerked violently as consciousness returned with a flash. Instantly, pain shot through her shoulder and she sat up like a shot.

"Easy, Paladin Martin," she heard a man say in a soothing voice.

Martin felt a gentle hand on her undamaged shoulder and turned to see a Humani medic smiling back at her.

"Where am I?" she demanded, looking around what appeared to be a medical bay.

"You're on the battle cruiser *Crasius Renus*, and I am medic first class Braun, part of Admiral Haxius's private medical team."

A dull pain enveloped her side and back as she became more aware of her. "How long have I —"

"Not long, Paladin," replied the medic. "Just a few days. When we found you, you were in rough shape, so we had to keep you under to work on you."

"Any other Guardsmen?" she asked, hopeful some of them had survived.

"I'm afraid not, Paladin," answered the medic.

Martin shook her head in frustration. Lowstreet was a good soldier. All of them were good soldiers. And they had died for not just one but two lies. First, the complete fallacy that was their own history and then the new lie that was the Saint's Word. "The Saint?" she asked.

"Don't worry about him, Paladin. Our combat troops have taken the two largest cities and have killed over thirty thousand of his followers in just two days."

"Lambs to the slaughter," pondered Martin out loud. "What about the Saint?" she asked again.

"He has seen that the power and might of the Humani military is no match for his backward followers," answered the proud medic. "His shuttle docked only moments ago to discuss terms with General Mellius."

"What?" replied Martin. She let out a groan as she swung herself out of the bed.

"What are you doing, Paladin Martin?" asked the surprised medic. "You should rest."

"That bastard won't surrender," she interjected. "Something isn't right."

"I don't under —"

"Where are they meeting?" grumbled Martin. "And where are my damn clothes?"

"In the starboard main hangar," replied the medic. "And you have a new uniform in the locker over —"

"Call security and tell them to clear the hangar," ordered Martin, stepping into a pair of pants and letting out a slight grimace from the pain of her injuries. "Now!"

"Yes, Paladin," replied the startled medic as he turned and ran toward a communications panel on the opposite wall.

Martin grabbed her belt, with Lieutenant Braxus's sword still attached, and quickly locked it in place. Gripping her service weapon, she ejected the clip. "Full mag," she said to herself, slamming it back into place and racking a round into the chamber. She had just pulled her shirt from the locker when the medic shouted across the room.

"The security office said they needed confirmation of a threat before they interrupt the meeting."

"Assholes," grumbled Martin as she mechanically walked to the comms panel and pushed the medic out of the way. "Whoever the dumbass is in the security office, this is Paladin Martin. If you don't call an alert immediately, I'm gonna come down there and put my boot up your ass!"

Almost immediately, red lights began to pulse at the exits to the room and the ship's intercom crackled before the announcement.

"SECURITY ALERT, SECURITY ALERT, SECURITY ALERT IN STARBOARD MAIN HANGAR, AWAY ALL SECURITY FORCES, ALL NON-ESSENTIAL PERSONNEL EVACUATE STARBOARD MAIN HANGAR AND REPORT TO AUXILLIARY HANGER ALPHA. THIS IS NOT A DRILL."

"Morons," said Martin loudly, rushing toward the door, throwing her arm through one of her shirtsleeves as she went.

Once in the outside passageway, she pushed her arm through the other sleeve and started to latch her buttons as she ran. Near the end of the passageway Martin saw four members of the security team rush into the elevator. "Hold that elevator!" she shouted toward them as the doors started to close. The door slid full open again and Martin rushed inside.

"Give me your comms link," she ordered one of the guards as soon as she entered the elevator.

The guard was startled and slow to respond.

"Just ... here," grunted Martin, snatching the link from the man's chest. "Who's Mellius's security officer?"

"Ummv…" stumbled the guard.

"Name!" she shouted.

"Uhv… Captain Velari," stumbled one of the guards.

"Captain Velari of General Mellius's guard, this is Paladin Martin, over," said Martin into the comms link as the elevator descended toward the hangar.

She repeated the call.

As the seconds passed, Martin looked toward one of the guards. He was staring at her.

"What is it?" she growled.

"Uh, I'm sorry, Paladin," he replied meekly. "I just noticed your feet."

"My what?" asked Martin, ready to punch the guard. The cold hard sensation of the tile on her bare feet suddenly registered. "Boots are for pussies." She turned away from the guard. Once she was sure the others couldn't see her, she mouthed *shit*, with a quick shake of her head before she activated the comms link again.

"Captain Velari of General Mellius's guard, this is Paladin Martin, over."

"Paladin Martin, this is Velari. Why did you call away an alert?"

"Just get Mellius out of there and clear the area," she replied as the elevator doors slid open on the hangar level.

Martin burst from the elevator and rushed toward a stairwell leading toward the main deck of the hangar. Skipping several steps, she quickly descended the ladderway and activated the barrier door which opened into the main hangar. As the door slid open, Martin pulled her pistol and stepped inside. Ten meters away stood General Mellius, his security team, and other officers. A few meters beyond was an old transport, no doubt the Saint's.

"What is the meaning of this, Martin?" shouted Mellius, his face bright red with anger.

"Where is he?" replied Martin, walking toward Mellius.

As she continued, Captain Velari stepped forward to block Martin's path.

"General Mellius is not pleased that you have disrupted his acceptance of the Saint's surrender," he stated with his hand on his sidearm.

"I don't give a shit what the general is not pleased with," she replied. "It's a trap, Velari. This guy isn't going to surrender."

"Nonsense!" shouted Mellius from a few meters away. "He has gotten a taste of Humani might and had his fill."

"You arrogant jackass!"

"You will not talk to General Mellius in that tone!" shouted Velari as he grabbed Martin's arm tightly.

"I …" replied Martin, grasping the captain's hand and wrenching it away from her body. "… will do what I please." She drove her fist into Velari's throat.

The captain fell to the floor as Martin continued on. "Where is he?" she demanded.

"How dare you!" shouted Mellius as he and his other guards took a defensive stance.

"I'm a Paladin, you pompous dick." She smiled. "And I answer to no one except the ProConsul."

Martin heard the doors to the old transport open and spun to her left. From the transport stepped two priests.

"General," said Martin turning toward Mellius. "Don't be an idiot. Get out of here an —"

"Paladin Martin, what a surprise," came a smooth, booming voice from the transport.

Martin turned again to see the Saint step from hatch, followed by four more priests.

"Get back in that transport, asshole," she ordered.

"Looks like your time with my followers did little for your attitude," he replied, stopping at the bottom of the access ramp.

"Please excuse Paladin Martin," interrupted Mellius. "I am prepared to discuss —"

"Mellius, shut your damn mouth! He's not here to talk!"

"It seems you cause trouble everywhere you go." The Saint took another step toward Mellius.

Martin leveled her pistol toward the Saint. "Not one more step!"

The priests responded to Martin's move and drew their weapons. In response, the Humani guards drew their weapons.

"Everyone wait!" shouted Mellius. "This man is a guest under my flag."

Martin kept her focus on the Saint but spoke to Mellius. "If you'd actually took your fat ass down to the surface, you would know these assholes don't surrender."

"Very good." The Saint looked toward Martin. "So, you do understand us."

"I understand you're a fake and a lunatic, Tali Vena," answered Martin. "I know who you are."

Martin saw the Saint pause and slightly turn his head at the sound of his real name.

"You might know who I used to be, but therein lies the beauty, the pure, cleansing beauty of the Word, my young Paladin. We all used to be someone else. But the truth of the Word transforms everyone who opens their heart. I was chosen by the Word to be the physical embodiment of its teachings. From that glorious day, until my last," he paused to let a slow smile form around the edges of his mouth, "Tali Vena ceased to exist and the Saint was born. Even for a non-believer such as yourself, you know this is true."

"Shut up!" replied Martin.

"Now Paladin —"

Martin fired a round into the Saint's leg causing him to stumble but not fall. In response the priest leveled their weapons toward Martin.

"Hold your fire!" shouted the Saint with a booming voice that echoed across the hangar.

"I'll have you on charges!" shouted Mellius.

"Such palpable displays of Humani character," said the Saint, his grin thinly veiling the pain from the wound to his leg. "The arrogant General Mellius and his minions. All you can see is the glory of accepting my defeat and pleasing your precious ProConsul Astra Varus, herself just a vassal of the Xen Empire."

He turned toward Martin.

"And you, my fierce Paladin, are so full of the same violence your civilization has exerted on the people of the Dark Zone for generations in the name of civil order and stability." He paused. "Stability!" he shouted before letting out a deep laugh. "Your single planet. One planet," he said, presenting an outstretched finger to Martin, "has sown fear, distrust, chaos, and suffering in the hearts of countless millions on dozens of planets." He paused again. "For a lie!"

"Shut up or I'll put a bullet in your brain," warned Martin.

"Of course," he responded. "Answer truth with violence. But kill me if you like. When you do you'll see that death will beget the truth."

Martin wanted to pull the trigger. But she could tell the Saint wanted her to as well.

"General!" shouted Velari. "We have reports that ships are launching all across the sector from Echo 4's moon and both Echo 3 and 2."

"We are under attack!" declared Mellius.

"No sir," responded Velari. "The ships seem to be setting courses for planets scattered across the Dark Zone. Hundreds of ships, sir."

"To all carriers, launch aircraft to intercept," ordered Mellius.

"Sir, several have begun to jump," replied Velari.

"What have you done?" demanded Martin, raising her pistol toward the Saint again.

"The Humani have sown the seeds of suffering and death," he replied. Martin saw a euphoric glow slowly cover his face as he continued. "Now it is time for you to reap the harvest." He extended his arms toward the overhead of the hangar. "As my followers spread across the known worlds to plant the seed of the Word, I will fuel their growth with my own blood."

"Son of a bitch," said Martin aloud, realizing why the Saint had agreed to come to the ship.

Martin fired but a priest had stepped in front of the Saint and absorbed the round. Spun around by the shot, the priest outstretched his arms to cover the Saint's front as the five others mimicked his actions, forming a cocoon around their leader.

"Open fire!" shouted Martin as rounds fired into the cluster of priests.

The automatic weapons of General Mellius's guards joined in tearing apart the priests' bodies.

After a few violent seconds the echoes of gunfire died away. Martin let the clip fall from her pistol and inserted another as she walked toward the pile of human wreckage. When she reached the bodies, she looked for movement and saw none. Holding her pistol toward the center of the mass, she grabbed the arm of one of the dead priests and pulled him from the pile, exposing the Saint.

He was still alive but barely. She grabbed his arms, extended them above his head, and checked his hands for any objects. She heard him cough and raised her pistol to his forehead.

"Do it," he smiled as blood flowed from his mouth. "And let it be done."

Martin ignored the Saint's plea and grabbed his shirt, tearing it open. Just as she had thought, a vest of gel explosives was strapped to his chest.

"No martyrdom for you today," said Martin. "Today you just die."

"And in death I become the Word," he replied with a bloody grin.

Something was still wrong. She knew the Saint wanted to go out with a bang a little bigger than some automatic weapons. *'If he had failed, why was he so pleased,'* she wondered to herself. "What are you hiding?" she said as she started sifting through his clothing and the vest.

"What are you looking for?" asked Velari as he and the other guards reached Martin.

"Get the general out of here!" ordered Martin. "And don't —"

Martin paused as she saw a small wire running from the vest to a sensor embedded in the Saint's chest. "It's wired to his heart," she said aloud. She looked up toward the Saint's face. His expression was frozen; he was dying.

"Run!" she shouted as she sprung to her feet and rushed across the hangar. Focusing on the barrier door, she pushed her body as hard as she could.

Almost in reach of the barrier door, Martin's body was lifted off the ground and slammed into the door as the gel explosives detonated, sending a massive blast wave across the hanger. Her vision blurred temporarily as she impacted the deck after bouncing off the door.

She rolled onto her back and pain shot through her previously injured shoulder. Holding her shoulder, she scanned the hangar. The explosion had set a nearby fighter and maintenance truck on fire and destroyed the side of the Saint's transport that faced the blast. Looking through the thickening black smoke from the fires, Martin saw Mellius stumble toward her. She rose to her knees just in time for him to collapse next her. Martin rolled the general onto his back and checked for his vitals. He was dead.

Rising to her feet, Martin quickly exited the smoky hangar and rushed past the flood of security and damage control troops as she made her way through the ship to *Renus*'s operations center. Martin entered the room and made her way to Admiral Haxius, who was relaying orders to other ships in his task force.

"Any more reports of detonations?" he asked intently to his communications officer.

"Yes, sir," replied the officer. "Explosions on Echo 4 moon and Echo 2."

"And casualties?"

"Unknown, sir. We are having trouble with our comms and many units haven't responded."

"Damn it," cursed the admiral.

"Admiral Haxius," interrupted Martin.

"Paladin Martin," he answered as he stood from his command chair. "Were you in the hangar? How is Mellius?"

"He's dead," she replied.

"Damn it," replied Haxius turning back toward his comms officer. "Lieutenant Skylar, inform General Vaal on Echo 3 he is in command of ground forces."

"We don't have comms with Echo 3," replied the officer.

"Well, get them. And pass the word to all squadrons to prepare to support medical evac from all forward bases."

"What's the situation, Admiral?" asked Martin, looking over the status screens in the operations station.

"The status is chaos, Paladin. Close to a thousand small crafts launched from Echo 4's moon, Echo 2, and Echo 3. We took out a few, but most jumped. It looks like their initial trajectories were all across the Dark Zone."

"That'll be his followers spreading the damned Word throughout the Dark Zone."

"With what plan?" asked the admiral.

"Nothing good for the Humani," she replied.

"Sir," interrupted Lieutenant Skylar. "More detonations reported on Echo 2 and now Echo 3." The officer paused to receive another report. "General Vaal's command post was at the center of the last detonation."

Haxius slammed his fist against the command chair. "Damn it!" He turned back toward Martin. "We've had at least five nuclear detonations on or near our positions. They are immolating their own troops and people to get at us."

"You'd better get ready for more," replied Martin. "In your haste to destroy your puppet, you have unleashed a firestorm likely to burn entire systems."

"Puppet? What are you talking about?"

Martin realized Haxius probably had no idea about Astra's plan. "You need to get your forces back onboard now, Admiral. Or you won't have any left."

Martin watched as Haxius leaned over his chair and gritted his teeth. "Lieutenant," he ordered, "inform all ground forces I am taking tactical command. To all forces … commence withdraw."

"From where?" asked the lieutenant.

"Everywhere!" shouted Haxius.

As the operations center began to buzz with withdraw orders, Haxius fell back into his chair. "And what will you do now, Paladin?"

"I'll go to Port Royal and continue my mission, Admiral," she replied. "I'm gonna need one of your transports and some damned shoes."

***

From her hovercraft, Astra Varus overlooked the work on a massive battle cruiser. A subdued smile came to her face as she read the name, still in the process of being painted on the outer shell of the recently completed command suite. "*Dominotra Varus*," she whispered as she read the name. The thought of a battle cruiser named after her father sending a rain of metallic death onto a Xen home world caused her subtle smile to expand.

"The *Dominotra Varus* is coming along nicely, ProConsul," reported the Association engineer in charge of the project. "Initial construction should be complete within two Humani years with final testing a year longer."

"Very well," she replied. "And the others?"

"The *Varus* class cruisers are scheduled for completion at two per year starting with the *Dominotra* and *Octavius* in three years. With the completion of the additional yards here on Dolus, that will increase to four per year for the last five years of construction for a total of twenty-eight ships."

"And the orbital destroyers?"

"The *Vengeance* class ships are also on schedule with the *Vengeance*, *Reprisal*, and *Fury* currently under construction."

"Excellent. And the training facilities?"

"We ran into a delay with flooding when one of the support beams failed in a wing under construction for ground troop training and berthing. We lost about five hundred workers and a week of schedule —"

"And I am sure you have a plan to regain that week," interrupted Astra with a cold stare.

"Of course, ProConsul," answered the engineer quickly. "The schedule will be maintained."

"Of course it will." She smiled.

"ProConsul," interrupted General Vispa. "I have just received word from the *Vulara* in orbit.

"What is it?" she snapped, letting her displeasure with the interruption show.

"I am sorry, ProConsul, but we have received a high priority electron spin message from Admiral Haxius."

"Is it done?" she asked eagerly. "Is the Saint dead?"

"Yes, ProConsul. But —"

"But what?" she asked, uneasy.

"He feigned a meeting with General Mellius and detonated an explosive vest, killing himself, Mellius, and several of other officers."

"Idiot," mumbled Astra. "Is that all?"

"No, ProConsul. At the same time as his death, it appears hundreds of vessels launched from areas under his control and his forces detonated close to a dozen nuclear weapons on the surface of Echo system worlds. Early estimates are sixty percent losses for ground forces including all three brigadier generals and most of the colonels."

Astra inhaled slowly. "And the escaping ships?" she asked quietly, barely holding back her rage.

"Haxius doesn't believe they were escaping, ProConsul," replied Vispa cautiously. "He believes it was an attempt to spread this religion of the Word throughout the Dark Zone now that the Saint is martyred."

"Religion!" shouted Astra. "It's a set of damned phrases our intelligence corps and the Association came up with to trick the mindless populations into submission…" She paused to take in a deep breath to control her already boiling anger.

"Apparently it has worked all too well, ProConsul," replied Vispa.

Astra turned and slapped Vispa across the face, her anger exploding into a rage. "Thank you for the enlightenment. Now we're going to have to kiss more Doran ass in order to free up more of our troops to deal with this shit and keep the plan on schedule."

"I am sorry," replied Vispa as he rubbed his face and struggled to hold back his own anger. "What are your orders?"

"We return to Alpha Humana immediately. Send my uncle Zari Varus to take command of the remainder of the ground forces."

"Of course, ProConsul," replied Vispa. "And Haxius?"

"Tell Admiral Haxius to set every inhabitable centimeter of the Echo system ablaze. Nuke every city and bombard the rest with the orbital destroyers. Any population greater than ten thousand will be attacked and destroyed. Have him bring any survivors here for modification and training or forced labor. I want the Echo system void of life when he is done."

Chapter 21

"All clear." Stone watched the last Association guard disappear around the corner of a distant passageway. He turned away from his vantage point and leaned against the wall, resting the butt of his rifle on the floor.

"That was too close," said Katalya.

Letting his rifle lean against his thigh and chest, Stone exhaled slowly. Katalya was right—almost every day the patrols became more frequent and they had to move more often. In the three weeks since their escape from the docking bay, Stone, Katalya, Orion, and Rickover had been on the run in the underground and vent tunnels of Port Royal's market polis. And the time had taken its toll. Stone's head felt cloudy from the lack of sleep, his mouth was sticky from dehydration, and his stomach ached from hunger.

"We can't keep this up much longer," said Rickover, grasping his wounded arm.

"Can you make another run tonight?" asked Stone, turning toward Orion. Her knowledge of Port Royal and its nooks and crannies had provided them just enough food and water to stay alive, but with the patrols increasing and Orion's friends dwindling, resources had run dry.

But Orion didn't answer. She had fallen asleep.

"Orio —"

"Let her sleep," interrupted Katalya softly. "We can talk about that later."

Stone was nodding his head in agreement when he saw Orion awake with a jerk.

"Are they gone?" she whispered, shaking her head to wake herself. "I …" she paused, the exhaustion making it difficult for her to form the words. "I can do some foraging tonight. Maybe I can find some more half-eaten noodles and drainage water." She smiled.

'*At least she still has her sense of humor,*' thought Stone, although that is probably all she would actually find. He was impressed with the endurance and determination of the group but was afraid it wouldn't last much longer. A few more days and even Guardsmen would be close to the brink.

"Can't we just give up and try to bribe them or something?" asked Rickover, unafraid to speak his mind. "It would be better than dying in this wet, muggy shithole."

"They killed TC," growled Orion. "We're not talking about giving up."

"So we just die? That's a great plan," Rickover replied.

"You're a coward, Rickover," spat Orion.

"No, captain," he retorted. "Just realistic."

Stone saw Orion lunge toward Rickover, and he quickly grabbed her.

"Son of a bitch," she groaned. "Let me —"

"Everyone relax!" ordered Stone. Maybe they had reached the brink. He needed to redirect their frustrations and to make sure they were more afraid of being captured than starving, so he decided to tell them the truth.

He looked Rickover directly in the eyes.

"If we're captured," he said coldly, "you'll be turned over to a Humani intelligence officer, who will interrogate you in ways you wouldn't have thought imaginable. You'll talk and then they'll put a bullet in your head."

Stone released his hold on Orion and leaned back against the wall. "You two will face the same if you are lucky. If not, you will end up sold into a Dark Zone slave ring or sent to Capro Prison."

"I won't live like that again," replied Katalya. "I will … they won't capture me alive."

"And you?" asked Orion.

"Astra Varus will most likely have me nailed to wooden poles and slowly skinned in front of a public audience to show the penalty for treason. They'll make sure I stay alive until all of the skin is removed and then they'll leave me to die and rot as a warning to others."

"We've got to find a way out of here," said Rickover.

"*Hydra*'s locked down and we can't release the locking mechanism without the code or getting into the terminal control room. Either way we would have to fight through Association and Guard troops."

"Can we try Hanagus and Bianca?" asked Katalya. "Maybe we can get another ship to smuggle us out."

"It's too risky," replied Stone.

"They know I did business with them. They would probably be watching," added Orion.

"Do we have another option?" asked Katalya.

"Yeah," answered Rickover. "Starving down here or waiting around for capture and apparently horrible deaths."

Stone looked toward Orion. She knew Port Royal better than any of them.

"What chance do you think we have of getting word to them?" he asked.

"Very little," she replied. "But we don't have any if we stay down here."

Stone knew it was risky. Almost too risky, but they wouldn't last much longer in their condition. Stone saw Orion bite her lower lip and furrow her brow in thought. He looked toward the others. Katalya and Rickover would go along with any plan as long as they made it off Port Royal. After a few seconds, he saw Orion look up toward him.

"Let's do it."

"When?" asked Katalya.

"Tonight," answered Orion.

***

Stone sat in a far corner of Hanagus's bar scanning the room. The music was loud and the crowd lively as it had been in both of his previous visits. Through the dim lighting, punctuated by bright flashes of strobe lights timed to the rhythmic music, he saw Orion cautiously approach Bianca. Even though the den mother of Hanagus's house of sinful fun had always come through, there was something about her that always made him uneasy. Hopefully, Orion would negotiate a deal and they could get back to Katalya and Rickover, who were still hiding in the underground at a nearby maintenance access. They had stayed behind to limit the attention they drew and to allow Stone and Orion to be quick and efficient since Rickover was useless in clandestine operations and Katalya, while a skilled warrior, wasn't wired to play the spy.

Stone continued to watch Orion as she stood facing away from Bianca, who sat leaning over the bar as if she were talking to the bartender. He had been in difficult positions before, but this was one of the worst. If Hanagus and Bianca couldn't get them off Port Royal, they would have to do something more ... overt. In the end, one or two of them might make it, but not all of them. This plan had to work. After a few minutes, Stone saw Orion grab a drink from the bar and slowly walk toward him.

He continued to watch in his peripheral vision as Orion, smiling and shaking her hips to the music, walked toward him and with a quick glance and a smile, turned and headed to the restroom. Stone exhaled heavily as he held his drink to his mouth. It looked like the negotiations had been successful. Now he would wait for Orion to leave and after enough time passed to limit suspicion, meet up with her and the others.

"Hey honey," Stone heard a soft, sultry voice say as a tall, slender mocha-colored woman with radiant blue eyes and jet black, shoulder length hair sat next to him.

"Hello," he replied, trying to play the role but keep his lookout for Orion.

"You here all by yourself, honey?" she asked as she slowly rubbed her hand over his thigh.

"Just been waiting for the right girl," he replied with a smile while he quickly glanced across the bar for Orion.

"Oh, I'm no girl, honey," she replied, sliding her hand over his groin. "I'm a woman," she whispered as she let her warm breath drift across his cheek before giving him a soft kiss. "If you want a girl, you'll need to go to the Playground Bar a few blocks down."

"No," he said trying in vain to control his body's response to her touch. "I'm in the right place."

"Not yet, baby," she smiled. "But you're getting warmer."

Out of the corner of his eye he saw Orion exit the restroom and head quickly for the exit. He leaned in toward the girl's ear but kept his eye on Orion. "What's your name?" he asked.

"Mandi," she replied with a whisper in his opposite ear. "What's yours, honey?"

"Joss," said Stone.

"What do you do, Joss?" she replied.

"A little of this and some of that."

Pulling his head back slightly, Stone saw a man rise from the bar and follow Orion toward the exit. Something was wrong; he could feel it and focused on the man behind Orion. As Orion passed through the exit, the man motioned toward a group of three others at a table near the exit.

"Hey!" said Mandi, placing her hand on Stone's cheek and turning his head toward her. "Are you listening?" she said bluntly.

The three men rose from their table and joined the first as they exited the bar.

"Sorry, honey," said Stone as he turned his head away from Mandi. "I just realized I need to be somewhere. And besides, I'm out of money."

"Broke asshole," cursed Mandi. "If you can't pay then don't waste my time. But you need to give me something. I've got —"

"Sorry," interrupted Stone. He rose from the table, dropped a five credit chip, and headed toward the door.

"Cheap prick!" shouted the woman over the loud music, but he ignored her and picked up his pace.

Stone quickly moved across the floor toward the exit, weaving between dancing patrons and brushing drunks out of his way as he focused on the exit. Stepping outside, Stone noticed the abrupt change from the cool, smoky air and low roar of noise over the loud music to the warm, damp humidity and chaotic street noise of the polis. He quickly scanned the area and saw the last two men who were following Orion turn down a street to his right. As the two men disappeared, Stone drew his pistol and loped after them.

He reached the intersection and tilted his head around the corner, leaning against the wall with his pistol ready. He saw the men transition from a walk to a run and draw their weapons as they disappeared around another corner.

Stone sprinted across the street to the opposite corner. As he turned the corner he saw Orion, just a hundred meters from the access to the maintenance area where Katalya and Rickover were hiding, struggling with the men. Orion was no slouch in a fight; she knocked one of the men to the ground before she was overpowered by the other three. As soon as she hit the wet, dirty pavement, one of the men grabbed Orion by her hair and pulled her to her knees. Stone overheard the men as he quietly moved closer.

***

Orion strained against the force of the man holding her hair and pressing down on her shoulder. Her jaw still stinging, Orion looked up toward another bounty hunter standing above her. His scarred and wrinkled face was partially covered by a scraggly beard. A ragged smile of poorly kept teeth became visible when he smiled.

"Where are the others?" demanded the bearded man.

"Bend over and I'll show ya," replied Orion.

The man slapped her across the face.

"Where?"

"Screw you," replied Orion, spitting blood from her mouth. "You might as well kill —"

"Fine," interrupted the man as he drew his pistol and placed it on Orion's forehead. "One million credits in hand is better than four in the —"

The man was cut short as a round from Stone's pistol ripped through his skull. Another shot rang out and the grip on her hair and pressure on her shoulder disappeared. Orion grabbed the pistol on the ground and swung it toward a bounty hunter as he ran for cover. She felt the repetitive recoil as she fired several times at the running man. Her fourth shot found the mark and the man fell. Orion turned toward Stone as he rushed toward.

"Behind you!" he shouted.

Orion suddenly felt a blow to her hand and dropped the pistol. Before she could react, she was

323

spun around and her head was forced backward by her hair. The cold, hard edge of a knife pressed against her neck.

"Let me go or I'll cut her throat," she heard the man behind her warn as Stone moved toward her. His weapon was drawn and his gaze locked on the man behind her.

"Stop!" shouted the man. "Or I swear I —"

***

Stone fired and watched the man holding Orion tumble backward.

"You good?" he asked Orion.

"Y-yeah," she replied, still recovering from the suddenness of Stone's shot. "Thanks."

"We need to move," replied Stone. "If they reported us or someone called in the gunshots, this area will be crawling with Association security and Elite Guard in minutes."

Stone heard a noise behind Orion and raised his pistol. It was Katalya, with Rickover in tow.

"Everyone okay?" she asked. "I heard the gunfire and —"

"We're good, but let's get back underground," interrupted Stone as he and Orion started walking toward the others.

"Did we make contact?" asked Rickover.

"Yes," replied Orion. "We're supposed to be at dock A-354 at 0200 tonight."

"Unless we're compromised already," murmured Stone.

"Well, we don't have much of a choice," grumbled a frustrated Orion. "If we don't get off here, we're dead."

As the group neared the access, Stone scanned the area for threats.

It was clear. Too clear. There should have at least been a few drunks stumbling around. "We need to get underground now," he said. "Something's wrong."

"It's shut," said Katalya as they reached the access. "We left it propped open."

"Where's the prop?" asked Rickover. "I put it here when we left."

"Then why is it over here?" asked a frustrated Katalya pointing to a metal bar about a meter from the access.

"Rickover, get that damn door open," ordered Orion.

Stone's gut was burning. "Katalya, you cover the right. Orion, you take the left and I'll cover forward while Rickover gets it open."

Katalya acknowledged and took cover behind a metallic power distribution box as Orion positioned herself next to row of dumpsters. Stone knelt and turned back toward Rickover. "And hurry. I don't think we're alone."

"What do you —"

A metallic *clang* drew Stone's attention. Looking to the ground he saw a grenade with yellow and green lining. Two more soon landed nearby.

"Gas!" he shouted. "Everyone move left!"

Stone looked for a target, but none had shown themselves. Quickly moving to Orion's position, he knelt beside her. "We've got — got to move —" Stone coughed as the gas started to burn his throat and cloud his thoughts. "— clear."

Orion nodded in acknowledgment and started to move forward when a single shot impacted her leg and knocked her to the ground.

"Get — get the others," coughed Orion, dragging herself back toward cover.

Stone turned back to see Rickover stumble clear of the smoke.

"Get down," he shouted. But the warning was unnecessary as the gas overcame him and he fell unconscious.

"Shit!" He moved toward Rickover, his own senses starting to fail.

Struggling to reach Rickover, Stone grabbed his arm and started to drag the unconscious engineer. He coughed and struggled to remain focused as bullets impacted all around him.

Suddenly, the burden of Rickover's body lessened and he looked to see Katalya across from him, holding Rickover's other arm.

"Let's —" She coughed heavily. "Let's go."

Stone saw a body emerge from the smoke behind Katalya. It was a Guardsman wearing a gas mask.

"Behind —"

Before Stone could get out his warning, Katalya sensed the movement and turned just in time for the Guardsmen to crash into her body, sending the two tumbling into the smoke.

With Katalya no longer assisting and the gas taking its toll, Stone dropped to his knees. Looking up, he saw another Guardsman above him. The Guardsman swung his leg toward Stone's head, but he raised his arm to block and then grab the attacker's leg. Once he had control of the leg, Stone reached forward pulled the attacker's other foot off the ground causing him to fall backward. Stone pulled himself up the man's body and quickly pulled the mask off his face, followed by a punch to the jaw.

Rolling off the Guardsman, Stone pulled the mask over his face. He was taking a deep breath when he saw a flash of movement to his right. Still suffering from the gas, he turned to see another Guardsman rushing toward him. Quickly — as quickly as his body would let him — he pushed himself off the ground and prepared for the next attacker.

Out of the haze of the smoke and Stone's cloudy vision, he saw a flash of red hair in a ponytail.

"Emily!" he shouted but his voice was muffled by the mask.

She was on him quickly.

He raised his arm to block a punch from Martin, but a bolt of pain radiated in his ribs as she countered with a knee, causing him to stagger slightly to the right. Through his mask Stone saw Martin pivot in preparation to send her left foot against his knee. He raised his leg to block the kick but in his weakened state he couldn't react to Martin's right hand as it crashed against the side of his head. Dazed, he felt his head snap to the right against the power of her punch and he fell to one knee. Before he could stand, Martin grabbed his mask and ripped it from his face. The smoke instantly burned his throat and forced him to close his eyes. In the burning darkness, he heard a muffled growl through Martin's mask and then felt the jolt of a boot to the side of head as darkness enveloped him.

***

Stone's head ached and his throat and nose radiated pain from the gas as he slowly came to.

Through his blurred vision, he saw Orion and Katalya sitting across from him, handcuffed and restrained. As he regained his senses, he realized he was also bound. He scanned the compartment. Two Elite Guard soldiers stood at both ends of the compartment. Looking more closely, he noticed the familiar layout and modifications of the transport. They were on *Hydra*.

"So were gonna ride our own ship to our death," he heard Rickover mumble. "Perfect."

He turned to see the engineer next to him, then tilted his head backward and pressed against the headrest as he inhaled heavily. Maybe it was going to be crucifixion for him after all. *'At least Mori made it.'* But as he looked across to the frustration on Orion's face and the anxiousness on Katalya's, it was little consolation.

"You're one hard son of bitch to track down," came a familiar voice.

Stone looked to see Martin enter the compartment.

"Humani bitch!" cursed Orion.

"Easy there, Ter." Martin smiled. "It would just be a shame if you were to die before you meet ProConsul Varus. She has been looking forward to meeting all of you."

"Astra is alive!" blurted Stone. "I saw her ..." He looked toward Orion. He could see her frustration turn to anxiousness.

"Oh, she's alive, Traitor. No thanks to your Terillian whore putting a bullet in her brain," said Martin as she leaned in toward Stone. "Seems like she managed to slither away, but don't worry, I'll find her."

Stone's mind raced. Astra was alive. And Mori, not Orion, had shot her.

"And your son's alive too," added Martin.

"Son?" Stone's head grew heavy. There was no way ... then he remembered the night she had woke him in his sleep. The night before everything changed. "No!" he shouted. If it was true, the thought of his own flesh and blood growing up under the guidance of Astra Varus — he instantly grew sick. His head spun and he wanted to close his eyes. "Why would you say this?"

"I'm not the deceiver!" Martin shouted. "You're the one that turned on your people. On your son!" she added as Stone felt the burning sting of her open hand across his cheek.

The slap brought him out of the confusion. "Emily, you know me," he pleaded. "You don't understand. We — all of us — have been lied to. The First —" His head recoiled from a powerful blow to his jaw.

"You abandoned your people and I'll personally drive the first stake into your hand when you are crucified."

"But you —"

He felt another blow from Martin, one so powerful he almost lost consciousness.

"If you try to talk to me again —" Martin paused and pulled a knife from her vest. "I'll cut your damn traitorous tongue out myself."

The blood began to pool in his mouth and his heart sank into his stomach.

"Corporal!" shouted Martin. "Did that damn engineer get this bucket's systems up and running?"

"Yes, Paladin Martin," replied the corporal.

"Excellent, time for everyone to go."

"Everyone?" asked the sergeant of the Guardsmen in the compartment. "I thought we —"

"No thanks," replied Martin. "You guys can head back to Desro and get back to your real mission. I'll deliver these packages to the ProConsul ..." She turned again toward Stone. "... for unwrapping."

"And the engineer?"

"He can go too," added Martin. "The reactor is up so I don't need him."

"Yes, Paladin," replied the sergeant as he stepped toward Martin. "Paladin," he whispered just loud enough for Stone to hear. "It might not be my place, but are they even going to make it Alpha Humana?"

"It isn't your place," replied Martin. "And I haven't decided yet."

"Yes, ma'am," he replied with a salute before turning to his men and ordering them out.

***

The rumble of *Hydra* as it cleared the atmosphere and gravitational pull of Port Royal resonated through Stone's body.

His eventual torture and death were far from his thoughts as he feared for a galaxy where Astra Varus was the Humani ProConsul — one where she raised his son. And he struggled to understand why the secrecy about who shot her.

"Why?" he asked, looking across to Orion.

"What?" she asked.

He could tell she knew what he was talking about. He stared into her eyes.

"Why?"

"Stone, you need to understand —"

Orion stopped mid-sentence as Martin stepped into the compartment. Stone watched as she walked toward him. After a long stare, she leaned over and undid his cuffs but left the bindings in place.

"Now that we're set on course," she said, "it's time we, uh, talked." She pulled her knife and leaned in close to Stone's face.

His heart started to race. If this was it, at least it would be Martin. The warmth of Martin's breath on his face and the pressure of her knife against his throat caused him to close his eyes.

"I'm going to ask this once and if your people — if I — mean anything to you, it better be the truth."

Stone nodded his head. "I've never lied to you."

"Did you know?" she growled through her teeth as Stone saw a tear quickly roll down her cheek. "Did you know about the Xen and their deal with the First Families?"

She knew! Stone's eyes opened wide and a flash of relief exploded through his body. The words exploded from him. "I didn't find out until after Juliet 3. Mori, the Ranger, told me when we were stranded in the November system and then Cataline and Astra confirmed it. After that I couldn't … I just didn't know —"

"And that's why you left … with her?"

"Yes. I needed to find a way to help but didn't know how."

"So you turned to the Ters instead of your own people?" she asked angrily.

"I thought you were dead. And Jackson … I didn't have anyone else to trust."

"Well," she said as she stood erect and took a step backward. "I'm alive. After Jacks —" She paused and exhaled heavily. "After lying in the mud and dirt and blood in Juliet 3, I crawled my way out and came back to my people ... our people."

"I —"

"Our people!" she shouted. "Not these Ters." She waved her knife in the direction of Orion and Katalya.

"We're right here, ya know," said Orion, tired of Martin's derogatory comments.

"You shut your damn mouth," ordered Martin, pointing the tip of her blade toward Orion. "I don't know you and if you hadn't figured it out, killing Ters is kinda my thing."

"You have to believe me," interrupted Stone. "I want what's best for our people. The Terillians have only been defending themselves against the Xen — against us — for generations. The best way to help our people is to work with them and find a way to bring an end to this war."

"Us? Our people?" asked Orion in Akota so Martin would not understand. "Do not forget the truth ... *You* are Akota."

Stone could see the anger in Orion's face. He knew the truth and felt his vision had helped ease his transition, but Martin's presence brought a rush of old feelings back.

"That'll be enough," said Martin as she turned toward Orion, "or we'll see how well you spit your gibberish with a few teeth missing. As for you," she continued, turning back toward Stone, "it's interesting your first thought was to abandon your people."

Looking into her eyes, Stone knew that what she really meant was *your first thought was to abandon me*. "I just want to do the honorable thing," he confessed. He didn't know what else to say. And it was the truth.

"Of course you do," replied Martin as she cut Stone's bindings. "But did you ever think instead of running away to the Ters, we could, just maybe, bring this war home to our people so they can see the truth themselves?"

Stone struggled for the words. The collision of his new Akota life with the best of his old Humani one had his emotions in turmoil. Trying to reconcile the two and understand the deception regarding Astra and the news he had a son drained him. He could only stare blankly toward Martin.

"But for now," continued Martin. "I'm with you." She turned toward Orion and Katalya. "And I guess that means them, too." She released Rickover from his restraints. "What do you do?"

"I'm the one that keeps this bucket flying," he responded. "And unless you're planning on shooting me, I'm gonna go see what those apes did to my engine room."

Martin nodded her head and Rickover turned and rushed toward *Hydra*'s engineering spaces.

"That guy's odd," stated Martin with a glance toward Stone.

"But brilliant," replied Stone, still unsure of what to do or say after the sudden turn of events.

"Hmm." She turned toward Orion. "You must be Orion, the pilot."

"I must be," replied Orion coldly. "And you must be a Hanmani murderer."

Stone's heart skipped. "Orion, wait," he interjected.

"Let her talk," replied Martin as she presented her palm to Stone. "Let's hear it, pumpkin," she said to Orion. "But remember, I'm the one that got you off Port Royal. Oh, and if you call me Hanmani one more time, I'm gonna knock your Ter teeth out. I am Humani."

"Do you expect me to just pretend hundreds of years of murder and aggression by your people just evaporate because you, what, changed your mind?"

"No," growled Martin, slamming her hand against the bulkhead above Orion's head. "I want you to remember all of it. And remember that I have killed Ters —" She paused. "A lot of them, in the name of the Humani and the Xen." Martin leaned into Orion's face. "But then also remember when I found out the truth I risked my life to save your Ter ass."

"Or to infiltrate our side," responded Orion. "It's pretty convenient."

"Convenient." Martin laughed. "You little —"

"Wait," interrupted Stone. He looked toward Orion. "I would trust her with my life. She would never deceive me."

He could tell Orion understood the jab, but she continued.

"Well that's just great for you," replied Orion as she leaned over to look around Martin. "I might need a little more."

Stone saw Orion lean back into her seat, look up toward Martin, and smile. '*What is she gonna say next?*' he wondered.

"And don't call me a fucking Ter, you savage. I'm a Terillian, at least to you — if you can pronounce a word that big."

"So, these are your new friends?" Martin asked turning toward Stone.

"We've all been through a lot," he said, trying to ease the tension that hung in the compartment.

"Don't worry, sir —" Martin paused. She had called him sir out of habit. Stone could see the frustration in her face. She was just as emotionally torn over everything as the rest of them, she just wasn't going to show it.

"Don't worry," she continued. "I'll play nice if they do." She turned back toward Orion and spoke in perfect Terillian. "That is if this Terillian can refrain from calling this Humani savage a Hanmani."

Stone could see the surprise on Orion's face. How would she have known one of Martin's many skills was a near fluency in standard Terillian Confederation language?

"Fine," replied Orion with a flat look on her face.

"Glad you're willing to agree to stop insulting the person about to free you," said Martin as she released Orion's restraints. "You're welcome," she added when Orion stood.

The two women stared at one another for what Stone thought was an hour.

"May I check on *my* ship?" asked Orion flatly.

"Feel free," retorted Martin. "Since I just freed you."

The two stared at each other for another very long second before Orion gave Martin a derisive smile and turned toward *Hydra*'s controls. As Orion disappeared through the compartment door, Martin stepped in front of Katalya.

"And this one. What's your story?"

"Emily," interrupted Stone, placing a hand on her shoulder. "Just let her go."

"No!" shouted Martin quickly as she spun around.

Startled by her response, Stone felt Martin push his hand off her shoulder. For a tense moment she stared into his eyes before stepping close to him.

"You don't get to call me that, or act like everything is back to the way it used to be," she said through her teeth. "Not yet."

"But —"

"Damn it, sir." She stopped him. "I can't ..." She took another deep breath. "Just prove to me you're worth this."

Stone knew Martin well enough to know it was going to be a long time before he and Martin were back to the way they were before, if that was even possible. "Understood," he replied. "Her name is Katalya. She is Mori's, the woman that I ... I'm with. She's her sister."

"Hmm. And her ears and teeth?"

"Why don't you just ask me?" grumbled Katalya.

Martin motioned for Katalya to continue.

"I, and my people, are the bastard children of the Xen's attempt to genetically alter their slaves."

"So you're from Dolus?"

"Dolus?" replied a confused Katalya. "Venato."

Stone tried to clarify. "They were on Venato before we destroyed their base a year ago."

"Well, I don't know anything about that, but a little red-headed canary from the Association told me Astra Varus is building an army of genetically altered soldiers underneath Dolus. Then a transport landed on her and squish, no more canary."

"Astra's doing what?"

"Some master plan to take out the Ters ... Terillians and then eventually go after the Dorans and Xen too."

"She's insane," replied Stone.

"Hey, she was your fiancée."

"Was. Now I'm ... anyway, we need to get to Hotel and get this information to the others."

"Then I guess that's where we're going," replied Martin.

***

Stone entered the cockpit as Orion and Martin, the latter acting as the navigator, set up *Hydra* for a jump to the Hotel System.

"You seem to know what you're doing," said Martin to Orion, "for a Ter."

"First, I'm Akota, you Humani ape. And second, I'm the best pilot you're ever gonna see."

"I don't know what the hell an Akota is, but you are good. Even a Humani ape can see that."

"Smartass bitch," replied Orion in Akota, with a smile.

Martin returned the smile. "More gibberish." She looked back toward him. "To meet up with the —"

"Mori," said Stone. "Her name is Mori."

"Fine. Mori," huffed Martin. "And I'm guessing that a-hole with the tomahawks is there too."

"Thay."

"Hmm." Martin smiled. "Bet they're gonna love seeing me again."

"Don't think love's the right word," said Orion.

"Well, this is gonna be exciting," replied Martin.

"We'll need to figure out how to do this," warned Stone. "I don't think anyone is prepared for more surprises."

Chapter 22

Stone's heart raced as he stood at *Hydra*'s access after she landed onboard the Akota carrier, *Moon Harvest*. His excitement at seeing Mori again was tempered by the fear of both her and Thay's reactions to Martin. And there was Orion's and Mori's deception about Astra. '*Why didn't she admit it?*' He was so wrapped up in his thoughts he failed to move when the door opened. Across from the gangway stood Mori, with Thay and Magnus in the background, but he stood firm. Suddenly, he felt the brush of Katalya rushing past him and across the gangway. Stone watched as Magnus stepped forward and she leapt into his arms. He also watched as Mori placed her hand on her sister's hair before turning toward him. A huge smile was on her face and her incredible green eyes were bright as stars.

Move! he told his legs, but they didn't respond.

Mori began walking toward him. Finally, as if awakening from a deep sleep, his muscles responded and he stepped toward. As they neared each other, the powerful mixture of yearning and trepidation was almost crippling and he slowed his pace. Focusing on her eyes and the thought of her comforting embrace, he again started to pick up his pace.

Suddenly he saw her expression turn from one of happiness to confusion and then rage in an instant as she drew her pistol.

"You!" she shouted as Stone saw Thay pull a tomahawk from his waist and rush toward him.

Martin had emerged from *Hydra*'s access.

"Wait!" shouted Stone as he outstretched his hands toward Mori and Thay.

"Get out of the way!" shouted Mori angrily. "What is she —"

"Stop!" continued Stone. "She helped —"

"She killed my brother!" shouted Thay, rushing past Mori toward Martin.

As Thay neared, Stone stepped in front of him.

"Move!" shouted Thay as he put his hand to Stone's chest to push him aside.

Stone could see the hatred emanating from Thay's eyes and coursing through his entire body.

"Just wait!" pleaded Stone as he shifted his body to remain in front of Thay.

"Don't make me go through —"

Frustrated, Stone shoved Thay backward and drew his sword. "Everyone just stop!" he shouted.

"Let 'em pass," he heard Martin say confidently.

"What are you doing?" demanded Mori as she stepped closer, her pistol still pointing toward Martin. "What have you done?"

"So, you pause when our life is in danger," growled Thay, "but don't hesitate for this murderess?"

"Everyone just shut up!" growled Stone, dropping his sword. "I'm not fighting anyone … no one is fighting anyone. Just let me talk," he pleaded as he looked toward the furious Thay and the confused and frustrated Mori.

"Why is this animal with you?" replied Mori.

"Animal?" laughed Martin.

Stone quickly turned toward Martin. "For once, Emily, please just keep your mouth shut for a minute."

"Fine," grunted Martin through her teeth. "But —"

"Quiet!" interrupted Stone before turning back toward Thay and Mori. "She has found out the truth, just like I did, and helped us escape Port Royal."

"She did," agreed Orion as she stepped onto the gangway beside Martin. "I don't know what she's up to, but she did get us off Port Royal."

Relieved Orion had spoken, Stone continued. "She has joined us."

"Whooaa," interrupted Martin again. "I haven't joined anything. I came for you, sir, and these Ters ... these Terillians just happened to be there."

"He is one of us now," spat Mori as she slowly holstered her pistol. "So if you have come for him, you're going to be disappointed."

"Perhaps she has come for death," added Thay, gripping his tomahawk tightly.

"Let's go then!" taunted Martin. "Prove that you are the savages I know you to be."

"Savages!" shouted Mori as she stepped closer. "You have the audacity to challenge us onboard our own ship."

Martin smiled. "It's not a challenge, pumpkin. No challenge at all. This one," she continued as she pointed toward Thay, "nearly drowned himself trying to kill me and you, sweetheart, had to blow up the whole building you were in to keep me from killing you ... how did that work out for ya?"

"I don't know, how's that leg and elbow working out for you?" replied Mori, returning a satisfied smile.

"Why don't you come find out?" teased Martin, drawing her sword.

"Damn it!" shouted Stone as he drew his pistol and fired a round into the overhead of the hangar. The sound of the blast and the ricochet of his bullet was still echoing through the massive compartment as he continued. "Martin, stand down and shut up!" he ordered as if she was still a young lieutenant. To his surprise, she lowered her sword. He then turned toward Mori. "Mori, do you trust me?"

"Yes," she replied flatly. "But —"

"Good," he interrupted. "If you truly trust me, then you trust her."

He could see the anguish and frustration on her face.

"But she —"

"*She*," said Stone before Mori could finish, "has never deceived me."

Looking into Mori's eyes, Stone could see she was beginning to understand the statement went beyond the current situation. Slowly, he could see Mori's body start to relax. He then turned toward Thay. Stone could see that Thay's breathing was labored from the anger that still flowed through him. His chest was heaving in and out and his gaze was locked on Martin. "Thay, I know your need to avenge your brother is real, but don't forget your dream. Would you have been given the vision if fate was going to deliver her to you?"

"But the one that took his life is right here!"

"Maybe you had the dream because this was going to happen. You have been released from your mourning and now you meet again. Perhaps it isn't to be as enemies." Stone could tell Thay began to consider his words. "And how many brothers have you killed?" he asked calmly. "I've killed my share ... we all have."

As Thay stood silent in contemplation, Stone looked back toward Martin. He saw her return his gaze. She had been silent too long, especially for her. He hoped she would say what needed to be said.

"I have killed," stated Martin. "I have killed dozens, probably hundreds and have done so proudly for my people." She paused to sheath her sword slowly and step toward the others. "But I now know I was killing for a lie." She stopped less than a meter from Thay.

Stone's body tensed as the two warriors stared at each other.

"You can blame me," continued Martin. "I have been an instrument of death for the Xen and Humani leaders. Or you can let me help you fight the real murderers."

Stone's gaze was locked onto Thay's face. He knew Thay's hatred for the Humani was strong and his desire for revenge was still palpable, regardless of his vision.

Thay spoke grudgingly. "For now, Red Wolf."

Martin stepped closer to Thay, her eyes still locked on his. "I believe this is yours," she said as she presented a tomahawk from behind her waistbelt. "I thought I would be returning this to you in a very different way, but here."

Thay snatched the tomahawk from Martin's hand and without a word turned toward Stone. "You still have a lot to prove," he said. "And she is still a stranger."

Stone nodded in acceptance. He was just happy no one was trying to kill anyone else. He turned back toward Mori and waited for her approval. After a short, awkward silence, she spoke.

"Fine," she conceded. "But she is your responsibility."

"Of course," responded Stone.

"And she doesn't go anywhere without a guard." Mori paused again and turned toward Martin. "Without three guards."

"Fine," grunted Martin, giving Mori a sarcastic smile. "Thank you for your hospitality."

"Hmm," said Martin as she turned back toward Stone. "We don't have time for any more of this. We have a briefing in fifteen minutes about the information we gained from the Association."

"Dolus?" asked Stone.

"How did you know?"

"From me, the one you don't trust," interjected Martin.

Stone saw Mori's head snap back toward the direction of Martin. "So, you knew?"

"Just found out," replied Martin. "Found out the same time I learned of the First Family deception. Then I came for my colonel."

Stone felt another uncomfortably long silence as the two women glared at each other.

"Well," said Mori. "No need to call him colonel any longer. Tyler is here, safe and sound, and you can help him by staying onboard *Hydra* until you're called for."

"Called for?" huffed Martin, stepping toward Mori.

Stone's heart raced as the two warriors stood so close they were almost touching.

"Don't forget," whispered Martin just loud enough for Stone to hear, "you're not the first relationship he's ever had. And how did the last one end? Oh, yeah, you shot her in the face while she was carrying his son." Martin turned toward Stone. "You know where I'll be *when* you need me."

As Martin walked away, Stone sensed Mori's gaze on him.

"Tyler," said Mori softly, "On Alpha Humana, that woman, she was going to —"

"It doesn't matter that you did it, or the reason," interrupted Stone. "You want me to trust you and accept this new path, but you won't fully open up to me. Not about Astra, or the Dance, or when we lost Henry ... what else are you keeping from me?"

"Tyler —"

"She," added Stone as he pointed toward *Hydra* and the emotion from his last statement began to boil over, "has never given me a reason to doubt her."

"Then maybe you should be with her?" blurted Mori.

"No! Ino'ka, you are missing the point. I want to be with you, but I need to trust you ... to truly trust you, not just in combat but in everything."

"It's complicated, and you are new to our ways."

"The truth," replied Stone, "is never complicated. How people deal with it is."

"She has you second guessing yourself," warned Mori angrily.

"No," retorted Stone, "she has me second guessing us."

Mori stepped back from Stone. He could see a mixture of rage and anxiety on her face. He had hurt her, but she deserved it.

"I never meant to give you a reason to distrust me," she said as a tear formed and ran down her cheek. "Don't you understand what I'm risking by being with you?"

"No!" replied Stone, frustrated. "I don't know because you won't tell me."

"You have only been with me for a year and you have only recently begun to understand what it means to be Akota."

"I know what it means to love you. I know what it means to be willing to give my life for you."

"I feel the same way, Tyler."

"But still you keep secrets."

Mori clenched her jaw, looked up toward the overhead, and let out a long breath through her nose. "Your black and white world is great in theory, Tyler. But sometimes black and white only leaves two options, and I don't believe … I'm not ready to believe there are only two options for us."

"I don't even know what options you are talking about!" shouted an exasperated Stone.

Stone felt her back away with a jerk from the suddenness of his outburst. After another deep breath, she stepped close to him again and placed her hands in his.

"The options are being with you and being a leader of my people someday or being with you and never fulfilling what I am told my destiny is," she said softly. "It all depends on how I, how we, perform together. I can do this without you, but I'd be miserable." She paused. "So, if it's between leading the Akota someday and being with you, I choose you."

"What are you talking about?"

"If my vision and those of some of our elders are true, and I act with wisdom, generosity, bravery, and endurance, I may one day become a shirt-wearer. The four shirt-wearers are the cultural and political leaders of all Akota." She paused again, drew a deep breath, and bit her lower lip. "But our relationship can either solidify my chances or destroy them completely, depending on what you do."

"I don't understand," replied Stone. "How does my action determine if you can lead your ... our people."

"That's my point, Tyler. You don't understand ... yet." Mori's hand touched his cheek gently. "It will just take time."

Still confused but relieved she was actually talking to him, Stone spoke again. "What is it that you want me to do? I'll do it."

"I can't tell you," she said as she lowered her head briefly before looking back into his eyes. "If I tell you then the journey you must take can't be completed and I'll have to choose now between you and my destiny with our people."

"So I'm not part of your destiny?" he asked as he moved her hand from his cheek but still held her hand in his.

"I think you are in my destiny. I dreamed of a great warrior lost in the prairie that would come into my life, challenge me, and eventually allow me to complete my circle of being, which will allow me to finally obtain all of the character traits of a Shirt-Wearer. I think you are that warrior … I know you are. But you must develop without my help in order for the destiny to be fulfilled."

"So, you're asking me to just accept there is something I will do that will determine both our fates and your status with all Akota, but I can't ask you about it."

"Yes. For now." She smiled. "I know it's not easy and, given the deception of the Humani leaders, trust is something that must be earned."

"Yes, it is."

"I also know that she has long ago earned that trust. But that was your former life, before you realized you were Akota. Maybe someday she will have the same realization as you, but I doubt it. But for now, please be wary of her influence, Tyler. She ties you to a world you no longer belong to."

"But she is no different from me. She can see things as I have begun to … she just needs time."

"She is not like you," warned Mori. "I can see it. Even if there is truth in her intentions —"

"There is," he interrupted.

"Even if there is," continued Mori, "her path is straightforward. She does not see other paths or avoid pitfalls. I fear she will never accept who she truly is and accept her Akota or Iroqua heritage. Even if she fights with us, she will never be one of us."

"Don't ask me to choose," he replied. "I shouldn't have to … I can't —"

"I'm not asking you to today, Tyler. But someday you will need to. For now, I'm only asking you to remember who you have become and not let her drag you back to who you were before … for us." She stepped in closer and wrapped her arms around his waist. "I have made mistakes, I know. And I will make more." She looked up at Stone. "But please believe I will do anything for us and *our* future … which is the future of the Akota people — your people."

"I'll try," replied Stone as he returned her embrace. "And I will try to understand why you can't tell me what I will need to do … someday."

He slowly moved his hands to her waist and gently broke their embrace. "But no more secrets. Never."

"Never," she replied.

Stone leaned forward and pressed his lips to hers for a slow, soft kiss.

***

Stone could feel Mori's hand on his as he sat next to her in the large briefing room onboard *Harvest Moon*. Also seated at the table were Orion, Thay, Magnus and Katalya, as well as several Akota field and flag grade officers.

"Where's my seat?" came a familiar voice as Martin strode into the room.

"You can stand," replied Thay without looking up from the table.

Stone looked on as Martin, with three guards in tow, confidently paraded across the deck despite the air of anger and hatred for her that hung heavy in the room. "Lively crowd," she replied, reaching the bulkhead and falling into a leaning position.

"I didn't think they would let her in the briefing," whispered Stone.

"I convinced them to let her in," replied Mori. "Since you trust her, I took responsibility for her."

"Thank you," said Stone, giving her hand a light squeeze.

"Of course, with some restrictions," continued Mori.

"We'll need your weapons before the senior officers arrive," Stone overheard one of the guards say to Martin.

"Are you fu …" Martin paused and looked toward Stone. "Fine." She pulled her pistol from its holster and let it hang from her finger as she presented it to the guard. She then handed over two knives and a short stabbing blade embedded in her belt. "There ya go, buddy."

The guard remained in front of Martin.

"What?" she snipped.

"Your sword."

"Not gonna happen," she replied. "Unless you can take it from me."

Stone closed his eyes and inhaled deeply. Martin definitely walked her own path.

"I'll be happy to!" declared Thay, pushing himself from the table and turning toward Martin.

"Stop!" shouted Mori as she stood. "Thay, sit down. You are a guest among the Akota and this Humani —"

"Name's Martin," interrupted Martin loudly.

Stone inhaled deeply again. Sometimes Martin was just an asshole. He looked up to see Mori's fists clenched so tightly her fingers were white as she fought to maintain her composure.

"Martin is a guest of mine. If you insult or challenge her, you do the same to me."

"Fine," replied Thay, still looking at Martin. "But one day you and I will finish what we started on that riverbank."

Martin blew Thay a kiss before responding. "Looking forward to it." She smiled before she turned toward Mori. "And I'm not giving up my sword."

"Very well," conceded Mori, "but please remember you are also a guest and I ask ... I demand your respect as well."

Martin slowly pushed herself from her leaning position and stood straight and tall. "Fair enough."

"Thank you," replied Mori as she returned to her seat.

"Thank you," whispered Stone.

"She doesn't make things easy," murmured Mori.

The sudden sound of a large door opening near the head of the table drew Stone's attention. As the door opened three high-ranking Akota flag officers entered the room with the former First Family general, Nero, at their side. Instinctually, Stone started to pop to attention but remembered his earlier embarrassment and stopped himself.

"Good evening, everyone!" declared the admiral in the center.

"That is Fleet Senior Admiral River, our senior flight officer and a shirt-wearer," whispered Mori.

"Let's begin," continued Admiral River. "Thanks to Ka-itsenko Ino'ka and her team, we have gathered intel that changes the scope of the war as we know it. They have discovered a significant threat to not only the Akota people, but the entire Confederation. The Humani, apparently unbeknownst to the Xen or Dorans, have started work on a secret fleet underneath the water surface of the gas planet Dolus on the Humani side of the Dark Zone."

Stone heard a low rumble move across the room.

"There is more," said the general standing next to River. "The increase in the slaver operations and the spread of the religious movement known as the Word seem to be part of a Humani and Association plan to supply a large army to augment the fleet being built on Dolus."

"What is the status of this movement?" asked an officer from the crowd.

"There must have been some disruption," answered River. "Intel shows several Humani battle groups operating in the area."

"He's dead," shouted Martin from the back as the entire room turned to face her.

"Excuse me," replied River.

"The Saint ... the guy they propped up as their messiah — he's dead."

"Oh," said River. "Our Humani guest. And how do you know this?"

"I saw him blow himself up and take a First Family general with him," she answered. "But then his followers started nuking their own populations to take out Humani troop concentration centers and launched hundreds of ships from Echo System throughout the Dark Zone to spread the Word. I'm betting Astra Varus will be looking for recruits somewhere else, but those followers are bona fide nut jobs and are going to cause trouble wherever they go."

"Interesting news," replied River.

"And news that will complicate everything," added the general next to River. "And as our guest said, we are assuming the Humani ProConsul will most likely continue her efforts."

'*You have no idea*,' thought Stone.

"And that leads to the biggest threat," said River. "It appears the Humani and the Association have been working on a virus that will significantly degrade human, Doran, and Xen life forms alike and devastate populations. After this happens, she will release her fleet and an army genetically altered to be resistant to the virus on the Confederation."

Again, a low roar consumed the room.

"Quiet, everyone," ordered River. "With this serious threat in mind, we have laid out the initial planning for a major assault. The largest in our lifetimes."

Stone's attention was drawn to a massive digital screen, which illuminated above Admiral River and the other senior officers standing at the head of the table. On the screen was a stellar map showing the Gateway Station and boundary to the Dark Zone as well as Alpha Humana and Dolus.

Admiral River continued. "It is estimated that the Humani secret fleet and troops will not be combat ready, nor the virus active, for several years, but we have decided to strike early."

"When?" asked a colonel from the group.

"Tentative planning is for eleven standard months. I will turn the details over to General Noe."

"Thank you, uncle," replied Noe as he stepped forward. "First, as Shirt-wearer River mentioned, this will be our largest single attack in over two centuries and it would not have been possible without the Iroqua matrons' agreements to supply warriors to relieve some of our combat troops in less active regions so they will be available for the assault."

"I only hope this is the first step to full military support and open involvement in the war," added Thay from his seat.

Noe acknowledged Thay's comment with a nod and continued. "Our initial objective will be to move through the satellite grid at subjump speeds to prevent deactivation of our reactors by the Gateway defensive systems."

"But subjump speed will allow the Humani to concentrate their forces and meet us at the Gateway Station," stated a fleet captain from the table.

"True," conceded River. "And we will expect heavy casualties."

"I have volunteered to lead the assault," added the former Humani General Nero as he stepped to the front. "The losses will be heavy, but we must take out the station to allow the main force to attack Dolus. This is the only option available since we cannot obtain the required daily frequency settings to allow jump speed travel through the Humani side. I believe there are still First Family members that want to resist Xen rule and can obtain the frequencies, but I have been unable to get any agents in position to contact them."

"You have supporters on Alpha Humana?" interrupted Martin again.

"Yes," replied Nero. "Not all First Families want to remain under the yoke of the Xen or even the ProConsul."

"You know this to be true?" asked Martin, stepping up to the table. "Are you confident there are people on our home planet that will support us and can provide the frequencies?"

"Yes."

"Then I can be your agent. I will make contact and get the frequencies," offered Martin as the room again erupted.

"Everyone, keep it down," ordered Noe as he turned toward Nero. "Will this give you the opportunity you have been looking for to carry out your proposed plan?"

"Yes," replied Nero. "If Martin can contact the right people quietly and get the information … this could be the day I have been waiting for."

"Revolution?" asked Stone from his seat, unable to remain silent.

"I'm in," added Martin.

A strange sense of excitement rushed through Stone's body as he saw Nero, River, Noe, and the other general talk amongst themselves while the room again began to rumble with a dozen other conversations. After a brief moment, Admiral River turned to face the room.

"Please excuse us," he said. "We will need to pause this briefing for another twenty-four hours, but I need all fleet admirals and division commanders to remain, as well as the Ka-itsenko, Mr. Stone, and our Humani guest."

"What's this about?" Stone asked Mori. "Why are we included?"

"I don't know," replied Mori.

Stone wondered what this special meeting would bring as the rest of the officers quickly left the briefing room. In a few moments the attendance had dwindled to the senior officers, including five fleet admirals and four division commanders, along with Stone, Mori, Thay, and Martin. All were sitting around the large table in the center of the room, except Martin.

"Please join us," asked Admiral River as he motioned for Martin to take her seat.

"Guess who's moving up," said Martin as she bounced to the table and sat in the chair next to Stone.

With Mori and Martin flanking him, Stone felt an invisible force tearing him apart as if they were opposing forces of nature.

"This changes everything," said Nero to start the meeting. "If Martin can return to Alpha Humana and retain her status, she can make contact with key opposition leaders."

"I left Port Royal alone with the colonel and the others as prisoners. If we can come up with a story about them escaping and that keeps me on the planet for a while, I can do it. But it will have to be believable."

"And if you can be discreet as you make the contacts," added Nero.

"Discretion is my middle name," replied Martin as she plopped her legs onto the table.

"Is she for real?" whispered Mori to Stone.

"She likes to put on a show," answered Stone quietly. "But she'll do what she needs to in order to complete a mission."

"If you can pull this off. This will be the new plan," said Nero, illuminating the large screen.

"Once you have support of the First Families — and I will give Martin the details after the brief — then you'll need to find a reason to head back into the Dark Zone in about seven standard months in order to give us a debriefing and set a final assault date."

"If I tell them Stone is still alive, Astra Varus will expect me to keep hunting for him," replied Martin.

"That should work," answered Nero. "Admiral Carsis Plaxis will be key. He must be with us."

"Admiral Plaxis is a dissenter?" asked Martin, her shock evident.

"Yes," answered Nero. "I am assuming he is still in command of two of the four battle groups assigned to Alpha Humana defense."

"He is," replied a still stunned Martin.

"Plaxis will proceed on a training mission to the edge of the Dark Zone near the Gateway Station. When he is there, as soon as the next day's frequencies are passed, he will send an electron spin burst message with the required frequencies to my attack group. As soon as they are received, I'll pass them to the other two groups. The first assault force, identified as Task Force Scout under command of Admiral Willow, will perform a combat jump and engage and destroy the Gateway Station."

Admiral Willow rose to address the group. "I will need ten battleships and two carriers uploaded with additional attack and fighter craft, along with another … fifteen escorts. We will greatly reduce the troops onboard the carrier to support the larger loadout of the air assault elements. That should be sufficient if we take them by surprise."

As Willow sat, Nero continued. "With the Gateway boundary down, and the Humani unaware of our knowledge of Dolus, the next group should take Dolus completely by surprise. Admiral Evergreen, with Task Force Raven, will carry out the assault on Dolus.

Admiral Evergreen then rose to address the group. "As we discussed under the previous plan, I will have twenty battleships and four carriers, also with increased air assault loadouts, and about twenty-five escorts. As soon as we reach Dolus, we'll launch recon patrols to identify the access points to the underwater stations. Once identified, we will begin launching deep penetration nukes with remote charges. They should be able to quickly dive to the ocean bottom and then embed themselves into the floor, where we will detonate."

"And," added Nero, "with the Humani keeping the Xen and Dorans in the dark about Dolus, they will most likely respond to Dolus and the Gateway Station with their entire Humani defense fleet, half of which will be under the command of Plaxis and not engaging. That will open the door for my force to assault Alpha Humana itself. My group, Task Force Eagle, will include fifteen battleships, thirty carriers, and sixty escorts. Onboard the carriers will be ninety thousand troops. We will also have fifty transport carriers with an additional one hundred thousand troops. If Martin is successful, we can possibly double that number with military support from the resisting families on the planet itself. The goal will not be to occupy the entire planet, but I believe we can gain control of at least two regions and most importantly, the capital of Mt. Castra. Once we have the capital, we can send out the truth via Senatorial citizenry comms links and let the Humani people determine their own fate."

"This plan has a lot of risks," replied an admiral sitting across from Nero. "What if this Humani fails?"

"If she fails, we can still slug it out at Gateway Station and attack Dolus like the original plan," answered Nero.

"What if she's found out and then forced to talk?" asked the same admiral.

"I won't fail," replied Martin. "And nobody forces me to do anything."

"You say that now," answered the admiral.

"She may fail," replied Nero. "But she is a Guardsman — one of the best. She won't talk."

"Will the Association not inform the Humani they have lost a council member? That could cause them to fear the information has been leaked," asked another admiral.

"We are confident the Association is invested too deeply and would fear the Humani response if ProConsul Varus found out. As usual, they will keep quiet and try to hedge their bets. That is also why we will not retaliate against Port Royal for their clear violation of neutrality. That will also help to convince the Association that we do not know their plan," replied River.

"What of the others on Alpha Humana?" asked another officer. "What if they talk?"

"They won't know enough," answered Nero. "Martin will be the only one to know everything. And the others won't act without her signal. The only other linchpin is Admiral Plaxis, and I trust him, as well."

"There is no doubt risk," added Admiral River. "But if we can pull this off, we destroy the Gateway Station, stop the ProConsul from unleashing genetic warfare on the Confederation, and possibly bring the Humani into open revolt against their government, maybe even the Xen. It's too much to pass up."

"So it's decided?" asked Nero.

"I'll need to confer with the other Shirt-wearers, but I think they will approve."

"Excellent," replied Nero. "Now we need to get Martin ready to play the chameleon. A chameleon that will open the door to victory from the inside."

***

"They have to believe it," huffed Martin.

"I know, but this isn't easy," replied Stone.

"Look, the only way they are going to believe you escaped is if I'm torn up. You know I wouldn't give up without a fight — well, without losing a fight — and I don't lose many fights." Martin paused and tilted her head slightly. "Actually, I don't lose fights at all."

"Just punch her already," interjected Orion. "The transport is waiting to pick us up. If this crazy ass plan is costing me my baby, I at least need to see this Humani get her ass kicked."

"Fine," replied Stone as he landed a right hand across Martin's jaw.

Martin stumbled backward and spat blood from her mouth. "Seriously, sir," she replied. "You hit like a girl. They have to believe this. Maybe I should have one of these Ter bitches hit me."

"You mouthy cow!" yelled Orion, reaching across Stone and punching Martin.

Martin's head snapped to her right, but she looked up with a smile. "You hit pretty good for a pilot ... but that ain't saying a lot." She turned back toward Stone.

He could see her teeth coated with blood as she spoke.

"Come on, sir, we don't have all day. Stop being a pussy."

"Do you ever shut up?" asked an exasperated Mori, walking over to Stone. "Are you going to do this or not?"

"I am. I just —"

"Screw it," declared Mori as she grabbed Martin's arm and pulled her body downward while crashing her knee into Martin's nose.

Stone heard Martin's nose crack loudly. Her head recoiled and she stumbled backward against the *Hydra*'s bulkhead.

"That's more like it," smiled Martin as blood began to stream down her chin and onto her shirt. "I didn't realize you swung that way, Ter. But if you want to keep giving me kisses you should ask first."

Mori let out a groan as she brought her foot against Martin's knee. Martin fell to her knees and Mori quickly followed with a sweeping kick against the side of her head. The impact knocked Martin to the deck, but she slowly pushed herself to her hands and knees.

"You're getting there, pumpkin," mumbled Martin through her swollen cheek and mouth. "Maybe —"

Before Martin could finish, Mori slammed her foot into Martin's ribs.

Stone let out an involuntary gasp as he heard the sound of Martin's ribs crack. He knew at least a few ribs were broken.

Martin rolled onto her back and sucked in a deep breath to control the pain.

"That's prett —" Martin paused to spit a mouthful of blood on the floor as she rolled onto her side and slowly stood. "That's pretty good," she continued.

Stone could see the left side of Martin's face already turning purple; that was in addition to her broken nose trickling blood and her swollen cheek.

"One more," Martin taunted Mori. "Right here where your daddy kisses me."

Before Stone could react, Mori pounced. She knocked Martin backward into a nearby seat and leapt into her lap. She then delivered a series of blows to Martin's face.

"Stop!" shouted Stone as she pulled Mori off Martin's battered body.

"That bitch had it coming!" growled Mori as she twisted her body free of Stone's grasp.

"She doesn't know about your father," said Stone. "She's just trying to rile you up."

"I already hate her," blurted Mori. "So she doesn't need to say a fucking word. In fact, I'd rather she kept her mouth shut."

"That ... was good," mumbled Martin, barely able to speak. "But that's not enough," she added as she slowly stood once again.

"What?" asked Stone. "You're a mess."

"Not long term," she coughed and tensed her body from the pain of her broken ribs. "Need to lose something ... if I have to have the medics regenerate something that will keep me home long enough to make the contacts."

"Regenerate?" asked Stone, but he knew what she meant.

"She wants you to cut a hand or something off," added Mori coldly. "Makes sense to me."

"I can't do that," replied Stone.

"Yes, you can," said Martin. "They have to believe this story or they'll kill me."

"She's right and you know it," added Mori. "It'll take months to regenerate a hand. That will be the perfect excuse to keep her on Alpha Humana."

He knew it made sense. There was no way Martin would have allowed a prisoner to escape without taking more than a beating. Logically, the mission called for it. After a deep exhale, Stone slowly drew his sword as Martin rested her left hand on an armrest. He looked down toward her bruised and bloody face.

"You can do this sir," said Martin, looking up toward him.

"Do it," added Mori.

Stone closed his eyes and let out a groan as he swiftly brought his sword downward toward Martin's hand.

But he stopped just short of making contact. He couldn't bring himself to do it.

"Do it!" shouted Martin.

Stone gripped his sword so tightly he could hear the sound of the leather bindings compressing against the force of his hands. She was right. He had to do it. Raising his sword again, he took a deep breath and looked into her eyes. She wanted him to do it. His body tightened as he tried to force his arms to move. But they wouldn't respond. "Damn it!" he shouted as he threw his sword across the cargo bay. "I'm sorr —" Stone stopped as he saw Martin's eyes shift toward Mori.

"Come on, bitch!" shouted Martin. "I know you want to."

Stone saw the flash of Mori's sword followed by a shriek as Martin fell backwards and her left hand fell to the floor.

"Son of a bitch!" declared Orion. "Did that just —"

"It had to be done," replied Mori as she looked toward Stone. "You should get some meds in her and stop that bleeding before you put her in the escape pod."

Stone quickly moved toward Martin. He knelt next to her and placed a rag over her gushing left forearm. He pressed tightly but the blood quickly soaked through and began trickling onto the deck.

"Give me the meds," grunted Martin as she pointed to a nearby medical pack.

He quickly grabbed the pack and applied the coagulant to her wound. Almost instantly the flow of blood slowed as the bubbling gel began to interact with her blood, causing it to quickly clot.

"There," said Stone as he leaned back on his heels.

Stone felt Martin grab his shirt with her remaining hand and pull him closer. "Pain meds would be nice."

"Shit," he replied, grabbing a neuro injector from the pack and shoving it into her shoulder.

"Another," demanded Martin.

Stone nodded and injected another dose.

As Stone watched, Martin let out a slow breath as she slowly took control of her pain.

"Hey Ranger!" shouted Martin in Mori's direction.

"What?" asked Mori, wiping Martin's blood from her sword with her sleeve.

"Come here."

Mori let out a sigh and slowly walked toward Martin. "I only did what you wanted, Guardsman," stated Mori with a content smile as she stood above Martin and Stone.

"Of course you did," replied Martin. "You're just supporting the mission."

"Glad you see it that way," replied Mori as she knelt next to Stone. "And I hate to admit it, but you took that well."

"Anything for the mission, right?"

"Anything," agreed Mori with another smile.

"Good," grunted Martin as she snatched a knife from her vest with lightning speed and drove it into Mori's thigh.

Stone fell backward from the surprise of Martin's attack as Mori let out a groan and brought her right hand against Martin's temple.

"Fucking bitch!" she yelled as she stumbled to her feet and drew her pistol.

"Whoa!" laughed Martin.

"Emily? Why?" asked a shocked Stone.

"The mission." Martin smiled as she looked toward Mori, who was pointing her weapon toward Martin with one hand while putting pressure on her wound with the other.

Stone could see blood starting to stream down Mori's leg.

"You know they wouldn't believe I let any of you get away without drawing blood," continued Martin as she held her bloody knife toward Mori. "Now we have blood. Thanks for volunteering."

"Screw you," said Mori, slamming her pistol into its holster.

"You might want to stop that bleeding," offered Martin.

Ignoring Martin, Mori turned toward Stone. "You should probably load her into the escape pod now. I'll launch the two empty ones after I fix this damn wound. After that, I'm getting ready to transfer to the transport ship docked with us."

"I'll get her ready."

"Don't be long." Mori turned and limped toward the aft escape pods.

"Don't be long," mocked Martin as Mori disappeared down the passageway.

"Stop it," said Stone, helping the wrecked Martin to her feet. "She's important to me."

"Fine," huffed Martin. "Just get me to the pod."

Stone supported Martin as they made their way the short distance to the forward escape pod. Once there, he opened the access door and gently helped Martin into the pod.

"Here's a full med pack to go along with the one in the pod. The food packs and water —"

"I think I can figure it out, sir."

"You don't need —"

The sound of gunfire drew their attention and Stone felt Martin attempt to pull herself from the pod.

"Don't worry," said Stone as he placed his hand on Martin's shoulder to prevent her from exiting the pod. "Orion is firing some rounds into the cargo bay, hanger bay, and a few other spaces to make it look like there was a gunfight as well in case they find parts of *Hydra* when they find you."

"I bet that Ter pilot is hot about having her ship blown up just to put the finishing touch on the deception. I can only imagine what that crazy engineer —"

Stone laughed. "Yeah, he refused to come out on this run. Called us butchers. Orion had to slip something in his drink last night so he would be out when we left the carrier."

Stone saw Martin let out a laugh, but her expression quickly shift to a somber, determined gaze.

"If this works, sir, it could change everything," she said.

"It could, Emily. And you don't need to call me sir anymore."

Stone felt Martin's right hand grasp his forearm.

"You'll always be a Guardsman. Don't let these people ... don't let her change who you are. Even if we fought for a lie, the Oath we took still holds true."

Martin's words tore at him. She was right. But so was Mori.

"I understand," replied Stone. "But all Humani are descendant from the Terillian people."

Martin's grip tightened.

"Our ancestors might have been Akota or Terillian or whatever, but we — including you — are Humani. I'm my father's daughter, a citizen of Mt. Castra, and a member of the Elite Guard sworn to die for our people. The deception of the First Families doesn't change the Oath we took one bit. And when we defeat them and the people have a chance to determine their own fate, it will be a Humani, not an Akota that will lead them."

"But —"

"Sir ... Tyler," Martin interrupted as Stone felt her move her hand from his forearm and cup the back of his head as she leaned forward. "Don't let these people change you. Even if they think it's for the best, they — she — wants you to become something you're not in order to meet their own agenda. That is not what our people need." She pulled Stone even closer. "I believe in you and will die for you because of the man you are, not because of something I want you to become. And our people, the Humani, will do the same. For you."

Stone didn't know how to respond. His head spun from the emotional tug-of-war between Martin and Mori. Both thought he was to become something far more important than he believed he would, or maybe could, be. Every step he had taken toward becoming Akota, toward his life with Mori, had been just been challenged by the one Humani he respected above all for her dedication to her people. His head began to ache. "It's complicated" was all he could say.

Martin laughed. "You're making it complicated, sir. You always let your brain override your gut and make things complicated. It might have helped you navigate the First Family bullshit, but your gut is what made, what makes, you a great leader. And you know the truth is pretty damn simple."

"*It's time*" came Orion's voice over the intercom. "Get her off my ship so we can kill my baby."

"We should get you launched," he said. "When you're far enough away we'll detonate the charges and blowup *Hydra* so it looks like you blew the ship when you were injured."

"Let's do this," replied Martin as she activated the closure and the pod's door slid shut.

"See you in a few months," said Stone into the pod's intercom link.

"*Don't lose the man I know you to be by trying to become what someone else wants,*" warned Martin, speaking into her intercom.

"Emily —"

Before he could finish, Martin activated the jettison lever and disappeared into the darkness of space as the boundary closure slammed shut.

He let out an exhausted breath as he stared at the armored boundary door where Martin had been seconds ago. It would be months before they would meet again, and he had no idea who he would be the next time they met.

About the Author

Brian Dorsey is a retired Naval officer and is currently a nuclear engineering instructor for a naval shipyard and part-time US history instructor for Vincennes University. When not spending time with his family, Brian enjoys reading and researching US and Native American history, watching good TV shows or films (anything by Joss Whedon), camping, hunting, and working on his next writing project. He is married with three adult children.

Current books available in the Gateway Universe

Gateway (Gateway Series Book 1)
Cold Planet (A Gateway Universe Story)
Saint (Gateway Series Book 2)
Uprising (Gateway Series Book 3)
Rise of the Wolf: Katalya's Story (A Novella)
Schism (Book 4)

www.mountaineerwest.com